SKIM

SKIM

JAMES G. PATTILLO

SOHO

Published by
Soho Press, Inc.
853 Broadway
New York, NY 10003

Library of Congress Cataloging-in-Publication Data
Pattillo, James G., 1944–
Skim / James G. Pattillo.
p.   cm.
ISBN 0–939149–50–8
I. Title.
PS3566.A822S55   1991
813'.54—dc20   91–6442
                                                              CIP

Book design and composition by
The Sarabande Press

To Shelly, who was present at the creation.

SKIM

CHAPTER

1

"THEY STICK MONEY IN your posing brief," Richie said. "Cop a little feel, pretend they're touching you by accident. Housewives and like that."

He took a deep breath, exhaled steadily, and straightened his arms. The barbell rose off of his chest and came to a stop. "Spot it," he said. Richie was proud of being able to keep his voice from tightening with the strain.

Dominic put his hands on the barbell, lifted a fraction, and guided it into the rest.

Richie and Dominic had been lifting together for a year or so. Before that, Richie had been lifting for, was it three years? Or four? Richie had gotten into lifting at San Quentin, doing the middle term for attempted arson. Stupid district attorney thought he was pulling a fast one, charging it as "arson of an inhabited structure" instead of extortion (which was what it was, torching a little mom-and-pop grocery because they hadn't paid the money for insurance). The D.A. thought he was being smart because the sentence for arson was longer—three, five, or eight, instead of two, three, or four.

That was before some of Richie's friends had leaned on one of the witnesses, and the witness couldn't be found for the trial, so the D.A. had to let Richie plead to attempted arson because he couldn't prove his case for shit.

The D.A. had the last laugh though, stuck Richie with a five-year enhancement for a prior serious felony conviction. Serious felony, for Chrissakes, when he'd only done six months county jail for it. How was it fair for them to stick you another five years for something you already done the time for it? How was that fair?

So Richie did four and a half years, got credit for seven (two for the attempted arson, plus the five-year enhancement), and got into weights while he was inside.

Dominic undid the keepers, slipped a twenty-five-pound plate off of each end of the barbell, and put the keepers back. Richie got up off the bench, and Dominic lay down and put his hands on the barbell.

"So," Richie said, "you don't got anything for me do this week, maybe I'll go up Vegas, catch the Mr. Universe semifinals." He lifted the barbell off the rest and let Dominic take it.

Dominic inhaled, held his breath, and then exhaled as he pressed the barbell up to arm's length. He let the barbell down across his chest, then inhaled and pressed it up again. He didn't answer until he'd finished his reps, and the barbell was back on the rest. Then he sat up, reached for his towel, and wiped the sweat off of his face.

"I got a couple little things," he said. "Uh-huh. Couple of little things." Taking it slow. "Don't you feel, you know, weird, up there, front of a bunch of women, nothing on but a little pair of briefs, about the size a jockstrap?"

"Weird, what's to feel weird about? It's like it'll be a Tupperware party, or a bachelorette party, and the hostess maybe has shown them a porno film, and wants a good-looking hunk there, impress her friends." Richie glanced across the weight room, checked out his reflection in the mirror on the far wall. His stylist had lightened his hair last time, putting gold highlights in the brown curls. Not obvious peroxide blond like a lot of guys had, but understated. Classy.

"Like," he said, "you stand around, smile a lot, and then usually the hostess, she'll wait until all the other women go home, then she'll say something, let you know she's in the mood. So you get laid, and get paid for it too. What you got? Delivery?"

Dominic threw his towel at the barrel in the corner of the weight room. He missed. "Nah," he said. "Just, like, a reminder on a place that's behind with its insurance."

"Uh-huh," Richie said. Richie liked deliveries better than reminders. People were tensed up for a delivery, but not uptight, hysterical, like they could get during a reminder. And the best thing was deliveries for gram dealers that were women. What it was, Richie could tell the ones that were turned on by the situation: this big, good-looking guy, that was a *criminal*, bringing them a couple ounces of coke. Waiting to see if he'd make a move on them. And Richie gave them what they wanted, even when they were pretending to be reluctant. He could tell they liked it. Liked it rough.

He'd guessed wrong, though, a couple times. The prior serious felony—the one they popped him the five-year enhancement for— that had been a forcible oral copulation beef. A girl he was sure was really into it, turned out not to like it at all. Or she changed her mind after, more likely, and left Richie with a two-year suspended sentence—six months county jail and two years probation.

"What kind of place is it? The reminder?" Richie said.

"A motel. One down on Sepulveda."

"What're they buying insurance for?"

"Girls. Most of the trade's hookers. They don't want any noise, any fights, anybody getting out of line, attracting attention."

"Uh-huh," Richie said. He wiped the back of his neck with his towel and started for the showers.

"Your director is a thief, is that what you're saying?"

"No." Maurice shook his head to show that wasn't what he was saying. "That isn't it at all. What I'm saying is that . . ."

David Pike pushed his hand six inches across the desk toward Maurice. When the hand stopped, the index finger was raised, pointing at Maurice. It was a good gesture. Maurice stopped talking and admired it. He decided to use it the next time he argued with his director.

"Then," Pike said, "what do you call it when you give someone control of a checking account and money disappears out of the account?"

Maurice shook his head again. "It hasn't disappeared. It's just not accounted for. And normally I wouldn't be worried, but things are kind of in a slack period lately, and I couldn't afford to lose the dough."

Pike stood up and crossed to the window. He glanced through the blinds, into the slanting afternoon sunlight, then paced back and forth in the space between the window and the desk. Not so much pacing, Maurice thought, as prowling. He couldn't sit still and listen to you, could he? The man was being paid for his time, and couldn't sit still and listen.

Maurice, on the other hand, sat very still. Not checking the knot of his tie, not shifting in the chair, not playing with his reading glasses. Spyros Skouras always said, when you lie to someone, sit still and look him in the eye. Maurice sat still and looked Pike in the eye, at least when Pike was looking in the right direction.

Pike sat on the windowsill and folded his arms. "How much did you say? Seventy? Eighty?"

"No." Maurice sighed. "Not nearly that much."

"How much then?"

"More than fifty. That's all I can say for sure."

"You're right, Maurie, that's not theft. It's foreign aid, that's what it is. So why are you here? Isn't the whole thing an accounting problem?"

Pike was looking out the window again. Didn't he have a boat there, in the marina? What was he doing, trying to see if his boat was still there? He could at least sit down and talk face-to-face, if you were paying him for his time, couldn't he? The old studio heads, Mayer, Sam Goldwyn, if they had a lawyer that prowled around, got on your nerves like this guy, they'd have fired him in a minute. Or maybe, Maurice decided, they'd have had a vice president fire him. He looked like you wouldn't want him to get personally mad at you. Big guy, two, three inches over six feet, almost two hundred pounds, all of it bone. Hard blue eyes. Limped a little, which made him seem, not crippled, but dangerous, like a bull with a couple of banderillas in him. Had a droll story about how he came to get shot in the foot that, between the lines, told you he'd been some places and done some things. Mid-thirties maybe, maybe younger. Hard to tell.

"Isn't it, Maurie? Isn't it an accounting problem?"

"I'm seventy-seven years old, I don't know when I need an accountant and when I need a lawyer? It's accounting if we got the books, the canceled checks, the bills. *Get*ting the stuff—that's the legal problem."

"Uh-huh. Let me ask you something, Maurie. I thought the producer handled the money. What's the director even doing on the checking account?"

"Because," Maurice said, being as patient as he could, "this isn't some big studio. This is just me producing a picture. And the way I set it up was to let the director write a lot of the checks. Is that all right with you?"

"Sure. Sure, Maurie, it's fine. Let me ask you something else. Do you have a distribution deal already on this movie?"

"No. Why should I? The picture isn't made yet. What could I show to a distributor? A screenplay?"

"And so you invest money you can't afford to lose in a film with no distribution arrangement. Didn't you sit here and tell me, when we incorporated this production company, that unless the distribution is committed ahead of time, there's no way to be sure you'll break even on the film no matter if you get it finished? On top of that, you let the director have sole signature authority on the checking account? Not even a second signature required, none of that stuff? Maurie, there's a screw loose here somewhere. How many movies did you tell me you've made?"

Maurice nodding, thinking: The guy is good, he's close, he's real close, and he doesn't even know he's there. Saying: "Produced, not made. I produce pictures, I don't make them. The director makes them. Fifteen, twenty years ago, I produced a lot of pictures. *A lot.* Not so many recently. In fact, this is the first picture I've done in maybe two, three years—and I wouldn't be doing it if I didn't need some income. Okay, it was stupid, I know. But I'm telling you, I've worked with Mickey before: three, four times. And I just . . . well, I did it, okay?"

The lawyer finally getting down to business, coming back from the window, sitting down at the desk. Saying: "Have you asked for what you want?"

"Yeah, I've asked."

"And what happens?"

"Nothing happens. The bills're not at the studio, the checkbook is at the bookkeeper's that does the payroll checks, figures out the deductions. Always some excuse, never any records."

"You're paying these people, aren't you? I mean, it's your money? Have you said, 'Listen, I want the records. I'll be here tomorrow at ten, you have them ready.' Have you done that?"

"Well, it's not that easy, you know . . ."

"What's not that easy? You think this director is ripping you off, there's more than fifty thousand missing, and you can't just say, 'Give me the financial records?'"

"David, it's not missing. It's just not accounted for at this point, and I don't want Mickey to think I'm implying that the money is stolen, because . . ."

"Because that's exactly what you do think. So why not say so?"

"Because for one thing we're in the middle of a picture, and if I say things that sound like accusations of stealing, and my director stalks off the set in a huff, then where am I? I got a half-done picture and *all* the money is down the drain. I can't afford that."

The lawyer shaking his head, saying: "Since when is a half-done film a problem in this town? You could stick your head out the window and spit, half the people you'd hit're directors. There are more out-of-work directors in this town than there are pigs in Iowa."

"So now he knows all about the film industry," Maurice said, nodding and speaking to the air. "Get an advance commitment for distribution, fire the director, get a replacement to finish the picture. Let a lawyer work on one movie deal, incorporate one lousy production company, he knows more about the industry than people have been in it thirty, forty years. Will you to tell me all about the motion picture industry, Mr. Lawyer?"

"Maurie, I'm not trying to tell you how to run your business, I just—"

"Keep still, Mr. Smart Guy. If you don't know enough to tell me, then listen. Maybe you'll learn something. It's not so simple, finding a director. Mickey is not just your average director. Mickey is special, because—"

"Sure, special," Pike said, half under his breath. "Special because of a well-developed ability to make money disappear."

Maurice waited, one eyebrow raised, hands spread, a silent comedian playing exaggerated patience. Louis B. Mayer always said, Don't tell the lawyers anything. Just the bare bones of the deal. They don't need to know *why* and *what for*. Just *who* and *how much*.

The lawyer Maurice usually used, old Sid Stoddard, he just did what you told him: no back talk, never asked why. But Sid was cutting down his practice—who wouldn't, after the second coronary—and he recommended this Pike guy. Said he was smart, too. Actually, what Sid had said was, "Pike spent some time in Army Intelligence, or one of those outfits. Maybe he's seen enough sneaky things tried enough different ways to even keep up with you, Maurie."

But a little of the *why* could be useful. Get the guy pointed in the right direction. Pointed away from places where Maurice didn't want him poking around.

Maurice let three or four seconds of silence pass before he laid his hands flat on the desk and sat forward slightly.

"You're ready to listen now? Okay. Have you ever crossed the speaker wires on a stereo? Plugged the left speaker into the jack for the right speaker, and the right one into the left jack, and then played a piano concerto?"

"What has that got to do with anything?"

"I'm telling you *what*, if you care to listen. It's the same music, right? Same notes, same tempo, same everything. But every now and then there's a passage, let's say, where the theme is supposed to start off on the right, in the orchestra, move across in front of you and finish up on the left, in the piano. And if you crossed the leads, what happens? The sound starts in the middle, in front of you, moves off to the left where the piano's supposed to be, but it's the orchestra that's playing. Then the sound disappears, pops up way off on the right, where it should be orchestra, only it's the piano that's playing, and then it moves back, and finishes in front of you. It's weird. It doesn't feel right.

"Well," he said, "that's how Mickey is. You see some jerk, that has a lot of those self-congratulatory awards from the Guild, do a scene. Then you see Mickey do the same scene—maybe Mickey is the A.D. or the second on some clunker a big studio is doing and the director gets tired after fifteen takes and lets Mickey do the scene.

"It's," he said, "it's like uncrossing the speaker wires. Same set, same dialogue, same actors, maybe Mickey has a grip move one piece of furniture, flags a light a little bit, has an actor hold a pause a beat longer—and all at once, it isn't just a movie, it's real life. Huston could do that, on a good day. And Bergman, most of the time. *That's* what I don't want to lose."

"So what am I supposed to do about it?" Pike said, surrendering. "If I go ask for the books and records, how is that less of an insult than if you do it?"

Maurice had it all worked out. The money was Maurice's money, all right, but it had been run through a corporate account—the little production company that Pike had incorporated.

"You formed DCI, you're in the minutes as assistant secretary. Mickey doesn't know who the stockholders are, or who the officers are. Anybody checks with Sacramento, they find you on the articles as incorporator, right? Let's say you represent the other stockholders, my silent partners—which I haven't got—and *they* want to know what's going on. So you're asking for *them*. And then if Mickey gets upset . . ."

"Ah," Pike said. "I like it. You ride in on your white horse and say it wasn't your fault, it was the other guys' idea, don't worry about it, etc. etc. Well, it's thin, but maybe it'll play. Where am I going to put on this little piece of improv?"

"I'll have to find out. My picture is on hiatus for a week, and Mickey is shooting a public interest piece about alcoholism. They're in one of the big studios. The studio is donating the space, taking a tax write-off. I'll get you the address."

Dominic drove. That was fine with Richie. He could sit and look out through the smoked glass, watch the people, they didn't even know they were being watched. Dominic had this Mercedes 4-door, an undertaker's car. Black, all the chrome blacked out, and the smoked windows. A nothing car, right? What kind of class did it show driving around in some family sedan, looked like it belonged to a funeral parlor? Not like Richie's car. Richie had a Jeep—maroon, with yellow pin-striping, and Marchal driving-lights on the roll bar. Understated. Classy. But practical, at the same time, like for if you needed to drive through mud or something.

Sometimes, when Dominic drove, Richie would look at him and try to figure him out. The flat, tilted eyes were Oriental, and the straight black hair and yellow skin. Fine so far. But most Orientals were small people. Dominic was over six feet and weighed about two hundred. Then the name. Nakamura, that sounded Oriental all right. But Dominic was a Chicano name, or Italian, or one of those.

Richie had asked him, one time, wasn't Dominic an Italian name? Dominic nodded and said yeah, named for Domenico Scarlatti. As if Richie should know who Domenico Scarlatti was. Richie thought maybe he was a Cuban who had played center field for the Mets for part of a season and then blew out a knee and went back to the minors—but he wasn't sure. Dominic had this ring, too. Like a high-school class ring. Richie had asked him one time where was the ring from? And Dominic grinned and said a junior college he once went to. Richie asked which one? And Dominic said Leland Stanford Junior University. Richie didn't think junior colleges had class rings, but Dominic had this look when he said it, like it might be some kind of joke, so Richie grinned too, like he got the joke, and said, yeah, right.

Dominic pulled over to the curb and Richie got out and walked into the lobby of the motel. Everything looked like it was bolted down, or bulletproof. There wasn't a reception counter; there was a window, like in a drive-in bank. Green-tinted glass, slot at the bottom to push the money through, little speaker at the side. Richie pushed the button under the speaker. A woman in a flowered housedress came out of a door at the back, holding a napkin in one hand and chewing something. She'd have lifted in the same weight class as Richie—two-twenty anyhow—but soft. Two hundred-plus pounds of Jell-O jiggling around on these tiny little feet, making a nylon-rustling noise as she walked.

"Mrs. Wessel?" Richie said.

The woman wiped her mouth and swallowed. "Yes?" she said. She said it like she might want to say no if it turned out what you wanted was going to be a problem.

"I have a message for your husband, Mrs. Wessel. From Mr. DiAngelo." There wasn't any Mr. DiAngelo, but that was the name Dominic always told him to use. Mr. DiAngelo wants this, Mr.

DiAngelo doesn't like that. Made it sound like the Mafia, besides giving people someone to blame things on. And always be polite, Dominic said. Call people Mister and smile and be cool. That way it was more impressive.

The woman swallowed again. "He's up the motel," she said. "Checking onna maids. They're cleaning up onna second floor." She gestured vaguely over her shoulder. "You wait here. He'll be down'n a while."

"Thanks, sweetheart," Richie said. "I'll just run up and talk to him a minute."

The motel was laid out around a courtyard. In the front of the courtyard was parking, and in the back was a nearly dead swimming pool with a scummy ring around the tile, and trash floating in it. Richie could see a cart with a bag for dirty linen standing on the second-floor balcony. He walked up the stairs and along the balcony. The doors of a couple of rooms were open, near where the cart was parked. A vacuum cleaner was whining inside one of the rooms.

A short little man bustled out of one of the open doors. "Then the south side, Louise," he called back into the room, and started along the balcony past Richie, but Richie put out his arm and the little guy stopped. Stopped and looked at Richie. Self-important, sure of himself. Trying to puff out his chest, but doing nothing but bulge his stomach. Richie wondered if the little guy made it very often with his wife. Richie couldn't figure out how they'd do it: woman the size of one of those Japanese wrestlers, what were they called—sushi wrestlers? That wasn't right, but some name like that. And this little guy like a plucked chicken. Swallowing now, his Adam's apple bobbing up and down his neck.

"Mr. Wessel?" Richie said.

"Yes?" the guy said. Like his wife, saying it as if he might want to say it wasn't him, once he found out what you wanted.

"I'm from Mr. DiAngelo. You know you're behind three weeks on the insurance money, and he asked me to—"

The little guy was shaking his head. Richie wasn't even finished with what he had to say, and already this geek is shaking his head, no, no, no.

"What am I paying for?" the guy said. Talking fast, like if he said his piece first, then you wouldn't be able to finish what you were saying. "We had Vice in here Saturday night. They busted four girls and threatened to bust me for 'keeping a house of assignation,' whatever that is. So whatever I was paying for, I'm not getting it."

"—come by and talk to you about it." Richie finished. "Now, it sounds like you think you have a problem. Let me ask you, have any of the girls had a fight with each other? Anything like that? Has one of the johns beat up a girl? Anybody broke up any of the furniture?"

He waited, but the guy didn't have anything to say. "How about when Voochie cut that other pimp in that argument about who owned that Korean chick? Didn't we take care of that for you? You want to keep those kind of things in line, you got to keep your insurance paid up."

The little guy deflated, shrinking like a balloon losing air but still shaking his head, no, no, no.

"The bank just raised the variable interest rate," he said. "On the loan. Another two hundred a month that costs me. The linen has gone up. Almost double. That's one of Mr. DiAngelo's companies that I have to get the linen from. And the City has put some kind of sewer bond on the property. With all that, I'm going in the hole a grand a month, without even saying that the building needs a new roof, which will cost twenty or twenty-five thousand. So I can't pay. Look, no hard feelings, huh? I'll just have to take my chances with those things happening, okay?"

Richie nodded. "Yeah, I see that you have a problem. I wish I could help you, I really do. But see, Mr. DiAngelo . . ."

The geek wasn't listening. Richie could see his eyes had glazed over, and he wasn't listening. He had made up his mind, and he was just waiting until Richie finished talking, and then he was going to say he was sorry again, and keep saying it. It was too bad. Richie had hoped it wouldn't go this far.

"That your car down there by the office?" Richie said. "That blue Camaro?" Pointing, getting the guy to turn his head.

"Huh? Where?" the guy said. "Where? What's wrong with my car?" Turning to the railing and looking down into the courtyard.

Richie got one hand in the guy's hair, and one into his belt, in the small of his back. Clean-and-jerk, and the guy was off the ground and over Richie's head.

"*Hey!*" the guy said. His voice had gone squeaky. "Hey! What the hell . . ." as Richie threw him over the railing above the courtyard.

He yelled all the way down. The yell chopped off, at the bottom.

Then there was silence, except for the whine of the vacuum cleaner.

Richie walked back along the balcony, down the stairs, and into the office again. He pushed the button by the speaker grille.

The woman shuffled out of the back and came up to the inside of the sealed teller's window. "Yes?" she said. "Yes? What is it?"

"Mrs. Wessel," Richie said. "Your husband fell off the balcony. You should go and see if he's hurt. And you'll want to make sure your insurance stays paid up, in case something like this happens again. You should make sure to keep Mr. DiAngelo paid on time."

Richie walked out of the office, leaving the woman turned to stone, the back of one hand pressed against her mouth.

He had walked two or three blocks along the street before Dominic slid the Mercedes to a stop next to him. Richie climbed in the front and shut the door.

"How'd it go?" Dominic asked.

"No problem. Puffed-up little fuck. Threw him off the balcony. Landed in the swimming pool. He was thrashing around in there, so I guess he isn't dead. You wanna cruise by Rogelio's, see if there's any chicks there?"

"Nah," Dominic said, concentrating on his driving, sliding the big car through the traffic. "We got one more reminder."

"Who's that?"

"In Westwood? You remember, you been over there a couple times. They been pretty good up to now, but they didn't have the money there the last time. We had to wait a week."

"Uh-huh," Richie said. "You sure? I seen that blonde there last night. The blonde with the brown eyes that you liked. Rogelio said she asked about you."

"Oh yeah?" Dominic glanced at his watch. "Well, maybe we could just swing by. Check it out. We can always remind the Westwood people on Friday."

"Sure," Richie said. "Sure. That'll be fine."

CHAPTER

2

AN AIRPLANE HANGAR, YOU would have said. Big rolling doors, arched roof trusses, no windows. A hangar, for sure. But hangars have room for airplanes to taxi in and out.

A factory, then. Factory buildings are jammed together with only narrow asphalt driveways between them. But factories have windows, or glass roofpanels.

So a gymnasium, maybe, or an indoor swimming pool.

Or a sound stage.

Pike had parked his car in a lot a half block away, at which point the directions had become a little vague. The car was a six-year-old Porsche 911 with a bad case of rust in the fenders and rocker panels. The car had belonged to Pike's ex-wife, who had brought it to California from New York, where it had spent its early years acquiring the rust. The ex-wife had left the car, along with other castoffs of their marriage, and gone back to New York, taking with her only the proceeds from the sale of the house, which had been awarded to her in the property settlement. Pike still drove the car because it was cheaper than buying a new one. Besides, he liked it, although he sometimes worried that it was a California cliché.

Leaning their shoulders against the wall outside the door of the sound stage were two girls. Production assistants, or makeup or wardrobe. Both of them had Styrofoam coffee cups and were in identical poses: one leg bent at the knee, the sole of the foot resting against the wall. Closest to the door was a brunette, slender, with long hair to her waist. She was wearing jeans and a man's blue work shirt, and smoking a cigarette. The other was a shorter blonde in pastel green slacks and a matching sleeveless blouse.

Pike nodded at the girls. Neither so much as blinked in reply, but the blonde glanced at her watch and said, "We'd better get back."

The other girl tossed her head, rippling that fantastic hair. "We got time. Owen won't start without us. Besides, I want to finish my cigarette."

Pike had his hand on the door handle. He stopped for a second.

"I just wish he wasn't so mean in front of everybody on the set," the blonde said.

"Excuse me," Pike said, still with his hand on the door handle. "I'm looking for Mickey McDonald's set."

"He only does it because he's nervous," the long-haired girl said. "It comes across as hostile, but it's his own insecurity. But you can't ever let him see that you know that. Just look him in the eye, and say, 'Oh, yes, Owen,' and smile. You'll be fine."

The blonde nodded. She wasn't sure she liked what she was hearing. "Yeah," she said. "Yeah, well . . ."

"Excuse me," Pike said again. "I'm sorry to bother you, but . . ."

Both girls looked at Pike and in that split second he decided he knew them. He'd seen them before, a dozen times. Seen them by the hundreds around the fringes of the movie industry. If you'd sent out a casting call for a soft-drink commercial, they'd have been among the three hundred hopefuls, all in their early twenties, who'd have showed up. And if you were a bigshot casting director, you'd have rejected the blonde immediately. Her eyes were too close together, and she pouted when she talked.

The long-haired one, when you looked carefully at her—looking through the first impression—you'd have thought, 'Well, the nose is maybe a tiny bit too big, and she's a shade heavy in the tush.' And if you were casting this soft-drink commercial, you'd have said, "Sorry darling, we can't use you." And she'd have had an answer, flip, wry and mocking. And you'd have looked again at the quick light of intelligence in the eyes, and wondered: Can we use her for the toxic waste piece, as the concerned young mother? And then you'd have thought—still being the big-shot casting director— 'Nah, in a meat market like Hollywood, we can get one that's a straight ten on looks *and* comes across as smart too.' But maybe as a consolation prize you'd have put her in the soft drink commercial anyhow. Stuck her in the background in a bikini with a beach ball, told her to arch her back and look starry-eyed. And when you saw her after the shooting was finished, and tried to hit on her, because she owed you for the job, she'd have stuck that nose in the air, and turned down the corners of that wide mouth, and told you to fuck off.

And all of that was in a glance, and a sentence spoken in an undertone to another woman.

And in the next second, Pike thought: Maurice is right. I incorporate one lousy production company and I think I know everything about the movie business. Have to cut that shit out.

The long-haired girl, still looking at Pike, squinted slightly against the smoke that rose from her cigarette. "If you're looking for Mickey McDonald's set"—she took a drag on her cigarette and exhaled through her mouth and nose at the same time— "you came to the right place. It's inside there. You can't miss it."

Pike pushed through the outer door, into the pitch blackness of the light trap, shoved open the inner door, and stepped into the sound stage. There could have been five sets inside, or fifty, but only the one just inside the door was lighted. The rest of the interior faded into a muddled obscurity, in which the lighted set was a tentative island of normality surrounded by coils of cable and camera dollies.

The set replicated an office conference room—big table, a dozen identical swivel chairs, couch at one end of the room with some bright throw pillows. In the rear wall was a dummy window, lighted to simulate slanting late-afternoon sun. Two men in business suits were sitting on the couch, doing absolutely nothing.

Other people, more casually dressed, drifted to and fro around and across the set. No one seemed to be in charge but it was hard to tell, because no one was doing anything except milling around. But there was a wiry, angry-looking man in one of those wood-and-canvas chairs that people call director's chairs. He was sitting down to drink his coffee, while everyone else was standing up to drink theirs, and he had a porcelain cup instead of Styrofoam. That seemed enough for a start. Pike stopped in front of the angry man, who sipped his coffee and glared.

"Excuse me, are you Mickey McDonald?"

The man snorted into his coffee cup. "No, I am not Mickey McDonald. Do I look like Mickey McDonald?"

"I don't know what Mickey McDonald looks like. Can you tell me where to find Mickey McDonald?"

"How should *I* know? I have to keep track of everyone *else* on this set, at least I do *not* have to keep track of the director. The director has to keep track of the director. We are having a coffee break. I have no idea where Mickey is. But I can tell you that when we start shooting, Mickey will be right *there*." He pointed at a spot on the stage near his feet.

"Could I talk to Mr. McDonald for a minute?"

The angry man put his coffee cup down on the floor and snorted again. "We're in the middle of a shot here. You can't talk to *any*body until we get through."

"And when will that be?"

"Who knows? One more take? Five more takes? Who knows?"

"Is it okay if I wait?"

"Who *are* you?" The angry man looked at Pike and didn't like what he saw. "And how did you get on the set? And why do you want to see Mickey anyhow?"

"David Pike. I've got a letter from another production company that Mr. McDonald is shooting for—the film that's on hiatus? I showed it to the security guard. I'm the lawyer for the company—the production company, I mean. I need to talk to him about some financial matters. Mr. McDonald."

The angry man smiled to himself. He was vastly amused by something but wasn't saying what. "Just don't get in the way," he said. "Stand over there and keep out of the way."

Over there was next to an anonymous piece of equipment that was covered by a canvas shroud. Pike folded his arms and stood next to the shrouded object. There was a kind of tidal motion toward the set and its immediate surroundings. People drifted past, tossed cups into wastebaskets, sat down at consoles, picked up pencils and clipboards. Pike tried to decide which of the new arrivals was Mickey McDonald. Maybe the guy in the fringed buckskin shirt with the necklace of wooden Ashanti beads. Or the one that Buckskin was talking to—nervous, intense, drumming his fingers on the sound console.

The angry man was fussing around, looking through the viewfinder of a camera. He stepped away and glanced right and left.

"Well now," he said, sarcastically. "Well now, if we're all here, maybe we can begin?" He waited a moment, the sergeant-major pausing after calling the battalion to attention. "If you don't mind, people," he said loudly. "Quiet please! Let's have it quiet on the set."

He paused for effect. It had already been quiet on the set. Now it became a fraction quieter. He lifted his chin. "Stand by . . ."

The long-haired girl from outside stepped forward from somewhere behind Pike. She touched the cameraman on the shoulder in passing and came to a stop near the angry man.

"Roll camera," she said. Her voice was husky but penetrating.

The cameraman glued his face to his viewfinder. "Rolling," he said.

The long-haired girl looked across to the far side of the set. "Roll sound."

The man in fringed buckskin had donned a pair of earphones and taken a seat at a console. He put one finger in the air and revolved it rapidly. "Speed," he said.

"Mark it." This came from the angry man. Someone clacked a clapstick in front of the camera.

The long-haired girl looked around the set, just a quick glance. "Action," she said.

In a stagy way, one of the actors got up from the couch and crossed to the dummy window. He leaned both arms on the sill and stared out into the imaginary middle distance. There was some dialogue about alcohol problems and how a local treatment center had helped one of his colleagues. The dialogue ran to a conclusion.

"Cut," the long-haired girl said, tossing her head so that her hair rippled.

The angry man was standing next to her. "Beautiful, Mickey. That was beautiful. The best yet. Do the next setup?"

"No." The girl stood for a moment, tapping her foot. Then she walked onto the set and picked up a throw pillow from the couch. She spoke to one of the actors. "Ed, when you stand up, I want you to knock this onto the floor. About . . . here." She dropped the pillow on the floor, near the couch. "Then, when you go across to the window, kick it, and then step over it, and go to the window, okay? And Tom . . ." She turned to the other actor. "This is the president of the company, right? You're making a suggestion that could save his job, his marriage, maybe save his life. You're humble. Resolute but humble. Think humble."

She turned and walked off the set. "All right, one more time."

They went through the whole rigmarole again. The scene played again. The conversation unfolded. The actor on the couch rose to his feet in agitation, knocked the pillow to the floor, blundered over it, and fetched up against the window. Somehow, his tripping on the pillow made the whole thing real. It wasn't actors, it was two friends having an awkward discussion of a sensitive issue.

"Cut," the long-haired girl said. "That's it. Next setup."

The angry man bustled forward. "All right, people. Scene three, the hospital. Let's move it. Talent—break for thirty minutes."

The long-haired girl turned to Pike. "Now what is it you want Mickey McDonald for?"

"I thought you were a grip."

"You mean outside? Don't try to kid me. You thought production assistant. Most of the time people think I'm some production assistant who's sleeping with the director."

"Sorry."

She tossed her head and the long hair rippled. She knew it looked good, and she knew that you watched it, but she still did it. She was that kind of woman.

"Don't sweat it," she said. "I'm used to it."

The smog made for great sunsets. The suspended particles refracted enough light that the air itself glowed with a hot, pumpkin-colored light, like the inside of a foundry. The molten glow flowed through the blinds and threw dark shadows on the far wall of the office. Pike put a finger between two slats of the venetian blinds and pushed the lower slat down to make a hole to look through. He squinted down at the basin of the harbor, then let go of the blind. The slat snapped back into place.

"Why didn't you tell me the director was a woman?" he said into the phone.

"Didn't I?" Maurice said. "Yes, I did. I'm sure I did. What difference does it make?"

"What difference? What difference! Maurie, I'm all wound up to deal with a *guy*, maybe lean on him a little, tell him, come on, let's go right now and get the financial records, and here's this slender little thing, looks like she's about eighteen."

"No, no. She's got to be thirty, or around in there."

"Maurie, I don't care how *old* she is. What I'm saying is that I went to talk to a guy and it was a girl instead, and you didn't tell me that."

"I'm sure I told you, David. Positive of it. But let's not argue. Did you get the records?"

Pike sighed. "I didn't get anything yet, but I got an appointment to go over on Saturday, to pick up the paperwork."

"And she didn't mind? I mean, she wasn't upset about letting you have the records?"

"No. Not a bit of it. Straightforward business deal. You want the financial records, yessir three bags full, and come on Saturday after softball practice. Of course that gives her two days to come up with something creative—if we're worried about that."

Maurice grunted. Pike wasn't sure if that meant they were worried about her cooking the books or not. "She said she doesn't have an office." He prompted. "Does that sound right? Said to meet her at her apartment."

"Yeah," Maurice said. "A lot of them don't. Free-lance directors. They have an office address, mostly it's just a phone and a place to send mail to. She'd probably keep her records at home."

There was a tap at the door of Pike's office. When it opened, Sid Stoddard strolled in, holding his pipe in one hand. Stoddard was the senior partner in the firm. He always wore his jacket, even in the office, and his courtly manners, wispy white hair, and frail physique made him seem benign and ineffectual. This was an assumption adversaries made only once and regretted ever after. Stoddard slid into one of Pike's client chairs and began loading his pipe, tamping the tobacco with his thumb.

Pike raised his eyebrows inquiringly, but Stoddard made a staying gesture with one hand: keep on with what you're doing, I'll wait.

"Uh-huh," Pike said. "Maurie, this still seems like a lot of hassle over a little thing. One more time, tell me, why couldn't *you* have just asked straight out for the records?"

"All right," Maurice said. "All right. I'll give you another reason. I said I'd worked with Mickey before. It's more than that. In some ways, Mickey is like one of my own children. No, closer than that. Mickey is in and out of my house all the time, comes over for tennis, comes to use the pool, or just to talk. My own kids I haven't seen in what? Not since I divorced their mother, married my third wife, rest her soul. So if I ask something that can be construed as an accusation of stealing, then I offend somebody who's one of my few close friends. That I care about. I don't have so many friends anymore that I can afford to do that. Anyhow, I don't believe anything's been stolen, I just want it checked out."

"All right," Pike said. "All right. It's your nickel, we'll do it your way." He hung up.

Stoddard slipped his tobacco pouch back into the side pocket of his coat. "I had Maurice Baranowitz in my office this afternoon," he said. "Complaining about you."

"This afternoon? How could he have been in your office this afternoon? He was with me this afternoon. And that was just him. On the phone."

"He said he'd been in to see you. Ducked into my office on the way to the elevator."

"Sid, why do I get a funny feeling with that guy? Like he's telling me about one thing and using it to hide two other things."

Stoddard shook his head. "Maurice is just that way. Maybe he had to be that way in the old days around this town. Maybe he still does. He's stayed independent, made a good living, and ended up well off, and none of the majors ever was successful in taking him over, or running him off. Being forthright and open wouldn't have helped him a whole lot."

"So what was he complaining about?"

Stoddard always sat the same way, back erect, both feet flat on the floor. Never leaned or slouched. Now he frowned at his shoes, then took out a handkerchief and dusted the toe of his left shoe. They were lace-up shoes—Stoddard never wore loafers or shoes with buckles. Pike had a picture at home of his grandfather wearing a pair that looked exactly the same. He'd showed it to Stoddard once.

"You," Stoddard said. "Says you ask too many questions and don't want to do what you're told."

"And you said?"

"I said you didn't always do things the same way that I would, but that nobody complained about the results—just sometimes about the body count."

"Thanks a lot." Pike filled a glass of water.

"David, David. Don't be huffy. I was admitted to practice in 1933. We did things differently then. Had a different approach. Of course you do things differently now. As well you should. If the guys on the other side don't behave like gentlemen—and more and more these days they don't—then I see nothing wrong with giving as good as you get. What's the expression? 'What goes around comes around'?"

Pike, irritated, but trying not to let it show, said, "So tell me, Sid, am I off the case, or what? What is this all about?"

Stoddard hadn't lit his pipe. He gestured with it. "Gently, gently. Who said anything about you being off the case?"

"You said Maurice was complaining about me. It doesn't take a great brain to guess what comes next."

"David, usually you're very smooth. A strong advocate, but smooth. If Maurice is complaining to me, I have to wonder: what's going on? Why is the client unhappy when we're here to make him happy? So I'm asking. That's all. Just asking."

"Uh-huh. Well, there's not much I can tell you. It's like I said. Maurie's got this funny look, all sincere and wide-eyed, looking straight at you. Like he's pumping you full of shit and hopes you don't notice."

Pike shook his head and frowned. "You know how it is sometimes. You're cross-examining a witness, you ask a simple question, and you get back an answer that doesn't quite fit. It isn't wrong, it's just a little bit out of whack. And you get this feeling, 'Ah ha! Something is under here. Let's just push on it a little, and see what we find.' That's how I feel around Maurice. So I push a little more than maybe I would ordinarily."

Stoddard got to his feet. "All right. Just so you know he feels you pushing. So now you can do whatever you think best."

"Was that all, Sid? He just complained?"

"All that was of any importance. He was curious about you."

"Curious about what?"

"Why do you care?"

"I don't know." Slowly, thinking as he went. "Maybe because if I know what he asks about me, I could try to figure out what it is that bothers me about him. What'd he ask?"

"What you'd done before you came with the firm, that kind of thing."

Stoddard had taken out a box of matches. He opened the box, selected a match, and slid the box closed again. Waited while Pike thought, frowned, and then thought some more.

"All right," Pike said finally. "I'll try to ease up the next time I see him. Take it a little easier. That satisfy you?"

Stoddard struck the match and held it to the bowl of his pipe. He spoke between aromatic puffs. "Whatever you think best, David. I'll leave it entirely . . . up to you."

Pike watched the door close behind Stoddard, and then swiveled his chair to face the window. The sun was lower, but the hot orange light was the same. Most of the cars down on Lincoln had their headlights on. Pike stared out the window, not seeing the view, thinking.

Stoddard had brought Maurice to Pike's office for the first time maybe nine or ten months before. Pike had come back from an appointment and found Stoddard sitting on the corner of his desk, swinging one leg back and forth, and stuffing the bowl of his pipe. Perched in one of Pike's client chairs, not saying a word, was a dour, sallow-faced little man with hair so black it was obviously dyed. Pike waited to see what they wanted. Stoddard pointed at the dour man with the stem of his pipe. "David, meet Morris Baranowitz. Morrie, David Pike."

"*Maurice*," the sallow man said. "I had it changed legally, Sid. It's Maurice now."

And only after this had been firmly established did he extend his hand to Pike. A limp hand, not much of a shake, saying at the same time—petulant, querulous—"Sid, why can't you just keep on handling my stuff? It isn't ever much, and we won't have to reinvent the wheel with some new *hohem.*"

Pike didn't speak Yiddish, but he knew a *hohem* was a smart-aleck kid. If that was how the guy felt, he could stuff himself, and take his business elsewhere too.

Feeling as he did, Pike tried not to participate in the little act he and Sid had developed for those moments when Sid was handing over a client. He left Sid to play both parts himself. Only Sid wasn't having any of that. He'd talk for a while and get something wrong on purpose, so that Pike would have to correct him, and then he'd prod his young colleague into filling in more detail.

Sid did what he always did—skipped over law school or anything else that was really relevant, to how good Pike might be at what the client was going to pay him to do, and dwelt at length on Pike's youthful folly: four years in the CIC, the Army Counter-Intelligence Corps. Went into excruciating detail about the training at Fort Holabird, Maryland, all the dirty tricks stuff, codes and microdots, and how to use Oriental dirty-fighting techniques to beat the shit out of spies and saboteurs and other Enemies of the Republic. Dwelt on Pike's tour with the Intelligence Support Activity at Fort Belvoir, that was supposed to rescue the hostages from the Tehran embassy. (And did its part pretty well, thank you very much, Pike thought. Got into Tehran, rented trucks, had keys to the embassy gates made. And then the Navy began crashing helicopters all over the fucking desert and the whole operation ended up a shambles.)

The recitation was calculated to show what a tough son-of-a-bitch Pike was, although what that had to do with being a good lawyer was another question entirely. Maurice hadn't wanted Pike working for him then, and apparently he still didn't. Well, fuck Maurice.

CHAPTER

3

"YOU GET *NATIONAL GEOGRAPHIC?*" Dominic asked, munching greens.

Richie didn't get *National Geographic.*

"Well, I don't either, but there was one in the barbershop, about these wolves in . . . I think it was Alaska or somewhere. And there were these pictures. There's like four wolves and these caribou. You know what caribou are?"

Richie didn't know what caribou were.

"They're like a deer, you know, with horns." Dominic held his fingers to his forehead, demonstrating. "Anyhow, these caribou—there's millions of 'em. *Millions.* They like migrate or something, and as far as you can see there's nothing but caribou. Anyhow there's, like I said, four wolves. And in about five minutes the wolves have dodged around, and made a fake here, a fake there, and got one of the caribou and killed it, and they're eating it, and the rest of the caribou are just running by, past where the wolves and the dead caribou are, not looking left or right, just running by the wolves eating on one of their buddies."

They were in this health-food restaurant on Sunset, the restaurant that was in the last scene of *Annie Hall*—Woody Allen is in the parking lot of this restaurant and some cop is hassling him because he doesn't have his driver's license. Dominic liked it because he was into health food, at least sometimes. Mostly he liked red meat and booze, but occasionally he'd go on a health-food kick for a day, or even two days, and eat alfalfa sprouts and whole wheat. Dominic was eating some kind of vegetarian sandwich, and Richie was eating a burger. Richie didn't get health food. Richie also didn't get it about the wolves and the caribou. "I don't get it," he said.

Dominic smiled. He felt a little sorry for Richie. The man was so slow. Had to have things explained to him. Things that were obvious, if you just looked at them. What it was, was he was dumb. Dumb but dangerous. Dangerous *because* he was dumb. Couldn't figure out how to put a deal together without help, but give him directions, point him at something, and look out!

The way Richie and Dominic met, a little over a year ago:

Richie had decided that going back to Bakersfield after San Quentin was a bad idea. Bakersfield was a nothing place. The whole San Joaquin Valley was one big nothing. But when he was due for release, a guy Richie knew at Q told him about this club in West Hollywood. The guy'd worked there. They had mostly yuppies in there, in their late twenties and thirties. Thought they were cool and tough and with it. Stood at the bar and ordered tequila shooters and talked about "dead meat" and "hardball" and looked at their Rolexes and ordered another round. Only sometimes they could get out of hand if they got into too much White Lady, and tried to *act* tough. The club liked to have somebody there to quiet them down.

So Richie went to L.A. and got a job at this club, and didn't have to do anything but stand around, wearing a tux, and look mean, maybe once a week help quiet somebody down and stuff him in a car.

One night he's standing out front, talking to the doorman and the guy who parked the cars, and this Mercedes pulls into the driveway. The car is all black, dark windows, all the chrome blacked out, and Richie says to the doorman that it looks like a hearse. And they're having a laugh, and this Oriental guy gets out, looks right at Richie, and throws his car keys at him. Says, "I'll be back in a half hour. Park it where it won't get dings in the doors." And walks into the club.

The doorman is there, he's got this long coat that divides in two in the back, with all gold braid on it, and a stupid hat, and the parking-lot guy is there, he's got this white jacket, and a pad of claim checks sticking out of his pocket, and Richie in a tux. And the guy throws the keys right at Richie. Now how stupid was that? Guy can't even tell the outside help from the inside. Or Richie could have even been a customer. How did the guy know Richie wasn't a customer? Or maybe he didn't care. Maybe he thought he could just order people around, tell them what to do, no matter who they were. Well that was bullshit.

A lot of Richie's problems had started with his temper. When he was playing football in high school, varsity even in his freshman year, he spent so much time in juvie, the coach threatened to throw him off the team, but never did. If Richie was there, the coach always played Richie in the games. The time in Juvenile Hall was mostly for fights. Someone would say something, or Richie would see them looking at him funny, and he'd bust them in the mouth. And when it was all over, he couldn't really explain why it had been so irritating, but it happened again the next time just the same way.

But after Q, Richie had cooled down a little. Tried to take things a little easy, not be on the muscle all the time. So when the guy threw the car keys, Richie thought about busting him in the mouth. But instead he caught the keys, walked around the back of the Mercedes, got in, started it, and drove away. Went down on Sunset, sat in a bar and popped a couple beers, watched some TV, and finally, around nine o'clock, drove back to the club.

The manager was there, out front under the awning over the driveway, and the guy whose car it was—big for an Oriental, almost six feet and two hundred easy—and the doorman, and the guy who parked the cars. All of 'em standing around, talking to one another. And right away, when Richie gets out of the car, the manager goes, "Do you know what the sentence for grand theft auto is in this state?"

Richie goes, "Well, I don't see where there's any theft, the guy gives you the keys."

And the manager goes on, whining and fussing. And the Oriental guy, the one who owned the car, he comes around the driver's side, where Richie is, and he's pissed off.

"You asshole," he says. "I told you half an hour, I meant half an hour. You got any idea how much it's going to cost me because I missed a meeting because you had my wheels?"

Richie says, "No, and I don't care either."

And the guy says, "Yeah? Then maybe this'll help you understand." And he throws a punch at Richie.

Now the guy is not bad, but Richie has been spending two, three hours a day in the gym at Q with some guys could have wrote the book about streetfights, and he's better. So pretty soon the guy has a bloody nose, and he's going to have at least one black eye in a day or two, when it has time to bruise up good, and Richie is fine, not a scratch on him.

Then the manager, he takes the Oriental guy inside, to get ice in a towel for his nose, and as they go in the door, he says to Richie, showing off in front of his customer, "You're out of here, you understand? Pick up your check on Friday."

But Richie, he doesn't plan to be anywhere around on Friday, in case the customer puts in a beef to the cops and they're there waiting when he comes to pick up his pay. He's learned a couple of things, so he goes, "The California Labor Code says, it says, if you fire somebody, you got to pay them on the spot the wages you owe them. That seventy-two-hours crap is for if they quit. And in cash money, no checks."

So Richie is waiting for the manager to bring him his money, standing around out front. Only he isn't talking to the doorman and the parking-lot guy anymore, because they're afraid the manager will think they're on Richie's side, and fire them too. They're down at the end of the driveway, pretending they don't know Richie, when the guy comes out, the one who owns the car. He's got a dish towel held up against his nose, and he's keeping his head tipped back, trying not to get his nose started again, and he has this envelope in the hand that isn't holding the towel. And he says to Richie, kind of muffled because of the towel, "This is for you, your money," and holds out the envelope to Richie. And then he says, "I talked to the manager about you. If you want a job, I think I can use you."

Richie says, "Oh yeah? Doing what?" Thinking: Sure, Jack. I bust you in the nose, and you're going to do me a favor?

And the guy says, "Driving, for starters, and maybe some other things. I have an industrial laundry business, and a couple of sidelines. Get in. Let's talk about it." And he hands Richie the keys to the Mercedes, and the envelope, and gets in the passenger door, and sits there, with his head tipped back, and the towel under his nose.

Richie stands there, with the keys and the envelope in his hand.

Finally the guy slides across to the driver's side of the car, and opens the door from the inside. "You think I'm going to do something funny, is that it?" he says.

Richie doesn't say anything, just stands there with the keys and the envelope in his hand.

The guy pops open the glove box of the Mercedes, takes out an automatic pistol, and lays it on the driver's seat.

"Here," he says. "If you're worried I'm going to do something funny, you can hold this while we talk. Now get in the car, will you?"

And that was how Richie met Domenico Scarlatti Nakamura.

They had a deal going now. Richie drove Dominic when Dominic wanted him to, and did reminders and deliveries, and made between eight and twelve bills a week, sometimes more.

"So, Dominic," Richie said. "I don't get it about the caribou."

Dominic thinking, "How can the man be so slow?" said, "What have the wolves got? They're outnumbered, right? Outweighed, right? One of those caribou weighs as much as all four wolves put together. If a couple of those caribou get together and decide to stomp on a wolf, it's good-bye wolf. But the caribou don't have organization. They don't work together, the way the wolves do. And as long as it stays that way, the wolves can have dinner anytime they want. That's you and me, Richie." Thinking: I'm a wolf, but I don't know what he is. Not a wolf, but maybe a bull. Yeah, a bull, with dull, slow strength and that awesome rage.

Pike was invariably amused when he saw a reference to Malibu in a magazine or in the caption of a photograph. The reference was usually to Malibu as being the place where movie stars lived, with tennis courts and stables, and acres of landscaped hillside sloping down to the blue Pacific.

Maybe there really was some of that, but mostly it was quite ordinary people striving to live in the way they thought famous people might, and looking out of the corners of their eyes to make sure that they were being noticed.

This part of Malibu didn't even rise to that level of ambition. The houses were in a style called California ranch, which was really no style at all, unless sliding aluminum windows and heavy shake roofs could pass as an architectural statement. Most of them did have a little land around them — a quarter or even half an acre — but it was rarely landscaped and usually covered with the native chaparral. Maybe they would have sold for four hundred or four-fifty, the ones with bigger lots and a pool, but they would have sold for almost as much in Van Nuys, or San Fernando, or Palos Verdes.

When they were rented, they rented for three times what Pike paid for the rent-controlled one-bedroom in Santa Monica that he thought of as home. At least he'd thought of it as home since the divorce. That was why this house was such a good deal. It was owned by a tenured professor at Pepperdine College who was on sabbatical, poking through archives in Madrid, doing research for the definitive work on the politics of Aragon and Castile and the effect thereof on the third voyage of Columbus. The professor hadn't wanted his house left vacant, or rented again to tenants who might paint the master bedroom purple or throw the kind of parties that ended up with the sheriff being called. The professor was a friend of a friend of a friend, and the upshot was that Pike was house sitting, making sure the algae didn't take over the professor's swimming pool, nor the weeds choke his flower beds.

Most mornings Pike would run down the hill to Highway One, and then along it past the shopping center at Trancas, almost to the entrance of Zuma Beach. It was about a mile and a half down, or maybe closer to two miles, but that was the easy part. Then, in some kind of existential shift, the way back, up the hill to the house, was definitely all of two miles, and maybe more.

Pike had gotten into running for the exercise, but found that he continued to do it not just for that reason but because it provided time to think—time away from the phone, away from talking to anyone, away from doing anything but being alone with yourself. Pike had a theory that a lot of the hassles in which people found themselves could be worked out, if people would just take twenty or thirty minutes a day and be alone with themselves.

He had tried to explain this theory once to his ex-wife, Amanda, before she became an ex. Amanda was a clinical psychologist and felt proprietary about theories that dealt with what went on inside peoples' heads. She had therefore explained, succinctly, just why his theory was ill conceived, lacked definition, and ran contrary to accepted clinical thought. Pike had thanked her for her views (which had not changed his theory one iota) and continued to run three miles a day whenever he could.

He was almost home, only a hundred yards from the house, at the place where the street branched off and led steeply uphill, when a teenage boy came out of the house that was next down the hill from where Pike was house sitting. The boy came out into the clear early light, onto the tiled front porch. He left the front door open and started along the driveway toward the street. Coming down to the road to get the morning paper, Pike assumed.

Pike passed the end of the driveway, pushing it, trying to get the three miles—or maybe it was closer to four—done in something approaching six minutes per mile.

"Sir! Excuse me! Excuse me, sir!"

Pike broke stride and stopped, breathing hard. Bent one arm and buried his face in the crook of his elbow, wiping the sweat with his sleeve. "Yes? What is it?"

It wasn't a teenage boy. It was a girl, or a small woman. Short blond hair, as short as a man's. Maybe an inch or two over five feet. A small-boned face. Plain features. Eyebrows startlingly dark against the pale skin and blond hair. A kind of loose-jointed stance, thumbs hooked in the pockets of a pair of faded jeans. A casting director would have grabbed her in a minute, to play the girl next door. The one who never has a chance at ending up with the lead. Someone's kid sister.

"I'm sorry. This is really dumb." Her voice had a slight nasal twang. "But the garbage disposal is stuck, and I can't get it loose with this damn little wrench and I wondered if you could help me, before I have to call a plumber."

Her "damn" had two syllables: "Da-yum."

Pike had a little breath back now. He bent his other arm and wiped his face again. "Glad to take a look. Can't promise anything, though. I can usually manage to get everybody in the room wet if I try to change a faucet washer. I'm Dave Pike, and you're . . ."

"Mildred. Mildred Dossfelter. But for God's sake call me Dossie. I hate Mildred."

"Uh-huh. I thought the Foleys lived here. Have they moved?"

"Oh, no. Millie—Millicent Foley—is my sister. My folks were into M-names. We have one other sister. Her name is Mabel, can you believe it? I mean, even for sodbusters, Mildred, Millicent, and Mabel are pretty bad. If they'd had a boy they were going to name him Matthew or Mark or Marshall. Daddy really wanted a boy.

That's why all us girls got electric trains for Christmas, and .22 rifles for our birthdays. We kind of got raised as boys."

"Uh-huh," Pike said, feeling overwhelmed by the rush of words. "And where are you from?"

"Muleshoe." Looking at him for a moment. Gray eyes. Nothing startling, just clear gray eyes. They were the best part of the face, set wide apart, a little fleck of gold in the left one, about six o'clock, in the iris.

Seeing his lack of comprehension, she said, "You don't know where that is, do you? Northwest of Lubbock about fifty miles. Or southwest of Amarillo about the same distance, if you like that better." Then, seeing him still confused, "In the Panhandle. North Texas."

"Ah," he said. "That explains the accent." And was startled when she blushed a furious red.

She had an Allen wrench. Mild steel, not hardened. It went into a hole in the bottom of the disposal unit, under the sink. Whatever was jammed into the disposal was in there tightly enough that the soft metal of the wrench merely bent and didn't break the jam loose. Pike slid out from under the sink, stood up, and looked into the drain.

"What were you running through it?"

"Seeds from a papaya. You wouldn't think they would be hard enough to jam it. I mean, they're so itty bitty." She looked into the drain, too. The top of her head didn't come up to Pike's shoulder. He could smell her hair. A clean soapy smell.

Pike reached into the disposal and poked away some of the mass of round, shiny black seeds. In the center of the opening, down in the bottom, was what looked like a half-inch hex nut.

"Look," he said. "This Allen wrench is no good. But there's a nut in here, and I've got a socket set up at the house. Let me go up and get a couple of sockets, and maybe we can break this thing loose."

She wouldn't hear of it. Had no idea it was such a big project. Didn't want to take up his time, cut into his day. She'd call a plumber; they'd take care of it in no time.

"Hey!" Pike said, cutting her off. "Hey! It's no big deal. It'll take five minutes. I'll be right back."

He jogged the rest of the way uphill to the house. Thought about a shower, compromised on sponging off with a washcloth and putting on a clean sweatshirt. Took the tray from the top of the toolbox with the graduated row of sockets and the ratchet handle, and walked back down the hill.

The sun was pretty well up now. A couple of red-tailed hawks were hanging in the air, a hundred feet above the chaparral. Occasionally one of them would give a lazy stroke or two with his wings. There were mice and pocket gophers that lived in the chaparral, and as Pike watched one of the hawks folded his wings and stooped, disappearing into the brush.

It was all very quiet and peaceful in the clear early light—except, Pike thought, for whatever had been on the receiving end of the hawk's stoop. He shrugged and went into the house, calling, "Mildred? Dossie? I'm back."

A half-inch socket worked fine. Broke whatever it was loose on the first try. Pike flipped the wall switch and the disposal whirred into life. When he turned around from the sink, she was pouring coffee. Had the table set for two with plates, linen napkins, cups and saucers. Warm croissants in a basket in the center of the table, and a half-papaya on a plate at each place. Insisted that he should stay for breakfast. Wouldn't take no for an answer. She was staying with her sister for a few weeks. Thought it was beautiful. The ocean, the hills. Only thing was, there was a crack in the pool. It had been drained while they fixed it. What a drag, you know? If there weren't a pool at all, it would be fine, but having one that didn't work—How long had he lived up the hill?

Just for a few weeks. He was taking care of the place for a professor who was on sabbatical. Had a place of his own in Santa

Monica, but it was more like a place to crash while he was going through a divorce. He'd kept the boat, a thirteen-foot sailboat. And her car. She got everything else.

The house he was taking care of had a pool. It was full, and the solar heater worked. She could come up and use it any time she wanted. Just ring the bell and if he wasn't home, go on in the backyard and make herself at home.

That was nice of him. She might do that. She was getting out of shape, not being able to swim. Did he really have a boat? And it was a sailboat? Maybe she could go out on it sometime. She'd always wanted to learn how to sail. Never had the chance before.

"Sure," Pike said. "We can take it out some evening when the wind has died down a little. That's the way to learn—small boat, sheltered water inside the harbor, not too much wind. Of course you usually get wet. C-13s turn over pretty easily and everybody dumps a couple of times until they get the hang of it."

"Could we really do that sometime? I'd love that. But don't do it if it's any trouble."

"No trouble," Pike said, "I'd enjoy it." He caught sight of his watch. "Good lord! Is that the time? I've got to be downtown to pick up some accounting records in a half-hour. I'd better run. Thanks for breakfast."

On the way into town it was the eyes Pike remembered. Clear and grey, with a level, open gaze and a way of looking at you as if what you were saying was profound and important and original.

CHAPTER

4

THE PHONE RANG THREE times . . . five times. Why didn't Nico have an answering machine like normal people? Nine times . . . Then you could leave a message and go do something else, instead of having to call him back. Thirteen times! Pike started to hang up, and then heard Nico's voice, hurried, abrupt: "Hello? Who's that? Hello?" sounding confused, like he wasn't quite there, or maybe just out of breath.

"Nico, it's me. Dave Pike. Are you free to accept a professional engagement?"

"Dave, Jesus! I was clear outside. Had to run all the way back." The voice was more under control now, and Pike decided Nico was only out of breath, and not drunk. "No, I'm not free. I charge by the hour."

Special Agent Panayotis Nicolasiou had been FBI liaison to the Intelligence Support Activity. That meant he was supposed to blow the whistle if ISA ran amok and started bugging Green Peace phones, or reading the Iraqi ambassador's mail, or doing anything else that smacked of domestic intelligence.

It wasn't that the FBI didn't believe in doing these things—it merely wanted to do all of them itself, and not let other agencies horn in on its own particular preserve. The situation could have been prickly, but instead of being pissy about it, Nico had shown Pike many useful things—for example, how to pick a cylinder lock with a bent wire and a penknife, and how to tap a telephone. They had polished off a few hundred beers together, too. Then Nico had been transferred to the Bureau's L.A. field office, and got into the sauce a little too heavy, and the Bureau found him surplus to requirements. Nico liked the climate in Southern California better than in his native Michigan. There weren't nearly so many mosquitoes, so he stayed, and used his accounting degree to get a job with a tax-return preparer in Santa Monica. He sometimes did audit work on the side—and did it very well, too, when he was sober.

"Cute, Nico. Very cute. What I mean is, are you able to, uh, does your schedule, uh . . ."

"You mean am I sober or am I drinking?"

"Yeah," Pike said, "that's what I mean."

"Fuck you, Pike."

"Does that mean yes or no?"

"What's it to you?"

"I need a quick run-through on some bank records and invoices. I don't want to pay some CPA to do it and then get a five-page letter about why the material submitted doesn't meet his audit standards, instead of a sensible answer. Are you interested?"

"How quick is quick? I couldn't start to do anything about it until maybe Tuesday. Then I could work on it full time for a week or so."

"That's quick enough."

"You want to send me the stuff? Have a messenger bring it over?"

"Yeah. As soon as I get it."

"As soon as you get it? What the fuck is this? You want a quick run-through on something you don't even have yet?"

"Yeah, well. I'm picking it up today. If you can't start until Tuesday, I'll have it for you in plenty of time."

"Fine. That'll be fine. Look, Dave, I'm sorry about getting huffy. I just . . ."

"Fuck you, Nico," Pike said. He tried for just the right tone—one that would tell Nico it was okay.

Nico laughed. It didn't sound very hearty, but at least it was a laugh. "All right. Talk to you when you get the stuff then."

"Wait," Pike said. "I almost forgot. Is there any truth to the rumor that the Dukakis campaign people had you tapped as head of the FBI if their man got elected?"

"Fuck you, Pike," Nico said. But this time there was no bitterness in it, and he was chuckling as he hung up.

Richie parked his Jeep down the block. Dominic said never to drive right into the driveway where you were going, or park in a visitor's spot. That could attract too much attention, or somebody could remember the license number. Dominic always said it was better to arrive on foot, people didn't know where you came from.

Richie got out of the Jeep and walked back up the street. It was shady, like a lot of streets in Westwood. Big old trees hanging over the sidewalk and meeting in the middle of the street, the kind with big leaves, like on the Canadian flag, and fuzzy balls on them instead of fruit, and bark that scaled off in patches like a jigsaw puzzle.

The address was an older fourplex, two up and two down. Richie had been there before, quite often as a matter of fact, and knew that the woman lived on the second floor in back. He walked up the driveway, took the stairs two at a time, and pushed the button for the doorbell. Dull sound of chimes from somewhere inside. Sound of cars going by in the street. Couple of kids yelling as they rolled past on skateboards. Richie pushed the button again. Looked like she wasn't home.

Back in the Jeep, Richie sat for a minute. Dominic said never wait around. Dominic said people noticed you waiting, and then they remembered. If the person you wanted to see wasn't home, hey man, no big deal, cruise by Rogelio's, have a beer. Then come back.

Richie got out his key and switched on the ignition. He put the Jeep in reverse and started to back up. And there she came around the corner and along the street, driving one of those funny little low cars that might have room inside for two people, as long as neither of them was carrying a purse or anything. The hood ornament was a three-pronged fork. Probably a foreign car. They were all foreign cars these days, not like a Jeep. Made in the U.S.A.

The little car turned into the driveway of the apartment house and disappeared behind the building. Richie switched off the ignition, pocketed the keys, and walked back up the sidewalk.

She didn't see him coming, she was bent over, reaching into her car for something. Sensational ass the woman had. Richie stopped and admired it. When the woman stood up she had a baseball glove and a bat in her hands. That explained the clothes she was wearing—those baseball socks with straps under your feet, and tight blue pants (knee britches really), and a little hat. She stood, holding the bat and glove, her head tipped. Listening. Richie listened too, and heard, very faintly, what could be a phone ringing. The woman set the baseball glove on the roof of her car, leaned the bat against the door, and broke into a run, fumbling in her purse for her keys.

Richie watched her sprint up the stairs. Great legs, but the ass—sensational.

She got to the top, yanked her door open, and disappeared inside, leaving the door standing wide. Richie followed, his boot soles rasping on the concrete treads.

He went straight across the little landing at the top of the stairs, and into the open door of the apartment. Just inside the door was a couch, and leaning her hip against the couch, talking on a cordless phone, was the lady. She was facing away from the door, didn't even see Richie.

"All right," she said. "All right. Call me at the studio Monday, then." She put the phone back onto its base unit and turned around, seeing Richie, bunching her eyebrows in a frown.

"Well, hi there, sweetheart!" Richie said, stepping up close.

Very stern, cold movie lady, looking hard at him, saying: "I don't think I heard you knock. Whatever you're . . . selling, I don't have time for it."

"Come on, sweetheart. Don't be that way."

"How clearly do I have to say this? I didn't ask you to come here. I want you to leave. Now!"

"Now, sweetheart, you don't mean that," he said, picking her up, and dropping her over the back of the couch, onto the cushions. She squealed. Not a scream, but one of those noises women make when they sit down and the chair isn't there.

Richie vaulted over to land on top of her. Her hat fell off.

"Lookit how comfortable we are here," he said, nuzzling the side of her neck.

The woman pushing at him with her hands, saying, "Get off me! Don't you understand English? I want you out of here."

Pike had been early. He had parked in the shade of the sycamores, gotten out of the car, and walked back up the street to the address. Checked the apartment number. Rang the bell and waited. Rang it again. No answer. Softball practice probably didn't have a time limit. Pike walked down the stairs and to the far end of the block, enjoying the dappled shade under the trees. Almost like a Midwestern street, the big old trees arched over the roadway. A couple of kids on skateboards came by, rattling across the joints in the sidewalk, shouting to each other. Pike walked on past the driveway and down to the other end of the block.

A silver Maserati took the corner, skidded a little, corrected, and came fast along the block. Pike turned to watch, and sure enough, halfway down it turned into a driveway. Hard to tell from where Pike was, but it looked like the right driveway. Pike headed back.

Coming along the sidewalk from the other direction was your typical cowboy iron freak—creep with bleached hair, cowboy boots, and a silk shirt with pearl buttons open halfway to the navel to show his pecs. Had a neck on him that was thicker than his head was wide. He'd gotten out of a Jeep that should have been self-conscious, the way it was all tarted up with metallic paint and pin stripes.

Blondie turned into a driveway. Pike turned into the same driveway. At the back of the driveway, in a little parking area, Mickey McDonald was getting out of the silver Maserati, turning around and bending over to reach inside for something. Then she stopped, cocked her head as if listening, and trotted up the flight of stairs.

Blondie followed Mickey up the stairs. From the bottom Pike could see her talking on the telephone. Blondie was standing behind her. She finished, turned. She and Blondie spoke. Her tone was strident. Then Blondie picked her up and tossed her over the back of a couch, and she screamed.

Pike was up the stairs and in the door in four long steps. He leaned over and tapped Blondie on the shoulder, stepping carefully back out of reach. "Excuse me," he said.

Blondie was up off the couch in a heave. Mickey got up more slowly, straightening her shirt and shoving the shirttail into her pants.

"I don't want to interrupt you," Pike said, "but I have an appointment with Miss McDonald. Who might you be?"

Blondie licking his lips, glancing sideways at Mickey, saying: "I'm a friend of hers. We're friends. Aren't we?" looking sideways again at Mickey for confirmation.

No answer. The look from Blondie was a little uncertain, yet insistent.

"You don't want to talk to this guy," he said. "Do you. We were just having fun, horsing around. Tell him."

Mickey found her voice. It was very small, not at all like the confident, husky voice Pike had heard her use on the set. "I would like you to leave. I've been saying that since you walked in here."

Blondie putting on a show, getting a hurt tone in his voice. "Hey, what gives? We're friends. Tell him."

"I said . . ."—she stopped and cleared her throat—"that I'd like you to leave."

Pike thinking, Oh shit, here we go. I could say his lines, and he could probably say mine. It's as fixed as a Noh play. I ask him to leave, and he tells me to fuck off, and somewhere down the line he takes a swing at me. Look at the size on the bastard—used to people backing down, doing things his way because he outweighs them by seventy-five pounds. I *don't* want to get into this. Saying: "It is Miss McDonald's apartment, and if she asks you to leave . . ."

Blondie spinning around, glaring straight at Pike, with what was probably supposed to be his frightener's look. "What business is it of yours, fuckface?" Frustrated and bitter, but finding a target now: "Why don't you just take your sad ass out of here while you can still walk?"

Pike sighed and backed up a step, palms up. "Let's not get unpleasant about it, shall we? We're all adults here, right? And it is Miss McDonald's apartment, and if she asks you politely to leave . . ."

Pike ducked under the wild roundhouse right that Blondie threw. A punch so hard that it spun Blondie halfway around so that he had to stagger a step to keep his balance. But he recovered and came on another step, swinging a left that Pike slipped, backing out the door, turning, and trotting down the stairs to the yard.

Wonderful, Mickey thought, walking across to the door and looking down into the yard. How do I get so lucky? What have I done to deserve this? Now the big guy will kill the lawyer in my backyard, and there will be cops all over the place, and it will all be just *won*derful.

She went out and stood on the landing. The big guy had gotten into the driveway, so the lawyer was cornered in the backyard. The lawyer was going around the yard, looking for another way out. He wasn't going to find one. There weren't any. The pyracantha hedge was forty years old and the solid mass of thorns was over ten feet tall. The big guy watching, smiling, waiting for the lawyer to try to come past him.

Richie watched the geek looking for a way out of the backyard. Damn hedge was solid all the way around, except for the driveway, and Richie was standing in the driveway. Geek would have to come to him, walk right up to him. Richie watched him moving around the backyard, limping a little. Guy didn't look scared, though. He looked—Richie wasn't sure, but it seemed like—pissed off. But not at Richie, more like pissed off at himself for making a mistake. Turning around now, and coming across the yard toward Richie.

"You want to say you're sorry?" Richie said, moving to head him off. "Get down on your knees, say you're sorry you interrupted me? Cause maybe then I'll let you out of here alive."

Guy stopping five feet from Richie, looking at Richie with cold blue eyes. Guy was pretty sizable, six feet plus, one-ninety maybe, but no definition, where his arms showed in his short-sleeved shirt. No bulk, nothing to worry about. Saying, "You stand aside, friend, and we'll call it square. You stay in the way, who knows what'll happen?" Very calm voice. Dead level. But a lot of guys could fake it, pretend to be cool when it was all a bluff. Richie feinted to the left and then lunged at the geek, swinging with his right fist.

Shit! Pike thought. Absolute drizzling shit! Concentrate so hard about getting down the stairs ahead of this creep you forget to *think*, and let him jump over the railing halfway down and get between you and the driveway. Dumb, dumb, dumb! Now there was no way out except to go around and around with him. The creep coming on now, feinting to his left, but only a feint, his feet and his shoulders saying he was going to lead with his right.

Pike ducked and circled away. Blondie recovered and swung

again. If he ever hit anything with a punch like that, he'd probably break his wrist. On the other hand, whatever he hit would be pretty well destroyed, too. Here he came again, right, right, left, right. Pike ducked the first two, used a wrist block on one, and took one on the shoulder. Tried again to circle left, get out to the street—but Blondie moved to stay in the way.

"The matter with you, scumbag?" Richie said. "Afraid to stand still and take what's coming? And it's coming, never fear. You can run, but you can't hide." Moving in again, swinging.

Pike ducking, bobbing and weaving. Blondie would make a mistake sooner or later, give him an opening to get out to the street. Nobody could do everything perfect in a fight. There'd be an opening in a while. Or that damn woman would have the sense to call the cops.

Just have to wait it out.

It was a jab with another jab on top of it. Pike blocked the first one. Saw the second one coming too late, sailing in, right on the money, bouncing off of his cheekbone. Found himself on his face on the driveway, pushing at the concrete, trying to get up, Blondie behind him saying, "There we go. Now we're getting somewhere. We'll just help you up and get back to work."

Pike feeling himself getting back to his feet, but slow, so slow, and Blondie standing there, and a fist floating in, and felt his stomach exploding, and fell back against the side of the silver Maserati, and slid down onto the concrete, and started to get up again, important to get up, not to just lie there, scrabbling at the side of the car with his hands . . . and one of his hands found the smooth aluminum handle of a Louisville Slugger official slow-pitch softball bat.

Got his hands on the bat, got his feet ready, and came up and stuffed the fat end of the bat a foot deep into Blondie's stomach, just above the belt.

And reversed and laid the fat end against the point of Blondie's shoulder, looking for the notch at the end of the collarbone. And reversed again, and laid it against the ribs on the opposite side.

Watching the smile go off of Blondie's face. Watching the eyes start to shift, getting worried. Pike starting to get his breath back. Hell of a pain when he inhaled, but the breath coming easier now. Standing up and trying to use the pain, focus it on Blondie. Breathe and focus.

Mickey leaned on the railing and watched. First the lawyer tried to talk to the big guy, but that didn't work. Then the big guy started swinging. For a while the lawyer stood up to it, doing tricky things, ducking and twisting, trying to work around and get out of the driveway. Then the big guy landed one, and then he landed another, and it was going to be lights out for the lawyer. The big guy picked him up and belted him again, and he wasn't even trying to duck anymore, and he fell down, against her car. And then he got up again . . . and he had something in his hands, something shiny. Her softball bat! He was holding it, not on his shoulder, like you would in a game, but across his chest at an angle, like you'd hold one of those Oriental fighting staffs.

The big guy jumping around, waving his arms and making noises, like, *hah* and *hunh,* every now and again, and trying to take a swing at the lawyer. And the lawyer talking to him, telling him to calm down, to take it easy, pivoting smoothly, keeping his face toward the big guy, holding the bat.

And every now and again, the lawyer would hit the big guy, with the bat. Across the shins, on the thighs, on the forearms, on the biceps. Poking him in the stomach with the end of the bat, doubling him up, rapping him across the back, until the big guy turned and began a kind of hobbling run out of the driveway, and out of sight around the corner of the building, with the lawyer limping along behind him, until he, too, disappeared.

And a minute later, here he came again, the bat on his shoulder, around the corner of the building, stopped by her car, took the glove off of the roof, and started up the stairs. Mickey thinking here it comes: he's thought up some kind of macho bullshit line he's going to lay on me. "I think these are yours, ma'am?" that kind of crap.

But he didn't. He just limped up the stairs, dropped the bat and glove on the floor inside her front door, and stood there for a second, looking around.

"You got a phone?" he said.

"Sure," Mickey said. "That portable right there."

"Who do you call here? LAPD? Or is it the sheriff?"

"Wait a minute," Mickey said. "What do you want to call the cops for?"

The lawyer straightening up from where he was bent over the phone, looking at her slowly, raising one eyebrow, saying, "That creep comes in here and jumps you, with God knows what in mind, and then pulls a Rambo on me, and you ask why call the cops? Well, I don't know, maybe they'd come out and sell us a ticket to the Police and Firemen's Ball."

Mickey found her purse and dug through it for her cigarettes. Shook one out of the pack and lit it. Thinking, how do I handle this so it doesn't get out of control? How much do I have to say? Looking at the lawyer and saying, "How much do you know about the movie business?"

The lawyer shaking his head, saying, "Not much. And the more I find out, the more I wish I never had anything to do with it, why?"

Mickey took a drag on her cigarette. "Just call Maurice, will you? Let's just call Maurice, tell him what happened, and see what *he* says, okay?"

CHAPTER

5

A BIG ROOM, BEEN there since the building was built in 1923. The room was a Walgreen's five-and-ten-cent store then, if anyone cared. The ceiling maybe eighteen, twenty feet high. Pressed tin squares, floral-patterned. Not that you could see the ceiling, of course, even in the daytime. The windows had all been painted over, and no sunlight came through. The light came from hanging lamps, and it was all down low, on the tables, leaving the upper part of the room in hollow obscurity.

The lamps hung to within three or four feet of the tables, lighting the green baize so it was brighter than emeralds. There was no juke, so the room was quiet, except for the solid click of balls, and the muted hum of voices.

Dominic leaned into the light at the end of the table, squinted at the balls, and then stood up. Moved around to the side of the table and looked again, measuring the angle from the cushion to the side pocket. He picked up his beer from a coaster on the side of the table, took a swallow, and then, with the bottle still in his hand, touched the side pocket of the table with the tip of his cue. "Six," he said. "Over there. So, you had a little trouble, huh?"

"Nah," Richie said. "Not trouble, really. Who said anything about trouble?"

Dominic put his beer down on the coaster, bent over the table, and just missed the side pocket with the six ball on a two-cushion shot. "Shit!" he said. "Least I didn't leave you much. You tell me you didn't talk to the woman, and you say no trouble. If there wasn't no trouble, you'd been done this afternoon, there'd be no need you talking going back there."

Richie walked around the table, bending over to sight at one pocket or another across various clusters of balls. He chalked the end of his cue and dusted a little talc on his fingers. "Not my fault," he said. "I get there, I'm talking to the woman, and she's got this guy jumps me with a ball bat."

"Only one guy? And alls he's got's a baseball bat?" Dominic shook his head, not believing what he was hearing. "You shoulda took it away from him and showed him a couple things. Teach him to mess around with things don't concern him."

"Look," Richie said, "he got in a couple of solid shots before I even knew what was going on, got me off balance, and even then, I landed a few good ones. That's one dude will be sore all over in the morning, for sure. So what do you think?"

Dominic had his beer in his hand again, taking a swallow, glancing at the level in the bottle. "She still needs to be reminded, right? Have her money there when she's supposed to, right? And then there's this guy with the ball bat. Well, that's two separate problems. Unless they're playing house together, something like that?" He looked at Richie and raised one eyebrow.

Richie shook his head. "I don't think so. I never seen him there before."

"Okay. So we remind her. Then find out who he is, where he hangs out, maybe take a baseball bat over there, stick it up his ass. Or just leave him in the trunk of a car. You gonna shoot, or what?"

"Yeah," Richie said. "Yeah. Eleven back there in the corner, off the thirteen. So should I get Titch or one the other guys and go back there tonight then?"

"You think it needs two of you, or what?"

"No, no." Richie took his shot and missed. "Why should it need two of us? I go back, remind the woman, find out who the geek is, where he hangs out, like you said. Then, couple days, Titch and I go see him. How's that?"

"Sure," Dominic said. "That sounds fine. You want to finish this round? You seem kind of"—he made a vague gesture with his cue—"like you're not into it."

Richie shrugged, elaborately casual, trying not to show he was so stiff he could hardly bend over to take a shot. "I don't care."

"Fine. That's fine." Dominic liked to watch Richie, liked to stay one step ahead of him. Know what he was going to say before he said it. "We'll call it a draw. On your way out, ask Rogelio to send me another beer, will you?" Dominic began taking the balls out of the pockets, setting them up for another break, as Richie racked his cue and headed over toward the bar.

"Water? Soda?" Maurice paused with the glass in his hand.

"Water's fine, Maurie."

Maurice poured carefully from a carafe, and crossed the room to set the drink on the coffee table in front of Mickey. Picked up an ashtray from the bar as he passed, and set that next to the drink. Found his way back to the bar around the jumble of furniture; glass-topped tables, and rattan chairs with cushions slipcovered in a floral print. "David? How about you?" He was taking his time, didn't seem to be in any hurry to get down to what they were there to talk about.

"Just a beer for me, Maurie." He didn't want to push them. They'd known each other a long time. Maurice had said she was closer to him than a daughter. But after the initial five minutes of concern over Mickey's visitor, Maurice had swung back to social politeness. Back inside himself somewhere, thinking about something, being polite on the surface.

"I got Carta Blanca, I got Heineken, I got Sapporo, I got San

Miguel . . ." The perfect host, concerned only with catering to his guests. And Mickey was no help, sitting there sipping scotch, with one long leg crossed over the other, swinging the free foot. Occasionally running a hand through her hair.

"Whatever's closest to the front of the refrigerator. Maurie, if you don't mind . . ."

"David, take it easy. Here, try this." Maurice put a brown bottle on the table near Pike's chair. "Sapporo. Great beer with sushi, if we had any sushi, which we don't. But we got pretzels, we got some peanuts, I can open a can if you'd like, or there's . . ."

"Maurie, can we just get down to it?" He had cross-examined hostile expert witnesses, run interrogations in the CIC, and the worst, the all-time worst, was trying to make a social conversation move in the right direction. It was partly the lack of structure, and partly that no one was really in charge.

"All right, David, all right. Mickey, you need anything?"

Pike looked at Mickey. Mickey saw him looking at her, uncrossed her legs, crossed them the other way, and winked. "No, Maurie. Maurie, if it's okay, I think we've kept David waiting long enough. Do you want to explain this, or shall I?" The voice coming back, almost to the penetrating, husky tone she'd had the other day at the studio, not the subdued little-girl voice from when the guy was at her apartment.

Maurice sighed, lifted his drink and took a sip, and then sighed again. "You said the guy was a collector?"

Mickey nodded. The long hair rippled in the reflected light from the patio.

"For DiAngelo?"

Mickey nodded again.

"DiAngelo's been getting paid on the new picture?"

Mickey nodded.

Maurice shook his head. "Then we can't call the cops. It's out of the question."

Pike put his beer bottle down on the table. Too hard, because both

Maurice and Mickey looked sharply at the bottle. He stood up and moved across the room to the sliding glass doors, open to a patio where a pool filled with lime Jell-O lay absolutely still in the afternoon sun. Turned and faced back into the room, saying, "Jesus Christ . . ." Stopped and got it under control and started again, but still on the edge. "Maurie, who the *hell* is this DiAngelo guy, and what entitles him to have goons running around half-raping women in their own apartments?"

Maurice was looking everywhere but at Pike, not comfortable with the topic and not hiding it well. "DiAngelo is a lot of things. DiAngelo is probably into shylocking, and probably into drugs, and for sure into protection."

"Protection? Maurie, do you mean like Edward G. Robinson playing a tough guy in some gangster film one of your buddies made in 1932? Give me a break!"

Maurice sighed, moved back behind the bar, and splashed a little more scotch into his glass. He held up the glass and looked at the level, then added water. "David, I'm trying to tell you, if you'll listen. I've never seen this guy DiAngelo, but I can tell you some stories. Last year there was an independent producer doing a picture. Competent director, decent actors."

Turning to Mickey, "Mickey, you remember Peploe doing that screenplay by that English guy, what was his name?"

Mickey shook her head, and Maurice shrugged. "Doesn't matter. Anyway, the producer refused to pay anything to this DiAngelo, and that was the end of his picture. Never finished shooting."

Pike was too close to the light from the patio, and Maurice was too far back in the room. Couldn't see Maurice's face, only a dim blur. He moved away from the windows, back to his chair, making himself sit down, speak calmly. "Maurie, what are you saying? This is California, not Chicago. What do you mean, 'that was the end of the picture'? End how?"

"I think it was the catering people, wasn't it, Mickey?" Maurice had stayed behind the bar, leaning his forearms on the polished wood. "One of the unions that wasn't directly involved in the production. They raised a fuss over some point like how much overtime the dishwashers were entitled to, and the next thing there was a picket line, and the electricians wouldn't cross it, and it was all over."

Then, seeing Pike was incredulous, Maurice went on, "Shooting a picture isn't like going to the grocery store for a can of peas. At least not if you're an independent and don't have cameramen and lighting technicians and all that on the payroll all the time, and sound stages lying around whenever you want. Even with the majors, the actors are under contract, and they're going to be on your set for a certain length of time, and then they're under contract to go somewhere else. So you've only got them for so long. And the costumes are made, and the sets, and you've rented a sound stage, and the electricians and the cameramen are hired and it all comes together, and for however many days it lasts, you hope to get a whole picture in the can. But if something holds it up, and messes up the shooting schedule, like one trade pulling a strike for a week, why, a whole picture can go in the toilet."

"And you're seriously telling me that Hollywood pays protection money to the unions? Or to some gangster connected with the unions?"

Maurice smiled. It was a very sad smile, all in the mouth, and none of it in the eyes. "David, where have you been? Even the majors, they had IATSE and Willie Bioff, and then when Bioff started his car one day and went straight up, it was somebody else, and now they deal through Sidney Korshak. He calls himself a labor lawyer. Maybe you've met him, if you're political. Jerry Brown knew him, when he was governor. Ronald Reagan knew him. He gave money to their campaigns. Went to the fund-raising dinners in a tuxedo. And other people knew him, too. Johnny Roselli, who ended up in a fifty-five gallon drum floating in Miami Bay. And Fratianno. And Jake the Barber. And a bunch more I could name. And that's the majors, they do it all very nice through lawyers. But the little operators, independents like me — sure we pay. It's cheaper to pay than to risk the loss of a picture."

"Uh-huh." Almost losing it again. Looking at Mickey and taking a breath to calm down. Looking at the long legs, the mocking smile, the nose that wasn't really too big, but just right for the face. "And so that means the goons that work for this guy DiAngelo can just do whatever they want? Is that it? What is Mickey supposed to do, go home and wait and see if maybe the guy decides not to come back?"

"No, no, no. I'm sure there's some kind of misunderstanding. I mean, if you've paid him . . ." Maurice paused for a moment and looked at Mickey, who nodded vigorously, so that Maurice also nodded, once, to himself. "Then there's no reason we can't expect them to behave themselves. We'll just have to get word to DiAngelo to call off his dog. It's only when they aren't paid that they get out of hand."

"And how is that supposed to happen? Getting word to DiAngelo to call off his dog?"

"Mickey? Shall I call them?"

Mickey shaking her head, saying, with that husky voice, "If you don't mind, Maurie, I'd rather do it myself."

Maurice came out from behind the bar and sat down in a chair facing Mickey. Leaned forward and put his elbows on his knees, confiding. "Mickey, look. I've never met this DiAngelo, but I know a guy named Dominic Nakamura, what kind of name is that, I ask you? He's the right-hand man for DiAngelo. Let me get the word to him, okay?"

But Mickey wasn't having any of it. She wanted to do it herself. They argued back and forth, and Pike watched. Enjoyed watching her toss her head, glare at Maurice, give as good as she got. Only it was like watching a kid argue with her father, after he's made up his mind. He's going along, letting her run, enjoying the game, but he's going to do what he's already decided to do, no matter how it comes out.

And sure enough, when Mickey excused herself to go to the

restroom, Maurice barely waited until she was out of the room before grinning at Pike and saying in an undertone, "I'll take care of it. Call Nakamura. She can call him, too, that won't hurt. Isn't she a dandy? Didn't I tell you she was good? What do you think of her?"

"I like her. She's quick, and she's damn spunky."

"She comes across as all tough and ballsy. Fools some people. Even fools herself sometimes. But she's really very sensitive. That's what makes her good at what she does."

"I won't argue with that."

"Besides being a nice person."

"That, too. Maurice, are you trying to sell her to me?"

"No, no. Not at all. I just want you to see why she's important to me."

And as Mickey and Pike were leaving, Maurice walked them to the door. And when Pike stood back to let Mickey precede him, he glanced at Maurice, and Maurice glanced back, and winked slowly.

She drove well. Stayed in second, third at the most, on the winding streets. Downshifted at the stop signs, tapped the brake, and flicked the tach around the dial accelerating away. Looked straight ahead out the windshield, or out the side windows at the cross streets. Didn't have that almost-universal female habit of turning to look at whoever she was talking to, inviting agreement, taking her eyes off the road.

"I don't think I said thanks." The tone offhand, casual. Then she did turn to look at him for a second, aviator-type sunglasses hiding her eyes, before she looked back at the road. Clean profile framed by the long hair rippling in the breeze from the open window. "For coming up when I screamed, I mean. A lot of people would have just . . . no, let me finish."

Lifting her right hand from the gearshift and resting it for a moment against Pike's shoulder, cutting him off almost before he knew he had been going to say anything. "I realize it could have turned out very badly. I mean, that guy was *huge!* And I stood there like an airhead and didn't do anything. However important Maurice thinks his picture is, it would all look different if we were visiting you in the hospital. So thanks, okay? Really."

And another microsecond of blank gaze from the aviator glasses.

She waited a moment for a reply. When Pike was silent, she touched his arm again. "You're awful quiet. What are you thinking?"

Pike grinned. "That you're the most interesting woman I've talked to since I happened to meet Sandra Day O'Connor at a testimonial dinner."

She grinned back. "And did you save her from a dragon?"

"No such luck. We shook hands. I asked if I could get her another drink. She said no thank you. Then a court-of-appeal judge came up and they began to argue about federal sentencing guidelines, and that was that."

"Poor David," she said. "And so you lost your chance to contribute to the development of the law."

And then she had made the last turn, too fast, skidded a little, but corrected, and then turned into the driveway and rolled to a stop. And they were out of the car, slamming the doors, when she looked at him across the top of the car, leaning one hand on the silver edge of the roof. And the huskiness was back in her voice, but a different huskiness. Softer, somehow.

"Why don't you come upstairs. I'll pour you a drink. And say thanks again. More thoroughly."

She was serious, or she was having fun, and it could turn out okay either way.

"Sure," Pike said. "I'll accept a drink. And that'll give me a chance to pick up the canceled checks and stuff."

She had been enjoying herself, teasing him, and all at once, at the mention of the canceled checks, she wasn't enjoying herself anymore. She looked back at him across the roof of her car, turned down the corners of her mouth, and then led the way upstairs to her apartment.

"There's some wine in the refrigerator. Pour me a glass, will you?"

"The glasses are . . ."

"The cupboard above the stove."

When Pike turned around with the bottle in his hand he thought—he wasn't sure, but he could almost swear—that she'd unbuttoned the top button on her blouse. There was more than a hint of cleavage there. In fact, there was damn near half a breast visible through the opening in the fabric. He tried to keep from looking too closely. "You have a corkscrew?" he said. His voice was funny, and he cleared his throat.

"In the drawer to the left of the sink."

Pike opened the bottle, poured two glasses, and handed her one.

She raised her glass and made as if to clink it against his. "Cheers." She paused a moment. "So. What now?"

Pike cleared his throat again. It was definitely hard to keep his voice level. "Maybe you could see if you have the canceled checks?"

It had been the wrong thing to say. She went from teasing lightness to blazing fury in a microsecond. "What is it with you?" she snapped. "What is this fixation you have on those goddamn checks? I've seen you looking at me. So why don't you do anything but look?"

"It's an ethical problem."

"Sure, sure. Don't give me a bunch of fuzzy philosophy or some other kind of bullshit."

"No philosophy. I'm a lawyer. There're rules I'm supposed to follow. One of the rules says I don't fool around with the people on the other side of a case, because if I do, then the people on my side of the case can't tell if I'm really on their side anymore. It's not worded exactly that way, but that's what it means."

"On the other side of a case? What case? What other side?"

"The canceled checks and stuff. My clients have decided, for whatever reason, that they want an audit. If it turns out there's some money missing from the bank account . . ."

"There isn't. Not. One. Cent." She tapped her forefinger on the counter in time to her words. "It's all there."

"Then the sooner we go through the stuff and make sure of that, the sooner I can take you up on your kind offer."

"Besides, who'd know?"

"You and me."

"So?"

"So that's two people too many."

"Are you always this stuffy?"

"No. Only sometimes."

"Uh-huh," she said, "I'll bet." Then, crossing the room and squatting next to a cardboard box on the floor, "Here. Here's the checkbook. These are the bank statements. The checkbook is balanced to the last statement, by the way. Let your clients look at it all they want, they won't find anything out of whack."

"How about the invoices? Bills and stuff?" Pike said.

Mickey raised her eyes to the ceiling and then rolled them at Pike. She stood up and put her fists on her hips. "Jesus Christ! Do you want copies of the toilet paper we used in the porta-potty on the set too? I don't have the invoices here at home. I'll get them from the bookkeeper. You can have them tomorrow. Is that all right?"

Pike nodded. "Uh-huh," he said, "that'd be fine."

"Do you know what burns me about this whole thing?" Mickey said. She was still mad, and it showed. Showed in the way she bit off her words, in the quick gestures as she lit a cigarette and puffed out a jet of smoke. "Do you? I'll tell you. This is all part of what's happened to the industry. It isn't about *art* anymore. It's about the bottom line. It's all accountants and lawyers. Can you name me one kind of artist, one other medium, where accountants watch you as you create and they make decisions that the artist should be making? Can you?"

She didn't wait for a reply and her voice rose as she went on,

making jerky gestures with her cigarette. "Did Picasso have accountants watching him while he painted? Did Rodin think about
return on investment when he bought clay and hired a model? *Hell*
no! They practiced their art, and created their work, and didn't even
really worry about whether or not it sold.

"But," she said, "in the film business, even if you're a big name,
you still have to fight over burn ratios, and time on location, and
worry about whether it will go over budget. Even on a piece of trash
like this film I'm doing for Maurice, the accountants and the lawyers are after you all the time.

"Then what happens when the film is finished?" she said. "Film
is the only medium where it's got to click right *now,* when it's made,
or never. How many years did stuff from Picasso's Blue Period sit
around before people said, 'Hey, this is great!' But it's not that way
with a film. A film either gets shown, and makes it, or it goes in the
can in a warehouse somewhere. It's not out there, on display, where
people can look at it day after day and then say, 'You know, it kind of
grows on you . . .' Well, let me tell you something, buster, I've had it
up to here with this shit! I have an option on a new novel by a major
American novelist, and I'm going to raise my own money to produce it, and do it right, not half-assed. And I'm not going to let a
goddamn accountant or a lawyer even come downwind of the
production."

When she was talking about film she had a different quality—an
absolute confidence in her own opinions. A definiteness. It was a
consciousness of superiority as serene as if she had just given a cello
recital in Stockholm to a standing ovation, and chatted afterward
for a half hour with Carl XII and Queen Sylvia. That conveys the
degree of confidence, but gives too relaxed and triumphant a picture. Perhaps it was more like the surgeon waiting for her anesthe-
siologist and the rest of her operating room team to join her in the
VIP lounge, en route to Sofia where Todor Zhivkov was hospitalized
and waiting for treatment.

"What's a burn ratio?" Pike said. He'd done it before, ask a witness to explain something he'd said to derail him, get him off his high horse.

Mickey blinked at him for a moment. "Do you care?" Then, half to herself, "Why do I care if you care? All right, filmmaking one-oh-one. A burn ratio is the ratio of the number of feet of film you burn—waste—to get one foot of finished film. Like if you have the budget to shoot each scene six times, and take the best one of the six, then that's a burn ratio of six. If you could shoot it ten times, that'd be a burn ratio of ten. But it's not quite the same as the number of takes, because some scenes you shoot once and you use them, and some you shoot twenty times, and then shoot them again. It's the overall ratio of the feet of film, like I said."

"Thanks," Pike said. He had the cardboard box under one arm and was sidling toward the door. "Shall I call you about the in-voices, or . . ."

"I'll call you," Mickey said. "Tomorrow."

This time Nico answered his phone on the first ring. "Hey, Davey," he said. "Change your mind? Decide to have one of the big eight do it? Peat, Marwick? E and E?"

"Don't kid yourself, Nico. I've thought about having one of the majors do my accounting work, just to avoid the abuse. And I would, too, if I thought they could do it as quick as you can. That, and one other little thing. I need a license number checked. You still know people who can do that?"

"Sure, but why not just send fifty cents to the DMV like any other citizen?"

"Because you know people who can do it in real time on a computer, and I don't want to wait two weeks for an answer."

"Is it a California plate?"

"Yeah. 1RRA326. It's a Jeep. Can't tell you the year."

"Got it. That all then?"

"Well . . ."

"I rather thought not. What else?"

"When you get a name, see if he's got a sheet. And if he does, get a copy, and find out for me who I can talk to who's busted him a couple of times."

"All right," Nico said. "You don't want much for fifty-five an hour, do you?"

"Fuck you, Nico," Pike said, and hung up as Nico began to laugh.

CHAPTER

6

NICO REACHED OVER AND slapped the alarm clock into silence. Lay there for moment feeling the familiar fear: was I drinking yesterday? Then a small feeling of satisfaction: no, I wasn't drinking. Then a feeling of dissatisfaction: I wasn't drinking yesterday, but I was drinking less than two weeks ago. Finally, a dull feeling of hopelessness: it took so much energy to stay away from it, so much strain to build up anything significant, like, say, six months of being sober. And it was so easy to blow the six months in five minutes with one drink. One drink that led to another and then to another.

Oh well, one day at a time.

Nico rolled out of bed and walked down the short hallway to the kitchen. The mobile home was smaller than most apartments, but Nico preferred it to an apartment because of the space.

Not the space *in* it, but the space around it.

The mobile home sat on a concrete pad in a mobile home park, along with fifty or so others like it. Or almost like it. Some had an aluminum roof over their tiny patios. One or two had fences around their minuscule yards. There were even a couple of dual-wides, occupying two pads with a yard on both sides. But however much alike they were, or however different, at least none of them had a common wall. None of them had a roof that was somebody else's floor. The ten or twelve feet between one of them and the next wasn't much, but to someone from Michigan's rural Upper Peninsula it was the difference between a home and a tenement.

In the kitchen Nico ran water into the pot and emptied the pot into the top of the coffee maker, then measured in coffee. He pulled the cellophane off of a package of sweet rolls and put two of them in the toaster oven.

While he waited for the coffee to brew and the rolls to heat, Nico sat down at the table in the dining area. On the floor near the table was the pile of copies of canceled checks, invoices, and bank statements that he'd gotten from Pike. Today was Tuesday, and he'd told Pike he'd start looking at them today. No time like the present. Nico began to sort the pile and arrange items on the table.

When the bell on the toaster oven rang, he got up, put the sweet rolls on a plate, and checked the coffee. Still not ready. He sat back down at the table.

Wasn't there something else? Pike wanted a license number run too. Better get on that. He had written the number on a slip of paper somewhere. Nico looked on the cork-board near the phone where he pinned notes to himself. Not there. Looked in the drawer with the phone book. Not there. Padded down the hall to the bedroom and looked through the slips of paper in his shirt pocket. Not there. Finally looked in his pants for his wallet. Folded up inside was the slip of paper with the number. On the way back through the kitchen, Nico opened the refrigerator, took out the carton, and poured a glass of juice.

Back at the table, he sipped the juice and bit into a sweet roll. Nico didn't know anybody at CII, the California Identification and Information Bureau. But that didn't matter, since any police agency could tap into CII's data bank. The best guy to call was probably Tonello. Nico had done some favors for him in the old days. Nico picked up the phone and punched out the number for the Forgery Detachment at Parker Center. He asked for Lieutenant Tonello.

"Forgery, Tonello."

"Tony? Nico. Run a license number for me?"

"Uh-huh. And what are you going to do for me?"

"I'll owe you one."

"You already owe me one about fifty times."

"So this'll be fifty-one. If you'd stop arguing, you coulda done it already."

"I don't know why I put up with this shit," Tonello said. "What's the number?"

"1RRA326. Oh, and Tony—when you get the name, run it and see if he's got a sheet."

"Sure, Nico. Any other little thing you'd like? Motorcycle escort on your way to lunch? A stake-out on your girlfriend's pad? Anything else?"

"Complicated stuff I can't trust you not to fuck up. Just run the number and the name, will you? Most times the computer manages to get those things right."

"Up yours, Nico. Where'll you be when I get this?"

"At home. You got the number?"

"Yeah. Talk to you." There was a click and Tonello was gone. Nico hung up the phone and went back into the kitchen. The coffee was done and he poured himself a cup and sipped it. Too strong. The coffee maker was new and he still hadn't figured out the right proportions for the way he liked his coffee. He ran a little water into the cup at the sink and sipped again. Better.

There was a window over the sink. Outside the window was the patio of the trailer next door. The owner of that trailer had planted sweet peas around his patio, and the trellis, which was almost against Nico's window, was covered with pale blossoms. Why did people plant sweet peas? Flowers looked faded when they first bloomed, and didn't get any better. Probably the same reason people went to work for the FBI. They didn't know any better. Or they didn't have any other ideas that day. Or it was there. Nico had never been so bored for so long in his life as when he'd worked for the Bureau. The boredom had accounted for the drinking, at least partly. So in a way, what they'd fired him for was the Bureau's fault to begin with. Should have tried that argument on the special agent in charge when he had his termination interview. Oh well, as they said, there's no justice, only Justice. Nico carried his cup into the

dining area and began sorting through the invoices, bank statements, and other papers laid out on the table.

Richie carefully loosened his grip on the woman's wrists and slid
his hand down to the front of her blouse. What was her name? Was
it Susan? Or was Susan the one that was getting married, that the
party was for? This one was the hostess, and her name was something else . . . it was . . . Richie wasn't sure, but he thought it was
Penny. It didn't really matter that he didn't know her name, he
never called them by name, he always called them "sweetheart."
But he wanted to know her name so that he had something to call
her inside his head, when he thought about her, without having to
think about her as "the woman."

Lightly, gently, he began stroking the fabric over Penny's left
breast—if her name was Penny. At the same time, Richie's other
hand continued rubbing, stroking and squeezing the inside of her
thighs, her stomach, and between her legs.

Penny lay for a moment with her wrists crossed above her head,
where Richie had been holding them. Then she swung her hands
around and down, and began to squeeze at the front of Richie's
posing brief. "Mmm," Richie said. "Mmm, that's nice. I like that."

From the chair in the corner, where Richie had put his clothes
when he changed into his posing brief, came the insistent *beep-beep-
beep* of his telephone pager.

Richie thought it was pretty clever, the way Dominic had it set up.
Dominic never left a message or a number on the pager. Dominic
said the cops had ways to listen in, if they thought you were using a
pager for something they were suspicious of. Then they heard your
messages and knew what you were doing. What Dominic would do,
he would just dial the number of Richie's pager. Then Richie had
another number he had to call back, that connected with an answering machine. Richie thought the number might belong to an
old girlfriend of Dominic's, who kept the answering machine in her

apartment for Dominic. Before he beeped Richie on the pager, Dominic would have called the machine from wherever he was, and used his remote access code to leave a message of what *other* number Richie should call to find out what Dominic wanted.

The cops would never know about the answering machine, because it wasn't around anyplace that Dominic or Richie ever went, and even if they found out about it and put a tap on it, they couldn't react quickly enough to put a tap on the *other* number that Richie made the callback to. At least that was how Dominic had explained it to Richie. And if the old girlfriend ever listened in to the messages on the machine, all she'd hear were some telephone numbers, and the numbers changed from day to day anyhow.

The only problem was that when Dominic used the pager he wanted a callback *now*, not in five or ten minutes.

When the pager first went off, Penny went rigid, one hand still on the front of Richie's posing brief. But as soon as she figured out what the noise was, she relaxed and started again, squeezing, scratching at the nylon brief with her nails. Richie nuzzled his face into the side of Penny's neck for a moment, and then he stood up off the bed.

"Hey!" she said. "Hey! Where are you going?"

"Sorry, sweetheart. I got to make a phone call. You got a phone in the kitchen, don't you?"

"Dom? Richie. You beep me?"

"Yeah. I just got a call from this old guy that I know that's in the movie business. Maurice Baranowitz his name is. I don't think you know him. Anyhow, he said he had a complaint to make. Said his production company was paying us for insurance on a movie, and then some goon—that's what he said, 'some goon'—went over and roughed up his director. He's all bent out of shape and says he's always paid up before, never made any waves, and now what gives? You got any idea what he's talking about?"

"No idea at all, Dom. I don't think we have any insurance coming in on any movies right now. I don't know what he could be talking about."

"How about those people in Westwood? The woman you went to do the reminder on the other day? When the guy jumped you with the baseball bat. Wasn't that some movie deal?"

"Oh," Richie said, making the connection. "Yeah, but . . ." He stopped to collect his thoughts. "Yeah, but see, that isn't insurance, it's well, you know . . . They didn't have the fifty thou there, so we had to wait a week for them to round up the money. That was what the reminder was about. You remember."

"Yeah, I remember that. But what is this shit about roughing up his director? That must be the guy with the ball bat, huh?"

"Oh no. The woman, Mickey McDonald, the one I went to remind—that I still got to go back and remind. She's the director."

"Ah," Dominic said. "Well, I don't know that it makes a whole lot of sense that way either. So, if Mr. Baranowitz calls me back, I'll just have to tell him he hasn't paid us for any insurance on his movie." Dominic paused for a moment, and Richie could imagine him holding the phone like he sometimes did, pulling at the lobe of his ear with one hand and thinking. "But what about it?" Dominic said. "Should we get paid for it? Insurance on this movie, I mean."

"I don't know, Dom. I mean, we've been moving a lot of product through those people. Maybe it would . . . I mean, maybe we wanted insurance too, maybe they'd be, you know, upset. Like if they're our customers, then don't they get something for that?"

"You mean get something besides the product? Be serious. How far are they along in shooting this movie, do you know? They been taking product from us for a while, like four, five months, isn't it?"

"Yeah. Yeah, about that. I think they're nearly done. Just reshooting a couple of scenes, like."

Dominic was silent again for a moment, considering. "Nah," he finally said. "Nah, I don't think it's worth it. Let's leave it alone. But if you hear that this company is doing another film, you tell me right away. Then we can get in at the beginning, get paid for some insurance."

"Sure. Sure, Dom. I'll do that. Was that all?"

"How about that reminder? When are you going to take care of that?"

"Tonight. I'm going over there as soon as I'm through here."

"Through where?" Dominic wanted to know. "What you got going?"

"A bachelorette party. I did some lifting, did some stuff like that. I got the hostess in bed now."

"Uh-huh," Dominic said. "You got a line on who the guy was yet? The one that had the baseball bat?"

"No. Not yet. I'll find out when I do the reminder."

"All right," Dominic said. "Talk to you later. *Bon appetit.*"

"Okay then," Richie said. He didn't know what *Bon appetit* meant. He thought maybe it was Japanese for "good luck," but he didn't ask.

When Richie got back to the bedroom, the woman had gotten up, put on a housecoat, a kind of orangy-pink quilted thing, with a lace collar and cuffs, and was sitting at a little bench in front of a mirror, brushing her hair.

"Hey, sweetheart," Richie said. "Sorry about having to take that call. Now, where were we?"

The woman looked at him in the mirror, one hand raised, still holding the brush. "Let's forget it, shall we?" she said. "It wasn't really such a good idea anyhow."

"Hey, don't be that way. I said I was sorry." Richie crossed the room, scooped the woman up off the little bench, turned, and tossed her onto the bed. She squealed as she landed, and pushed the skirts of the housecoat down over her knees.

The squeal reminded Richie of something. Of being in a similar situation recently. It took him a minute to figure out that it was at the movie director lady's house, when he'd tossed her over the back of her couch, she'd squealed the same way. But while he was thinking, he knee-walked across the bed, flipped up the skirt of the housecoat and straddled the woman's hips. Pam. That was her name, not Penny. It was Pam. She was pushing at him now with her hands, hitting him in the shoulders, ineffectual little blows, like she was trying to hammer on something with her fist, not real punches. Saying she didn't want to, and he should get off her, and it was her house, and things like that.

Richie caught at Pam's wrists, got one, and held it, and then got the other one, and held them both in one hand. With his other hand, he reached down to where he'd flipped up the skirt ofthe housecoat, and began to stroke and knead at her thighs again.

Most people think the coast of California runs north and south. This is generally true, but west of Santa Monica, at least as far as Point Dume, the coast bends and runs almost east and west. So the late afternoon sun, low on the horizon, hung right in the center of the windshield as Pike headed out the Pacific Coast Highway toward Malibu. Off on the left—when you could see it through the jam of beach houses—the blue Pacific curled and licked at the sand.

It was almost dinnertime, but what was there in the house to eat? He was almost sure the lettuce was gone. Out of tomatoes, no meat, maybe a potato or two left in the bottom of the vegetable bin. It was like an evening in D.C., coming home from a night class at the law school, stopping at a supermarket to do the shopping. It had probably begun then—getting divorced from Amanda.

The Army had been fun for a while, and then okay for a while, but it wasn't anything he wanted to stick with for twenty years. On the other hand, an undergraduate degree in poli. sci. wasn't much of a qualification for anything else.

He'd decided to go to night law school at George Washington, thinking it would be like taking a night class in arc welding, or something else that you might do for amusement. Of course it wasn't just one night class, it was two or three, five nights a week, but that had seemed like it would be all right. And after all, Amanda was working and taking classes for her master's, so there should have been no problem.

Except that there was a difference between one person in the house studying, and getting ready for exams, and trying to concentrate, and two doing it. Whatever the difficulties were of spending time together, and paying attention to one another—doing, as it were, the daily gardening that kept a relationship green—it was much worse when two of them were studying instead of one. Not twice as difficult, but maybe four times. When he had some free time, she had a paper due. When she had free time, he had an exam. And it would be okay, it was just temporary, they'd work it out—only somehow it wasn't, and they didn't, and things had never been the same again.

Pike swung off of PCH at Trancas and parked in the lot at the Trancas market. Hell of a way to spend a Saturday night, pushing a shopping cart through a supermarket looking for dinner. On the other hand, it was better than sitting alone in a restaurant. He got a cart and began working his way down the meat case, looking at pork chops and chicken.

"Hah!" a voice behind him said. "What are you doing here?"

It was Mildred—Dossie. Also pushing a shopping cart, although hers was nearly full.

"Looking for dinner. And stuff for the rest of the week."

She nodded. "Hell of a way to spend Saturday night, though, huh?"

"Yeah." And then, seeing a kind of hesitant expectancy in her eyes that made it all right, "Look, if you're not about to rush out to a, ahem, commitment for the evening, why don't I get a couple of steaks, and you can come up to the house and help eat them?"

She hesitated for a fraction of a second, looking at him with those big gray eyes. Then, "Could I go for a swim first?"

"Sure."

"And bring something? Say a salad? I'm good at salads."

"Sure."

"I'll be there before you are." And with that she was gone down the aisle of the market, trundling her cart.

When Pike got to the house, the gate to the backyard was standing ajar, and he could hear the sound of splashing, and the slop of water against the side of the pool. He walked around the house to the patio. Dossie was in the pool, swimming laps. She swam with a lot of energy but not a lot of style. Pike went through the house to the kitchen and got a couple of beers out of the refrigerator, then went back out the sliding glass doors to the deck. Walked around to the shallow end of the pool and set one of the beers on the concrete that was still warm from the afternoon sun.

Dossie finished the lap she was swimming and came to a stop, then stood up in the shallow water. She slicked her hair back with both hands and looked up at Pike. With her hair plastered down that way, she looked about twelve years old. Or maybe it had something to do with the clean lines of her face and the absence of makeup.

"Whoo!" she said, "ten minutes and I'm bushed."

"You want a beer?" Pike pointed at the bottle on the deck with his toe.

Dossie put both hands on the edge of the pool, jumped and turned, and sat on the deck with her feet hanging in the water. She was wearing a dark green Speedo tank suit with straps that crossed in back—a serious swimmer's suit. She picked up the beer, twisted off the cap, and took a long swig. She put the bottle down on the concrete, put one hand over her mouth and burped, and then giggled.

"You won't tell my sister, will you? She thinks drinking beer is only for shiftless no 'count folks. The only drink for a lady is bourbon and branch water."

Hoisting herself to her feet, she left wet footprints across the deck to where she'd put a towel over the back of a lounge chair. She picked up the towel and scrubbed at her hair, then wrapped the towel around herself like a skirt. Why did women always do that? They bought these bathing suits, wore them in the pool, and then, as soon as they were out, they wrapped a towel around them. Must be some deep inner part of the female psyche. Should work up a theory about it, maybe try it out on Amanda. Call her in New York, and say, "Oh, by the way, I have this theory . . ." Once upon a time she would have laughed and played along, suggested embellishments for the theory. Now she'd probably say, "David, don't be ridiculous," in that prissy voice she could put on. Have to find someone else to try out the offbeat ideas on.

Dossie was working her feet into a pair of sandals. Pike watched the play of muscles in her back as she balanced on one foot, running a forefinger around inside the strap of a sandal. She stood up and turned around. "That was great. But am I ever out of shape. I haven't been swimming enough."

"Come over any time you want, and use the pool."

And there was another level look from those gray eyes. "You mean it? Don't say it unless you mean it, 'cause I'll take you up on it."

"Sure I mean it."

"Okay. Well, I better get started on the salad. I brought some stuff. Which way is the kitchen?"

"Inside and to the right. But take your time. I have to light the grill and let it heat up."

"Great. That'll give me time to create." And she walked into the house, slim in the green tank suit.

When Pike went inside after lighting the gas grill, Dossie was sitting on one of the stools at the counter, looking moodily at the countertop. Arranged neatly in front of her were a salad bowl, a head of lettuce, two carrots, an onion, two tomatoes, two lemons, and a bottle of olive oil. Pike walked across the kitchen to the cupboard where he kept the grill for the barbecue. He got the grill out of the cupboard and brushed it with oil. When he glanced at Dossie, she hadn't moved. She chewed thoughtfully at the side of her thumb and sighed.

"Not much progress on the salad, huh?"

Dossie sighed again and glanced up. "Dave, can I talk to you a minute?"

"Sure. Let me go and put this on the barbecue and I'll be right back."

"Could we talk now? Before you do that?"

"Sure." Pike put the grill down in the sink. "What is it?"

"The other day? When you helped me fix the garbage disposal? That wasn't an accident. I wanted to meet you, so I plugged it up myself and then waited until I saw you out running, and then asked you to fix it. I'd seen you drive by, and out running sometimes, and I wanted to meet you, so I just . . . well . . . I did it, okay? Are you mad?"

Pike stood blinking at her, shaking his head, suddenly seeing the whole thing in another light. "Mad? Me? Mad? Why should I be mad?"

"Well, I don't know. I might be mad if someone did that to me. I mean, I don't think *I* would, but some people would."

"Flattered maybe, but not mad."

"Is it okay then?"

"Sure it's okay. Don't worry about it."

"Super!" And with a great show of energy she jumped off the stool and began shredding lettuce and chopping carrots and onions.

Pike took the grill outside and put it on the barbecue.

Richie parked his Jeep down the block. Almost in the same place as that afternoon. Was it only that afternoon? Starting to get dark on the sidewalk under the overhanging limbs of the trees. Walked up the sidewalk toward her driveway.

All the way driving over Richie had been thinking. Thinking about the smartass with his baseball bat. The smartass had been at her house. She must know who he was and where he hung out. Richie was going to enjoy asking her, particularly if she didn't want to tell.

Or maybe the smartass'd even be there. Find them both at the same time. Richie had brought along a little equalizer. Two well-seasoned oak rods, an inch and a half in diameter and eighteen inches long, joined at one end with a short length of nylon line—a nunchaku. Richie had spent hours practicing with the nunchaku. He could break boards with it, smash bricks. And if you used it like a nutcracker—put someone's arm or hand between the two wooden rods and squeezed—Richie had tried it on his own hand one day, just to see. It had brought tears to his eyes. He'd brought some rope too, and some strips of material torn from a T-shirt. There was enough to tie both of them up, if the smartass was there. Use the T-shirt material for a gag, keep the smartass quiet while he took care of her. Then take care of the smartass later.

Got to the driveway. Kept to the grass at the side, off of the concrete. Dominic said try to walk quiet, so people didn't know you were coming. You could get a lot of advantage in a situation, just popping up where someone didn't expect you.

Around the corner of the building, into the backyard, still on the grass. Took the stairs with just the tips of his toes, careful not to scrape his boot soles on the concrete treads.

Now came the hard part. Dominic said that people always hid a key somewhere around near their door. The thing was, was figuring out where they'd hide it. Besides, if they heard him and came out while he was on the stair landing, it could get nasty. Or if they just sat tight, called the cops. Richie lifted the doormat and looked underneath. Ran his fingers along the molding over the door, and felt on top of the porch light. Nothing.

There were potted plants on the little stair landing—the kind with fat green leaves and big, thick stems. Being very careful not to make any noise, Richie lifted each pot and looked underneath. Nothing. Maybe it was hid in one of those phony hollow rocks. Fuck.

Richie stood on the stair landing and looked around. There were no more places to hide anything. Maybe she didn't leave a key outside. Or maybe it was someplace else. Richie went down the stairs on tiptoe. Along the side of the driveway, against the grass, was another row of potted plants. Richie lifted them one by one.

The key was under the third pot.

The key was corroded from being under the pot, and it was hard to get it into the lock. Being nervous made it harder. Richie's sweaty fingers slipped on the key. Almost had it. What was that noise? Someone inside? Richie froze, listening. No more noise from inside, but now the key was stuck and wouldn't turn. Shit! Wiggled it gently. And again. And again.

And then the cylinder turned, and the door was open.

Richie held the door barely ajar. Stood up, took a deep breath, and stepped inside, his nunchaku ready in his hand. The living room was lit by a lamp on an end table. Nobody was there. Maybe they were in the bedroom. Maybe he was balling her. Tiptoed down the hall. Drapes were pulled, couldn't see into the darkness in the room. Reached around the doorjamb and flipped on the light switch.

Nobody. Shit!

Went quickly back through the apartment, checked the bathroom, the kitchen. Looked like she wasn't home. Richie looked in her refrigerator, helped himself to a glass of wine from a bottle that was open. Found a comfortable place in the corner of the living room and sat down to wait.

CHAPTER

7

"Not interrupting anything, am I?" the voice said. Female voice, husky but penetrating. Pike looked at his watch. It was a little past nine, and he'd just come back inside from getting the Sunday paper.

"No," he said. "Should you be?"

"Sunday mornings are a little dicey sometimes—depending on what you've been doing the night before." There was more than a hint of challenge in the way it was said.

"Only what the dog did in the nighttime."

Which was unfortunately true. After what had seemed to be a promising beginning, the evening had turned to a bovine end product. Dossie had been tense and skittish, and had gone home early, pleading a headache. All of which left Pike more than a little confused. Why had she told him about plugging up her disposal? And once she'd told him, why turn shy and disappear? It made very little sense, but then Pike had found that he had a tendency to fall off on the curves when he tried to follow the twists and turns of the female mind.

"Well then, Mr. Holmes, perhaps you'd like some things that you came to get yesterday but I didn't have ready for you?"

"The invoices and stuff? You got them already?"

"I went and picked them up from the bookkeeper. Thought I'd bring them over. Sort of give you a chance to reconsider." The challenge in the tone and phrasing was even more evident.

"Well, I . . ."

"You really are stuffy, you know?"

And then, in one of those mercurial changes that she seemed to be capable of, becoming soft and contrite: "I'm sorry, I don't mean that. I'll just bring the stuff out and leave it with you, okay?"

"You don't need to do that. I'll come get them. I don't want to put you to the trouble . . ."

"Don't worry about it. I've got to see a friend of mine in the Colony for lunch, so I'm going to be out in Malibu. I'll bring them by on my way. Besides, I have a favor I want to ask you."

"Oh. Okay," Pike said. "By the way, did you talk to this guy DiAngelo yet?"

"No. I really haven't had time. Maurice insisted that I go back and spend last night at his house, but that's such a drag. None of my clothes are over there, and Maurice is worse than a Jewish mother. So I'm moving back to my place tonight. I'll see you in a while. Around ten thirty, maybe."

Pike was in the driveway vacuuming the floor of his Porsche when the silver Maserati braked to a stop. He stood up and shut off the vacuum. The driver's door of the Maserati popped open and a pair of very long legs came out of the door. Looking at the legs—legs encased in sheer nylon—Pike realized he'd always seen Mickey in pants, never in a skirt.

The difference was definitely worth looking at. She was dressed like a model, or maybe people going to lunch with a Hollywood acquaintance dressed that way too. Pike wouldn't have known. Beige suede skirt with matching beige suede car coat—wide lapels, double breasted. Black nylons, black heels, a tight black scoop-neck blouse out of some knit fabric, and her long hair done up in a bun under a black hat with a flat crown and a round brim.

She reached up and gave the hat a tug, pulling the brim low over her eyes, then walked around to the passenger side of the Maserati and opened the door.

"These are the invoices." She indicated a cardboard box on the seat. "If you wouldn't mind carrying them, the box is kind of dusty and I don't want to get dust on my skirt."

She stood to one side as Pike lifted the box out of the car. Looked around at the house, the mile of view down the hill to the Pacific, the gray silhouettes of the Channel Islands almost sunk in the morning haze. She pursed her lips and nodded.

"Not bad. No wonder people like to live out here."

"Yeah," Pike said. "If they can afford it, which I can't. I'm just house sitting."

"Oh well. Better that here than owning your own in Compton or Downey. What's the yard like, do you mind if I look?"

"Help yourself. There's a gate at the side there." Pike followed her around the garage and into the backyard as she picked her way across the stepping stones in her heels.

"Yesterday you said," Pike addressed her back, "that you had an option on a new book by a major novelist."

She was looking around at the landscaping. "Yeah. I did. This is nice, it's all native plants so you don't have to water it, right? And having those rocks around the pool so it looks more natural."

"You still have to water it," Pike said. "At least those things that look like iris down past the pool need to be watered. Agapanthus or whatever they are. I was just curious who it was. John Fowles maybe?"

"Uh-uh. I said a major *American* novelist. Fowles is English. And that diving board. It isn't just your average home-type board. It's a one-meter competition board."

"How do you know? Alice Walker then?"

"I used to dive competitively. In college. I said a novelist, not a propagandist. I meant someone who writes literature, not someone who tries to shove an agenda down your throat."

"Ken Kesey?"

"Maybe."

"John Irving?"

"Maybe."

"John Updike?"

"Maybe."

"Why are you being so cute about it?"

"Because the option is about to expire, and I've got to renew it, and I don't want anyone else bidding against me."

"I'm not about to bid against you for the film rights on a novel."

"Maybe not, but you're a lawyer who represents people who are in the film business." She twirled her finger as though indicating a group. "The stockholders in this production company, who are being so paranoid about their money, right?"

Pike nodded and she smiled a tight little smile. "Let's just say that if you can be professional about what you do, why, so can I. And if you don't know whose novel I'm buying, you can't make a mistake and tell the wrong people."

She had turned and was looking at him from under the brim of her little hat. "I'm sorry. I don't want to be unpleasant about it. Get off on the wrong foot when I'm about to ask you a favor."

"That's okay," Pike said, shrugging. "I wasn't feeling hassled. What's the favor?"

She was still looking at him from under the brim of her hat. "I'd like," she said, "to borrow a gun. Maurice said you'd have one."

If you had given Pike fifty guesses, borrowing a gun wouldn't even have been on the list of alternates. It came as a complete surprise. He took a breath and let it out slowly.

"What," he said, "do you want a gun for?"

"That should be obvious. In case that guy comes back."

"I don't really know how to say this, but just borrowing a pistol won't keep him away. Like having a compass in your pocket won't keep you from getting lost in the woods. You've got to keep it where you can get at it, and you've got to be willing to use it."

"I think I can handle that." Very flat voice. Sounded like a line from a movie. Debra Winger in *Black Widow* maybe.

"Uh-huh," Pike said. "Have you ever shot anyone?"

"No." And then immediately, as a challenge, "Have you?"

"As a matter of fact," Pike said, "I have. But that's really neither here nor there. Have you thought about buying a pistol?"

"I tried. It takes a two-week waiting period. Does that sound right? Unless they were just jacking me around. And I need it now. Tonight. So I asked Maurice, and he said he was sure that you'd have one you could loan me."

Her gaze had softened and turned pleading, and Pike remembered the way her voice had changed, gotten small and lost, when Blondie had been in her apartment.

"All right," he said. "Give me a minute, I'll dig around and see what I can find." He carried the box of invoices with him and went into the house. Dumped the invoices on a chair in the den and began looking through the drawers of the desk for a souvenir that he'd hung onto. Finally found what he was looking for, a bundle wrapped in an oily rag. He carried the bundle back outside.

She was still standing by the pool, looking cool and elegant. Pike put the bundle on a poolside table. "There you are. Be careful, there's oil on the rag. You don't want to get it on your suit."

"Wait." She looked the tiniest bit nervous. "Can you show me how it works?"

"Sure." Pike unwrapped the rag from around the pistol and held it up for her to see. "This thing here? This's the safety. If that red dot is showing, it's ready to fire. If it isn't, it's safe to put in your purse. Pull this back here and let go, like this, and that loads it. Then just point it and pull the trigger. Don't mess around with the sights if you're in the same room with the guy. Don't try to hit him in the head, or anything fancy. Just point with your hand at the middle of his chest."

He reversed the pistol and held the butt out toward her. There was a slight hesitation, and then she took it from him.

J A M E S   G .   P A T T I L L O

"Do I have to cock it or anything?"

"Not after the first time. It'll cock and reload itself each time, until all thirteen rounds are fired. So just keep pulling the trigger until he goes down."

"Like this?" She held the pistol up and squinted experimentally across the sights.

"You can support your wrist with your other hand. That might steady it down some."

"What's this here?"

"It's a slide lock. Don't mess with it."

"What's it for?"

Pike remembering. Remembering the instructor holding up the ugly automatic pistol, looking around at the group of ISA officers, letting his face show just a hint of the career noncom's contempt for chair-bound officers. Droning in his bored instructor voice, "All right, boys and girls, this is a Model thirty-nine Smith & Wesson, but slightly modified, as you can see. This was originally done for the Navy SEALS, but we think it's a pretty nice pistol, so we use them too. Here we have raised sights, so that if you use a suppressor—some of you that watch late-night television may call that a silencer—the sights are tall enough to use over the top of the suppressor. Here we have a slide-locking lever, so that the sound of the slide going back and forward is avoided. Note, please, that in this mode the pistol is firing single action. That is, you will have to unlock the slide and cock it by hand to fire the next round. And here, we have a special subsonic nine-millimeter round. As some of you may know, a lot of the noise from a pistol shot is just the bullet going supersonic. Use a subsonic round and the noise is significantly reduced. For example, watch that glass jar there at the end of the range."

And the class watched as the glass jar dutifully flew into pieces with no more noise than the glass breaking—not even the usual *pop* of a suppressed pistol shot.

Looking at Mickey and saying: "If you're trying to shoot some-

8 4

one and not let anyone know it, it locks the slide so the action doesn't cycle, and there isn't any noise of the action working. Don't worry about it. You won't need it."

"How about bullets?"

"You're going to shoot one goon, not start a war. There's thirteen in the clip. If you can't do it with thirteen, it can't be done. Either the guy is Godzilla, or you aren't hitting him. In either case, more bullets won't help." He wiped the slide and the frame with the rag, wrapped the pistol in the rag again, and held the bundle out to her.

"What are you doing?" she said. "Wiping off your fingerprints?" The question was delivered in a blasé tone that tried to assume complete familiarity with such matters, but only revealed a certain naïveté.

"Not in the way you seem to mean. It's metal. There's salt in perspiration. Metal rusts. There's oil on the rag. If you can, try to keep it oiled."

"All right," she said. She took the bundle and put it in her shoulder bag. "All right. I'll get it back to you in a couple of weeks, when all this is sorted out. By the way . . ." She tilted her head so that the brim of her hat almost hid her eyes, and gave him a slow glance. It was a gesture so studiously artificial that it had to have come from a script. ". . . Would you mind if I went for a swim in your pool?"

Pike started to laugh, but converted it into a cough when he saw she was serious. "Aren't you supposed to be meeting someone?" he asked.

"Yes, but not until lunch. There's bags of time."

"It's your funeral. Come on inside and we can find you a suit and a towel." He crossed the patio to the sliding glass doors that led into the living room. As he rolled the door open, the front doorbell rang. Pike glanced back at Mickey. She had not followed him, but was standing near one of the patio tables at the side of the pool, taking off her coat. Leaving her there, he crossed the living room, went down the hall, and opened the front door.

Dossie was on the doorstep. She was wearing a short terrycloth robe—just a long shirt, really. In a string bag she had a bottle of suntan oil and a paperback book.

"Hi," she said. "I hope you don't mind. You said I could come over any time. I would have just gone around through the gate but I saw another car and thought you might have company."

"Not really," Pike said. "Just someone bringing over some invoices and stuff that need to be audited."

"Oh. That's okay then." Dossie stepped into the hall. She lowered her voice, "Dave, I want to apologize about last night."

Holding up her hand, palm out toward him. "No, let me finish. At the time, it seemed as if I were just being too forward, I mean practically inviting myself over here, and then telling you that I'd intentionally plugged up that disposal just to meet you, and I was afraid, well . . ."

She was looking everywhere except at Pike. All at once she did look at him, a direct, level gaze, ". . . It just seemed too much like I was coming on to you, okay? So that's why I left in such a hurry after dinner. Then when I got home, it all began to seem a little silly. I mean, I plugged up the garbage disposal so I could meet you, so why am I fussing around behaving like a simpering schoolgirl? So I thought I'd come over and see if we could start again. Just forget last night, and start where we were."

She stopped, a little out of breath after this long speech, again avoiding Pike's eyes.

"Sure," Pike said. "I mean, I don't think you need to apologize. We had dinner, you said you had to leave, and that was it. I didn't think anything of it."

Or at least he wasn't going to say so when she was so obviously upset about it.

"Okay then." She seemed to regard something as settled, although Pike wasn't sure what. He got a long look from those gray eyes. "So I came over for a swim, if that's all right."

"Sure. Fine. Go ahead."

Pike stepped back, and Dossie walked past him, down the hall and into the living room. She began telling Pike something about her sister—not the one she was visiting, but the other one—talking a blue streak over her shoulder as she walked. She shrugged out of her robe and tossed it on a chair in passing. Underneath the robe she was wearing the same green tank suit as the night before. Started toward the doors out to the patio and the pool. In the middle of the room she turned to stone, staring off into the distance.

Trying to figure out why she'd frozen like that, Pike followed her gaze, across the room, and out through the glass doors, and saw Mickey arising from the pool ladder, like Aphrodite from the shell—naked as an egg. Mickey reached the top of the ladder, ran a hand over her face to wipe the water from her eyes, and then strolled around the end of the pool toward the diving board. Droplets of water glinted on her breasts and flanks as she walked.

Dossie was still frozen in the middle of the room.

Mickey climbed onto the board and stood, head level, looking into the distance. Took three steps in a proud, firm stride, and lifted off the board in a lovely, soaring arch with a sudden tuck into a perfect back one and a half somersault.

The entry was so clean that the splash didn't even rise above the pool coping.

Dossie turned and bolted past Pike toward the front door. Apologized profusely. Forgot something. Must leave. Picked up her robe. Disappeared.

Pike sighed and walked back out onto the patio. Mickey's suede skirt and coat were neatly folded on a chair, also the black blouse. The black heels were next to the chair, one standing, one tipped over on its side.

Mickey swam slowly to the ladder at the side of the pool. Climbed out, without so much as looking in Pike's direction, and walked back to the board. Climbed on and stood for a moment, hands at her sides, head level, looking at nothing. Three steps, stamp-and-lift, and another perfect back one-and-a-half.

Pike went inside again to get a towel. On second thought, he got two. Her hair'd be wet, and she'd need one, at least, for that. He carried the towels back outside and put them next to the folded clothes.

CHAPTER

8

NICO WAS SITTING IN Tonello's office at Parker Center, 150 North Los Angeles Street, the headquarters building of the LAPD, waiting for Tonello to get through telling a story and give him the rap sheet on the guy who owned the Jeep. Tonello always wasted fifteen minutes of your time telling some dumb story about something that happened to him before he made lieutenant and started to spend his time in a swivel chair. But Nico didn't want to make him mad by telling him to cut the crap and give him the sheet.

"The D.A.—stuck-up little bitch, but smart as a whip, just stayed in the D.A.'s office long enough to get her ticket punched and then went on to Justice, but that's another story—the D.A. says, 'What next transpired, Officer Tonello?'

"So I go, well, the deceased and the defendant, Leroy George Washington Carver Jones, they produced pistols, and ordered the storekeeper to lie on the floor, and they proceeded to take the money from the cash register. My partner and I thereupon emerged from our place of concealment and called on the defendant and the deceased to drop their weapons, which they failed to do. Shots were exchanged, and my partner and I placed the defendant under arrest, and advised him of his rights. Oh, and we called the meat wag . . . I mean an ambulance for the deceased."

Nico looked out the window of Tonello's office. Three floors below he could see the black-and-whites lined up in the parking structure, and farther west, across First Street, was the edge of Little Tokyo. Nico wasn't sure, but he thought he could see a little of the fountain on the corner of First and Los Angeles Street, in the grounds of the Otani Hotel. Or maybe it was just that he knew it was there. And further down First Street was the Sumitomo Bank Building.

"No shit," Nico said. "But what about this off-the-record explanation the defendant was going to give?"

"I'm coming to that. So I finish testifying and I'm excused, and they mess around for another hour or two with the rest of the prelim. Well, finally we get done with that, and the D.A. calls the defendant for his off-the-record explanation. So this big dumb bastard—as big as a linebacker, or maybe bigger—he gets up there and he says, 'Well, it wuz about like de officer say, we was robbin' de sto'. Only when de officers come out the back, there wasn't nothin' 'bout drop your weapons. What they say was, "April fool, mother-fucker," and then the shootin' started.'

"Well," Tonello said, "the judge just broke up. He had to take a recess, and then after ten minutes when he came back he was still chuckling every now and again, but finally he says, 'All right, counsel, I'll accept the plea on the basis you've worked out,' and we all go back to work."

"Yeah," Nico said. "That's pretty good. April fool. You know, I kind of think I believe the defendant's version more than I believe yours."

"Well." Tonello scratched his head and then looked suspiciously at his fingernails. "You're not as dumb as you look, Nico. I'll give you that. Here. This's what you're after."

He handed Nico two sheets of paper, stapled together. Nico took the sheets, glanced at them, folded them, and put them in his pocket.

"Thanks, Tony. By the way, you got anyone here who's arrested this bastard, or who knows anything about him?"

"I don't know. Let me see the sheet again." Tonello held out his hand.

Nico unfolded the sheets and handed them back. Tonello studied them for a moment.

"Couple different arresting officers, but the guy in the black-and-white won't know much about him. You want to talk to one of the detectives, or somebody in OCU that's tried to make a case on him. Simms, or maybe Jan Bokkie down in Organized Crime. Here, I'll see if one of 'em's in the building."

Nico held up his hand. "Tony, Tony, not so fast. I got some things to do, right now. If you don't mind, just give me the phone numbers, okay?"

Pike punched the lighted button on his phone. "Mr. Pike?" the receptionist's voice said, "There's a Mr. Baranowitz here to see you. He says he doesn't have an appointment. Shall I send him back?"

"Yeah," Pike said. I think he knows the way okay. Send him on back."

A moment later Maurice strode briskly into Pike's office. He looked around, chose a chair, and sat down.

"I talked to Mickey," he began. "She said she gave you the canceled checks and stuff on Saturday, and then took the invoices out to you on Sunday. So you got all the stuff, right? You got it all here?"

"I got it," Pike said.

"I, ah, was in this neck of the woods anyway. Thought I'd just pop in for a moment, pick up the stuff." Maurice crossed his legs and then uncrossed them again. "Since I was close. Since Mickey said you had it."

From the moment he had dropped into one of Pike's client chairs he had not been still. Smoothing the points of his collar, running his hand across his scalp to make sure the wisps of hair were in place, tugging at the lapels of his suit.

"Yeah, sure," Pike said. "It's right here. We can make a copy for you from the originals, and . . ."

"No." Maurice had gotten to his feet, shaking his head, "No. I don't want a copy. I'll just take the originals. I don't want to take up your time. I'll just take the stuff and get out of your hair."

"But, Maurie, I uh, I thought you wanted to have an audit done on it and I had . . ."

"Audit? Who said anything about an audit? I don't need no audit. I can look at it myself and find out everything that some auditor could tell me. Who needs to pay an auditor?"

He had been scanning the shelves of the bookcase and the surfaces of the desk and credenza, turning his gaze here and there with quick movements of his head. "Where's the stuff?"

"That cardboard box there in the corner."

Maurice crossed the room quickly, dropped to one knee, and opened the box. He located the checkbook and pulled it out, then continued to dig through the box. "The bank statements are in here too?" he said without looking up.

"Yeah. They're on the bottom, under the invoices. Should be in chronological order."

"I don't see any copies. Do you have any here?"

"Not here, I had . . ."

"Good. We don't need any copies."

Maurice pulled out a couple of envelopes and carried them back to Pike's desk along with the checkbook. He took the statements from the envelopes and spread them out. Made a production of taking a pair of reading glasses out of his pocket and putting them on. Then he began flipping the pages of the checkbook, muttering to himself.

"Maurice," Pike said, keeping a firm hold on his temper, "I thought you wanted these books and records so that we could have an audit done, to find fifty thousand dollars that was missing. Now you're telling me you *don't* want an audit?"

"That's right. I'll just take this stuff along with me. I need to look through it a little more thoroughly, but from a quick glance . . ."—he ran his finger along a line of figures on one of the bank statements—". . . it looks okay. The checkbook is balanced to the last statement, and the amount of money that's in the account seems about right."

"Maurie," Pike said, and now his temper was no longer under control, "wait a minute. Just because the balance looks right, that doesn't prove if the checks were actually written, or if they were written to the right people, or if we got to this balance another way. Now that we've gone to all the trouble to get the damn things, why not take the time to do it right?"

"What do you mean, do it right?"

"Have an accountant go through the books."

Maurice shook his head and frowned. "Because I know how these things should look, and it looks right to me. How many pictures have I produced, I need some accountant to tell me everything is fine only there's a fifty-cent error in addition somewhere and then hand me a bill for a thousand dollars for his time. No, no, no."

He shook his head more firmly.

"Maurie, you want to tell me what's going on?"

"David," Maurice said firmly, "you don't need that tone in your voice when you talk to me.

"Besides, whaddya mean,"—he switched to wide-eyed innocence—" 'what's going on?' What should be going on?"

"If I knew, I wouldn't be asking. But something is funny about this. You're worried about money being missing, only . . ."—Pike paused for a moment and then went on, more slowly, thinking it out—". . . only you're worried about something else, too, that's almost as important as the money. And you aren't telling me what it is."

"Nothing. There's nothing else," Maurice said, looking Pike right in the eye.

"Okay," Pike said, exasperated, but willing to give the old man his way. "We'll do it your way. Don't hire an accountant. But I already had, but I . . ."

"What?" Maurice said. "But what? You don't agree? Look, I told you. I got a feel for these things. This looks all right, and that's the end of it."

"All right," Pike said. "It's your money. Only why did we get all stirred up over the damn things in the first place?"

"It was a false alarm," Maurice said. "What can I tell you? What happened was, I got this notice that the interest rate on my credit line was going up two percent. *Two* percent, I mean, that's an insult.

"So I go in to see one of the vice presidents, give him hell about this rip-off they're doing with the interest."

He shook his head at the memory. "Asshole! So we're having this argument, and I say, 'We had a deal, and the deal was prime plus one, long as I kept a hundred thousand, short-term deposit.' And he says, 'That's what I'm trying to tell you. Your compensating balance's been below fifty thousand for two months.'

"Well." Maurice grimaced. "You know how it is when someone tells you something, you know it's wrong. You *know* it. You're indignant, you're self-righteous. And I say, 'Never mind my personal account, the business account, They been low lately, but how about the DCI account? That's over a hundred right there.'

"And," Maurice said, and grimaced again, "he's looking at me and shaking his head. Right then I got this feeling, like when I went on my brother-in-law's boat, huge thing he's got like a Winnebago only it floats, rolls back and forth, never stands still. Well, my stomach felt like when I was on that boat, hollow and sore, and like I wanted to throw up.

"And the vice president says, 'No it isn't. It's less than fifty.' Well of course he was right. Showed me the statement, with the balance. And that's why I wanted to see the canceled checks, the invoices, see what happened to the money. Because I got—I have a feel for where we are in the production, and how much should have been spent.

"But now,"—he flipped a page of one of the statements—"seeing the balance in these statements, it looks right. Even better than I expected with Mickey having to pay off that bastard DiAngelo.

There are one or two things that Mickey could have maybe prepaid that would have made the balance lower than it should have been for a while, but this is about right, what's in the account now. And the invoices look right, just flipping through them. So it was all a false alarm. You can forget about it."

"Speaking of DiAngelo . . ." Pike said.

"Yeah." Maurice paused and refocused his attention. "Yeah, right. I talked to his man Nakamura. They all think they're so smart. He can't just say sure, I know what you're talking about, we've made a mistake, I'll fix it. He has to play his little game. Doesn't call it protection. Calls it *insurance*. Says he doesn't really stay on top of which projects they're handling insurance for.

"Ha!" He turned and looked past Pike, scowling at the memory. "As if he didn't know all the time. Says he'll have to look into it, ask around. He'll let me know. Let me know! I tell you, I gave him something to think about. Told him just what I think of *gonifs* who take money and don't deliver."

Still bristling with righteousness, Maurice carried the box of canceled checks and invoices out the door.

Richie had been sitting in the woman's apartment again, ever since lunchtime, waiting for her to come home. He'd tried a couple of evenings, she'd never showed, so he figured she was sleeping out, and he'd catch her if he hung around in the middle of the day.

Only problem was, it was dull as hell, sitting there with nothing to do. But if he turned on the television, she'd hear it when she came home, know somebody was in her apartment. So he sat in her living room, in the dim light that filtered through the drawn drapes. He had a gym bag with him, with his nunchaku in it, and some rope and the strips of T-shirt material.

The room had a pleasant feel. Not as nice as Richie's apartment, but then his place had been done by an interior designer. Guy was a friend of Dominic's, only he was a fag, least he talked like one. But had good ideas about what colors to use on the furniture and the rugs to pull the whole thing together. Richie had a whole wall of stereo equipment he'd ordered from the Sharper Image catalogue, a rowing machine, a universal gym, and before it had been decorated it had looked kind of confused. But now it all seemed to fit together and had a high-tech, modern look. Understated, but classy.

When Richie thought of the dump his folks had lived in—probably still lived in—he had to laugh. Single-wall shack like they did for farm laborers, at night you could see the light from inside shining through cracks between the boards in the siding. Broken-down furniture like it had been rescued from the dump. And that cot in the living room with his father lying on it. Lying there ever since he'd reached into a tank of pesticide to get a spray nozzle somebody had dropped in there.

He'd been exposed to so much of the stuff from working in the fields, that getting it on his hands that one time set him off, and now he just laid there. On a good day he'd get outside, sit in a chair in the yard in the sun for an hour or two. Well, that was a long way away and a long time ago, and Richie was living good now.

Richie had eaten too much for lunch, had almost dozed off when he heard the rasp of a key in the lock. He got quickly to his feet and stepped into the hall to the bedroom, so he'd be out of sight from the door. Watched as she came in and did all the things people did when they got home. Put her mail down on a little table by the couch, shut the front door, put her purse on the table with the mail, put her keys in her purse. Richie waited until she had gone into the kitchen before he came out of the hallway.

CHAPTER

9

SHE HAD BEEN GLOWERING at herself in the mirror when the phone rang.

There really ought to be something interesting she could do with her hair. Get it up off her neck. She had a slender neck. A hairdresser had told her that once. 'Course he was gay, but she thought he was right, about her neck being nice. Too bad the rest of her didn't go with the neck. Her chest, well, forget it. Most men had bigger tits than she did. Not like Millie. Boys had started looking down the front of Millie's dress as soon as she was fourteen, sliding their eyes over her body from across the room, elaborately casual.

The trouble was, she'd cut the hair so short, there wasn't much that could be done except wait for it to grow out again. And when it did, it would be the same thin, wispy texture it had been before she'd cut it off, in an attempt to get it short enough that it would at least seem to have some body.

She hated it. If she had hair like Millie, thick, naturally curly, with a lot of body, well, you could do anything with hair like that. Millie had all the luck. Got the hair, the looks, the boys, the whole shooting match. Millie with her opinionated yuppie husband and her dumb yuppie house and her mindless yuppie chocolate Labradors that needed to be fed and exercised while Millie was on her stupid yuppie vacation down at Club Med in Cancún, which required Dossie to come from Texas to be sisterly and take care of the house and the dogs and—how crass to even think it, but yes—

to be respectful and admiring of all Millie's accumulated yuppie possessions.

She was frowsy and plain and even the three hundred dollars she had spent on voice lessons, trying to lose the north-Texas twang, had been a waste. As soon as she got excited, or upset, back it came, and people looked at her and she could tell what they were thinking: that here was a ditzy blonde with no chest and no looks and an accent that no educated person could listen to without his teeth hurting, like when someone scritched a piece of chalk on a blackboard.

And then the phone rang.

"Hello," she said.

"Dossie, hi. Don't hang up, okay?"

He must have read her mind, because that was exactly what she started to do, as soon as she identified the voice. It was that jerk that lived up the hill. She wanted to die when she thought about him. All lean and rangy with Marlboro man looks. Let her make a fool out of herself coming on to him. Lord! She'd pranced up there, thinking she was being risqué in her stupid tank suit, thinking maybe he'd rub suntan oil on her back, and he had some woman there who was completely naked! Naked in the middle of the day! And she wasn't even ugly! Looked like she could be in a perfume commercial, had hair all down her back. 'Course it was all wet, but you could tell, when it was dry, it would be all wavy and thick and heavy. And tits! Tits like you could kill for. He'd probably had a thing going with her the whole time. They probably laughed about it together, after Dossie left.

But she didn't hang up.

Halting, stumbling, he was giving an explanation of this woman—Mickey. It seemed her name was Mickey—coming over to deliver some financial records for some company, and inviting herself for a swim. It sounded lame. It sounded like something cooked up by a desperate philanderer to cover a lost afternoon. He must have thought she was dim, too, besides being plain, to buy something like that.

"Don't tell me that was all she came over for," Dossie said. She heard the brittle sharpness in her voice, and hoped he heard it too.

"Well, yeah. It was. That and she wanted to borrow a pistol."

"I'm sorry," she said. "I don't think I heard you right. I thought you said she wanted to borrow a pistol."

"That's right."

"Whatever for?"

"Well, there was this guy in her apartment who was apparently trying to — Or at least I thought he —. But then he turned out to be a goon for some gangster who's connected with some labor union. And her producer was going to call the gangster and tell him to call off his goon, but she wasn't sure that—"

"Can I ask you something?" Dossie said.

"Sure."

"You're a lawyer, right?" not waiting for him to answer. "You go to court, right? Stand on your hind feet, talk to rooms full of people. There's other lawyers there, too. Right? They try to pick apart what you say and turn it into garbage. You deal with that, right?" Waiting for an answer now.

"Yeah, that's right," he said. He said it slowly, trying to figure out where she was going with her line of questions; sounding like he didn't think he'd like it when they got there.

"Then why do you sound like a tryout for the second-grade play when you talk to me?"

"I don't know." He said it again, slowly, like he was really trying to think why it was. "I really don't know. Maybe it's because, well . . . I don't know. So anyway, as I was saying, I don't know if the producer got the word through, and I've been sleeping with a pistol under my pillow too, just in case the guy comes to pay me a visit."

"What does a gangster and a labor union have to do with a movie director?"

"It doesn't make a lot of sense to me. I guess he's been getting payoffs to leave the production alone. Otherwise they'd have labor trouble and not be able to finish the picture."

"Uh-huh," she said. "And why would he do that? The goon, I mean. Pay you a visit."

"Oh, didn't I say? He wanted to fight, and I uh . . . I hit him with a baseball bat. Several times, in fact. And he left in kind of a huff. I thought he might not be kindly disposed as a result."

She was silent for a moment, and then couldn't help herself and began to chuckle. " 'Kindly disposed,' " she said and began chuckling again. "A baseball bat. Whoo! Well all this's too complicated to make up, and just stupid enough to be true. Only . . ." She paused, and when she spoke she heard the hard edge back in her voice again. "You sure there ain't something between you and that lady?"

"Not a thing. Honest."

"Well, maybe I'll believe that." She heard the hard edge go out of her voice, and figured he probably did, too. "So, was that all you called for?"

"Well, no, actually. I was thinking you said once you were interested in learning to sail. Maybe you'd like to go out some evening. Like maybe tonight. It stays light until almost eight now, so we could go out after work, sail around for an hour or so, and then maybe have dinner."

"Uh-huh," she said. "And where would we do this? Out here in Malibu?"

"No. In the marina. Near my office. The boat I have—it's in a dinghy rack at Cal Yacht Club."

"Well . . ." she said. Inside her it was as if her feelings were bumping into one another, pushing and shoving and leaving her hot and irritated and breathless. If he had said another word, tried to persuade her, she would have told him to fuck off, leave her alone. But he seemed to sense that the best persuasion was silence. "Well, I don't know. It seems like every time we . . ." She stopped herself, and started again. "Well . . . all right. So I should meet you someplace, huh?"

"Good afternoon, sweetheart," Richie said.

She was standing by the refrigerator with a wine bottle in one hand and a glass in the other. Turned and stared at him, her eyes looking dark, as if the pupils were dilated.

"Scare you?" he said. "I'm sorry, I didn't mean to scare you. I just thought we should talk."

Mickey still hadn't said a word.

"I didn't like the way I was treated, last time I was here. Maybe you think I don't have feelings, like everybody else. I feel bad when somebody treats me like that. But hey, I'm not mad. I just have a couple questions to ask you, nice and polite, that I'd like answers for. Like who that guy was that was here, and where I can find him."

She put the wine bottle and the glass down. Shook her head like women did to get their hair settled like they wanted it. "I'm not going to tell you."

"Oh, I think you are." It was like a gin game, having the cards in your hand, knowing how the last three tricks were going to go down, but playing it out for the fun of it.

"No, I'm not. Get out of here." She started toward the near end of the kitchen, where there was a wall phone, or maybe she was headed back toward the living room where her purse was, Richie wasn't sure. But he was there in two steps, and grabbed her by one arm.

She tried to twist away, going first one way and then the other, but after a minute or two of wrestling Richie had her on the floor, flat on her back. Richie sitting on her, with his knees on her shoulders, her arms held down by his shins—the same way Richie's big brother used to sit on him whenever they had a fight.

She tried to move her arms. She tried to sit up. Her face got red and she breathed heavily from the exertion. "Get *off* me, you big oaf."

"Now, now," Richie said. "Don't bust a gut. You aren't going anywhere."

Then, his mood changing, "Hey, I got an idea. You wanna know what my idea is? If you're not going to talk to me about that guy that was here, there's something else we can do . . ."

Richie leaned over and caught hold of one of the handles on the gym bag he'd brought with him. Opening the bag and taking out a strip of T-shirt material, he wrapped it around Mickey's face and tied it into a gag. He had some difficulty, because she was twisting her head back and forth and jerking it up and down, but he did it thoroughly. Didn't want it to come loose, fall off.

With one of the pieces of rope from the bag he tied her arms together at the wrists, and then her legs at the ankles. It was awkward turning around far enough to reach her ankles while he was still sitting on her, but Richie was afraid that if he got off of her before he had her feet tied she might try to get up and run away.

When he had finished the last knot, Richie got to his feet, bent over, and picked Mickey up. "The bedroom's back this way, sweetheart, isn't it?" he said. "Let's just go look, shall we?"

She felt funny, going into his office. As if she had come for a job interview and noticed too late that she was underdressed. If she'd had her wits about her, she'd have told him to meet her outside, or at the place where the boat was.

Part of it was because she'd hardly ever been in an office, except for visits to the doctor, or the dentist, or if she went with Daddy to see one of the vice presidents, when Daddy had to sign something about the loan from the Production Credit Association. So offices were to her a place where, when you went there, you were one-down on whoever's office it was.

But he didn't make her wait. A woman came out, as soon as she gave her name to the receptionist, and led her through some doors and down a hallway and around a corner to a big office, much bigger than the vice president of the Production Credit Association in Lubbock.

He stood up right away, smiling, seeming really glad to see her, and came around the desk.

"Hi, you made it. Good. I was afraid the traffic would be bad this time of the afternoon."

"Oh, no." She shook her head. "It wasn't bad. Actually, I drove in a while ago. I've been kind of wandering around looking at the water and the boats. It must be wonderful having your office this close to the water."

He picked up his telephone, pushed a couple of buttons. "Celia, I'm going to sneak out a little early. I'll take the file on that Bookhalter motion and go straight downtown in the morning. See you around ten."

He was loading things into a briefcase. Files and loose papers. She wandered slowly around the room, looking at the books, and at the framed photographs and certificates hanging on the walls. She stopped in front of one of the photos. "This is you, isn't it? What's this on your face, makeup?"

He closed his briefcase and snapped the lock, then looked to see what she was looking at. "Sort of. It was camouflage, for running a night infiltration course. So your face didn't show up in the dark if they put a light on you."

"Who are all these other people with you?"

"Other guys I was in the Army with. All except for the one at the end. That's a guy named Nicolasiou. He was in the FBI at the time. Now he's an accountant."

"And why were you running a whatever-it-was course with the FBI and wearing camouflage paint?"

"It's a long story. Come on, let's go sailing."

He reached behind the door and pulled his suit jacket out of a cupboard, and they started down the hall back to the reception room.

"Wait," she said. "Isn't that your phone ringing?"

She could see him hesitating. "It's okay," she said. "I don't mind waiting."

He dropped the briefcase and his jacket into a chair on the way back into the office, and went around the desk to pick up the phone.

"Uh-huh. All right. What line? Hey, Nico. How are you?" Covering the mouthpiece of the phone, he smiled apologetically at Dossie. "It's an accountant who's working on an audit for me—in fact, on the one I told you about. The same guy who's in the picture there."

Even though he'd smiled at her, she could tell that his mood had changed. He was more contained somehow, harder. He listened for a long time, making notes on a pad. "Convictions?" he said. "Any convictions?" And then listened again.

"When?" He was looking at her. Looking appealing. Like he was asking her if something was okay. "Tonight? Nico, I'm taking someone to dinner. Can't we meet the guy another night? Uh-huh. Uh-huh."

She looked back at him and shrugged. If he'd called her and said they couldn't go to dinner, that something had come up, she'd never have believed it. She'd have been sure it was the woman, Mickey, or whatever her name was. But being there, seeing it happen, having seen the face in the picture, of the man who was on the phone— somehow made it all okay. Or maybe it was being in an office, being one-down, so that you had to go along with whatever the person whose office it was wanted. At that moment, she didn't care.

"Okay," he was saying. "Tell me where and I'll be there."

"This," Richie said softly, "is called a rolling hitch. It's a good knot to use to tie the cover on a load—like on a truck or something. It's good because you can slip it this way, but then it holds and it won't slip back."

He was using half-inch Dacron line. It was more comfortable—soft and didn't cut into the skin like twine or thin line would have done. He was using the line to tie Mickey's right hand to the headboard of her bed. Good stout iron frame, inch-and-a-half pipe, guaranteed to rip, wear, and tear, like they say. Mickey's left hand was already tied to the other side of the headboard. Her feet, tied together, lay in the middle of the bed. "What's that? You say something?" Richie turned from what he was doing and looked at Mickey.

Mickey hadn't said anything. She couldn't, because of the gag. Good strong fabric, but soft. That was important. Use things that were soft, didn't leave marks.

Mickey looked back at Richie, her eyes wide above the strip of fabric that bound her mouth. Then she closed her eyes and turned her head away.

"Here, sweetheart, let's move your feet over here."

Richie slid Mickey's feet across the bed, so that both of them were close to one corner. From a small pile on the floor—pieces of line and several more strips of T-shirt material—Richie selected a five-foot length of line, and tied it to one of the legs of the bed. He worked the free end of the line between Mickey's knees and slid it down to her ankles. Taking two turns around Mickey's right ankle, he tied the line off so that it held both of Mickey's legs close to the corner of the bed.

"You got anything to drink around here?" Richie glanced at Mickey, who still had her eyes shut, her head turned away. "Don't mind if I go look, do you?"

Richie walked unhurriedly into the kitchen, opened the refrigerator, and looked inside. Selected a beer and twisted off the cap. Took a swallow and set the bottle on the counter. Then got a glass and took the glass and the beer and went back to the bedroom.

"I found me a beer, sweetheart."

Mickey's eyes remained closed, her head turned to one side.

Again Richie worked a length of line between Mickey's knees, slid it down to her ankles, and then tied it to the other corner of the bed. "Now. I'm going to untie your ankles, but one foot is tied to this here leg of the bed, and the other one is tied to that leg, so don't get the idea you're going anywhere." He glanced at Mickey's face, but she still had her head turned away.

Richie untied the short line that held Mickey's ankles together. As soon as the line came off, Mickey yanked her left leg up and kicked at Richie, making a grunting noise at the same time. Since the leg was already tethered to the bed, the tether pulled the kick around, and it merely glanced off of Richie's shoulder. But Mickey yanked her leg back and kicked again, and then again and again, making a wordless grunting each time.

Richie pounced with both hands and seized the flailing leg, forcing it down onto the bed, and then over to the far corner. Swinging around, he sat on the leg, using his weight to hold it down while he shortened the tether and retied it. Then he stood up and looked at Mickey. She was spread-eagled on her back, tied hand and foot to the corners of the bed. Richie shifted his weight, put his thumbs in the front pockets of his jeans, and pushed them down a fraction, to ease the growing congestion in his crotch.

"Now, sweetheart, let's get you ready."

Slowly, gently, Richie began to unbutton Mickey's blouse. When all the buttons were undone, he pushed the fabric open, back over her shoulders, and then unsnapped the catch on her brassiere and laid the cups back. Mickey's breasts were covered with gooseflesh, the nipples crinkled and erect. Richie stopped and looked at them for a long minute, then undid the snap at the waist of Mickey's jeans, pulled down the zipper, and began to work the jeans down over Mickey's hips. It was a slow process, because Mickey had begun to writhe and wiggle, making a high, stifled whining noise through the gag.

The jeans wouldn't go down very far, because of the angle at which Mickey's legs were held by the ropes. But finally they were down halfway to her knees. Mickey had opened her eyes now, and

SKIM

they followed Richie as he stood up and began to undress. When he was naked, he walked slowly around the bedroom. Picked up a piece of T-shirt material from the pile on the floor, went back to the bed, knelt and leaned over, and wrapped the fabric around Mickey's head, tying it into a blindfold. Stood up and looked around.

"Now. What else do we need? Music, maybe? You want some music?"

Went to the stereo on the bedside table. Fingered the stack of tape cassettes. "What you got here, Linda Ronstadt? You like Linda Ronstadt?" He glanced at Mickey, who was turning her head from side to side, still making the whining noise. Richie inserted a cassette into the player, turned it on, and plugged in the headphones. Putting on the headphones he adjusted the volume so that it was loud, but not uncomfortable. That was important, not have it so loud it hurt. Then he slipped the headphones off and put them over Mickey's ears. "There, sweetheart, relax and enjoy the music."

Nico parked the Volkswagen around the corner. When he was with the Bureau, they'd usually park the Plymouth—or sometimes it'd be a Dodge—right in front, let the guy see it that they were going to lean on. Plain beige, or maybe gray. Blackwall tires. As soon as the guy saw the car, he'd think, Cop! It was part of the process, get them off balance, get them worrying, before you walked in and held the leather credential case up in front of their nose, let them look at the picture, the fancy green engraving on the card, watched their eyes as they found the words *Federal Bureau of Investigation*.

But with a Volkswagen—ten years old and rusty at that—Nico parked around the corner. Anybody saw that VW, they'd know damn well he wasn't official. They'd lock their heels, phone their attorney, cause more stink than Nico could stand right now.

Nico was wearing one of his Bureau suits. He'd kept a couple of them in the back of the closet, the way guys would keep their Class

A uniform, if they'd been in the Army, or their blues if they'd been a cop. And he thought of them as a uniform. They might as well have been. He could wear any of the ties with any of the suits, and not raise a word of complaint from the special agent in charge. He hadn't had to match his socks to his suits, because every pair he'd owned had been identical charcoal gray.

Now he wore what he liked. He saw Pike and other people looking at him sometimes, when he was wearing a checked shirt with a plaid suit. But that was their problem. If he liked the colors, he wore them, never mind if they went together.

So it felt strange, being back in the mud-colored Bureau suit with the drab tie. But that was the Look, and for this job he needed the Look.

He'd kept his credentials when the Bureau threw him out on his ass. The leather wallet, the laminated card that said he was Special Agent Nicolasiou. Nico watched the guy's eyes as he folded the wallet and slipped it back into his inside coat pocket. You could tell a lot from the eyes. The skin tightened, there were little lines there, and all at once they looked shifty. Or the skin went loose, and the eyes went round, and they looked scared. This guy was shifty. Definitely shifty. The other ones he'd talked to today had been bored, or scared or just busy, and everything had checked out. But looking at this guy's eyes, Nico decided maybe he'd get somewhere with this one.

The guy using a voice like he'd heard it on TV, saying to Nico: "You think you can just walk in here and start asking questions? I know my rights. I got a lawyer. You want to show me your warrant? Or why don't you get the fuck out of my office?"

Nico nodded pleasantly. Smiled just a little, to show he didn't take it personally. "Sure," he said. "Sure, I can do that. Better still, besides a warrant, in addition to a warrant, why don't I get a subpoena *ad testificandum*. Get a bunch of them. I got time for that. Your lawyer, I don't know what he charges you. Probably a hundred, hundred and twenty an hour, huh?"

Paused a moment to let the guy think about it. "Why don't you call your lawyer, tell him cancel what he's doing next week, come down the Federal Courthouse on Spring Street there, first thing Monday morning, meet you before you go in testify before the grand jury.

"Maybe," Nico said, "maybe you got somebody can come in answer the phone for you too. 'Cause all these people . . ."—sweeping his hand around the office, pointing at the women working at desks and filing cabinets—". . . they're going, they'll all be right there with you, waiting there, outside the grand-jury room. So they won't have time to tend to the phone. Maybe even make you the subject of the inquiry, instead of just a collateral source, that's going to confirm something for me."

The words came back to him, the gestures, the flat, dull tone of voice, the heavy, slow manner. Like throwing a baseball again after ten years. You never forgot how. They said they knew their rights, and you said, "Fine. I've got all week. And I'll keep *you* tied up all week, *and* your lawyer, *and* your employees, and waste your time with endless repetitive questions. Or . . ."—giving them a chance—". . . or we can do it the easy way. Just a couple quick answers, and I'm out of your life."

"Wait a minute." The guy was licking his lips, swallowing quickly too. "Wait a minute. Don't go off half-cocked. What'd you say? Just a minor source? You're not here to check up on anything I been doing?"

Nico had a hell of a time keeping the grin off of his face. But he did it. Kept his voice slow and dull as he said, "DCI. You did a fair amount of business with them back two-three months ago. You got copies of your invoices?"

The guy still nervous, but getting over it now, feeling a lot of relief. Saying: "DCI? DCI? Jesus Christ, why didn't you say so? Little punk outfit like that, you can have whatever I got on them *and* the horse they rode in on. What'd they do? What're you checking them out for? Porno, huh? I'll bet it's porno."

And Nico kept his voice heavy and dull, saying, "I'm sorry sir, I can't discuss the subject of an investigation. Now about those invoices . . ."

He was explaining what made a boat go, the action of wind on sails. There were all these words: *lift, drag, lateral resistance from the centerboard and rudder. Using crew weight to balance the boat against wind pressure on the sails. Tacking, jibing.*

She wasn't really listening to him. She was waiting to get in the boat and go sailing, and he seemed to see that.

"All right," he said. "Let's go give it a try. You get in the boat and I'll push it off."

For ten minutes he sailed around the basin near the yacht club, going through the explanation again: about watching the masthead fly to see the direction of the wind, tacking, reaching, running. Then he let her take the tiller. It was a little like riding a bicycle, because you had to balance the boat by leaning your weight back and forth. But you didn't have to peddle, because it went by itself. So maybe it was more like riding a horse, or going down a hill on a sled—a smooth, sliding rush.

The boat turned over for the first time within a minute after he gave her the tiller. There was a slight increase in the wind strength—not enough to pay any attention to if you'd been standing on solid ground. The boat had been tipped toward one side. As the wind increased, it tipped more, and then more. And all at once, it went completely over.

Both of them were wearing life jackets, and they popped to the surface immediately. She was laughing and sputtering. He showed her how to hold on to the edge of the boat, the gunwale, he called it, and lever it back upright, pushing with one foot on the centerboard. They sprawled back into the boat, dripping wet.

"Well, you said it was easy to turn over. But who'd have thought it was that easy? Whoo! I'm wet as a flea on a drowned mule. You want to drive it the rest of the way? Make sure I don't do that again?"

"Don't worry about it. It happens to everyone. Just let the mainsheet out, or head up and luff a little to keep it on the edge."

Whatever that meant.

She dumped it three more times in the next five minutes, but then went almost ten minutes before she did it again. It was a thing you had to feel, like how hard you could cut, roping a calf, before the horse got his feet tangled up and tripped, and left you with nothing to do but ride him into the ground. Only it was hard to get the feel. At one point, tipped over to a certain angle, you were fine. The wind held the boat over, and it felt as solid as a church. But a fraction more, and over it went.

He said she picked it up quickly. She didn't feel quick. She felt slow and clumsy, particularly when she didn't judge it right and turned it over. But he kept saying she was a very quick student.

The sun dropped gradually behind the buildings on the west side of the main channel, and the hot glare went out of the afternoon. In the cool, gray light she worked at dodging around the evening traffic—people out in powerboats, having a cocktail cruise, fishermen coming in from an afternoon on the water, sailboats coming and going. Most of the time she could feel herself smiling, turning her head quickly to keep an eye on the other boats, looking up at the masthead fly to gauge the wind direction. She'd get tense when another boat got closer than she liked, feel herself frowning, chewing on her lower lip. But then she'd tack away, or get back to a comfortable distance, and she could feel herself grinning again.

"We'd better turn around," he said finally.

"Do we have to?"

"We've been out a long time. We've come clear down the main channel. See the harbor master's dock across there? That's the last thing before the channnel out to the harbor entrance. And we still have to go all the way back."

"All right." She watched him while he wasn't looking. He looked around all the time. Sort of the way you looked at cattle when you were driving them, to see what they were doing, and what they were going to do, and what terrain was up ahead, and figure out what might happen. Not in a nervous way, but to stay ahead of things. He looked up at the sails, at the wake behind the boat, and at the bow wave, across the channel, around at the other boats. Ran one hand absently through his hair, which spilled through his fingers and was instantly disarranged by the wind again. There should be a word for how he looked. Not comfortable, that was too static, too inactive. Some word that meant relaxed, competent, and on top of things all at the same time.

"What do I do now?" she said.

"Nothing to it. Let the mainsheet run out, and turn away from the wind."

Dossie glanced around, waited for a fifty-foot powerboat to rumble past, and then turned the boat and pointed it back up the main channel.

"Okay," he said. "Now we're running almost dead downwind, right? Got the sail out on the starboard side. What would happen if you turned more to the right—far enough that the wind was coming from around the other side of the sail?"

She looked at the sail a moment. Looked at the masthead fly. "Then," she said slowly, "the wind would get behind the sail and blow it across from one side to the other."

"Right. That's called a jibe. It can be dangerous, if you don't see it coming, because the sail goes across just like that." He snapped his fingers. "From full out on one side, to full out on the other. If you don't get your head down, you could get hit by the boom, this spar here on the bottom of the sail . . ."—he rapped on the hard aluminum with his knuckles—". . . maybe knocked overboard. But if you do it on purpose, keep it under control, there's no problem. Give it a try."

She was afraid of it, at first. Like taking a horse over a jump, the theory sounded easy, but she had an idea there were a lot of things that could go wrong with the theory.

But after four of five jibes with no ill effect, she gained confidence, and continued back up the main channel, jibing back and forth through the other boats.

They were almost back to the Yacht Club when it happened. The boat was sliding smoothly along, with the boom out over the starboard side. Dossie was looking at a sixty-foot schooner that was motoring past, all white topsides and varnished teak. She turned her head to watch the schooner, and as she turned, her shoulders twisted and her hand moved the tiller slightly to port. The boat veered more to the right. She saw what was happening, tried to pull the tiller back, but too late. The wind had gotten behind the sail. In a fraction of a second, the sail had blown across to the other side. The boat rocked wildly for a moment, started to round up into the wind, and held, on the edge.

She felt it go. She knew it had gone too far and was going over, she had developed her feel for it that much. And sure enough, the boat turned over. This time, climbing on board, she noticed how cold it was, sitting there all wet with the wind blowing.

"You want to take it now?"

He shook his head. "Just before we get to the dock. I'll take it then. You're doing fine."

The remaining distance down the basin went by quickly. At the dock he took the tiller, rounded up into the wind, and came alongside. Dossie stepped off the boat, and he handed her the bow line.

"We can leave it tied up here. It'll be all right until we get dried off, and I'll come back and put it away. We can take the life jackets up and put them away on the way inside."

Richie sat down on the edge of the bed, his hip against Mickey's ribs. Mickey had stopped making the whining noise, but flinched away when Richie sat on the bed. Very slowly, very gently, using only his fingertips, Richie began to caress the outside of Mickey's thighs, then the edges of her breasts, spiraling around and around, inward toward the aureolae. At the first touch, Mickey jerked, strained against the ropes, and began making the whining noise again, but higher pitched, and more insistent.

Richie continued to caress Mickey's breasts, moving closer and closer to the nipples. Then, bending over, he took the right nipple in his mouth, sliding his tongue over the crinkled flesh, squeezing it between his lips. Mickey began to twist her head from side to side and continued to make the whining noise, interspersed with harsh grunts.

CHAPTER

10

PIKE WAS WAITING WHEN Dossie came out of the door of the women's locker room. She was wearing faded jeans and a polo shirt and some kind of running shoes with fancy graphics on the sides. Her hair was slicked down, and she looked twelve years old. Pike glanced at his watch. "We've got time for a drink before I have to meet these guys downtown. Is that okay?"

"Oh no. I mean, not here. I'm not dressed for . . ."

"C'mon," he said. "It's a yacht club, not a country club. They expect people to be dressed to go sailing."

"Well . . ."

She allowed herself to be persuaded.

They got a table at the side of the club bar, looking out over the docks. She talked about growing up on a ranch. Fifteen miles into town. Riding the school bus. Raising a lamb or a calf and entering it in the 4-H competition.

"I don't know why this happens to us," Pike said. "Look at the time. I've got to scoot to make it downtown."

"Do you want help? Putting the boat away?"

"No, that's okay. You're all cleaned up. It'll just take a minute."

"Well, all right. If you're sure."

He watched her walk across the lobby of the building and out the door, then turned and headed down the stairs to one of the doors on the lower level and outside. It was fading into twilight, and the wind was dying. Instead of a steady westerly, it was swinging to the south, and getting puffy, coming in fits and starts. People were strolling along the dock, some of them getting off of their boats, and some just out to enjoy the evening. Pike walked back down the dock to where the C-13 was tied up, untied the bow line, and stepped on board.

Nice kid, Dossie. Not exotic, or exciting, or sexy, in the way that Mickey was, but a nice kid. Wholesome. Not aggressive and insistent with her opinions, but had a gentle sense of humor. Could point out something ridiculous in a situation without making anyone the butt of it. She seemed to be in a better mood today. At least she hadn't been in a huff when she went home. Wonder if Mickey would be home yet. Maybe he'd have time to give her a call after the boat was put away.

The dinghy rack was farther down Basin F, past the club building. With the wind swinging to the south, the boat was being pushed against the dock. He'd have to sail out into the basin a little, then tack around and reach back to where the boats were kept. Pike slid under the boom and sat on the port side of the boat, to be able to balance the heel of the boat as it sailed away from the dock. Sitting on that side of the boat he could only see the feet of people walking along the dock.

Everybody wore deck shoes these days, whether they sailed or not. Made it hard to tell which of the disembodied legs parading past belonged to boaters and which were merely strollers—except for the obvious; women in high heels. Or there was even a pair of cowboy boots on somebody. Boots and jeans, coming along the dock, stopping for a moment, then coming on, right up to the edge of the dock, and as Pike ducked to look under the boom, there was Blondie standing on the dock, grinning down at him.

"Surprised to see me, asshole? Thought maybe I wouldn't know how to find you?"

"Well," Pike said. "I thought you might need help. But I figured we'd bump into one another again."

"Damn right! Why'nt you climb off that thing. You and me got some things to talk about."

Instead of answering, Pike kicked against the dock, shoving the boat away and out into the basin.

Blondie was quick. For someone who looked like he'd be completely musclebound, he was definitely quick. He stepped lightly off of the dock, onto the deck of the boat, and sat down. It was done as smoothly as if it had all been discussed ahead of time. Still grinning, he reached under the blue-jean jacket he was wearing, pulled out a large automatic pistol, and held it in his lap, pointing more or less at Pike.

Still the same jerk, Pike thought. The jacket, silk shirt, boots, the whole nine yards, even a cowboy hat. And, of course, the gun. Still the same jerk.

Pike had pulled in the mainsheet, and the boat gathered way and moved farther from the dock. Blondie twitched the muzzle of his pistol.

"Now turn this thing around and take it back to the dock there," he said. There was an edge of tension in his voice. "Then you and me can go somewhere quiet and have a little talk."

"All right," Pike said, thinking: would he risk it? Firing his pistol in the middle of the harbor? Most people thought they could just wave a gun around and the seas would part. They weren't ready for what would happen if they actually had to use one, and when it came to pulling the trigger, a lot of them balked. But Blondie looked just crazy enough that he might not care. Or he might be too stupid to have thought through what would happen if he did shoot Pike sitting on a boat fifty feet away from a dock in full view of a mob of people. So maybe it was better to go along with him. At least until something else happened.

"I'm going to turn the boat around now," Pike said. "The sail will flap some, so don't get excited."

"I'm not excited, asshole. Just take it slow and easy, no quick moves, right?"

Pike pushed the tiller and pulled the mainsheet out of the jam-cleat and began to let it out. The little boat curved away from the wind and off onto a run, paralleling the dock.

"I said . . ."—Blondie reached up with one hand and settled his hat more firmly on his head—". . . to go back to the dock. Over there, asshole, not just sail around out in the middle here."

"All right," Pike said, and he pushed the tiller over another ten degrees.

What happened next seemed to take no time at all. The leech of the sail fluttered slightly, and then a stronger puff of wind caught it, and the sail jibed, slamming across from one side of the boat to the other. As the sail reached the limit of its swing, the boat rounded up and immediately went over.

Pike went into the water. Ducked under and swam away from the boat, which he could see sticking down into the water. Ran out of air and came up maybe fifty feet away.

There was a floundering and thrashing on the other side of the boat, where Blondie was in the water. Pike swam around to keep the boat between himself and Blondie.

The boat had flipped closer to the south side of the basin than to the dock where they had started out. The thrashing and splashing continued, and Blondie swam across to the dock on the south side, grabbed onto the dock and hauled himself out. Pike noticed that Blondie had lost his hat, which was still floating next to the overturned boat. He also seemed to have lost his pistol. At least he didn't have it in his hand anymore.

Pike swam back to the boat, passing Blondie's floating hat on the way, flipped the boat upright, and climbed back on board. Pulled in the sheet, centered the tiller, and sailed back across the basin to the dock at the Yacht Club.

Came up into the wind next to the dock, stepped off onto the dock, tied up the bow line, and trotted up to the club to find a telephone. Across the basin, he could see Blondie, moving along one of the docks on the south side.

There was a pay phone in the locker room. Pike fished in his pocket for some change, looked up the number of the nearest sheriff's substation in the phone book, and dialed.

It took an hour for the sheriff to show up, take a report, and look for Blondie, who was, of course, long gone. And for Pike to take another shower, get dressed again, and put away the boat.

Nico said the place didn't have a name. Or at least not in English— just three Japanese characters on the front of the building, over the door. He didn't know the address either. He had said two or three doors down from the corner. Pike counted. Sure enough, the third storefront had three Japanese characters over the door.

Pike paused inside the door and looked around. Television set on a high shelf showing a baseball game. Colored light from two neon beer signs in the window reflecting from a smudged mirror on the backbar.

Nico wasn't one of the drinkers on the line of stools. Maybe in a booth at the side or in the back? Pike peered around the room, occasionally meeting the eye of one of the customers. Every one of them—except a couple who had a thousand-yard stare that re-garded unpleasant events in an imaginary distance—had a cynical wariness, a fishy-eyed look that said no one had ever told them the truth, or at least not all of it, and that includes you too, buddy. Most of the haircuts were unfashionably short, and there were more mustaches than in a random sample of the population.

Even from the doorway, through the haze of smoke, it was a cop bar. If a car had backfired in the street, thirty snub-nosed .38s and .357s would have appeared from ankle holsters, belt holsters, shoulder holsters, and other more imaginative places.

At least it was convenient. Parker Center was just across San Pedro Street, he'd seen it on the way in. Eight stories of blue-gray mosaic tile, built in that kind of tasteless blockiness that they called "modern architecture" in the fifties. You didn't even need to get your car out of the parking structure when you got off shift. Just walk out the back door, cross the street, and have a quick one before you started home. Or two. Or three.

Nico was almost at the back, sitting at a table and looking the way he always looked, which was like he was about to expire from tuberculosis. His face was pale and there were dark circles under his eyes. His hair looked like he had combed it sometime in the last week—maybe. Pike decided that Nico being liberated from the straitjacket of the Bureau's dress code was not necessarily a Good Thing. Nico was wearing a tie that featured both stripes and a paisley background, mostly in tones of green. His shirt had a fine red stripe, and his suit was a bluish-gray glen plaid, worn with scuffed brown-and-white saddle shoes. The overall impression was of someone who was color blind to start with and who had dressed in a hurry in the dark.

Sitting at the table with Nico was a guy whose face didn't go with his body. He was tall. At least six-four, and gaunt, and bony. But he had a round, red face that belonged on someone with a beer gut. And a pair of furious blue eyes.

Nico caught Pike's eye over the guy's head and nodded at a chair. Pike sat down, and the guy glanced at Pike and held out his hand. "Hi. I'm Jan Bokkie. You must be the one who wants to talk about my little friend Richie."

"If that's his name."

"What's your interest in the prick, if you don't mind my asking?"

"It's sort of personal. He took a dislike to me one afternoon and started swinging. Fortunately he only landed two or three punches. So I thought I should find out something about him—like where he lives, and what he's all about."

"You had a fight with Richard, and he only landed three punches? Somebody break it up?"

"Not exactly. I persuaded him it wasn't a good idea to keep on."

Bokkie raised one eyebrow. "And how did you do that? Shove a piece up his nose?"

"Not exactly," Pike said. "What does it take to get a drink in this place? There was a baseball bat lying around. I used that. He seemed to find it persuasive."

"Ha!" Bokkie said. "A baseball bat! You took on Richard with only a baseball bat? My friend, I don't call that smart, unless you busted his head wide open. He'll remember, and he'll be back. The waitress is over there, next to that table at the end."

"Yeah. He's already been back. That's why I was late. He showed up down at the marina with a pistol."

"And?"

Pike explained how he'd flipped the boat over and dumped Blondie in the harbor. Bokkie whooped and slapped the table.

"That's rich. That's really rich. Dump the son-of-a-bitch overboard. I like it. Only trouble, it's not a permanent fix, and he'll just be madder next time. You call the sheriff?"

"Yeah. But he was gone by the time they got there. I didn't know his name, but I gave them his license number. I had that from before. You think they'll pick him up?"

"Here!" Bokkie said. "Marlene! This man needs a drink. What are you drinking?" He had grabbed the waitress as she walked past the table. Pike asked for a beer.

"Nico, you ready for another?" Bokkie looked across the table. Nico grimaced and nodded. "Yeah, I guess so."

"Same thing?"

Nico nodded again.

"Don't know how you do it," Bokkie said, and then turned to the waitress. "A ginger ale for my friend here, and I'll take another margarita, only see if he can get a lot of salt on the rim of the glass this time, okay? Really a lot of salt."

"Well," Bokkie said. He stopped and watched the waitress walk away. "She lost some weight, you know? Not bad legs the way she is now. Well"—draining his drink, licking at the salt remaining on the rim of the glass—"if it was our jurisdiction—which is isn't, it's county—but if it was, we prob'ly wouldn't do anything."

"What do you mean, not do anything?"

"Just what I said. What's the charge? Brandishing a weapon? Simple assault? Do you know what the situation is down the L.A. County Jail? Do you? I can see you don't. Let me tell you about it. The voters won't approve a bond issue, you know, for a new jail, and they wouldn't want one built in their neighborhood if they did.

"So," Bokkie said, "so we got these old jails scattered around, most of them built back the fifties, when the population's half what it is now."

Bokkie patted his pockets, pulled out a crumpled pack of cigarettes, lit one, and stuck it in the corner of his mouth. As he talked, the cigarette jumped up and down. "But bless their hearts, the voters don't want us, be soft on crime. They want every mother's son spits on the sidewalk arrested and put away. So guess what? The jails're crowded. There's four prisoners'n a cell designed for two, most the time. So the ACLU filed this lawsuit, inna federal court, and some fair-minded judge made this order."

He shook his head and took a drag at his cigarette. "Order says, 'My goodness, this isn't right. We can't have a jail population more'n so big, and can't have anyone sleeping on the floor.' And all that happy shit. So what happens? You make an arrest. You spend two hours filling out stupid forms. You waste a day waiting around to testify and then being asked smart-aleck questions by some wise-ass lawyer. Say after all that the guy's convicted, the judge gives him thirty days. He gets to the jail, they kick him loose. Any sentence thirty days or less, they're just releasing them when they get to the jail. Ninety-day sentences they'll do thirty and be released.

"So," he said, "you got to ask yourself, why should anybody waste their time with brandishing a weapon? If the guy was there on the sidewalk when I got the call, I might poke him a couple of times with the stick, crack him alongside the head if nobody was looking, tell him to shape up. And of course I'd take a report from the citizen, make him feel like he's getting something, his tax money. But that's it." He took a drag on his cigarette and blew smoke at the ceiling.

"So are you telling me I should deal with him myself?"

"Not with Richie. I wouldn't recommend that. On the other hand . . ."—pausing to put the cigarette in an ashtray and take a sip of his drink—". . . you're doing pretty well so far. But I'd watch myself if I were you. Besides, the Department don't like vigilantes."

"Well that's very helpful," Pike said. "So what can you tell me about this guy? So far all I know is he likes to jump on women and supposedly works for some guy that runs a protection scam. Anything that will fill that out or tell me about him would be a help. And a good address, if you've got one."

The waitress arrived with their drinks. She handed Nico the beer and gave Pike the ginger ale, then saw the empty ginger ale glass sitting in front of Nico and corrected herself. There was a perceptible pause, and then Pike remembered what Nico had said: the detective talks, you buy the drinks. He dug out his wallet and dropped a bill on the waitress's tray and she went away to get change.

The detective touched his tongue to the salt on the rim of his glass. "Here's how," he said, taking a swallow of his drink. "Little Richard. Richie. Richard T. Morrissey. He's got a sheet as long as your arm. Nico probably showed you that. Only a couple convictions though. Comes from a little town up in the valley—Shafter. North of Bakersfield a few miles and little bit west. Nothing kind of a place. Truck farming mostly, cantaloupes and shit. Started getting in trouble when he was just a kid. Supposedly his old man was on some kind of disability, just lay around the house. Mother couldn't control the kid, and he went kind of wild."

"And he works for someone named DiAngelo, is that right?"

"That I can't say. He has a steady job, listed as a driver at Peerless Industrial Laundry. Least that's what they tell his parole officer when he calls to verify employment. That's where he's *employed*.

What he *does* is something else. Mostly he hangs around with a guy named Dominic Nakamura, slick Jap with a college degree.

"DiAngelo," Bokkie said. He tipped his head back and forth and made a face. "DiAngelo you hear about, but nobody ever seen him. I got half an idea he may be out of state somewhere. Or maybe DiAngelo's an alias for someone else, who can tell?"

The blue eyes grew even more furious. "I had cases on Richie couple times myself. Assault. Extortion. You can probably guess what happens. First, we got him in custody, he bails out. Then he has Jacob Wolfe representing him, smartest defense lawyer in town, usually just does dope cases, that's where the money is, or society murders.

"And," he said, and crushed his cigarette into the ashtray, holding it down long after it had ceased to struggle, "Wolfe usually doesn't even have to go to trial. The time the preliminary hearing rolls around, the witnesses have forgotten, maybe this isn't the guy, they aren't sure. So the bastard walks.

"That," he said, "that's when we got a good case going in, good witnesses. That don't say anything about the ones we never even busted him for, 'cause they'd never stick. Like, right now we got what may be a homicide at a motel, or maybe it's a strange kind of accident, guy died of internal injuries after a fall. We think Richie's collecting for Nakamura, protection on the motel, maybe had something to do with it. But the woman there, wife of the guy who died, she just looks at you and cries, won't say a word. So what can we do?"

"Hey," Nico said, breaking a long silence, "how about ex-con with a gun? How about that?"

"What," Bokkie said, "are you talking about?"

"Now. Today. This thing with Richie and Dave. Don't you state guys have some thing about ex-con with a gun?"

Bokkie shook another cigarette out of his pack. Got it going and placed it carefully on the ashtray. Looking into the middle distance, speaking in a rapid monotone, and apparently reading the words off of the beer sign behind the bar, he recited: "Section one-two-oh-two-one, California Penal Code. Any person convicted felony under laws the United States, the State a California, any other state, government, or country, or any offense involving violent use a firearm, or addicted the use any narcotic drug, who owns or has in possession, custody, or control any pistol, revolver, other firearm capable being concealed upon the person is guilty public offense, punishable imprisonment state prison, or county jail not exceeding one year, or fine not exceeding one thousand dollars, or both.

"Sure," he said, "sure, we got that, so what?"

"So can't the county use it on this Richie?"

"You got the piece?" Bokkie asked.

Pike shook his head. "It fell in the harbor and sank. At least I think it did."

"Anybody see the piece?"

"I did," Pike said. "And him, or course. Nobody else."

"Forget it," Bokkie said. He picked up his cigarette and crushed it against the side of the ashtray, rolling it from side to side, shredding the paper until the butt spilled into loose tobacco and ash. "Forget it. That's reasonable doubt right there. It was our case, we'd never even send a report over the D.A. for them file on."

"What about this guy Nakamura?" Pike said. "What's the deal with him?"

Bokkie leaned over and touched his tongue to the rim of his glass. "You could almost believe the guy's straight, you know?" he declared in a biting tone. "Broad-minded citizen, gives an ex-con a chance to rehabilitate himself."

He believes, Pike thought suddenly. He sits there and sips his drink, acts relaxed, talks about rehabilitation. But he believes. He can quote the statutes word for word, like a monk with his breviary. He sees himself as part of a crusade. Or not a crusade, an Inquisition. From the tone of his voice he might just as well be a member of a tribunal of the Inquisition, saying: This one is apostate, excommunicate this one. Burn that one at the stake.

"Nakamura don't—he doesn't have any convictions," Bokkie said. "Not even an arrest. Couple parking citations, maybe. College degree, runs an industrial laundry, Peerless, where Richie works. Dull, clean kind of business. No pun intended. Only DEA had this snitch, he was a punk worked for this group of importers, bringing in ninety-five pure from down Belize or wherever."

He paused and nodded to himself. "The snitch, he named Nakamura as a big customer of the importers. Buys coke, five- and ten-kilo lots. Steps on it, of course. They all step on it, all the way down the line. But this Nakamura applies scientific marketing techniques, the snitch said. Never sells less than fifty-pure. Customers can depend on it. And he has a brand name for his stuff. *Sendero Luminoso* or some such shit. Well, it might not be true, okay?"

Turning to Pike and then to Nico. Tipping his head to one side and raising his shoulders and his eyebrows to indicate doubt. But Pike knew he didn't have any doubt. He believed.

"I mean, there was no hard evidence, and you know snitches. They never tell you the truth, only what they think you want to hear. And they're not above using you to put the hammer on someone that they have a beef with, for whatever cockamamie reason. That could have been what this snitch was trying to do, his story about Nakamura. We never had a chance to get the details, really check it out, because the snitch turned up in a vacant lot in Burbank one morning with a plastic bag over his head, smothered. So you ask me about Nakamura, and I say, who knows?"

And after this long speech he lowered his eyes devoutly to his drink, and would not be drawn again, other than to provide addresses and similar statistical data.

CHAPTER

11

EVERYBODY STEALS.

Dominic was trying to explain that to Richie. He wasn't sure it was getting across, as a philosophical concept. Like, Richie really believed everybody literally *stole*. Looked around, checked to see if anyone was watching, and *took* things.

That wasn't what Dominic meant at all.

What he meant was, everybody is on the take. Everybody does something, when they can get away with it. Naturally most of the time it wasn't out-and-out theft. Prosecuting attorneys let hookers off, and then the hookers took care of them after. Ministers performed weddings, got paid for it, never put it on their income tax. Treated it as a gift from the grateful couple. Gifts aren't taxable, right? A former vice president of the United States took bribes in the White House, if you cared to remember Spiro Agnew.

Everybody steals.

Take real estate, for example. You might think, how could anyone steal a piece of land? You can't pick it up and make it disappear.

But the way it worked, you had a piece of property that was for sale. A buyer came along. You negotiated a price. Then you said to the buyer, look, we'll write this up as if you were paying a hundred thousand *more* than you're really paying.

The buyer said, you're crazy, we got a deal. I'm not paying a dime more than the price we said.

You told him relax, we just *say* you're paying more. We write the escrow instructions to say you're paying the actual price through escrow, and a hundred thousand more, outside of escrow.

The slow ones, that didn't catch on, they'd say, why should I do that? And then you'd explain. Because when you get around to selling the property, in a few years, you expect to make a profit, right? And you'll have to pay income tax on the profit. But if you have documentary proof that you paid more for the property, then your profit is smaller, see? So you pay less tax.

Everybody came out ahead.

Except, of course, Uncle Revenue. But hey, who's going to cry if the IRS takes it in the shorts?

Usually they didn't even ask what was in it for you. They were so tickled about having a way to stick it to the taxman.

That was what Dominic meant, everybody steals. Look far enough, or deep enough, and it was always there.

Sometimes when you were setting up a deal, the buyer would ask, if he was one of the smarter ones, what about your side of the deal, you going to report the inflated price on your income tax return, pay tax on a profit you didn't make? Dominic told them, you bet. They'd scratch their heads, say, what do you get out of that? Dominic would just smile.

What Dominic got out of selling property at an inflated price was a legitimate explanation for the large cash deposits which he made in the bank. An explanation that could be reported by the bank, all normal and proper, with nobody even raising a question about where the money came from. It came from the sale proceeds on this duplex, or the sale proceeds on that commercial building. You want to see the escrow instructions? Look at the closing statement? See, here it is, a hundred thousand cash, outside of escrow.

And the great thing about it was, you made money on the deals on top of it. If you bought right, the property went up in value, generated a nice profit be*sides* hiding the cash income.

"So, Dominic," Richie said, "I was wondering," and stopped.

They were lifting in the weight room Dominic had set up at the laundry, behind his office. They were doing curls. Richie went on doing curls while Dominic waited.

"Well," Richie said. The barbell moved up and down smoothly, regularly, but his voice was getting away from him, the words spilling out. "I was wondering, if I could have like, you know, a promotion. Maybe be sort of a manager for you. Keep track of the other guys, make the assignments. Mill in the cut before we do the deliveries, turn the money over to you."

Dominic, taking it slow, said: "Sounds like you've been thinking about this for a while."

"Yeah," Richie said. "Yeah, I have."

Still taking it slow, Dominic said, "Sounds like this is important to you."

"Yeah," Richie said. "Yeah, it is."

"Is there a particular reason?"

"Yeah. See, like I been thinking about getting married." Stopping and putting the barbell on the rest.

Dominic picked up the barbell and began to do his reps. "Married," he said. "Married?"

"Yeah, married. You know. Like, well, married. And if I was working inside, more regular hours, not any more money. The money's fine. But if I was inside, well . . ." Richie ran out of words.

"This seems kind of sudden. Do I know the lady?"

"I don't think so. It's somebody I known a long time. We've talked about it, and she, well . . ." He ran out of words again.

"She doesn't like you being a frightener, doing deliveries?" Dominic suggested.

"No, no, she never said that. In fact, she never said anything. It's just like this feeling I have. She's got a good job. Responsible. Makes good money. But it isn't the money, I mean, I make more now than she does. It's, well, she does like free-lance consulting stuff. And I just kind of feel like . . ." Once again, he ran out of words.

"Like you'd like to have an executive-type job too, so she wouldn't be one up on you," Dominic suggested.

"Yeah," Richie said. "Yeah, that's it. I knew if I could explain it, you'd understand."

"Well let's think about it," Dominic said. "And talk some more, okay?"

"Sure, Dom," Richie said. "Sure, that'd be great."

He came out of left field at you with something like that. You were thinking about rates of return, or about a give-back on a commission, and he came at you like that. Dominic had spent the morning on the phone with a series of real-estate brokers. The central coast was supposed to be the coming hot market. The demographics were right, people moving north out of L.A., looking for a place away from the crowds. Looking for an ocean view. Santa Barbara had been good for a while, but it was about topped out. At least Dominic thought so, although one of the brokers swore he had some nice single-family stuff there that had been going up at twenty percent a year. But Dominic didn't think there was much upside potential in a single-family residence that already cost three-fifty.

Better to look farther north. Oceano, or Pismo Beach. Maybe Arroyo Grande. Units up there were still below two hundred, if you looked around. At least that's what two of the brokers were telling him. He'd agreed to drive up one day the next week, look at a few places.

Of course he wasn't looking for himself. He only ran a laundry business, didn't own a single piece of property, except for his house. He was looking on behalf of Soryu Kogyo Trading Co., Ltd., a Japanese corporation, qualified to do business in California.

Which happened, by the way, to be the owner of the property where Dominic's laundry was located, so he wrote a rent check every month to Soryu Kogyo, mailed it to the downtown office of the Bank of Tokyo for deposit.

It had been fun setting up Soryu Kogyo. Taking the trip to Japan, hiring a Japanese lawyer, arranging for dummy directors and all the formalities. Too bad about the way the dollar had been going against the yen lately. That meant there was some loss on the conversion. But Soryu Kogyo didn't move all of its money to Japan, and what it did move it didn't hold there for long. Just enough money went to Japan to confuse things, make it difficult to track what profit from which sale went where, and exactly where the money came from for the next purchase.

Then the money turned right around and came back to California for reinvestment in the real property market. Like these residential units up north. Or a medical office in Saugus, or some beachfront units in Malibu, or odds and ends of commercial property scattered over the L.A. basin.

Five years out of biz school, and his classmates couldn't understand what Dominic saw in one small commercial laundry. When he'd go to a reunion, they'd all be one-upping each other with their jobs, they'd look at him funny. After all, they'd spent two years reading case studies, talking about marketing plans, finance, getting geared up to run major industrial corporations. Sallied bravely forth and signed on with Xerox, or Crown Zellerbach, or Bordens. A hundred grand a year and stock options, and live in Armonk, New York.

Four and a half million dollars worth of property, at current prices. That was what Soryu Kogyo Trading Co., Ltd., held. With the rent the properties generated, and the income from the laundry, and one thing and another, there was plenty of dough coming in from legitimate sources. And, God knew, it took enough of Dominic's time, keeping track of tenants, arranging for repairs. So Dominic thought every now and again that he might close down the nose candy business. Maybe hand it off to someone, take a piece of the action for a while, or just get out altogether. Why not? But not to Richie. Dear Lord in heaven, not Richie. Somebody who didn't need a road map.

At the beginning it had seemed like such easy money. He had the source, the connection with the importer who brought in the ninety-five percent pure stuff. He had the buyers. Richie and Titch, or one of the others made the deliveries. It should have practically run itself. But there were always problems. Late deliveries from the importer. The feds found part of a shipment. Jurisdictional disputes between Dominic's connection and other importers. Buyers who didn't have the money ready when they called for a delivery.

"By the way," Dominic said, "did you do the reminder or not? Those movie people?"

"Yeah," Richie said, and made a face, so right away Dominic knew something was wrong. "Yeah. I did the reminder. That part is fine. Only . . ."

"Only what?"

"Only the guy . . ."

"What guy?"

"I'm *tell*ing you, the guy that was there."

"The guy that was where when?"

"The first time. When I went to do the reminder the first time."

"Oh," Dominic said. "Oh, yeah. I remember. The one that had a baseball bat or something. Yeah. What about him?"

"I got his address from the chick, of where his office is. I got his house too, but I go to the office first. I follow him when he leaves. I wait until he's alone on this boat."

"Wait. What boat? What is this about a boat?" Then, in a moment of clairvoyance, realizing that Richie was close to the edge, maybe about to lose it, start banging his head against the wall, saying: "That's okay. Just go on and tell it in your own words. I'll wait and see if I still have any questions when you finish."

Thinking: Jesus! now what? Using Richie was like using any other tool. Some tools were better for some jobs. You didn't use a sledgehammer to crack a nut. And tools wore out. Lost their edge. Needed to be replaced. Or they even slipped and cut the hell out of whoever was using them. Maybe Richie was coming to the end of his usefulness. Maybe the thing to do was ease him out. Especially if he'd fucked this thing up, like it sounded he had.

So Richie told about the boat, how it turned over all by itself, ruined a nearly new pair of Tony Lama boots, not to mention a genuine Stetson.

"Richard," Dominic said.

Richie knew something was coming then. It was like his mother. Whenever his mother was going to say something to him that he wasn't going to like, she always called him Richard. Dominic did the same.

"Richard," Dominic said. "I want you to do two things: first, clean up your apartment, guns, dope, anything you wouldn't want the cops to find, they came and looked, get rid of it. Second, get out of town for a week. Take a few days off. Maybe go up Vegas, get a little sun, gamble. Take your fiancée, you want to. Here—" reaching into his pocket, peeling bills off of a roll, handing them to Richie.

"But, Dom." Richie stood with the bills in his hand, looking puzzled. "Why should I do this stuff?"

"Richard?" Dominic said. "Trust me, okay?"

"Look," he said, "you don't like Vegas, go somewhere else. Consider it a paid vacation. But what I particularly want is, is that you should stay completely away from this turd that's the lawyer for the movie people. You got that?"

"But, Dom," Richie said, "I can handle it. This guy is no problem. It's taken a while, I admit that. There been a couple things, well, you could call foul-ups, you want to. I admit that, too. But hey, this is some guy sits behind a desk, you know? I mean, gimme a break, okay?"

"Richard," Dominic said, "I'm not upset at you. And I'll think about your promotion, like you said. It's just, look: this guy has seen you a couple times, right? Knows what you look like. May be thinking about calling the cops, may already have called 'em.

"We don't," Dominic said. "We don't want you walking in on him, busting his head open, the cops are hiding inna closet, do we? You're valuable to the firm. If we're thinking about promoting you, well, we don't want you involved in something could get messy. So I'll take care of this, right? Arrange a little accident for him.

"And Richard,"—pausing and looking at Richie, the slanted Oriental eyes as black and as hard as marble—"just so's we understand one another, you will stay *away* from this turd, you got that?"

"Yeah, Dom. Yeah, I got that. Shit, no need to get bent outta shape about it."

There were really not that many ways to cook a set of books—take money and try to make it look like the money was still there, or like it had been spent on some legitimate expense. Once you learned the patterns, saw enough of them, it was like listening to music from another room. First you just heard an occasional thump from the bass. Then you could make out the tempo. Then you got a few bars of the melody, and from there you had it wired. You could whistle the rest of it, you knew when the guitar would start, and when to listen for the lead vocal again.

Like if it was a lapping scheme, you'd see the deposits on the bank statement on different dates from when they were in the checkbook. Not just one or two days, like a deposit could have been delayed in the mail, but weeks late, sometimes. That was because someone had taken some of the cash out of a deposit. Then they couldn't make the deposit, because it was short. So they held that one up, until they could take some cash out of the *next* deposit, to cover what they'd taken out of the first one. So when they finally made the first deposit it was late. But then the *second* deposit was short too. (And usually they took a little *more* cash out of that one, while they were at it.) So they had to hold the second deposit, until the *next* one came in, so they could take some cash from it to cover the second deposit. And so on. Once they got started, they just got further and further behind.

That was the pattern for lapping. There were other patterns. Each scam had a pattern: kickbacks, fictitious invoices, nonexistent payees, they all left traces in the books, if you knew what to look for.

Nico began to look through the bank statements. Not looking for any one thing in particular, just looking, feeling, waiting for something to stand out. He compared deposit dates shown on the statements with deposit dates shown in the checkbook. Compared cancelled checks with invoices, looked at the endorsements on the back of checks.

And right there in the second bank statement, like hearing a couple of beats from the bass, was the faint beginning of a pattern. So Nico knew what to look for in the next bank statement, and the next.

It wasn't a lapping scheme. It was even more simpleminded. Not simpleminded, dumb. All-time fucking stupid.

Checks made out to a company name, but cashed instead of being deposited. Not a lot, but one or two a month. And checks where there wasn't an invoice. Not a lot of those either, but one or two a month. Whoever did it was *dim*. Probably thought no one would notice because it wasn't done very often. Didn't know accounting from first base. Probably stupid enough to have some nice kickbacks going too, at the same time, and thought no one would ever know.

Nico sighed and scratched his head. Felt absently in his shirt pocket for his cigarettes. Then patted his other pockets before he remembered he'd stopped again. Somehow having a cigarette in his mouth always made him want a drink. And one drink led to another, and then another. What was that expression the Japanese had, about after the third one the booze was drinking the man, instead of the man drinking the booze? For Nico, it wasn't the third one, it was the first one that did it.

Nico sighed again and reached for a yellow legal pad. He began listing the names of the suppliers off of the checks. It took an hour and a half to finish, and the list filled five pages. At the top Nico listed separately the suppliers' names from the checks where there hadn't been a matching invoice. Then Nico took out the phone book and began looking up the suppliers, making sure that when a check had been written to Studio Lighting Service there really *was* a Studio Lighting Service listed in the book. He found one right away that wasn't in the book—Serv-U Catering. Then another an hour later—Locations Plus. And a couple of more after another half hour. That was part of the fascination of auditing. You checked page after page of figures, and everything was in place, everything was nailed down. But the next entry could suddenly be as sour as the soloist hitting a note half an octave off pitch. And the excitement was waiting for the next sour note to come along.

Nico found himself humming under his breath.

Bokkie had given Pike the same address for Richie as Nico had supplied from the CII computer. One that he'd moved out of six months before, according to the landlady. But the laundry had to know where he lived, if they reported to his parole officer. If they'd give that information out.

The address of the laundry was in El Segundo, just south of the airport. Pike took Lincoln to Sepulveda, to avoid driving all the way around the runways.

What had that business been last night? Pike had gotten home from talking to Nico and his cop friend and there was a message from Mickey on his answering machine: "David, this is Mickey. I need to talk to you. Call me right away when you get in. Doesn't matter how late it is, call me."

So he'd dutifully called her, and nobody was home. Left a message on her machine. Tried again this morning, still nobody home. And Maurice hadn't heard from her, had no idea what might be on her mind. So whatever she'd wanted, the ball was in her court. Symptom of the modern era—people talked to the machines, but never made contact with other people.

As he started down into the tunnel under the runways, the

airport was like a seal rookery on one of the Channel Islands. The same muddled coming and going, the same noise and confusion. Airplanes lay asleep in untidy rows, or hauled themselves slowly, painfully, around the taxiways, or fell howling out of the sky.

Sepulveda climbed out of the tunnel, and Pike got in the right lane and began looking for the cross street.

Ugly stucco buildings crowding up to the sidewalks. Fork lifts scurrying back and forth around double-parked delivery trucks. And finally, at the end of the block, a rolling gate in a chain-link fence between two buildings painted the same bilious shade of green.

Pike parked down the block and walked back. A neatly lettered sign said OFFICE, and a curving arrow pointed around the corner through the gate.

Inside the yard two laundry trucks nuzzled up to a loading dock. In one corner of the yard was a Mercedes sedan, with darkened windows and all the chrome sprayed black. Hurrying women shouted to each other in Spanish and pushed wheeled canvas carts piled with sheets and towels and tablecloths.

A flight of concrete steps led up to the dock. Pike walked up the steps and through a door.

The office was a bullpen with six desks, their periods ranging from early Army surplus to later garage sale. A woman at the desk just inside the door looked up as Pike came in.

"I was looking for an address on one of your employees," he said.

"And you are?"

Pike fished a business card out of his coat and put the card on the desk. The woman prodded it suspiciously with the eraser end of a pencil, peered at it for a moment, and then prodded it again. "Uh-huh," she said. "So?"

"So I'd like to get an address for one of your employees."

"Who?"

"A Mr. Morrissey. Richard Morrissey."

"What d'ya need it for?"

"Business. It has to do with a legal matter for one of my clients."

"I'm sorry," the woman said, "I can't give out that information. Wait just a sec." She raised her voice. "Tina! Buzz Dom and tell him someone is here looking for the home address on an employee and will he talk to the guy. An attorney. David Pike."

Another woman at the far side of the room picked up her phone and spoke into it. As she spoke, she looked at Pike. Finally she put her phone down. "You can go on back," she called. "That door over there."

There was an electric lock on the door, and it buzzed as Pike approached. As he went through, he noticed that the door had been sheathed in heavy-gauge metal and had a peephole in it. Behind the door was a short hallway with another door at the far end. Above the far door was a surveillance camera. Again the door lock buzzed as Pike approached, and again the door had been sheathed in metal and had a peephole. There was also a hole in the center of the door—a rectangular hole a couple of inches on a side, with beveled edges, closed by a metal shutter.

The transition was like one of those staged so artfully in the earlier James Bond films. Bachelor pad inside an oil storage tank. Book-lined office on a submarine. The room had no windows, but it was well lighted and tastefully decorated—would have been right at home on the forty-fifth floor of one of the office towers in Century City. Black leather furniture. Video wall with a big-screen TV and half a dozen smaller monitors. Concealed spots glinting on polished glassware on the bar in one corner. Another spot illuminated a tasteful oil of a stream running over boulders. The room was washed in the crisp sound of George Winston playing piano. And coming around the desk was a muscular man with Oriental features and an engaging smile.

"Nakamura," he was saying. "Dominic Nakamura. I'm the general manager. I'm sorry, I didn't get yours when they buzzed me. Wait, let me turn that down." He pointed a remote control unit vaguely at the wall and pushed a button. The volume of the music diminished.

Pike gave his name. The man held out his hand. Pike shook it. Firm handshake. Pleasant smile.

"You're looking for an address on an employee, that right?"

"Yes. On a Richard Morrissey."

"I see."

Nakamura indicated a leather sofa at one side of the room, then led the way and sat down. Good-looking summer suit, pleats in the trousers and a tie that looked like it had been designed in about 1935. Pike wasn't really into clothes, but he knew that pleats and Depression Era ties were the newest thing this year. And he thought, he wasn't sure, but he thought that if a suit had what looked like real buttonholes for the cuff buttons, it was usually handmade.

"Is Richard in some kind of legal trouble?"

"Oh, no. Not at all. He, well, he may be a witness to something. I'd just like to contact him, talk to him about it."

"I see," Nakamura said again.

As he spoke, a woman's voice came through an intercom speaker. "Dom, Tina. There's a guy out here needs a check. Can you come out and sign one?"

Nakamura looked at Pike and shrugged an apology. "No rest for the wicked, I'm afraid. Let me tell you about our policy on employee information. You aren't from Immigration, are you? Or the State? EDD or anything like that?"

Pike shook his head.

"A private attorney, right?" Nakamura said. "Not any kind of government agency?"

Pike shook his head again.

"Well then. We don't give out information without the employee's permission. Richard is on a route right now. If you'd like to wait a few minutes, the dispatcher will try to raise him on the radio, ask him if it's okay to give out his address. If they can't raise him, you can leave me one of your cards, we'll give it to him when he comes in, ask him to contact you."

"Fine. That'll be fine. Maybe you could help me with something else while I'm waiting."

"Be glad to. What is it?"

"I have a client, a motion-picture production company. DCI is the name of it. Apparently it's been making some payments to you, or to your employee, Mr. Morrissey. And there seems to be some kind of misunderstanding, and I'd like to clear it up."

Nakamura's face had lost all animation, all expression. The engaging smile had turned into an Oriental mask. "I'm afraid," he said carefully, "that I don't know what you're talking about."

"I'm not sure what to call it. Protection? Insurance? Some kind of payment to avoid having labor trouble on the set while they're filming."

Nakamura shook his head. "I don't know what you're talking about. I know that Richard has a record. Knew that when I hired him. But all he does here is drive. Period."

"You think I'm wearing a wire," Pike said.

A small smile returned to Nakamura's face. "Why would you do that?" he said.

"To trap you into admitting something that could be used against you. But I'm not. Wearing a wire *or* trying to get you to admit anything. I just want to get this straightened out before it gets out of hand. Any more than it already has."

"Mr. Pike, I don't know if you're wearing a wire or if you're not wearing a wire. Frankly, I don't care. I manage a legitimate business here. You want to talk about getting a volume rate on napkins and tablecloths, I can talk to you. You want to talk about some funny thing you think one of the employees is doing, well, they do what they want on their own time. I have no control over that. Or responsibility for it either."

"Uh-huh," Pike said. "All of the laundries in town have offices like this? Where getting into them is like getting into the money room of a casino in Vegas? You have a lot of aggressive salespeople come in here, try to sell you soap, get out of hand? You need a gunport in your door to keep a salesman from getting his foot into it? That why you have this setup?"

Nakamura was still smiling his small smile. "I don't think I need to discuss my office with you, Mr. Pike," he said. "You're welcome to wait out front to see if we can contact Richard. If you'll excuse me, I have some work to do." He stood and gestured toward the door.

Nakamura remained standing until he heard the lock click behind Pike. Then he picked up the phone and dialed a number. Ordinarily he would have had Richie make the call, but he'd sent Richie away. Have to get one of the other guys in to do Richie's little jobs for the next few days. Maintain the layers of insulation between Dominic and the unpleasant stuff that occasionally had to be arranged. Freddie maybe, or Titch.

The phone rang several times.

"Yeah," said a voice.

"I need to talk to Solly's friend," Dominic said.

"All right," the voice said. "When?"

"Today?"

"Sure," the voice said. "You know where to be?"

"Yeah."

"What time you want to do this?"

Dominic looked at his watch. "In an hour?" he said.

"He'll be there," the voice said, and the line went dead.

CHAPTER

12

"DAVID?" IT WAS MAURICE calling. Five minutes to five, and he'd have some question that would take twenty minutes to answer. People did that, called just before quitting time, asked a question, thought the clock stopped at five and they'd get their answer for free. Some of them even had the balls to call up and complain, when they found the call on their bill the next month.

"You haven't forgotten about tonight, have you? 'Cause that'll give me a chance to give you back these checks and stuff. I'm through with them, and you can give them back to Mickey."

That was the other thing they did, asked you to lunch, or to a cocktail party, and then, purely by accident, oh, by the way, just happened to think of it, brought up some legal problem they had. Pike hadn't figured out a good way to deal with that one yet. Sometimes he billed for the time, and sometimes he didn't, and whether he did or whether he didn't he felt like he was being imposed upon.

He *had* forgotten about the damn thing, in fact. Probably be a bunch of Maurice's eighty-year-old friends from the silent film days, standing around comparing tans and complaining about the service at Caneel Bay, or the prices in Grenada. Oh well.

"Right," Pike said. "Sure, Maurie. I'll be there. I was planning, I've got another commitment, I was planning to just stop by for a half hour or so, but I'll be there.

"By the way," he said, "I assume since you say we're giving the

SKIM

cancelled checks and stuff back that you didn't find anything
wrong?"

"It's like I thought. They're fine. No problem."

"Great. See you in a while."

It was worse than he'd expected. There were so many Jags, Mercs,
and Rollers that you couldn't park closer than two blocks away. But
that was okay, because of course there was a valet service to take
care of the car for you. Inside were a couple of dozen traditional
Beverly Hills ladies with their out-of-style hairdos, lacquered in
place like they'd come out of a plastic molding machine, wearing
pearls and flowered silk. Husbands out of Brooks Brothers. And a
leavening of beautiful people; thin, good-looking people who
didn't look anyone in the eye as they talked, but flicked restless
glances around the room, looking for a director or someone who
could do them some good. They were screen personalities.

The pool was lit up and the doors out onto the patio were open,
and there was a four-piece combo hidden somewhere in the plant-
ings, wrestling with Cole Porter. Both sides were losing. A barman
with a white coat was behind the bar, where Maurice had stood two
days ago (was it only two days?) when Mickey had brought him
over to talk to Maurice.

Pike got a scotch from the barman, took a canapé from a passing
waitress, and looked around for Maurice. He wasn't in the bar, and
he wasn't on the deck by the pool, and he wasn't in the living room.
Maybe in the room beyond.

The living-room crowd was mostly younger, and someone was,
or had been, smoking a joint, because there was a sweet tang in the
air as Pike edged through the throng.

A blonde with a spectacular chest and a petulant expression was
standing in a group with another woman and three men. "Paul,"
she said as Pike passed, "can we go home now? I'm bored."

"Later, sugar," one of the men said. "So you don't like it?"

"Like it?" a woman with her back to Pike said. "Like it? A good case of the trots would be better theater, and more fun besides. It's not *noir*. It's not anything like *noir*. If you call that *noir*, you'd call *The Tempest* a travelogue. He thinks if you shoot light slanting through blinds and smoke off a cigarette it's *film noir*. He doesn't know a thing about developing conflict within a character." She shook her head, and her long hair rippled. It was Mickey McDonald.

Pike edged around the group and looked in the next room. Maurice wasn't there either. On his way back, the group with Mickey in it had broken up. The bored blonde was towing one of the men off toward the door. Mickey caught Pike's eye, said something to her companions, and came across the room toward him.

"Hi," she said. "Were you looking for me?" She was wearing a strapless sheath dress of a dull black material. Velvet maybe? And a single strand of pearls. She had lipstick and eye shadow on, and she was stunning. She was unquestionably and incomparably the best-looking woman in the room.

"No." Pike carefully avoided looking down the front of her dress. It wasn't easy, but he did it. "Actually I was looking for the host. You seen Maurice around?"

"I think he's out by the pool."

"I looked there."

"Oh. Well, how about the tennis court. Did you look by the tennis court?"

"I don't know where that is."

"Down past the end of the pool, through the hedge there. You want me to show you?"

"That's okay, I can find it," Pike said. "I called you back the other day. After you left a message on my machine. You weren't home."

She tossed her head and sipped her drink. "I know. That's okay. It wasn't important. C'mon, I'll show you where I think Maurice is." She took his hand and started back through the house.

"Don't look like such a sourpuss," she said over her shoulder.

"Is it that obvious? I thought I hid it better than that."

"You don't," she said. "What's bothering you?"

"Ah, shit, I don't know. Cocktail parties where you don't know a soul except the host. Creeps who lift weights and wear cowboy hats. Smooth bastards who look you in the eye and lie to you. Decline of the Amazonian rain forest. Crime in the streets. Take your pick. Speaking of which, have you been bothered by that guy again?"

They were through the bar now, and out onto the deck, she still had hold of his hand, and was taking him around the groups of people, talking, drinking, laughing. The music was louder.

"Oh," she said. "You mean the one who was at my apartment? No, no problem. I called Nakamura, and I'm pretty sure Maurice did, too, he had his Jewish mother look when we were talking about it. Here. We go through here."

She indicated a concrete path through a narrow opening in a hedge. Through the gap Pike could see a lighted tennis court and a small one-story building, white stucco with a red tile roof. "Anyway," she said, "that seems to have fixed it. Haven't seen or heard of him since. Have you?"

"Sure did."

"Oh?" It was polite, but not curious.

"Yeah. He showed up on the dock yesterday when I got back from sailing. Jumped onto the boat with a pistol and wanted to go somewhere quiet and talk." Pike stopped on the path. "Mickey, I don't see a soul down there. I think we'd better look somewhere else for Maurice."

"Maurice has a kind of office thing in the cabaña by the court. Sometimes he goes in there and talks to people if they have to talk business during a party."

"And he won't mind if we walk in on him?"

"No, of course not. So what happened then?"

"I dumped the boat over, and his pistol sank."

She gave a bark of laughter. "I can just see it. Did he sink too, or can he swim?"

"He swims. What bothers me about it is . . ."

They had reached the small building. Reached it and started around it, toward the side that faced the tennis court. But Mickey stopped, and Pike almost bumped into her. She turned around and tugged at his hand, pulling him back the way they had come. "C'mon," she said. "I was wrong. Maurice is busy."

He was busy all right. From the glimpse Pike got, over Mickey's shoulder and around the corner of the building, it looked like he was halfway to consummation with a woman who was visible only as a tangle of skirts and tousled hair.

Pike allowed himself to be led back toward the pool. "Well," he said. "*Toujours gai.*"

"You can say that again." It looked like she was blushing, although in the outdoor lighting it was hard to tell. "So, it's bothering you, huh?"

"What, that? That doesn't bother me. It's his house, he can do what he damn well pleases."

"No, silly, about what you were talking about. With the guy showing up at some boat."

"Oh. Well. What bothers me is how he knew where to find me. I got his license number off of his Jeep, but he never saw my car, and we weren't exactly introduced. So he didn't know my name, or have any way to get it."

She stopped and turned around. Her eyes were invisible in shadow. "Except from me? Is that what you're saying? That I told him?"

"You. Or Maurice."

"That's a shitty thing to say."

"Not necessarily. One of you might have told him without knowing it."

She frowned, lifted her chin, and looked at him down that proud nose, getting a pissy tone in her voice. "I usually know what I'm doing."

"Don't get all huffy. Suppose Nakamura had someone follow Maurice until he went to my office, and then followed me from there. Or followed you to my house when you came out there on Sunday."

Sometimes he had the feeling that she overacted her mood changes. She went from offended to contrite in the blink of an eye. The vertical line between her eyebrows disappeared. The frown vanished, and her eyes and mouth went round. "Oh. I never thought of that. Oh. But . . ."

From contrite she went to thoughtful, with one eyebrow raised. "Why should he be after you? When I called that Nakamura, he told me it was all taken care of. And I'm sure Maurice talked to him too. So why should they care about you?"

"Your misunderstanding with them was business. Mine was more on a personal level. I'm guessing that even if you've straightened out the business part, that doesn't fix my personal problem."

"No," she said slowly. "I can see that. I guess it wouldn't. What are you going to do?"

"Beats the hell out of me. Maybe start carrying a pistol, instead of just keeping one around the house. Speaking of which, if you're through with the one I lent you, maybe I could have it back?"

"Sure. Only I don't . . . I left it home, I don't have it with me. But I'll get it back to you."

"Fine. No rush. Well, since our host is obviously going to be a while, I think I'll get out of here. Tell him I enjoyed the party and all, if you will."

"Wait. What time is it?"

"Six. Maybe a little after."

"Could," she said, "would you mind giving me a ride? I came with some other people, but they're going to stay for hours, and I'm beat."

"Be glad to. That is, if the valet people can find the car."

She was silent during the drive. A couple of times he glanced over at her, seeing her profile, or her face for a brief moment in the light from a streetlight. Once she sighed, and once she made a sound, a little puff of air through her nostrils. But although he waited, she didn't say a thing, except, "Left here," and "Take the next right."

He recognized the driveway and pulled into the parking area, parked next to her Maserati, and switched off the ignition. Opened the door and glanced at her as he started to get out. She was sitting with her hands folded in her lap, staring straight ahead through the windshield. Hadn't made a move to open her door.

He heard her say, the voice so quiet he thought for a moment he was making the whole thing up in his head, "Why don't you like me?"

He almost answered.

He would have answered, if he hadn't turned to look at her, seen her staring out through the windshield of the darkened car. But as soon as he had turned toward her, sitting with her hands folded in her lap, staring out through the windshield as if she could see in the dark, he knew that if he spoke, broke the silence, they'd have to start all over again. No, they had been here before, and she had fed him lines, and he had blown his replies. Now she was giving him another chance, but if he blew his lines this time, there weren't going to be any more chances. So he touched her cheek, cupped her chin, and turned her face toward him, bringing his mouth to hers and feeling her arms go around his neck.

They went up the stairs in silence, through the apartment, and into the bedroom. Undressed without a word, until she said, "Wait."

They were on the bed, the room lit only by the distant glow of city lights reflecting from the clouds. She sat up and turned on a dim light on a bedside table. Slid open a drawer in the table and took out a small wooden box. Opened the box and held it out toward him. The box had a mirror inside its lid, and was filled with a crystalline white powder. Resting in it was a tiny silver spoon.

"You want some of this?"

Pike shook his head.

"You don't mind if I use some?"

"It's your apartment," Pike said carefully.

She nodded once, picked up the spoon, and took a small amount of the powder into each nostril, then lay back on the bed and pulled him to her.

He wanted it to feel right. He didn't want to just *do* it, he wanted it to feel *right*, and to get lost in the feeling. But her eyes were shut tight, and maybe she was just doing it. Doing it with him, moving with him, or just letting him do it to her, because he didn't know where she was with her eyes closed so tight. He wanted to see her eyes and he wanted her to see him, to look at him so he would know it was right, and not just a woman thinking she was gaining an ally or taking a hostage the way women always gained allies and took hostages.

The answer he had almost given her, in the car when she said, "Why don't you like me?" was that he was just confused. After all, he had reason enough to be. He'd heard Maurice say money was missing, which meant she was a thief. He'd heard Maurice say money was *not* missing, so she was not a thief. More than that, Maurice had said to forget the whole thing, come and get the books, give them back to Mickey. So it was all over. There wouldn't be any more investigation, or any litigation.

And that was only the beginning of the confusion, because she was as witty and articulate and intelligent as Maurice had said she was, and damn good looking besides. And seemed to be interested in him. And apparently was horny. All of which made it easy to rationalize.

So the rationalization, the mood, or some other thing had saved him from getting into another conversation, from saying something that would set her off. Had let him follow her lead up to the point where he had wanted it to feel *right*. Where instead it had been somehow unsatisfying; hollow and empty.

She smoked a cigarette in bed after. Took the pack and an ashtray off the bedside table, rested the ashtray on her stomach, lit up, blew a stream of smoke at the ceiling. He went into the kitchen and got two glasses of wine, brought them back to the bedroom. She took one and sipped at it. Set the glass down, and then sat back against the headboard of the bed.

Did it feel disconnected because she'd wanted to do coke and he didn't? Or had it felt disconnected before? Pike wasn't sure. And wasn't sure that it mattered. He slid out of bed and began looking for his clothes.

"Where are you going?" she said.

"Home. I've got to get up early tomorrow."

She didn't seem to be at all disturbed. "All right," she said, and took another drag on her cigarette, letting the smoke trickle out of her nostrils as she sat naked against the headboard of the bed.

The red message light was blinking on his answering machine. He hit the button for playback. "Dave," the machine said, "Nico. I'm done. With looking at those invoices and stuff you gave me. You want a report? Let's say I come by your office end of the day tomorrow, around five. That isn't good for you, get back to me, we'll set up something else."

Pike got undressed, got into the shower. Stood under the flow of warm water and wondered why everything felt so disjointed. Maybe it was the way she said things. How did you tell what was real and what came out of a script? But so what? If she wanted to play, what was wrong with that?

Pike got out of the shower, turned off the light, and got into bed.

CHAPTER

13

"WHAT," PIKE SAID, "THE fuck is that?"

"What's it look like?"

"It looks like a pizza box."

"Well, what'd you have to ask for? It is a pizza box."

"Nico, what are you doing in my office with a pizza box?"

"What do you think? It's dinnertime. This's dinner. I thought you might like to eat out tonight, instead of having to cook, while I talk to you about this audit. So I brought dinner."

"Oh," Pike said. "All right. Just as long as you didn't have them put anchovies all over the whole thing."

"Over there on the coffee table a good place?"

Nico crossed the room and put the box down. "You look like shit," he said. "Somebody die or something?"

"No," Pike said. "Not exactly. Senior partner in the firm, guy named Sid Stoddard, had another coronary. His third. He's up at UCLA med center in the CCU."

"'Scuse me," Nico said, "while I get my foot outta my mouth. You still up to doing this? I can come back another time."

"Now is as good as any. Let's do it."

"That's what I like," Nico said. "Man of decision. Says to one come, and he cometh. To another go, and he goeth.

"Hey," he said, and modified his tone, "you really are kind of down, aren't you? Right, then. The way it was done, was, well, it was really stupid. You got anything to drink in here?"

"Yeah," Pike said. "Down the hall where the coffee is, there's a little refrigerator. Soft drinks in there. And fruit juice, I think."

"No beer?"

"Nico, this is an office, not a saloon. Besides, I uh, I thought you, well . . ."

"Weren't drinking? I'm not. I thought you always liked beer with pizza."

As Pike led the way down the hall, Nico said, "There's checks written, the payees sound plausible for a film production company—Serv-U Catering, Locations Plus, couple more names. But there're no invoices in the files, and I can't—I looked in the phone book—those companies don't—they're not listed. Not in this directory of film-industry service companies that I got either. This thing? this is a refrigerator?"

"Open it and see," Pike said.

"Coulda fooled me. I'da said it was a filing cabinet." Nico opened the refrigerator, selected a can of soda, and popped the tab. Pike grabbed a can and they turned and started back down the hall toward Pike's office.

"And," Nico said, "this is the big tip-off—these checks I'm talking weren't deposited anywhere. They were cashed."

"So?"

"So it's plain as print. Even a lawyer should be able to understand it." Nico's voice held the merest tinge of sarcasm. "Those companies never existed. Somebody wrote checks to nonexistent companies, cashed them, kept the cash. Then there's one other thing. Now this I can't prove, and I'm reaching for it, I admit that, but I think it happened here, because there're a lot of missing invoices. Kickbacks. They could have written a check for one amount, say a hundred dollars. But the actual invoice was for a smaller amount—say fifty dollars. Then they got a kickback from the company the check was written to.

"Now," Nico said, "I can't prove that without taking more time than you wanted to spend, and without, you know, subpoena the

books and records from the vendors—see what invoices they generated, match them with the checks they got. But even without the
kickbacks, we can say for sure, based on the checks that were
cashed and not deposited, that more money came out of the account
than was accounted for by the actual expenses."

"How much more?"

"It's really hard to say. I can document thirty, maybe thirty-five
thousand. That I can document. I *know* there's more, but I can't
document it. So figure maybe that much again that I haven't had
time to find. Or be conservative and say around fifty.

"But wait," Nico said. "Now comes the interesting part. This's all
in like April, all this with the checks I'm talking. A couple months
later, they did it the other way. An invoice comes in for a hundred
dollars, the invoice's right there in the file. And a check's written for
fifty dollars. But the next month the statement from the creditor
shows a payment of the full hundred—so *some*body gave the creditor another fifty in cash, to pay him in full.

"So," Nico said, "as far as I can tell, someone just made themselves a little loan. They squeezed out maybe fifty grand in cash
there, used it a while, and then squeezed it back in again. No blood,
no foul. Unless you're worried they might do it again and not put
the money back."

"How sure are you of this?" Pike asked. "Maurice said he looked
at the checks, invoices, all that stuff, and it was fine."

"Then he didn't look very hard. Maybe he's humping the quiff,
it's scrambled his brains."

"Nico," Pike said, annoyed, "he thinks of her as his daughter. He
doesn't hit on her."

"Well," Nico said, "excuse me all to goodness. Little sensitive
there, are we, chief? Maybe getting some of that yourself?"

"Nico . . ." Pike said.

"Forget it," Nico said. "Forget it. Forget I asked. Only, Dave,"—he
paused. "Dave, look, all right? Fuck 'em or don't fuck 'em, but don't
go all funny on me, okay? When the suspects suddenly start being

out of bounds, it makes it damn hard to investigate anything, you know?"

Nico tipped his head back and drained his soda. He put the can down. "Okay," he said. "Change the subject. How'd you make out finding an address for our little friend?"

Pike shrugged.

"That bad, huh?"

"Yep. Talked to his boss, this guy Nakamura, and nothing. He'd barely even admit that the guy worked there. Must have thought I was wearing a wire, because he wouldn't say anything about anything."

"So what now, chief?"

"I need to find that bastard before he finds me, and try to get something worked out with him."

"So?"

"So you're the former G-man. How do we find him?"

It was Nico's turn to shrug. "Burgle the place he works and look for an address in their files? Too risky. Take too long to find it, 'cause we don't know where to look. Hang around across the street until he shows up for work and then follow him home? Or follow the boss-man until they meet up? Hire a couple off-duty blues to watch the place? Or all of the above. I can make some calls, you like. Maybe spend some time myself."

"You got time for shit like this?"

"Hey, what are friends for? Besides, I'm not real busy right now. You know," he said, and stopped.

"What?"

"Nothing."

"Don't give me 'nothing.' What is it?"

"I don't know, does it ever bother you?"

"What, thinking that some asshole is hiding in the bushes getting ready to blow my head off? It bothers the hell out of me."

"Not that."

"What then?"

"You know, the whole thing."

"Like what?"

"Life with a capital L, and that kind of stuff. I used to get this feeling. It was always the same feeling, and it had three parts. Part of it was surprise, surprise that I'd gotten so far up the ladder from where I'd started. Part of it was fear; being afraid that I'd make a mistake and lose it all. And the third part was sheer, stark terror that it might all go on and on, just like it was, day after stultifying day, forever. You ever get that feeling?"

"Nico, what is this? I thought you were a free spirit now. Quit the Bureau. Free-lance. Work when you want. What're you thinking all this kind of stuff for?"

"Forget it. Forget I brought it up. I'll make some calls tomorrow, see if I can find some guys want to make some money sitting in a car staring at a laundry."

Richie glanced down the driveway. The silver car stood at the end, where she usually parked it. Good. She was home. Richie walked along the driveway to the parking area, picked up the third flower pot, lifted out the key, and started up the stairs.

A hostess in a full skirt and ruffled peasant blouse led Dominic to a table, left a menu, and went away to get him a drink and some chips and salsa.

Dominic had been to Mexico. Several times, in fact, and he'd never seen a cantina that looked like an American restaurant designer's idea of a cantina. The gay display of serapes and bright woven straw animals. The stiff, self-conscious photographs from the revolution of 1910; blank-faced men with floppy hats and bandoliers of cartridges, standing or on horseback, or grouped around a water-cooled Browning mounted on the back of a Model T Ford.

Dominic waited. Watched a busboy clean up some lettuce and chopped red onion that had fallen from the salad bar, and waited some more. When he was halfway through his second drink, a slim man came in, spoke to the hostess, and stood for a moment looking around the room. The man was wearing a jacket with narrow lapels, a dark shirt and a narrow leather tie, and trousers that nipped in at the ankles. When he saw Dominic the man made a vague gesture that could have been a greeting and came toward Dominic's table. He stopped and put one hand on the back of a chair.

"Solly said," he began. "Solly said you was looking for somebody."

"Maybe I was," Dominic said. "But that don't mean I wanted to sit *here* all night. Next time you talk to Solly, you want to tell him something for me? Tell him when I ask him find someone for me, I want them now, not next fucking year. The fuck have you been?"

"Look, don't get on my case, all right?" the man said, straightening the knot of his tie.

"You think I got nothing better to do, sit here all night, wait for somebody to show up, they're home, trying to figure which shoe goes on which foot? I don't, I haven't got time for shit like this."

"Hey," the man said in an injured tone. "I'm a professional, not one of your niggers. I didn't get my reputation from goin' to some school. I got it 'cause I'm good at what I do. But I get paid for what I do, and I don't get paid to take shit offa nobody. You want something that's in my line, we make a price, I do the job."

The man straightened his tie again. "Whyn't you call Solly, see if he can find you somebody else knows how to do what I do?" He turned away from the table.

"Hey!" Dominic said. "Just a goddamn minute! Don't get so wound up, okay?"

The man turned back, rested both hands on the table, and leaned over toward Dominic. " 'Wound up'?" he said. "Wound up! *I'm* not goddamn wound up. The one who's wound up is, is *you*. I get a call

from Solly, will I meet a guy, I get through with my other business, I
go where the guy is, and I get a ration of shit? And I'm wound up? I
don't think so."

"All right," Dominic said. "All right. I'm sorry. I got a little out of
line there. I apologize. It's Kashkin, right? Am I pronouncing that
right?"

"Right," the man said, extending his hand. "Dmitri Kashkin. You
mind if I sit down?"

"Sure," Dominic said. "Fine. Great. Here,"—waving at the
waitress—"let's get you a drink."

"Cars," Kashkin said. "Cars is what I do mostly. But I can do
anything you want. I done lots different things. Suitcases, brief-
cases, I done a chair once, done a medicine cabinet, done a diving
board. Did a dog once. That," he said modestly by way of explanation, "that was with a radio control."

"What do you like to use?" Dominic said.

"You name it. I'll use anything. I used fertilizer, different commercial stuff, C-4, Semtex. That's from Czechoslovakia. Pretty good
stuff, behaves nice. You name it, I used it."

"But what do you *like* to use?"

"Depends on the job. Some jobs, you want plastic. Some you
can't use it. Depends entirely on where it's got to go and what it's got
to do."

"Uh-huh. Well how'ud you do this guy I told you about?"

"Have to look, wouldn't I? Can't just say something off the top
your head, 'use this, do that.' You want this guy, right? This one
guy, not his wife, girlfriend, the mailman, someone stops by for a
drink. That mean's gotta be something he does personally, him*self*.
How I know what he does I don't know the guy? Can't do the diving
board he don't swim. Can't do a briefcase he don't carry one. No,
no . . ." He shook his head.

"You," he said, "*you* tell *me* what you want done. Then I do that, and you got 'zactly what you asked for. Don't work, that's your lookout, 'cause you got what you asked for.

"The other way is," Kashkin said, "you want *me* decide how to do it, then I take a look, I decide what to do. Then it's my nickel, it don't work. Not," he said, "not that I'm saying that's likely, but it can happen. It has happened. It don't work, then I take care of it, fix it up for you. Do it again until it's right."

"Uh-huh," Dominic said. "Well, that sounds like the way to go, where you pick how to do it and all. I think I heard five?"

Kashkin closed one eye and twitched his mouth. He opened the eye again. "You think," he said in a reflective tone, "you think the Raiders'll move back Oakland? I don't like 'em moving these franchises around, you know? One week Oakland, next week L.A., next week back Oakland again. Why don't they just fahcrissake play ball, and quit all the goddamn moving around?"

"I thought," Dominic said carefully, "that we were talking prices here."

"That's what I thought, too, but if you don't want, you know, be serious about it, well, hey, might's well shoot the shit about football. Or maybe you got something you'd rather talk about?"

"All right," Dominic said. "How much was it? I forgot."

"Thirty," Kashkin said. "I decide how to do it and guarantee results, it's thirty. Five is you tell me what to hit."

"That's kind of steep, isn't it," Dominic said. "I mean, five sounds about right, but thirty? Thirty is steep."

"Not for what you get. You might say, well, costs five to try it once, should be maybe ten results guaranteed. That'll leave five try it again, it don't work the first time, right? You'd be wrong, though. Somebody almost goes up in a puff of smoke, the heat is on. Cops start running around all over the place. And he gets real careful. Starts pushing doors open with a stick before he walks in, gets one of those remote-control things turn his car on with.

"That means," Kashkin said, "well, you can see what it means. It's five, six times as hard to make it work the second time. But that's what you pay for. I stay around, keep on it, and I get it done, guaranfuckingteed. You ask around, ask anybody, they'll tell you. They'll tell you something else too, for free. Kashkin don't haggle over prices. It's thirty, or it's five, depending on how you want it done, and that, that's it."

"Thirty is kind of steep for what I'm dealing with here," Dominic said. "This is not such a big deal that I want to drop thirty on it. It's more like a minor annoyance.

"Let's," Dominic said, "do it the other way. You said cars're good, right? Suppose you do his car."

"All right. That'll be fine. You got an address and stuff for this guy?"

The box with the congealed remains of the pizza was folded up in Pike's wastebasket. The aroma of cheese and garlic still lingered in the room. Nico put his feet up on the coffee table and stifled a burp.

"You know," he said, "it doesn't make sense."

"What?"

"I mean, you said she was paying protection, right?"

"Absolutely. That's what got me involved with this goon I'm still trying to find."

"Well, what'd she pay it with? I mean, all the money that went out, came back. So where's the payments?"

"In cash, maybe?"

"Nah. No cash withdrawals from this account."

"One of the checks then? Like one to a caterer, or something that would look legitimate?"

"Won't work either. I checked 'em all out. Any check that didn't look legitimate, I checked it out. And all the 'funny' checks are included in the fifty grand that's been paid *back*. So if she paid protection, they paid it back."

"I don't think they do that," Pike said. "At least I never heard that they do. So then she wasn't paying protection."

"But she told you she was, right? So why'd she do that? Can't be to explain missing money, because there isn't any money missing. So what else?"

"It came up," Pike said, thinking it through, "when that goon was at her apartment. Don't call the cops because we're paying protection and we don't want the cops messing in it. So maybe she was trying to hide some involvement with him."

"Maybe she's humping him," Nico said. He looked at Pike warily. "If I may be permitted to make such a crude suggestion."

"Nico, Jesus! This is a guy who looks like he moves his lips when he reads. She wouldn't be interested in him. But say she was. So what? Nobody'd care about that. Maurice doesn't care who she sleeps with. *I* don't care who she sleeps with. Besides, it was the cops she didn't want involved, not Maurice. She *told* Maurice. It's got to be something bad, something criminal."

"Uh-huh," Nico said, grinning like a shark. "I'm with you there. I see what you're thinking. If you need a big hunk of money so bad that you steal it, and then you pay it back in a few weeks—well you bought something, and then sold it, and made a profit. And there's only a few things you buy and sell that quick, right?"

"Right," Pike said. "All of which raises an interesting point. Why didn't *Maurice* want the cops involved in this? Was it just what he said, that he didn't want his film messed up? Or was he involved in whatever she was doing?"

"Good question," Nico said. "By the way, the film's a porno film, I assume you knew that?"

"It's what?"

"A porno film."

"Wait, this film that they're making? Is a porno film?"

"All the way."

"How do you know that?"

"Two ways: first, from talking to the people who were on location. The caterers. The people did the lights. Some others. And second, I watched part of it."

"How'd you watch part of it?"

"At the editing studio. You'd be surprised how much you get away with, you wave an I.D. in someone's face. I don't think it was a finished film I watched. They said it wasn't 'locked' yet, whatever that means. They have all these words; *answer print, workprint, composite.* One of those things, they ran part of it for me."

He raised his eyes toward the ceiling and shook his head slowly. "And let me tell you, it's *hot.* Hot, but high class—like a girl's on call for a grand a night. There's this one scene I remember, this girl comes in the room, looks real innocent. Real young. She's wearing this robe, very demure, carrying this red rosebud in one hand, couple fern leaves in the other. She goes across the room, puts the rosebud in a vase, stands there arranging the fern leaves around it. This guy comes in, puts the moves on her, she's kind of holding him off, like she ain't never done this before. But after a while their clothes are off, they're on the bed, and the guy is hung like a goddamn horse. So just about the time I'm thinking, shit, she'll never get that whole thing in there, why, she does. And they're getting it on, and you can see next to the bed, on the nightstand there, in the vase, in perfect focus, the rosebud opens and blooms. It was a nice touch.

"Course," he said, "naturally, it wasn't all so refined. There's other parts, five people squirming around on each other like nightcrawlers in a bait can. But somehow it came across as quality stuff. Nothing sleazy, nothing vulgar. And *hot,* let me tell you."

"Ah, shit!" Pike said. "I incorporated that company. My name's on the articles. And it's porno? Shit! I'm going to have to dump Maurice as a client."

"For what? No law against porno, far as I know."

"Nico, I saw something in the paper the other day, the D.A. got aggressive, brought a pandering prosecution against a couple of producers."

"Pandering," Nico said. "Producers are like the guys who round up the money for a movie? How is a producer pandering? I don't get it."

"Oh, come on," Pike said. "It's no more convoluted than some of the things you did at the Bureau, going after someone for violating the victim's civil rights instead of murder, 'cause murder wasn't a federal crime. Here, instead of it being a pimp gets a girl to turn tricks for money, it's a producer gets a girl to fuck for money in a film. Either way it's obtaining a female to engage in sex for hire. What's confusing about that?"

"Nothing," Nico said. "Now that you lay it out."

"So, I'll have to tell Maurice to take his business somewhere else."

"Why do that? Guy pays his bills, don't he?"

"Nico, are you dense today? If he'd done it before I represented him, and then walked in here and wanted a defense, one of the guys that does criminal law would have defended him, no sweat. But there's a difference between defending someone for something he did last year, and being there while he does it. It doesn't matter that porno is legal, if the D.A. files on it as pandering. Pandering, in case you don't remember, is *not* legal.

"My name," Pike said, "my name is on the articles of incorporation of that company as incorporator. I could be charged as a co-conspirator, accessory, any damn thing. You remember what it's like when a prosecutor goes on the rampage? Indict everybody in the room, and sort it out later who was just there to deliver the takeout Chinese.

"Well, no thanks," Pike said. "I don't want that, and I'm not taking any chances of that happening. So I'm going to dump the client."

"Well, that's your business, I guess. But coming back to the topic at hand, what is this guy? Maurice? Is that his name? What is he hiding when he tells you to lay off the heavy lifter? That it's a porno film?"

"I don't know," Pike said. "The simple thing would be to use the same explanation for both of their behaviors, if it fits. If she's dealing drugs, then he's dealing drugs. But how well does that fit, really?

Why would he blow the whistle on all this in the first place, get me into it, if he was really involved in drugs? With him, he could have believed her and just didn't want the cops messing up the protection deal on his film."

"Maybe," Nico said, not convinced, but thinking about it. "You could ask him. But if he *is* dealing drugs he'll say he isn't, and if he *isn't* dealing drugs he'll say he isn't. So asking him doesn't go anywhere."

"I don't really care," Pike said. "Being involved in one criminal conspiracy at a time is enough for me. If the film's porno, then I'm firing the client, and I don't care if he's dealing drugs too, or not."

She couldn't move. Could only roll the slightest bit from side to side. Hands and feet held spread-eagled to the corners of the bed. Couldn't make any intelligible sound through the gag, just a kind of grunting. Couldn't even see who it was that was doing it, because of the blindfold.

It was the most liberating thing she had ever felt.

She could scream at the top of her lungs and no sound came out, except a kind of whimper. Strain her arms and legs until her muscles quivered with fatigue, and nothing stopped the steady, sliding, pushing in her groin. She couldn't stop it, couldn't help it, and so wasn't responsible for it, and could let go and experience it to a degree that she never achieved otherwise.

And then the sensation grew too intense, her muscles went rigid, and she went over the top, jerking and twitching, howling against the gag, until the spasm faded.

He pulled the blindfold and the gag off first, as he usually did. Mickey blinked and shook her head, licked her lips. "Untie me," she said. "I want a cigarette."

"You shouldn't oughta smoke, sweetheart," he said. "It's not good for you. Ruins your wind, and it can . . ."

"Richard," she said, "give it a rest. I want a cigarette. Untie me."

"Okay, okay, don't get all in an uproar. I'm doing it." And he began working on the knots that held the rope on Mickey's wrists.

"Richard," she said, "when you leave, I've got some money I need you to take for me, pick up the next load."

"I don't think I can," Richie said.

"What do you mean, you can't? Why ever not?"

"Well, but see," he paused. "See, I'm supposed to be on vacation. Dominic told me to take a week off."

"Richard, it's not like you'd actually be *work*ing. All you have to do is take the money, bring back the stuff. It's just like all the other times."

"Well, I don't know," he said.

"Richard, don't give me a hard time. How am I supposed to get the money to Dominic? How am I supposed to get the stuff? I don't have time to fool around with some new delivery person I don't even know. No. Absolutely not. I don't care what he told you. You take the money, and you bring me the stuff."

"All right," Richie said. "All right. I'll do it. Don't get all bent out of shape.

"Sweetheart," he said after a moment.

"Yes, Richard, what is it?"

"Have you thought any more about what I said?"

"About what?"

"You know."

"Richard, I told you before. I am not going to marry you. I am not going to marry anyone. I am not at a point in my career where I can even think about marriage."

"But I love you."

"That's very sweet of you. But you know what I told you when we started seeing each other. No questions, no excuses, no promises. Right?"

Richie was sulking. He didn't answer, just went on untying the knots on Mickey's ankles. When he finished, he stood up. "Sweetheart," he said. "Sweetheart, look at me."

He waited until Mickey was looking at him. "See?" he said. "What you see's what you get. This's me. There isn't any more. I don't read fancy books, and I don't, I can't discuss films with your friends, that're in the movie business, talk about symbolism and layers of meaning. And I don't play tennis or ride horses. I work for a guy and I get paid pretty good, and this is what I am.

"I know what you are," he said. "I know you're a lot more'n I am, to the people you know. You can run things, and plan things, and order people around, and make things come together. And I like that, being with someone's able to do those things. But see, all of those people you work with, they're different from me, for two reasons."

"First," he said, "first is, they're different because they could get along without you, it came to that. When you really come down to it, you got squashed by a truck tonight, they'd find somebody else, finish the picture, direct the next one, shake their heads, say, too bad about Mickey McDonald, she was so young and all. But they'd do it. They'd get along without you just fine.

"I wouldn't," he said. "I can't, don't know how to say it, can't find the words to tell you, but I can't get along without you. That's the first thing that's different.

"Second," he said. "Now let me finish here, second is, *you* can get along without *them*. But you can't get along without me. What I do for you, nobody else can do. I know you see other guys. I know when you're gone for a day or two, get vague about where you been, I know what you been doing. Sometimes it bothers me, and sometimes I can handle it better. But I also, I also know, that none of them get you off like I do. And more important, you know it, too. Isn't that right?"

He stopped and waited for her to answer.

"Richard," she said, "I'm not going to argue about this here. Everything you say may be true, but I am not marrying anybody, okay? Now hand me my blouse, I've got to be somewhere."

"No," Richie said. "I don't think you need to be anywhere right now except right here." He swung one leg over her as she sat on the bed and straddled her legs. Caught at her wrists and pushed her back onto the pillows.

"Richard," she said, "let me up. Stop that, goddamn it. Oh God. Oh."

She let herself into the backyard through the gate, feeling nervous, but thinking it should still be okay to use the pool. He'd invited her, told her it was okay. Come any time, he said. Then she'd run off the day the naked woman was there. But the point was, *she* was the one decided to split. *He* hadn't said, "Fine then, be that way," or not to come anymore, or anything. Nothing like that.

In fact, he called her up, all flustered, said don't hang up, and asked her out sailing. Apologized very nicely. So it was probably still okay to use the pool.

All the same she felt a little funny, swimming her laps, with the blank windows of the house watching her. And then lying on her towel in the sun to dry off, almost like sneaking into someone's yard to pick apples off of their tree, or to shoot at a bird with your BB gun. If someone had come out of the house and yelled at her, she wouldn't have been surprised. Would just have grabbed her towel and scooted around the corner of the house and out the gate.

What she'd rather, if she had her d'ruthers, would be for him to come in the way he had that first time, hand her a beer, and then go in the house and light the barbecue. He was interesting to talk to. Interesting, but fun too.

She had her sandals on, was picking up her beach bag, stuffing the towel inside, when she heard the car in the driveway. She stood for a moment, thinking. Slipped out of her wet suit and stuffed it in her beach bag, put on her cover-up, and walked around the house. Got there just as he was closing the door of his car.

"Oh," he said. "Hi. I see you had a swim."

"Yeah, she said, "I did. It was nice. Invite me in and offer me a beer, why don't you?"

He opened the front door. Stood back for her to enter. Led the way to the kitchen.

"Beer's in the icebox," he said. "Glasses are in that cupboard. If you don't mind, I'm going to go change, get out of my suit. Make yourself at home." He left her in the kitchen and went down the hall, toward the back of the house.

She got a beer, opened it, and went into the living room. Put the bottle on the coffee table and looked around. You could tell a lot about people by where they lived. At least momma said so. She wandered slowly around the room, and then into the den, that was just down the hall, careful not to touch anything. Looked at the books. Looked at the pictures and framed nautical charts that hung on the wall, and at the furniture.

He was a neat housekeeper, you could tell that. Other than that, the problem was, she didn't know what was his stuff, and what belonged to the guy who owned the house. If the books belonged to him, then he must read a lot. Some of them looked like law books, so she supposed they were his, but how could you tell? And probably the framed charts and photographs of sailboats were his. He was into boats, after all. The charts looked like they had been used before they'd been framed. They had stains on them, and figures jotted in the margins, and pencil lines and funny symbols.

Pike thought about taking a shower, decided that was too big a production. Hung his suit in the closet, put on a pair of jeans and a short-sleeved shirt. Slipped his feet into a pair of thongs and headed back for the kitchen. He found Dossie in the living room, standing by the bookshelves, her hands in the pockets of her beach cover-up. She had the beginnings of a tan, pale gold, and freckles across her nose. She had high, hard breasts under the cover-up, and the wet, slicked-down hair. And the gray eyes that were Dossie and no one else.

She was quiet for a while, then cleared her throat: "So, Dave, how long did you say you were married for?"

"I didn't say. Forty-six, forty-seven months, maybe a little over."

"It sounds like a long time when you say it that way."

"Sometimes it *felt* like a long time."

"Any kids?"

"No."

"Why not?"

"She was in school. No time. Then I was in school too. Even less time. And then it was over. No time."

"Uh-huh," she said. "What happened?"

"I don't know," he said. "Sometimes I'm not sure anybody knows."

"Your idea or hers?"

"Hers. No. I don't know. It just sort of happened."

"And you're happier now?"

"Yeah," surprising himself, because he didn't think about things like that: compare this year with last year, see how the trend line was moving. "Yeah, I'd have to say that I am. Though it took a while. I mean at first it wasn't fun at all."

"The other day," she said. "When we went sailing? What was it you had to go and do afterwards?"

"Oh," he said. "Go and meet a policeman and get some information about that guy I told you about. The one that was getting protection money from the movie company."

"And did you? Get the information you wanted?"

"Some. But not enough to be able to find him, which was supposed to be the point. You know, he was there, the night we were sailing. Showed up when I was putting the boat away."

He told her the story, the third or fourth time he'd told it. He'd worked a little humor into it, a few gestures. Gotten quite a laugh from a couple of people. She didn't laugh. Sat on the couch and looked serious. Sat forward, put her beer on the coffee table, and looked him in the eye.

"So," she said, "what're you going to do about it?"

"I don't know. Try a couple of other things. See if I can find him."

"And when you do?"

"I don't know. I can't make any sense out of all this. I don't even know the guy. I don't give a big rat's ass about him. Why should he care about me? There has to be some way to work it out."

"Suppose he finds you before you find him?"

"I don't know about that either. I try to stay loose, not walk in any dark alleys. And I'm sleeping with a pistol under the pillow. What else can I do?"

"Tell the police? What are you laughing about?"

He hadn't been laughing. At least there hadn't been any humor in it, just one of those noises you make at an appropriate point in a conversation. "Sorry," he said. "It isn't funny, is it? I tried telling a cop. He explained to me very carefully they didn't have the manpower to assign me a bodyguard on the off chance something bad might happen to me."

"Can't they arrest him?"

"Apparently not. Look, why don't we talk about something else, okay?"

"Sure," she said. "Fine. Tell me about those charts on the wall there, why do they have things written on them?"

"They're places I've gone. Souvenirs, like." He pointed across the room. "That one was a bitch of a trip on the Channel Coast. Rained for two straight weeks."

"Then why put it up to remind yourself?"

"Well, it wasn't all bad. Did a lot of sitting in cafés in these little French fishing towns, drinking a glass or three of wine, deciding if you wanted to go out and get wet, getting to the next town to do it all over again. That's why it has all the marks on it, from where glasses were put down. And the wine stains."

"And those pictures out in the hall?"

"Oh," he said. "Those. Well—" pausing. "You want to go out and look at them, or just talk about them from here?"

"I want the whole tour," she said. "Let's go look."

They worked their way along the hall. He talked about the boats, what they were, why he had pictures of them. The last two pictures were just outside the door to the bedroom. She looked through the doorway into the room. There were two dressers, and a queen-size bed with a pastel comforter on it, and sliding doors out to the patio, with curtains pulled to one side. She upended the bottle and drained her beer. She looked around the room and took a deep breath. She opened her beach cover-up. Under it, she was naked.

"So," she said, and squared her shoulders, "you wanna fuck?"

She seemed nervous, and that made him nervous. Trying to act natural and not think of the movie director, not think at all. There was no reason to worry about Mickey. Why should he worry about Mickey? He hardly knew Mickey, and besides, she hadn't even been there. She'd been off somewhere inside her head. He'd known Dossie longer. Or at least better. Or felt he had.

He put his arms around her. She felt small, pressing against him. Small compared to, who? Amanda? Or Mickey? But she *was* small, with a delicate angularity. She had her head turned, her cheek resting against his chest. She felt good against him. Then she lifted her face and looked at him, her face solemn, her eyes calm and gray, and very big. She stood on tiptoe and kissed him, delicately at first, then getting into it, her mouth open now, still a little nervous, he could feel it, but eager at the same time.

They made love on the professor's pastel sheets, in the professor's bed, with an upholstered headboard looming out of sight in the darkness. They made love immediately, as though they were to-gether finally after they had been away from each other for a long time—but awkwardly, because it was a first time, learning, getting to know one another. Once they bumped noses, and grinned at each other. And when he entered her she made a sound—a catch in her breathing—a sound that said she was there, right there, and not somewhere back inside her head, watching the dancing shadows in some room of her mind. Pike moving with her, involved, but watching her at the same time, seeing a face that was her face, but a face she would never have recognized, if she could have seen it. The thin, girlish-looking half-adolescent gone, replaced by a woman arching up under him, thrusting, her breath rasping in her throat, her head thrown back, writhing, gasping.

Pike held her, seeing the outline of her cheek and shoulder against the dim light through the sliding glass doors. He wanted to hold her very close and keep holding her. He heard her say, in a drowsy murmur, "That was d'licious." He thought of things he could say, but didn't say any of them. It was too early to say the serious things, but too serious to say something flip. He hoped she felt the same way; felt that it was better to say nothing at all, just to be close, to hold and be held.

It struck him—maybe it was only in his mind—but it came to him that she was *real*. Her feelings, her reactions, what she said, they were all what she really felt and what she really thought. And with Mickey it was different: the lines, the moods, the reactions. Everything was always well-acted, and fit the plot—but it wasn't necessarily *real*.

She sat up, leaning against the upholstered headboard, the sheet falling away from her breasts. She saw him looking at her and smiled. "Can I ask you something?"

"Sure."

"What about, what's her name? Mickey?"

"Oh," he said. "Mickey."

He'd never understood how they could do that. How women could read your mind, nail you on something you'd been thinking about. "Mickey's,"—what was she?—"it's hard to explain. On one level, she's right there with you, and on another level, it all feels like lines from a script."

"Do you go out with her?"

"No. Well, I mean, I haven't gone *out* with her. She . . ."

"Oh," Dossie said.

"I mean, I gave her a ride home once, is all. I . . ."

"She's beautiful. She has fabulous hair. And a figure, well . . ." Dossie looked down at her chest. "Well, we won't say anything about her figure."

"If you're into that kind of thing."

"Are you involved with her?"

Jesus Christ—

"No, she's not my type. Like you say, she's beautiful and all, and if that turns you on, fine. But somehow it only seems skin deep."

"Does she?" she said, looking at him seriously. "Turn you on?"

"Look," he said, "I know what you think, because she was out here that day you saw her in the pool. But she only came to bring some financial records, like I told you. And I gave her a ride home once, from a cocktail party."

"But does she turn you on?"

"You're just hung up on her because you happen to've seen her here, is that right?"

"I sound like I'm jealous," Dossie said. "Giving you the third degree and all."

"That's okay," he said. "Don't worry about it."

She turned her head on the pillow and gave him a direct look from those gray eyes. "I am. Jealous. I try not to be, but I am. Tell me," she said, "why did you go to law school?"

"Prestige," Pike said, "and money." Thinking: that was the other thing about women. They came out of the blue with these questions had nothing at all to do with whatever you were talking about.

"That's not all," she said.

"No. You're right. It was more than that. I wasn't enjoying what I was doing. And I wanted to try something else. And it seemed like law would be, I don't know, satisfying somehow."

"And is it? Satisfying?"

"Sometimes. Sometimes it's pretty frustrating. Things we would have just gone out and *done*, in the Army, you spend hours talking about doing them. And if you should, or if somebody else might, and what it'd mean if you did or if they did."

"See," she said, "you try to be cynical, but really you aren't. It wasn't just to be a bigshot and make money."

"Maybe," Pike said. "Yeah, maybe you're right." Thinking about it, trying to remember how it had started, why he'd decided to take the first night class—and why he'd kept on, once the first semester was over, even when it was plain where it was leading with Amanda—and how the time had gone by so quickly.

Richie parked his jeep in the yard, next to Dominic's Mercedes. Took the steps two at a time, and smiled at the ladies in the office, working at their desks. Picked up a phone and punched Dominic's intercom number.

"Dom? It's me. Buzz me in, will you?"

"Richie, well,"—taking his time, you could hear him thinking, deciding how he was going to react. The man did that a lot. Richie wished he could do it, too—let a situation develop, and all the time be *thinking* how to handle it. Something happened, Richie mostly *did* something, then thought about it after.

"Richie,"—friendly, but a little cool. "I thought you were off this week. Out of town."

"Yeah, Dom. Right. I'm on the way now. But I got something I need to give you."

"Fine. Come on in." The door lock began to buzz. Richie walked down the inside hall, had to wait a moment at the inner door until the lock buzzed. Stepped through into Dominic's office. He had the piano music playing again. He was on a big piano kick now, had a bunch of CDs, different piano players. Listened to them all the time. Sitting behind his desk in his shirtsleeves, working on papers, smiling at Richie across the room. But it was hard to tell when he smiled if he really meant it, with those hard, flat eyes.

"You, uh, you sure you want me to do this vacation thing now, Dom?"

"Yeah, I'm sure."

"And, uh, you really don't want me do anything about the guy was at the movie lady's house?"

"I'm sure. I already took care of it. Arranged an accident for him."

"Oh. That's fine. An accident?"

"Yeah. Guy Solly knows'll take care of that."

"Jeez, Dom, I coulda handled that, I mean, there'uz no reason why I couldn'ta."

"Richie, Richie. We talked about this. I explained it to you. I think it's best to do it this way, okay?"

"Sure. Okay. By the way, the movie lady wants another load. Three keys this time. She gave me the money. I got it here."

"I hope she's not in a big hurry. I'm going up Oceano for a couple days, look at some property. It'll have to wait until I get back."

"Well," Richie said. "I don't know. She was, she's always kind of in a hurry. I think she wants the stuff like right away."

"That's her problem. I was just down the stash yesterday, put a couple of keys together, and I ain't going again two days in a row. Besides, I got, I made an appointment to be up there, Oceano. I'll get it when I get back."

"Oh," Richie said. "Well. So, uh, who drove when you went, when you were down the stash?" He was surprised, and more than a little hurt. First the man sends him on vacation, when there was no reason for it in the world, and then he runs around doing things that Richie did for him, with someone else doing them.

"Titch."

"Uh-huh. Well, on this new load for the movie lady, you'll have the delivery to make. You won't want to do that yourself. And you'll have to make a trip to the stash, mill in the cut, all that. You know, with the car changes and all, well, I was thinking," he stopped.

"Hey," Dominic said. "Take it easy. I'm not thinking, trying to replace you. You were the one, remember, was saying you wanted to move up into management? You did that, you wouldn't keep on driving, making deliveries, would you? I explained why I want you to take a few days off—to protect you, because it looked like things were getting kind of involved. I been meaning to have Titch learn how to do the car changes, getting down the stash, and how to mill in the cut and like that. He's not nearly as smooth as you are driving, and not what you'd call fast on the changes yet, but he'll learn, okay?"

So then it was all right. Or at least it felt all right, when Dominic explained it that way. Except it was always hard to tell what he was thinking, and Richie had to ask: "Uh, Dom, you're not mad, are you? I mean, you said go on vacation, right? And bringing you the money from the movie lady, that's work, you know? But she insisted, and, like, what could I do?"

"Hey," Dominic said, "no problem. You used your head. Can't be criticized for that. If you want to be a manager, you got to use your head. Right?"

So then Richie decided it really was all right.

CHAPTER

14

KASHKIN HAD SPENT THE better part of a week following the guy around. Some people, they got paid to whack somebody, they went out and cowboyed the job, chased the guy down the escalator at Sears, spraying the shoppers with an Uzi, drove the wrong way down a one-way street on the way out. Those people, mostly, they ended up doing a deal with the prosecutor, testifying for the People of the State of California in a murder-for-hire prosecution on the guy who paid them.

Kashkin thought people like that were punks. Kashkin was a professional. So even though it was only five large that the Jap had paid him to do the job, he still did it right. Five large wasn't bad for a week's work, anyhow, so what was the problem?

So Kashkin sat outside the guy's house in Malibu, followed him in to the office, followed him when he went to lunch, to court, out to Malibu again in the evening. Got an idea how he lived his life, and what would be the best way to approach the problem. What the guy did was smart if you didn't like traffic. He didn't drive in the rush hour. He came in early, got to the marina by seven thirty. Worked all day, didn't leave for Malibu until six thirty, seven o'clock. Six at the earliest.

So the two likeliest places were the parking garage at the guy's office, or his house.

Some people, and these were the same people, in Kashkin's opinion, who cowboyed a job, they thought the quieter a place was, the fewer people, the better. They'd try to climb into somebody's garage at two in the morning. The guy's wife is inside, going Walter, Walter, what is that noise in the garage? The guy's Weimaraner is barking up a storm, and the Doberman next door. Porch lights are coming on all up and down the street, people putting their heads out, find out what all the racket is about. The private security patrol, they're writing down the license number of this strange car, parked there at two in the morning.

No thank you.

The more people, the better. People looked at other people, but they didn't *see* what was going down. Kashkin had wired a charge one time, put it in the car and wired it up, the car's parked on the street, broad daylight, corner of Second and Los Angeles. One block from Parker Center, Headfuckingquarters of the LAPD. And no one looked at him twice, just walked by on the sidewalk, kept their minds on their own scam. Besides, what'd it take, five minutes? Six, tops. Not more than that. Kashkin'd walked across the street, got a cup of coffee in the quick lunch joint on the corner, stood in the little park a block up, stirred the coffee with one of these little plastic sticks they had there, and watched the guy come down the sidewalk, get in the car, switch on the ignition, and get spread all over the street in little pieces.

So the parking garage looked like the best bet.

The lawyer came out to the reception room, looked very solemn. Sid was in the hospital, sure, Maurice knew that. But this was a different kind of solemn. The lawyer had called up, said they had to talk. Not tomorrow, not next week, but now. He'd said that first. Voice kind of different, hard, like, This is what I want, do it. Not trying to be rude, but not spending any time trying to be polite, either. Then, after, he said, "Oh by the way, Sid's in the hospital, had another coronary, I suppose you knew that." So he'd had something eating on him besides Sid having the coronary. Something that made him look solemn. A face that said the guy was doing something, that he didn't like what he was doing, but he was damn well going to do it.

Maurice thought about that as he followed the lawyer along the carpeted hallway and into the office. The lawyer gesturing at a chair, sitting down behind his desk. Rolling the swivel chair forward.

"You know," Maurice said, pulling his glasses away from his face, and looking over them and then through them, "I got these new glasses, it seems like everything is kind of bulged out at me. Makes it exciting to drive, let me tell you, try to judge distances when things are bulging at you."

Sam Goldwyn always said, Talk first. When there's a meeting, a discussion, whatever. Talk first. Even if you don't know what it's all about, or where it's headed, talk first. Get the bit in your teeth, run a while. The other guys in the conversation, at least it shows them that you aren't afraid of the meeting, of being there. Makes it seem like you don't have anything to hide. Besides, maybe you can control the conversation, if you talk first.

"So," Maurice said. "Sid, I understand, isn't so good. The thing with his heart again, huh? I had two like he did, let me tell you, you wouldn't find me the office anymore. I'd be on the beach down Barbados there, take it easy.

"I guess," Maurice said, "that means you have to change things around, here at the firm. Sid was managing partner, wasn't he? Reorganize and all that stuff. Shift responsibilities around. I imagine you have a lot to do, keep up with all that.

"You can't," Maurice said, "you don't want let it get to be all work and no play. You were going to drop by my place the other night, meet some people, have a drink. Relax a little. Then you never showed up. I still got the books and records that we need to give back to Mickey."

"Maurie," the lawyer said, "I'm going to have to ask you to take your legal work someplace else. I can't represent you anymore."

"Forgot to bring the stuff today," Maurice said, "but I'll get it all back to you. What? What did you say? What are you talking about?"

And now the lawyer was explaining: all about how he'd found out that the film Mickey was working on was a porno film. Which was perfectly legal, Maurice knew it was legal. He'd had that checked out. Nothing wrong with producing porno films. Except that prosecutors didn't like porno, and they were always trying to find a way to stop it.

For a while they'd had that thing about not transporting obscene matter through the mails, made it hard to distribute. Then they got all excited about kiddie porn, prosecuted anybody who had some actress up there, she'd been doing it two years before you hired her, but she was still under eighteen. And now this, some new thing about pandering, if you paid the actress to have sex with an actor.

Well what else did you pay them to do, in a porno film?

That was why he'd done it with a corporation. He knew there were these problems, or anyway *some* kind of problems, always coming along. If you didn't get a prosecutor after you from one side, you got too successful, and the wiseguys moved in on you from the other side. So do it with a corporation, let the director sign the checks, keep your name out of it, and avoid getting personally mixed up in the problems. That was how he'd stayed independent and made money as long as he had—think ahead and plan it so you stayed out of the sticky stuff.

Not that he'd done porno before. Never had. But for some steady income during a dry spell between projects, you couldn't beat it. Nothing flashy, no chance of a first week's gross that would be mentioned in *Variety*, but a nice little series, three, four porno flicks would pay the rent and keep you afloat until the next serious property came along.

At least that was what guys in the industry said.

And now this lawyer was telling him there was something wrong with that? Something about it being a criminal conspiracy, or it might be. That the lawyer might be prosecuted too.

Incredible! They were all the same, lawyers. They took your money, no problem there, but then they were always worried about keeping *their* skirts clean, and as soon as there was a problem, off they went and left you in the lurch.

Well, he'd always known that this guy might figure it out. Stoddard said he was smart. Still felt kind of sheepish, though, the guy throwing you out of his office like you came in to sell your sister or something.

"So," the lawyer said, "that's the situation. Now, I should explain one other thing that came up in the process of all this. Something that—really, it's how I happened to find out about this film being porno.

"When you asked me," the lawyer said, "to get you the books and records on this film, I got them. But I thought you wanted an audit done. So I had copies made, and gave the copies to a guy who, well, he has an accounting degree, but he never used it to become a CPA. He went to work for the FBI. He doesn't work for them anymore, but he still knows how to find out things.

"So," the lawyer said, "you came and picked up the books and stuff, but I'd already given copies to this guy. And he looked into things for me. And what he came up with was . . ."

"Wait a minute," Maurice said, fury rising up in him, swamping the sheepish feeling. "Wait just a goddamn minute here. I don't believe what I'm hearing. You gave copies, you hired an accountant, you didn't tell me about it? What the hell is this anyhow? I got half a mind to go to the State Bar, file a complaint about how you run your business, is what I'm thinking."

But the lawyer went on talking. And on top of the sheepish feeling because the guy had found out about the porno film, and on top of the fury that the guy had done things without telling Maurice about them, was a third feeling. It was the same feeling Maurice had when he went out on his brother-in-law's boat, his stomach hollow and sore, and like he wanted to throw up. Because what he was hearing was that Mickey had done some stupid kinds of things, that he ought to have seen, when he went through the books, but was too dumb to notice. Getting old, he had to admit it. Too old to notice when someone he trusted put it to him. Made checks out to businesses that weren't even there.

"Wait a minute," he said. "Wait just a minute, willya? I don't believe this. I don't believe she did this, what you're saying."

He believed it, all right. He believed that it had *happened*. What he couldn't believe was that *Mickey* had done it to him. Mickey, whom he treated like one of his own children. Closer than one of his children.

The lawyer went on talking. Explained how the companies didn't exist. Checks written to them and cashed, not deposited. Fifty thousand dollars.

"Yeah, but wait," Maurice said. "Not so fast here. That's how you do it. You can't just write a check to a gangster, pay him protection. You have to get the money some other way, pay him in cash."

The lawyer went on talking. Explained how all the money that was taken was put back. So none of it was missing. None of it had been paid for protection. It had been like a loan, and it had been paid back.

But the point was that he hadn't *known* about it. He would have loaned her money if she'd asked. Well, maybe he wouldn't've— hard to say. But that she would do this to him. *Mickey.*

"So," the lawyer said, "these are the files on your different matters. The corporate minutes, stock book, seal. If you'll just sign this receipt here that you have received these items."

Maurice signed the receipt. The lawyer stood up. He held out his hand. "I'm sorry, Maurice," he said. "Sorry that it ended up like this. Good-bye."

And somehow, Maurice found himself back in the reception

area, holding a thin stack of files and a cardboard box with the corporate minutes and seal and stock book in it.

He sat down in one of the overstuffed chairs, put the papers on the floor, and put his face in his hands.

The phone rang three times. Five times. Nico still didn't have an answering machine. Nine times. Still couldn't communicate with him like a normal person. Twelve . . . thirteen. And he didn't have the decency to call, let Pike know how he was coming with finding an address for Blondie. Fifteen times. Pike hung up.

What was the name of that CPA firm he sometimes worked for in Santa Monica? Kaplan and somebody? Or somebody and Kaplan? Had Nico given him the number? Pike slid the address book out of his pocket calendar and looked under the tab for *N*. Dialed the number and then had to wait while they fumbled around and tried to decide who would have been working with Nico, and who to ask.

"Sorry," the voice finally said. "Nobody here's seen him for, oh, it must be a couple of days. Do you want to leave a message?"

It wasn't like Nico. Sure, if he wasn't working on something, he'd drop out of sight for a while. But if he was on a job, he checked in like clockwork. Even joked about it. Gotta file reports, keep the resident agent happy, make him think you're earning your pay.

Have to drive by his place, see if he was there. Maybe on the way home.

There was a tap at the door of Pike's office. He looked up to see Sid Stoddard's secretary, Rae, who had been with the firm as long as Sid had, and was nine years older than God. "You were out of the office this morning," she said, "so you weren't here when Mr. Stoddard called in from the hospital. He asked if you would stop by there, so he could talk to you about filling in for him on a couple of cases."

"Did he say when I should come?"

"No. I think he was thinking after work today, because he said 'this evening.' But he didn't exactly say."

"All right. I'll go by on my way home. You have any files that I should take with me, or anything?"

"Mr. Stoddard didn't tell me to send any files. I think he just wants to talk to you, and then if you have questions tomorrow after you get back here and look at the files, you can call him back, or go up there again."

"Fine. I'll stop and see him."

She turned to go. "Uh, Rae?" Pike said. "Any word on how Sid's doing?"

When she turned back, Pike could see the strain she had been hiding. "That man," she said. "I don't know what to do with him. He won't slow down. He just keeps going and going. He says he's fine, but the doctors, they look at you when you ask, and you can tell. They think he's overdoing."

"I'll see what I can do," Pike said. "Try to get him to take it a little easier."

"If you would," she said. She sniffed, took a handkerchief out of the sleeve of her dress, and blew her nose. "Lord knows I've tried, and he won't listen to me." She went out into the hall.

It was almost four when Pike's phone buzzed. "Mr. Pike," the receptionist said. "Mr. Baranowitz is on the line for you."

Pike punched the button on the phone and said hello.

"David, Maurice. I, uh, I wanted to ask you a favor, if you don't mind."

"Maurie, sure, as long as it doesn't involve doing any more legal work for you."

"No, nothing like that. I wanted, I wondered if you would mind, I haven't told Mickey yet, what you found out. I called her, she's coming over here for a drink tonight. I wondered if you would come and bring the evidence that you have. Present it to Mickey, and see her explanation. Maybe there's an innocent explanation, okay?" Pike could hear the pain in the old man's voice. He knew there wasn't an innocent explanation, but he didn't want to admit it to himself.

"Maurie, if you don't mind . . ."

"Wait a minute," Maurice said. "I know what you're gonna say. And I do mind. You call me in, you make these accusations about someone that's, that I think of as very close to me, you won't even come and say it to her face? I call that pretty damn sneaky, that's what I call it."

"Uh-huh," Pike said. "She's your employee, she takes your money, you ask me to look into it, then you tell me not to do anything. Then, when I find out what she did, it's sneaky if *I* don't tell her? That makes about as much sense as Marxist economics."

"David," Maurice said. His voice shook. "I don't know if I can do this, all right? It's hard for me. I have an emotional connection here. You're a professional person. You have some detachment. Won't you do this for me?"

"No," Pike said.

"All right. I can respect that. What I'll do then" — Maurice's voice hardened — "what I'll do is, when Sid gets out of the hospital, I'll ask him to help me. Sid's been my friend for over twenty years. He'll help me out."

"Maurie," Pike said, "that is really low! That is really under-handed, putting that kind of pressure on me. But I tell you what. I believe you're low enough to do it. So to prevent the stress on Sid, I'll do what you want."

"David, I knew I could count on you. I knew you wouldn't—"

"Spare me the crap, Maurie," Pike said, breaking in on him. "Tell me what time."

"Six thirty. She'll be here at six thirty. At my place."

"Fine. See you then." Pike put the phone down and sat, thinking.

From Maurice's place in Bel-Air, he'd have to backtrack to UCLA to see Sid at the hospital. That wasn't too far out of the way. Then if he wanted to stop by Nico's, that was nearly all the way back at the marina. Who wanted to drive back and forth across L.A. all evening? Go and see Nico the next morning then, on the way in. But he'd need Nico's notes to explain what Mickey had been doing. So he had to go by Nico's *before* he went to Maurice's.

So do it the other way, kill three birds with one stone, swing by Nico's place on the way to visit Stoddard at the hospital, on the way to Maurice's. That made the most sense.

Kashkin had parked his own car out on the street. Wore a set of white coveralls, had some name embroidered over the pocket— Brad or Fred or something like that. Carried a toolbox had a couple stereo speakers in it, coils of wire and a volt/ohm meter. Anybody notices, you're just working on the stereo. Curbside installation.

Climbed up the stairs to the level where the guy had his leased parking stall. Guy didn't even lock his car, but then, lots of people didn't, they figured somebody steals the radio, why get a broken window besides?

Kashkin opened the driver's door and knelt on the concrete beside the car. Slipped an eighth-kilo block of C-4 under the driver's seat, tight against the seat track on the inside. Poked the wire runs under the floor mat, along the hump in the floor where the drive shaft would be, if there was a drive shaft. But this was a Porsche, had a rear engine, didn't have a drive shaft, so the hump wasn't so big. What'd they need a hump for at all? That was a question for another day.

Paused and took a look around. Nobody on this level of the garage. Rubber squealing somewhere as someone took the tight turns on the exit ramp. Traffic noise from outside. That was another thing punks forgot to do. Get so involved, what they were doing, they shut their ears off, someone walked right up behind them, put the arm on them.

Another eighth kilo up under the dash. The car had factory air conditioning, made a nice flat place to put the charge, on top of the part where the duct flattened out and led to the air outlets. Ran the wires from that one down, crimped the two sets of wires together. Peeled back the carpet and sank a sheet-metal screw into the floor pan of the car for a ground. Stripped the end of one of the wires, wrapped the bare end around the screw, and tightened it down. Pushed the carpet back into place.

Car noise, getting louder.

Kashkin sat up and took a look. A car came up the ramp, but continued on past, and up to the next level. Kashkin leaned into the car again, located the ignition switch, and peered under the dash. The air-conditioning duct that made such a nice place for the charge made it a bitch to get at the ignition switch. Kashkin turned around and slid into the car, lying on his back on the floor. Managed to get one hand and a pair of pliers up into the space under the dash. Snipped one of the ignition wires through and then stripped the insulation off of the ends. Twisted the end of one of the wires from the charge together with the ignition wires, and put a wirenut on them.

Slid back out of the car, got his volt/ohm meter, and checked the circuit. Not hot, no juice, but good continuity. Just like the doctor ordered.

Detonators last. Always detonators last. That was another thing punks did. Stuck the detonators into the plastic, connected the detonator wires right away to the wire runs. Went on happily connecting things together, and then got hold of one of the hot leads to the ignition, instead of one that was switched. Those punks, if they survived, they sometimes got off, the jury was sympathetic to someone didn't have no fingers left, or was missing an arm or blind or something.

Kashkin reached into his toolbox, got out the Styrofoam box with the detonators. Trimmed the leads on one detonator and poked it into the block of plastic under the driver's seat, molding the plastic tightly around the detonator with his fingers.

The empty soda can Kashkin had set against the metal door to the stairs clanked on the concrete and clattered as it rolled away.

Kashkin was out of the car and had the door shut in two seconds flat. Closed up the toolbox, duckwalked to an Oldsmobile that was three cars down, and took a look, just bringing his head above the windowsill of the Olds, looking through the windows.

And it was the *guy*. The guy that never went home, never used his car until at least six in the evening, coming out of the stairs, heels clicking on the floor. Fourfuckingthirty and he was coming out to his car. Maybe he forgot something. Maybe he just came out to get something out of the car.

Kashkin crouched behind the Olds and waited. Heard the car door open. Close again. Heard the starter crank. Crank again. Engine fired. Car whined in reverse.

Kashkin stood up and watched the car disappear down the ramp to the exit.

That was another thing punks did. Got mad. Into each life some rain must fall, right? No reason get all bent out of shape about it. Catch the guy at home, or finish wiring it up tomorrow. Or see where he was going, finish it there.

Kashkin trotted to the stairs and headed down.

Pike followed Lincoln north out of the Marina, toward Santa Monica. Cars crowding out of the side streets to push into the lanes that were already bumper-to-bumper, brake lights popping on and off ahead as far as the eye could see. This time of day, the traffic would be the same all the way up Lincoln to PCH, and all the way out PCH to Malibu.

Fortunately Nico lived in Venice, on one of the side streets jammed into the acute angle between Venice Boulevard and Lincoln, so there were only a couple of miles to cover before Pike could swing off of Lincoln, away from the stream of commuters.

As he followed the narrow streets past crumbling stucco duplexes and neighborhood markets advertising specials on hamburger and toilet paper, Pike decided that Newton's Third Law of Motion must apply to neighborhoods. As Marina del Rey grew and prospered and became ever more glitzy and upscale, Venice decayed and moldered, and became ever more tacky and rundown. For every action, an equal and opposite reaction.

Nico's VW beetle was parked next to his trailer. Good, he was probably home. But the windows were shut, curtains drawn. Maybe he was entertaining. Pike pushed the doorbell button. Pushed it again and again. Could hear the dull buzz from inside. Opened the screen and banged on the door with his fist. No reply. Went back down the two steps that led to the door and crossed Nico's tiny patio to the hibachi. Lifted off the grate and ran his fingers through the feathery ash in the bottom of the cast-iron firebox. Finally found the spare key that Nico hid there, wrapped in aluminum foil. Went back and unlocked the door of the trailer.

With the curtains pulled it was dark inside the trailer despite the afternoon sun. Nobody in the living room. Dirty dishes piled in the sink. Walked along the passage to the bedroom at the back. Felt around on the wall, found the light switch and flipped it on.

Nico was lying face down across his bed, fully dressed.

For a moment he continued to lie there, and then he rolled over and sat up, knuckling his eyes.

"You given up answering the door?" Pike said.

"Bitches," Nico said. "Fucking bitches." He picked up a glass from a bedside table, took a swallow from it, and made a face. "Goddamn ice's melted," he said.

"You want to expand on that?" Pike said.

"Ice," Nico said. "You know. Cold stuff. Get it inna 'frigerator. 'S melted."

"No," Pike said. "The other part, about bitches."

"Oh," Nico said. "Yeah. I got it figured out. Women. People're egocentric, right? Sometimes think you're important to another person. Like you probably used to think you're important to Amanda.

"Well," Nico said, "in fact, the other person's as egocentric's you are, and you're not really important to her at all. You're only important to yourself. Now listen close. Now comes the tricky part.

"You see," Nico said, "we're all *so* egocentric that we fool ourselves, on little or no evidence, *think* we're important to someone. Like you prob'ly thought you were important to Amanda there. But in fact you aren't, it's just your delusion."

He pointed at Pike, blinked, looked at his finger, and then turned it and pointed at himself. "*My* delusion," he said in an undertone.

"So *then*," Nico said, "when for some reason you start, you come to doubt whether you're really important this other person, check it out, examine the situation carefully, see if you are, why, guess what? You can't find no evidence you're important, 'cause there never *was* any. So you decide she doesn't love you anymore. Which is true, 'cause she never did." He raised the glass and took another swallow.

"This sounds like kind of heavy philosophy," Pike said, "to be floating around in a vacuum. Does it refer to anybody?"

"No," Nico said. "Not *any*body. *Some*body. Gina. Decided to get married. Not to me. Some other guy. Meets this guy couple months ago, now she up and decides to get married."

"Uh-huh," Pike said. "Well, I'm not sure, but I think your theory just trashed the basis of romantic love, and maybe some other things besides."

"Damn right," Nico said. He raised the glass and tossed off what remained in it. "*Damn* right. Never was any basis for it. Bitches. Fucking *bitches*."

He tipped the glass, looked into the bottom, and seemed surprised to find that it was empty. He put it down and began looking around, on the bedside table, across the room at the dresser. Finally he rolled over onto his stomach, groped on the floor behind the bed, and came up with a bottle of K-Mart vodka. He unscrewed the cap and poured the glass half full.

"You want a drink?" he said, holding the bottle out toward Pike.

"Ah, shit!" Pike said. "Ah, shit, Nico. Not again! Oh Jesus, not again.

"No," Pike said, getting his feelings under control. "I don't want a drink. Actually, I came by to see if you ever got a line on Richard Morrissey."

"Oh," Nico said. "Oh, that. Yeah. Well, I got something. I can't say for sure what it is, but I got it." He heaved himself up off the bed and went down the passage to the living room. Pike followed.

In the living room, Nico sprawled across the couch, grabbed a battered spiral notebook from an end table, and began flipping the pages.

"This guy's down the laundry a day or so ago?" he said. "What day's this? Thursday? Two days ago then. Off-duty blue that I got to sit there. Nakamura and this other guy come out—not the one you want, another one. The blue follows 'em. Nakamura acts like he's doing something sneaky. Gets on the freeway. Gets off. Drives around. Changes cars twice. The blue sticks to 'em. Said it looked like they didn't really have their act together. Like if they had one more driver, or had some more practice, what they were doing, it would've been impossible to stay with 'em.

"This blue's thinking something interesting is going down, 'cause they spend all this time farting around changing cars and trying to make it hard to follow them. They go east on Ten. North on Eleven. North on One-oh-one. You know that place on One-oh-one, just north of downtown, where the lanes divide, there's like this CalTrans yard in the middle, between the two sets of lanes?"

Pike shook his head.

"Well, there is. About Vermont, along in there, there's this place, five or six blocks long, where there's like seventy-five or a hundred yards between the two lanes. Fifty yards anyway.

"So," Nico said. "He gets off on Vermont. Winds around and gets on a street goes under the freeway. In between the lanes, he goes in this place, what do they call them? Public Storage? In there. Parks the car. Goes into one of the storage things. Stays inside a half hour. Comes out, takes One-oh-one north to Hollywood, Hollywood west to Laurel Canyon, and home."

"So?" Pike said.

"So that's it."

"That's it. That's it? So how does this get me an address for Morrissey?"

"Dave," Nico said. "You got to go with the flow, okay? You get hold the end of something, you pull on it, see what comes out from under the bed. That's police work. You don't get no neat answers. Now, this isn't an address like you want. But it's something."

"So what is it?"

"How do I know what it is?" Nico said. "I can speculate, make some guesses. Or you could go look."

"Speculate a while, why don't you, before I do anything."

"Okay," Nico said. "Speculation: What's gonna be in that storage thing? Maybe just old machinery from his laundry. But then, why all the hoopla when he's on the way there? Maybe papers and records. Guy's a shylock, needs to keep track, who owes him money, who paid. Guy does protection. Needs to keep track, who's paid, who hasn't. Don't just want to leave those kind of records lying around. That'd be worth hiding, and this guy's going to a lot of trouble, hide whatever this is.

"But somehow," Nico said, "I don't think it'd be that, either. Bokkie said, when we talked to him there, this guy's dealing. So I think maybe drugs. Coke."

"So you're saying I should go take a look? Is that it?"

"Not so fast," Nico said. "Let's assume I'm right, there's coke in there. Whatta we know about coke? One thing, it's worth a lot of money, coke. Two, it don't have no serial numbers on it, so's you can't tell yours from somebody else's. Three, someone takes it, the cops won't help you get it back. What's all that tell us? It tells us there ain't just gonna be some piddly alarm on there, rings a bell when you open the door. There'll be booby traps. Minimum would be a shotgun aimed at the door. More likely would be a claymore mine, or maybe three or four of 'em, wired up separately so anybody walks in there, or maybe the first three anybodies, gets his ass made into corned beef hash."

"How about guards?" Pike asked.

"I see what you're thinking," Nico said. "But you're wrong. You're thinking how you would protect the stuff, like to keep someone from stealing it. But see, you're thinking like it was something legitimate, like money, or gold. Like a bank. Everybody knows there's money in a bank, right? No news there. You went up to some wiseguy, said to him, hey, for a grand I'll give you a tip, there's money down the First National, he'd laugh his head off. Knowing the money is there isn't any big thing, because they got a right to the money. It's okay for them to have the money. The cops will come and help protect it, some wiseguy goes in and tries to take it.

"This's different," Nico said. "Stuff's worth more than gold, and you're not supposed to have it the first place. Cops want it, they'll grab you for it, put you away. Competition wants it, they'll fucking whack you out for it. And if either of them just finds out where it is, you're in trouble. So you say guards, you're thinking like somebody watches it twenty-four hours a day, changes shifts, all that?

"Nah," Nico said. "They don't do it that way. If you protect it with guards, take an army with you when you go there, well, then you're protected, but the guards, every one of them, and everybody in the army, they all know where it is. And someday one of 'em'll think it's worth a shot, stealing it, or else he'll get into trouble, trade what he knows for some kind of deal. Or sell what he knows to the competition.

"So, they mostly figure it's better to be a little thin on the protection, only have, only take one or two guys along when they go there. That way they limit the number of guys can drop them in the shit. So no guards.

"That still leaves," Nico said, "the matter of booby traps. You want to walk in there? Find out the hard way what they decided to use? Me, I don't. I wouldn't mind telling some guys get paid to do that kind of thing where it is, let them go in there, see what they can find. But I wouldn't suggest walking in there."

"Telling somebody like who?"

"Like Jan Bokkie. He'd know who to give it to. Or I could dig up a name, somebody with the Bureau who'd like to make some brownie points, impress the brass."

"I'll think about it," Pike said. "Give me the address of the place, and I'll think about it."

"All right," Nico said. "You think about it."

"Oh," Pike said. "I almost forgot. I need your notes and those copies of checks and invoices and stuff back."

"Sure. No problem. Just gotta find 'em." Nico got up from the couch and crossed the room to the dining area. He went around behind the table and began to rummage through several piles of papers that filled the space between the table and the wall, muttering to himself.

"Not here. Maybe inna bedroom." He disappeared down the hall. Several minutes passed.

Pike got up and went down the hall to the bedroom. Nico was sitting on the bed, pouring himself another glass of vodka. "Sure you don't want a drink?" he said. "I can't find the damn stuff anywhere."

Pike shook his head. He got down on the floor and looked under the bed. Nothing. "You looked in the dresser?" he asked Nico.

"Yeah." Nico lay back across the bed and stared at the ceiling. "I looked there."

Pike crossed the room to the closet. Leaned over and looked in under the clothes. At the back, all the way to one side, was a scuffed leather briefcase. He reached in and pulled it out.

"How about in here?"

"Beats the shit out of me. Take a look."

Pike opened the briefcase. Inside were the invoices and canceled checks. "This is it," he said. "You got a box or something I can put it in?"

"Take it," Nico said. "Take the whole thing. Bring the briefcase back when you have time. I don't need the damn thing."

"Okay," Pike said.

"And think about the other thing,"

"Okay," Pike said. "I'll do that. I gotta go. Got places to be."

Kashkin stayed behind the Porsche when it left the trailer park. East on Venice Boulevard in the golden afternoon light. Took I-405 north to Westwood, and trailed it east on Wilshire, and up into the UCLA campus. Followed it into a parking lot at the UCLA medical center.

Maybe the thing to do was go get a burger, head out to Malibu, hook it up when the guy got home. Or tomorrow in the parking garage. Or was it worthwhile trying it now? How long did people stay in a hospital, when they went in to visit someone?

CHAPTER

15

MICKEY FOLLOWED THE SWEEPING curves on Sunset, across the top of the campus in the dying light. Right onto Bellagio, through the Bel-Air gate. Where the hell was Richie? Couldn't get him at the laundry. They said he was unavailable. Couldn't get Nakamura. They said Nakamura was unavailable.

Give the big jerk a hundred and twenty thousand dollars, and he disappears. No reason to stand still for that kind of crap. Most people, they got the stuff in hand before they forked over the cash. It was all right for Richie to delay a few hours in bringing the stuff back, but two days! Forget it. She'd have a few things to say, the next time she saw Richie.

Followed Bellagio as it wound around the fairways of the Country Club, and on into Bel-Air, past big houses set back from the street, with old trees and well-kept lawns. Turned off at the cul-de-sac and parked in Maurice's driveway.

Got out of the car, went up and rang the doorbell. The door opened. Mrs. Bjorklund was standing inside. Her matronly face lit up when she saw Mickey.

"Miss Mickey," she said. "Come in, come in. Mr. Maurice, he is not here yet." She stood back from the door. "Mr. Maurice, on the portable telephone he calls. He can't go on the freeway with his new glasses he has, it takes him longer to drive home. In a minute he is here, I think. Please." She gestured, inviting Mickey into the house.

Mickey inquired about Mrs. Bjorklund's daughter, and asked

about her arthritis. Mrs. Bjorklund gave the same sort of answers that she always gave, describing new medication and new grandchildren with equal enthusiasm. Mickey made appropriate responses and asked further questions, thinking: Maurie sounded funny on the phone. Had a quaver in his voice, but was very jovial. Like he was trying to put a brave front on something he was upset about. Maybe somebody died. Maybe it's that old creep Maurie plays golf with, has to be eighty-five if he's a day. Casimir, "call me Casey," Kratzmeier. Old bastard can play eighteen holes without a cart, then pretends he needs to hold on to your arm, climbing stairs. Sliding his fingers around, getting a good feel of the side of your breast. Maybe he croaked. That could've upset Maurie, they were such buddies.

Mrs. Bjorklund went off to the kitchen, the social amenities having been observed, and Mickey went into the sun room and mixed herself a drink. She was sitting in one of the overstuffed chairs, looking out through the glass doors at a couple of leaves being pushed around the pool by the wind, when she heard the doorbell ring. Heard Mrs. Bjorklund talking to someone, and footsteps on the tile of the hallway.

And then Maurie's lawyer was standing in the doorway, looking like he'd lost his last friend. Mickey stabbed a half-smoked cigarette into an ashtray.

"Wait," she said, "don't tell me. I'll get the name. Your face is familiar. Didn't you do Mel Gibson's stunts in that film, what was it, *Lethal* something? Am I right?

"Now don't tell me. I'll get it in a minute. It starts with *D,* right? Doesn't it? Donald, Derek, Dean, David. That's it, David."

"Hello, Mickey," the lawyer said.

"I don't believe it," she said. "He remembered my name. How long's it been, three days? Girl likes to think, she's thrown herself at some guy's head, maybe the morning after he'll have the courtesy to call. Flowers would be nice, but in L.A. that's too much to hope for. Maybe in Paris, or in Florence, flowers. In L.A. you wouldn't expect flowers. But you could hope for a call. How are you, how's it going, enjoyed last night. At least that. Maybe even more. Maybe something mushy, little flirtation. But three days with nothing, my God!

"I checked my toothpaste," Mickey said. "Stuff says it's guaranteed, kill all the bacteria in your mouth, leave your breath smelling like a perfume counter. That can't be the problem. Checked the deodorant too. No problem there, at least not according to the fine print on the spray can.

"So," Mickey said, "I figure it must have been something I said, right? So tell me, what was it? I trash your politics? Insult your mother? What?"

"Give it a rest, will you?" the lawyer said.

" 'Give it a rest,' he says. Takes my clothes off, has his way with me, gets up without so much as a backward glance and stalks off, drops off the face of the earth for three days, and says 'give it a rest.'

"Three days," she said. "Three days I sit by the phone. Called the telephone company on the second day. Asked them to check, make sure my line was working, no problems or anything. Couldn't understand why I didn't hear from you. Had to be technical difficulties.

"Hey," she said, "maybe it was *your* phone. That's it! I never thought of that. You couldn't call because *your* phone was out of order, right? All this time I thought you didn't call because you were mad at me, or turned off, or grossed out or something, it's just because your phone was on the blink."

"Are you through?" the lawyer said.

"No," she said, lighting another cigarette and exhaling a stream of smoke. "No, I am not through. This may all sound like it's in good fun, but I am seriously pissed off here. And I want to know just what in hell happened to you that you get it on with me, and then just drop out of sight until I happen to bump into you at the house of a mutual acquaintance. So talk.

"You're not," she said, "You aren't still married. I checked on that. Asked Maurice. He was very clear on that. Divorced and done with it. Because it's just exactly like what happens when you go out with a married man. One roll in the hay, and pow! Back to wifey. Sees you on the street, says, 'Oh yes, hello, how are you?' like he never had his face buried between your legs.

"Maybe you aren't familiar with this phenomenon," she said, "not being female. But that's exactly what it was like. Like making it with some guy who's married. You want to explain that? Tell me why it feels that way?"

"I, uh, I've been busy," the lawyer said.

"Sure," she jeered. "Busy! Give me a break."

"I have," the lawyer said, and she knew she was getting to him. Heard the plaintive note in his voice and knew she had him on the defensive. "One of my partners had a coronary," he said. "All his cases, the deadlines, filing dates, all that stuff, that doesn't stop. Somebody has to keep all the balls bouncing. I've had to keep his stuff up to date besides mine."

She spent ten minutes sparring with the lawyer, letting him know she didn't appreciate the way he'd treated her, at the end of which Maurice finally came home and took him off the hook.

"I'm sorry," Maurice said, bustling distractedly into the room. "Sorry, sorry. Didn't mean to keep you waiting. It's these new glasses." He took them off and held them up. "Horrible things. Can't get used to them. I'm going back tomorrow, see if there's something wrong with the prescription. Can't judge distances with them at all. David, you don't have a drink. Mickey, my dear, get David a drink. What do you want, David, beer? You drink beer, don't you? Or would you like something stronger? Get me a scotch, would you Mickey? Just from Century City to here, and I feel like I've been in the ring with Sugar Ray Robinson. Thanks, Mickey," taking the glass she handed him and raising it to his lips. "Here's how.

"Would you mind," he said, "would somebody mind putting my car in the garage? Now that it's getting dark, I'll never be able to do it, and Mrs. Bjorklund can't drive. Never learned, can you believe it? Sixty years old and never learned to drive.

"It's," Maurice said, "it's the garage, too, you know? I just've never been comfortable with that damn garage. House was built in 1923. Cars were smaller then. Even before these glasses, it wasn't easy. Couple of times I may've even got too close, scraped a fender there."

"Maurie," Mickey said, "you sound like you're about to have a conniption. Why don't you sit down and finish your drink, and David and I will take care of it. Where're your keys?"

Maurice gave her the keys, but then insisted on going along. They all trooped out to the driveway. Maurice's car was parked in the driveway behind the two others.

"How about this?" the lawyer suggested, being all bossy and male. "I move Maurie's car, put it in the street, give you the keys to it. You move yours, put it in the street. I come back and move mine, and then you put Maurie's in the garage? That do it?"

"Too much switching around," Mickey said. "You back Maurie's car out in the street, just stay in it. I move mine, come back and move yours, and you put Maurie's in the garage."

"Fine by me," the lawyer said, and handed Mickey his car keys.

"Wait a minute here," Maurice said. "I am not a potted plant. And I am not senile, either. I can drive perfectly well. It's just the garage, judging the distance. Now that it's getting dark, that's a little hard with these new glasses. I can perfectly well move one of these. Backing it into the street, that's no problem."

"Uh-huh," Mickey said. "Sure you can. How much did it cost to fix Mrs. Conrad's Rolls after that garden party when you moved my car to let Buffy get past? No thank you, Maurie. You watch. David and I will take care of this."

"You guys fight," the lawyer said. "I'll go move Maurie's car." He walked around, got into Maurice's Mercedes, and backed it into the street.

"Mickey," Maurice said. His voice sounded strange, and he was looking at her like. . . . like what? Like he had appendicitis but was going to tough it out, stay on his feet despite the pain. There was a helpless appeal in his face. "Mickey, for Christ's sake, I am not a piece of furniture here."

"All right," she said. If it was so important to him, why not? She handed him the lawyer's car keys. "All right Maurie, move the damn car."

She got into her car, started it up, and waited, the engine idling. Saw Maurice in the rearview mirror, coming around the back of her car, getting into the lawyer's car. Fumbling around, looking for the ignition.

Mickey had seen any number of car bombs. On film, that is. Even filmed a couple herself. Or maybe three. They all looked pretty much the same. There was a tall, rolling, red-orange flame, and fenders and doors and other pieces blew off of the car and flew around. And then the car was enveloped in flames from front to back and burned merrily. The special-effects guys got a plastic bottle, about half-gallon size, filled it partly with sand. Then filled it the rest of the way with gasoline. Wrapped the bottle with Primacord, put it in the car, and set off the Primacord. That ignited the gasoline and threw the gasoline-soaked sand up in the air. That gave you the boiling, red-orange flame. Looked great on film.

This one wasn't anything like that. There was a bright, white-yellow flash, and the windows of the lawyer's car blew out, and that was it. No rolling tower of flame, no fire afterward.

And then there was the noise. It didn't sound anything like the charges the special effects guys used. It had a hard edge to it and you felt it through your feet, and it pushed against your lungs, and there was a rolling echo that faded away into the distance and left your ears ringing.

Mrs. Bjorklund had hysterics, of course. Flew out of the house, shouting, "What is it? What is it?" Saw Maurice lying on the lawn where the lawyer had put him after lifting him out of the car. Immediately began screaming. Screamed while the police came, and the paramedics, and the Bel-Air private patrol, and even a fire truck. Screamed until the paramedics, disappointed in their efforts to revive Maurice, took Mrs. Bjorklund with them instead, lying on a cot in the back of their ambulance, wailing louder than the siren.

A nice policeman came then and asked Mickey a few questions. She gave some kind of answers. Another policeman moved her car, had to drive it across part of the lawn to get around what was left of the lawyer's Porsche, and then handed her her keys and said she could go.

Instead of leaving, she went back inside, to make sure the house was closed up properly. She found some food on the table in the kitchen; Mrs. Bjorklund must have been getting dinner for Maurice. Put it into the refrigerator, turned off the lights, and locked up.

Pike stood looking around Maurice's front yard. The shell of his car stood forlornly in the driveway. The paramedics and cops and firemen had departed, to deal with the world's next emergency. Nobody seemed to be around. How was he going to get home? Maybe use Maurice's phone and call someone. Then he saw Mickey coming out of the house. He waited as she crossed the lawn toward him. "Can you give me a ride down to Westwood?" he asked. "Or someplace where I can rent a car?"

"You could take Maurice's car," she said, then stopped for a moment. "I was nearly going to say he wouldn't mind. I guess I should say he isn't going to be needing it." She laughed and then stopped herself. "Sorry," she said.

"I could," Pike said. "But then I'd still have to rent something, besides getting somebody to drive me back up here so I could return his car."

"Okay," she said. "If you want a ride, fine. Hop in."

"I can't believe it's real," she said, after they were seated in her car and moving.

"It is," Pike said. Thinking: It had to be real. They did it by the numbers, just like they always did. A uniformed officer had taken Pike aside after the paramedics drove away, taking Maurice's housekeeper and Maurice's body, shrouded in a blanket. Across the yard, Pike could see another officer talking to Mickey.

"Your name, sir?" the officer said.

The officer made notes with a ballpoint in a spiral notebook. He wrote down Pike's home and office addresses and telephone numbers.

"The Porsche's yours, that right?"

Pike said that it was.

"Do you know anything about what caused the explosion?"

"From looking at it," Pike said, "I'd say a half pound or so of plastic explosive, wired to the ignition switch."

The officer seemed to find it interesting that Pike would have that information. He eyed Pike in silence for some time. Finally he made some more notes and asked another question.

"Do you know of any reason anyone would put a bomb in your car?"

"Yes," Pike said, "in fact I do." And gave a five-minute replay of his recent involvement with Blondie. The officer wrote furiously. "Morrissey?" he said. "Richard Morrissey? You got an address for him?"

"No," Pike said. "I wish I did, but I don't. Not a current one."

"All right," the officer said. "That's all I need for now. I'm sure the detectives will be around, ask you some more questions."

"I know it's real," Mickey said. "It's just, I don't know—he showed me his will, you know? A year or two ago, said he was changing it, and gave me a copy of the new one. And I said to him then, Maurie, you're going to be around a long time, what is this? And he just said he wanted to get it done." She shook her head.

"I guess you'll be handling the probate? Or someone from your firm?"

Pike taking it slow, not wanting to get into it, said, "No, I don't think so."

"But," she said, puzzled, "he said you had his will."

"He said *I* had his will? He must have been mistaken. I never had his will."

"Well, not you personally. He said, 'the lawyers.' He gave me a copy of it, and said that his lawyer—the man who was his lawyer then, what's his name, Sid something?—that he'd written it, and I asked him what he'd done with the original, and he said the lawyers had it. So I thought you'd have it, since you took over all his cases. From the man who was his lawyer before."

"Well, I don't. What's more, the firm doesn't either."

"How do you know?"

"Because I looked."

"When?"

"This afternoon."

"How could you look this afternoon? He wasn't dead this afternoon."

Pike looking at her as she drove, seeing her face in the glow of the dash lights, and then seeing much more of it in the passing streetlights. Thinking, well, here we go.

"Because I had him come in this afternoon, and I told him I wasn't going to do his legal work anymore, and I had pulled every file we had on his cases, and I gave them all back to him, and there was no will there."

"Not do his legal work? Why not?"

"Because, with your help, he got me involved in what might have been a criminal conspiracy. Or at least it would have looked like one to a prosecutor."

"What are you talking about, my help? What criminal conspiracy?"

"This porno film you're producing."

"I'm not producing it. Maurie was producing it. His idea, his script, his money. He just hired me to direct it," she said, getting the relationship straight, as if it mattered.

"Producing, directing—makes no never mind to me."

"Well, then you don't know much about the motion picture business," she said. "But what was that about some conspiracy? What did that mean?"

"If somebody does something that's against the law, that's a crime. If two somebodies do it, and they agreed to do it together, that's a conspiracy. That's a separate crime."

"But," she said, "there's no law against porno films."

So Pike explained the district attorney's current crusade against pandering—interpreted broadly to include paying an actress to have sex with an actor.

"You're shitting me," she said. "That's sick. It's twisted. They can't possibly get away with that."

"Well, they have been, at least so far. And to anyone that didn't know, it'd look like I was helping him. I incorporated the company, I was on the articles, I was still an officer—assistant secretary. That's been more than enough to get other people prosecuted in the past.

"And," Pike said, taking a deep breath, "you being director'd be enough to get you prosecuted. So you might want to think about things. I mean, if you're maybe going to have cops crawling around on your movie set, they might find other things that you'd rather not

SKIM

have them find. You might want to, I believe the expression is, clean up your act."

"Like what?" she said. "Find things like what?" Putting on a blank and innocent expression.

"You're good," Pike said, "you know? Really good. Maybe you should have been an actress instead of a director. But it doesn't quite work when the person you're talking to knows it's an act.

"Find things," Pike said, "like that you're dealing coke on some kind of major scale, or even that you made yourself a little un-authorized loan of fifty grand or so out of one of Maurie's bank accounts."

There was a stunned silence in the car. Then she pulled over to the curb, parked, and switched off the engine. They were on Gayley, halfway down the west side of the UCLA campus. On the west side of the street were rows of apartment buildings. On the east side were the buildings of the campus. Sporadic traffic moved past.

"What did you say?" she said. "About taking money?"

"Spare me the injured innocence," Pike said. "I said you took fifty grand out of one of Maurie's bank accounts. I've got the canceled checks and invoices to prove it, and I've had an investigator talk to the guys who paid the kickbacks. And the reason Maurie wanted both of us to come over tonight was so he could brace you with it and see what you said."

"Uh-huh," she said, nodding to herself. "I knew something was wrong. That's why he was so upset. I thought it was because someone died."

"It wasn't that some*body* died," Pike said. "Some*thing* did. I think it was his relationship with you. And that's what had him upset."

And watched as she burst into tears.

Pike handed her his handkerchief, feeling like a fool, and sat while she sniffled, and blew her nose, and sniffled again, and blotted at her eyes. Finally she quieted down.

"What will happen now?" she said.

"About what?"

"About Maurice being dead. I don't know what you call it. About what happens to his property and stuff."

"I don't know. I haven't thought about it yet. I guess it depends on who inherits his estate."

"I think," she said, "that I do. Or at least most of it."

Pike laughed. "Well, isn't that ironic? In a sense, if you inherit his estate—assuming you're right about what the will says—then when you forged those invoices you were just borrowing your own money. So no harm. Of course there's still the little matter of your dealing coke."

"I notice," she said, icily polite, "that you didn't say you had any evidence of that. Besides, what if I did?"

"It's against the law."

"Oh, poo! It is not."

"Well maybe I misunderstood what I heard, but I had a guy read me chapter and verse on it the other day. Section one-one-three-five-oh of the Health and Safety Code. Possession for sale makes it a felony."

"That's asinine. That's just persecution. There is simply nothing wrong with cocaine. My God! It isn't as if it were heroin or something. It should be as legal as alcohol."

"You talk about it as if it were a public service."

"Public service? Sure it is. It's entertainment is what it is. Besides, creative people aren't subject to the same standards. They need that kind of stimulation, the ability to be able to stay awake to work on an idea when they're hot."

"I hope there aren't too many of them that think they're entitled to a different set of standards. They'll find out what Zsa Zsa Gabor found out when she got that traffic ticket—the ordinary people think the same standards should apply as apply to them."

She put the car in gear and pulled away from the curb in silence. After a block or so, she said, "Where do you want to go?"

"There's a Hertz on Westwood Boulevard. That'll be fine."

And she didn't say another word until she pulled up outside the rental agency. As Pike was getting out of the car, she asked, "What are you going to do?"

"About what?"

"David, all right? About all this," she took one hand off of the steering wheel and waved it in a vague arc. "About Maurice being killed, and about the other things you said." She looked at Pike, then looked away, and then looked at him again. "About Maurice's money. And what you said about thinking I was selling coke."

"It's not all one piece," Pike said, shrugging. "What I do about part of it will be different from what I do about another part of it. Part of it, in a way, well, it isn't any of my business. He wasn't even my client anymore. And yet in a way he was, when what the lawyers call 'the operative facts' went down. So that part, I just don't know.

"On the other hand," he said, "I can tell you what I am going to do about part of it. Dominic Nakamura and Richard Morrissey are going to take a fall. I don't know how yet, but it's going to happen. They wouldn't leave me alone, no matter how much I tried to leave them alone, so that's it. There is going to be a shitstorm, and they're going to be caught without an umbrella."

"Don't you think," she said, "haven't you thought that maybe that could involve me, too? I mean, if the police trace what they were doing as far as who bought from them?"

"I notice," he said, "that all of a sudden we're concerned that something might not be legal, that two minutes ago we were saying poo, it's perfectly fine."

"Will you just answer the question?"

"I can't tell you," he said. "It depends on what kind of records they keep. Depends on what kind of deal they're offered. All I can say at this point is that it's a definite maybe that you could be involved."

"Why do you have to do this?"

"Because they won't leave me alone."

"I'll talk to them," she said, brightening. "I can talk to Richard. He'll listen to me."

Pike shook his head. "I wouldn't believe it if they promised, cross their hearts and hope to die," he said. "Sorry 'bout that, but it's how I feel."

He got out of the car, stood at the curb, and watched her pull away into the traffic. Westwood traffic, BMWs and Mercedeses outnumbering Chevrolets and Fords.

CHAPTER

16

"I COULDN'T KEEP FROM thinking, you know?" Dossie nodded at the open curtains across the sliding glass door. "Wondering if he might come while we were here. Look in, see us."

They were under the sheet now, lying close, hips and shoulders touching.

"But just for a moment," Dossie said.

"What?"

"That guy you were talking about. The one you got in the fight with. That you think set the bomb. I worried about him seeing us. Then I," she said, "I got, uh, involved, and I wasn't thinking about that anymore."

"Involved," Pike said. His hand moved gently over the inside of her thigh, stroking her. "Is that what we're doing, getting involved?" And watched her blush, even her neck getting red.

She hit him lightly on the shoulder with her closed fist. "You know what I meant."

"I suppose I do. I got pretty involved myself there for a while," he said. "But I also think I could get involved."

"With me?"

"Of course with you. Who else did you think?"

She was in his bed. Next to him. Could see him next to her when she opened her eyes. Thinking about where she was, she could say to herself, What's going on? What am I doing here? Who is this guy? Or she could say, It's Dave, I know him. He's nice. She said to him, "Millie's coming back early. Did I tell you that? I was going to take a couple of weeks off, travel around. Then go back to Texas.

"She," Dossie said. "She's going to know that we're seeing each other." She frowned. "Why do I worry about my sister? I'm old enough to do what I want."

"Uh-huh," Pike said.

"But even so, I've always been concerned about what she thought of me."

"Uh-huh," Pike said.

"I mean, I'm an adult. There's nothing wrong with seeing some-one, if I want to. Right? I mean, people go on cruises, have a thing with somebody on the boat, never see them again. Nothing wrong with that, is there?"

"We could go on a cruise," he said sleepily. "Charter a boat down in Baja. Spend a week, or maybe two."

"Go on!" she said. "Don't give me a lot of bull."

"No. We could, really. Go from one harbor to another on the coast, or over to the islands. Anchor, snorkel. Take it easy."

She moved closer and snuggled against him, listening.

"Load up with provisions at the beginning. Stock plenty of beer. Maybe take some meat down frozen from here. The meat in Baja is not real good. Or catch fish."

"What kind of boat would we have?"

"Sloop. Thirty, forty footer."

"Where'ud we go?"

"La Paz to Loreto, Puerto Escondido. Any of those places around there."

"I'd like that," Dossie said. Getting into it, treating it as if it were something they were planning together. She thought, briefly: But what'll Millie say? Then made an effort and stopped worrying about Millie and what Millie would think and say. If she concen-trated, she could make herself feel almost comfortable, at peace. She could close her eyes and think about doing things without having to explain. For a moment she pictured herself doing whatever she wanted, just doing it, not thinking about doing it or worrying about doing it. She tried to imagine an island and the boat. But she saw herself explaining to her sister, justifying herself.

Oh wow! Mickey thought. Oh wow! *Residuary beneficiary.* That was what the copy of the will said. Residuary beneficiary. After he left the prints of his old films to the motion picture museum, along with his scripts and some junk. And a hundred thousand each to a son and a daughter he hadn't seen in ten years.

Residuary beneficiary. The old house in Bel-Air, on an acre and a half. And almost three square blocks of West L.A. real estate, right in the path of the high-rise development that was marching down Santa Monica Boulevard toward the Pacific Ocean. She knew he owned that stuff. Plus there'd be bank accounts, stocks, bonds. Who knew what all?

The film that won the Palme d'Or at Cannes the year before had been made for $1.2 million. She'd only been ten percent there, or a little more. It was going up quickly, of course, and there was the money Maurice owed her on the film she was directing. So it would have only been a matter of time. But now! Now she could borrow twice that much on a mortgage on the Bel-Air house tomorrow.

Not too fast, though. Wouldn't do to rush into things. Take up the option on the book first, and get someone started on the screenplay. Then look around, see who was going to be available in, say, six months. Line up a couple of cameramen, start making up a list of names for a crew.

It was all going to be peaches and cream.

Except for one problem: what was the goddamn lawyer going to do? He'd been all funny the night Maurice got blown up. Well, you could understand some of it, I mean, it had obviously been meant for him. But that was no reason to come down all over her. She'd paid back what she'd borrowed from Maurice. Every cent. And as for the thing with the coke, well, my God! Who cared about that? Everybody did that.

Still, it was a blessing in disguise Richie had been so slow bringing back the last load she'd paid him for. Couldn't trust what the damn lawyer was going to do. Too dangerous to fool around with it anymore. The thing to do was call Richie and cancel that order. Get the money back from him. Stay completely away from coke for a while. Like the lawyer said, clean up your act. Besides, who needed to sell coke anymore?

Mickey giggled and looked at the copy of the will again. Residuary beneficiary. Wow!

She picked up the phone and dialed. Listened to the ringing, and then heard the message machine pick up. "Richard," she said, "this is me. Call me right away, do you hear? Right away. I need to talk to you before you do anything, you understand? Call me just as soon as you come in."

She put the phone down. Residuary beneficiary.

Maybe it was just from being scared.

You got scared, and when it was over the adrenaline had to go somewhere, so it went into being mad. Whatever the explanation, the more Pike thought about it, the more pissed off he got.

When you did someone's legal work, you became involved with him. You were on his side, but in a much more intimate sense. His problems became your problems, and the solutions that you worked for, those were your solutions as much as the client's.

What was that line? Bogart had delivered it in *The Maltese Falcon*. Something about when somebody kills your partner, even if he was a son-of-a-bitch, you have to do something about it. Something like that. Maybe it applied to clients as well as partners. Maurice *had* been a son-of-a-bitch, and he wasn't even a client, at least not when he'd been killed. But that didn't change the way it felt.

And it got more personal than that. Blondie, or whichever one of his little friends had planted the bomb, had been aiming at Pike. No question about it. So, wait for the cops to plod through it, find Blondie, read him his rights, turn him loose on bail? Hell with it. Nico said this storage place was the end of something. Let's pull on it, see what it's attached to.

Pike tapped on Mike Blaylock's door. Blaylock looked up from his desk. "Davey, come in, come in. Hell of a thing about Sid, huh?"

Pike sat down across the desk from Blaylock. "Mike," he said, "I need a photographer to do some stuff for me on the q.t."

"We aren't," Blaylock said, "We don't do that anymore."

"Do what?"

"Do," Blaylock said, "You know, all that sneaking around and taking photographs in bedroom windows and all that. Those of us, that is, who practice, ahem, domestic relations law.

"We don't need to anymore," Blaylock said. "Got no grounds anymore, divorce. Just 'irreconcilable differences,' which, if one of 'em says it's there, it's there. Don't need to prove adultery, or like that. Plus which, it doesn't do any good anymore. Used to be, if you could show you had the 'innocent spouse,' well, fine. Judge'd divide the community property, give your side more than half, teach the adulterous bastard on the other side a lesson.

"Alls it did," Blaylock said, "alls it did was *both* sides pointed the finger at each other, and *both* sides proved they were *both* shits. So when they rewrote the law however many years ago there, they took all that out. Straight fifty-fifty on the community now, and no grounds. Don't need photographs."

"Not even for custody?" Pike said. "Don't you need to prove, you know, somebody's fooling around, or whatever, keep them from getting custody of the kids?"

Blaylock sat up in his chair. "Where have you been the last twenty years? We had a sexual revolution, case you didn't notice. Least California did—can't say about the rest the country. Nobody

decides custody anymore based on who's sleeping with who. Even
if they're gay, longs they don't do it in the living room in front the
kid, doesn't matter. The stuff that would make a judge sit up and
take notice, he's thinking about custody, I mean, that stuff you
couldn't take a picture of, it's all psychological now, not who they
sleep with."

"Well, if you say so."

"Talk to Fred, or one of the P.I. guys, they use photographers for
accident scenes, stuff like that. Or for following somebody around,
guy says he's all crippled up from the accident, get a picture of him
doing a double back flip off the high board."

"All right," Pike said. "I'll try that."

"Sure. Do that," Blaylock said. He lowered his voice and leaned
forward over the desk. "By the way, what it was you really came in
about?" He paused. "Don't worry. I'll vote for you."

"Mike, what in hell are you talking about?"

"As managing partner."

"Mike, Jesus! Sid's not dead. And if he were, I wouldn't be
running for managing partner."

"Bullshit! He may not be dead, but you don't think he's ever
coming back to work, do you?"

That slowed Pike down. Probably a good guess. But it didn't
change how he felt. "Listen to me, Mike. If nominated, I will not
run. If elected, I will not serve. That clear enough?"

"Have it your way, Dave. Just keep in mind you can count on
me."

Pike left, shaking his head. He walked down the corridor, around
a corner, and looked in at the door of another office. Fred Higgins
was inside. Higgins did P.I. defense, mostly of aircraft crash cases.
He had four depositions spread out on his desk. He was sticking
colored plastic paperclips on the side of the pages. He looked up over
the tops of his reading glasses. "Dave," he said, "long time and all
that. Come in. Set. Tell me, as my kid says, what's shaking."

"I was talking to Mike," Pike said.

"Crazy Mike. What's he up to now?"

"He's got me running for managing partner."

"Well, that figures."

"Fred, Christ, not you too? 'Figures' why?"

"Because you're the best guy for the job."

"Since when is that any criterion for anything? Besides, it's fifty percent bureaucratic nitpicking, fifty percent truckling to a bunch of prima donnas, and fifty percent headaches."

"You've got too many fifty percents. Anyhow, Mike has a personal reason he wants you to get it."

"Like what?"

"Because he wants your office. He figures, you go to managing partner, take Sid's old office, then he bids for yours."

Pike shook his head. "Byzantine, that's what he is. He'd fit right in in the Politburo. Well, to business. You got a photographer you recommend?"

"You going to use him to testify? Or just to get the film?"

"What's it matter?"

"It matters. Believe me, it matters. Maybe you got some accident scene photos, and they're taken a particular time of day, when the light just maybe puts a very black shadow over a driveway or something. Explains how your guy happened not to see the other car. I got one guy, wears a coat, tie, earnest, kind of dumb looking. You want somebody to explain to the jury how these photos are a fair representation of the scene, he's your boy. Looks 'em right in the eye, says 'Oh yes, this's how it is. Looks just like this.' Also, when the other side tries to trip him up, point out how these photos weren't taken, the accident wasn't even at that time of day—well, he's fast on his feet. He'll think of a reason why the pictures were taken then, and it wasn't your fault, and it wasn't his fault— nobody'd try to make it look different than when the accident happened. Gee, no, never.

"Okay," Higgins said. "That's one guy. Then I got another guy, I wouldn't have him testify on a bet. Kind of an over-the-hill hippie, you know? Hair in a ponytail, only it's all going gray now. Drives this van with Peace and Love and all that happy shit painted on the side of it. And he's absolutely crazy. If you need someone to hang in the wheel-well of an airplane while it takes off and get pictures of the landing gear as it comes up, he'll do it. And get good clear shots too."

"I don't need testimony," Pike said. "Sounds like your hippie is the guy for me."

"St. Clair his name is. Eugene St. Clair. Likes to be called Saint. I'll get you the number. And, Dave,"—he paused a moment and looked at Pike over the tops of his glasses—"I'll vote for you, too. For managing partner."

It was one of those days. Fucked up from the word go. First Richie overslept, missed his flight out of Vegas, had to sit in the airport forty-five minutes and take a later flight. Then he went to get his Jeep out of short-term parking. Threw his bag into the back, yawned, and rubbed his eyes. Four days in Vegas, and he was thrashed. Yawned again and stretched and got into the Jeep and the battery was dead. Had to wait another forty-five minutes while triple-A came and jumped it.

With all the delays, it was rush hour. No sense even trying to go up 11 to downtown, get on the 101. That'd be like a parking lot, going through the interchange there. Even going up the 405 to Santa Monica Boulevard was stop and go. And across Santa Monica to West Hollywood was the same.

His apartment was behind a house in West Hollywood. Once it had been the back bedroom and the garage for the house. Then someone had walled up the connecting door to the bedroom, finished the inside of the garage, and rented it out. Richie drove into the driveway and stopped. Got out of the Jeep, hoisted his bag out of the back, and froze. His door was standing open.

Come back from four days out of town, and your front door is open. He dropped the bag on the concrete of the driveway and slid around to where he could take a look through the open door. Two men were in his living room, moving around. Fury filled Richie's head.

Then, just before he went in there and strangled both of them, another man walked into view, wearing a blue uniform, a badge, and a gunbelt. A cop. The fucking cops were in his apartment.

And what do you know, they had a search warrant. They showed it to him when he carried his bag inside. He didn't bother to read the printed part, just what was typed, where they had typed in what they were looking for.

And he found himself thinking: smart. Dominic is so smart. Because what was typed on the warrant was: blasting caps, explosive, wire, batteries, timing devices, information or literature about explosives or bomb-making. The geek must have had his accident, and first thing the heat comes looking for Richie. And surprise, he isn't home. He's been out of town, and can prove it. And doesn't know the first thing about what happened to the geek, except that it didn't take a genius to figure out that apparently the guy got blown up by a bomb. And because of Dominic, he wasn't even fucking in town. All right!

They wanted to know where he'd been. He took the folded-up receipt out of his wallet and stuck it under their noses. Laughed in their faces. Listened to them tell him not to leave town, and laughed again. They couldn't do shit, and they knew it, and he knew they knew.

So they made a mess of things, to get even. Threw things around, dumped drawers out. Turned furniture over. Richie kept his cool, got some orange juice out of the refrigerator, sat and sipped it and waited until they were through and left. Then, right away, he picked up the phone and called the laundry to check in.

The girls were all well trained. Dominic had them trained. They knew it was Richie, they knew the voice. But all they'd say on the phone was Mr. Nakamura is not in at this time, would you like to leave a message? So that didn't tell him shit. Was Dominic still up north in Oceano, looking at property? Maybe he'd set that up to give himself an alibi, too. Had to hand it to old Dom. He did something, he did it for two or three reasons, not just one. But maybe he was back?

What to do? Go see Mickey? Check things out with her? He'd thought maybe he'd make Mickey jealous, taking off to Vegas. Didn't call her, wasn't around where she could find him. Show her how important he really was.

The message light was blinking on the phone machine. Hadn't noticed it before, he'd been working so hard on staying cool in front of the cops. Played the messages back. Couple calls about being Mr. Muscle for parties. And one from Mickey, call me right away. Maybe she'd changed her mind. Maybe she missed him. Picked up the phone and dialed her number.

"Sweetheart? It's me, Richie."

"Richard," she said, snotty tone in her voice, not being sweet at all, "where in hell have you been? I've been calling you for four days."

"Oh," he said nonchalantly, "here and there. Here and there. I was, I went up Vegas a couple days. Just got back and found your message. What's the deal?"

"I'll tell you what the deal is,"—still sounding snotty. "You have some money of mine. I want it back."

Richie had a sudden twinge of guilt. Dominic said never to talk business on the phone, and particularly not on your own, personal phone where you lived. The cops would have that tapped for sure. Calling Mickey was supposed to be a social call, and now she was turning it into business.

"Uh, sweetheart," he said, "can we talk about this another time? Maybe lunch today? Could we?"

"No," she said. "You've stalled around enough with this."

That wasn't fair. He hadn't stalled a thing. The man said take a week off, he took a week off. No stalling there.

"Well, uh, see," Richie said. "I, uh, a deal is a deal. I don't think I can get your money back."

"Richard, that is crap and you know it. That was a cash-and-carry deal, and I didn't get my merchandise."

Richie relaxed a little when she said that, "merchandise." He'd been afraid she'd say *coke,* or *girl,* or *blow,* or one of the things that meant drugs. But "merchandise," hey, nobody'd figure that out. That was cool.

"It's been four days," Mickey said. "I only gave you the money because I trusted you to go and get the merchandise and bring it right back. But four days, that's too much. The deal's off, and I want the money back."

"Well," Richie said, "the, uh, the merchandise is already ordered. It isn't like a department store. This's special-order stuff. Once it's ordered, well, you've bought it."

But she wasn't taking that kind of an answer. "Richard." Her voice hardened. "I'm not asking you, I'm telling you. You go and get my money, and bring it back to me. Now. Today."

"Hey," Richie said, "chill out, don't get all stressed here. You don't have a problem. There's been a little delay, I admit that. But no problem. The merchandise is on it's way. You've as good as gotit."

"Richard," she said, "we are not communicating here. I'm telling you I don't *want* it. What I want is my deposit back, and the quicker the sooner. You understand that? Merchandise no, money yes. That clear?" There was a click as she hung up. Richie shook his head and put the phone down. She could be a hard lady when she got it into her head.

So forget going to see Mickey. Not in the mood she was in. Take a spin by the laundry, check in. Maybe Dom'd be there by the time he got in. And he needed to go by the stash, pick up his gun, that Dominic had made him leave there. Felt naked without it. Wasn't supposed to go anywhere near the stash without doing all the car changes, all that razzle-dazzle stuff, make sure he wasn't followed.

So, he'd get Titch or someone to go down there with him, if Dominic wasn't around.

If Dominic was there, he'd talk to him, see about getting the lady her money back. Never heard of anyone ordering the stuff, paying for it, and then wanting the money back. He didn't think Dominic'd go for that. But he'd ask.

And it wasn't even 10 A.M. yet. What a day!

"Five bills," St. Clair said. "In advance. That's if, that's if it only takes the one afternoon, right? Plus expenses, I have any. Extra for the prints, right? You look at the proof sheets, tell me what ones you want blown up, then you pay for that."

"All right," Pike said. "When can you fit this in?"

"You tell me, man. This afternoon? Wednesday any time. Or Thursday morning. Or you tell me what other time you want, I'll see I can fit it in."

"How about this afternoon?"

"Fine by me, man. I'm going to need one helper. Carry the camera bag, hold things for me. You furnish the guy or I hire him. I don't care. Another hundred if I hire the guy."

"Suppose I come and do it?" Pike said.

"Your funeral, man, you know? Up to you. Tell me again what kind of place it is?"

"Like I said. Mini-storage. The one in the middle of the 101 freeway, near Vermont. Stucco buildings, three or four of them in a fenced yard. Electric gate into the yard, punch in a combination and it opens. Long, narrow buildings, two story. Row of metal roll-up doors along each side. No windows. Storage rooms on the second floor, that open off a hallway in the middle. Open stairway at each end of each building goes up to a door to the hallway."

"And this one's ground floor, or second?"

"Ground floor."

"Uh-huh," St. Clair said. "How do we get in this gate?"

"Rent one of the storage things. I'll take care of that."

"Alarms? Are we worried about alarms?"

"I'd assume so. If what I think is there is in there, then it's probably got alarms all over it. Or worse. Maybe booby traps."

"I can dig it," St. Clair said. "Groovy. So we don't go in the door. We do it another way, like go in through the roof."

"All right," Pike said. "Tell me where to meet you."

"My place. I'll have everything we need in my van."

CHAPTER

17

RICHIE STOOD UNDER THE northbound lanes of the freeway and watched the guy climb the stairs at the end of the building. It was the same guy. Fucking cops got it wrong as usual. Geek was supposed to be dead, cops are looking for who whacked him, warrants, the whole nine yards and he's walking around *alive!* Couldn't goddamn believe it. And he was at the *stash!* It was impossible, but there he was. Richie had driven by, seen him coming out of the door of the office, at the storage place, with another guy. A scruffy-looking one. Parked the Jeep, walked back, and stood and watched him start up the stairs.

Dominic hadn't been at the laundry. Still in Oceano. And Titch wasn't around. Nothing to do. So Richie decided to run by the stash, pick up his gun. It was one of Dominic's biggest no-nos, going there without taking all the precautions to make sure he wasn't followed. But hey! who'd know? So here he was, standing under the freeway, listening to the big diesels roar past overhead, and watching the geek go in the door on the second floor.

Dominic had said to leave it alone. He was pretty definite about that. But if Richie was going to be an executive, he'd have to act independently, wouldn't he? Wouldn't always be able to check things with Dominic, clear all the decisions before they were made. Besides, how could he check things with the man, he was still out of town? Wouldn't be back until Saturday, and that was another whole day.

Richie could feel the suppressed fury boiling in him, keeping him on the edge all the time. Asshole had made him look dumb, not once, but twice. And whatever Dominic said, that was before the guy had turned up at the stash. If Dominic knew that, he'd tell Richie to do something about it, and damn quick, too. He could handle it. He had the address. Some place out in Malibu. It should be easy enough to find. Or just take care of it here. While they were inside the storage place. Maybe that'd be better?

"We walk down the hall, right?" St. Clair said. "On the way, I pace off how far it is from the end the building to the unit you want."

"All right," Pike said.

"We put the bags and shit in the room you just rented, right? We take a look at the door of the unit that's above the one you're interested in. I wait in the room you rented while you go back and get the door open. Bolt cutters, kick it in, however you want. Then I come back and in we go."

"I thought you were getting paid to do this," Pike said. "How come I'm getting the door open?"

"I'm getting paid to take pictures, man. The fee don't include breaking and entering. You don't want to do it, hey, that's cool. I'll go out, hire me a guy, come back and do it tomorrow."

"No," Pike said. "No, fuck it. I'll do it."

"That's the spirit," St. Clair said. "Here, this bag's the tools."

It was a canvas bag that had been white once, but now was a dirty gray, with an abstract pattern of grease stains. It had two loop handles, one of which had torn and been mended with a piece of rope. The handles cut into Pike's hand as he walked. The bag was heavy enough that Pike had to walk lopsided carrying it. He stopped at the top of the stairs to change hands, and then followed St. Clair through the door.

"Ought to be about here," St. Clair said, nodding at a door. Pike put the tool bag down and changed hands again, taking the opportunity to look the door over. There was a hasp and a laminated steel padlock. He picked up the tool bag and they continued down the hall and into the room he had rented and put the bags on the floor.

"You want some bolt cutters?" St. Clair asked.

"No," Pike said. "If we cut it off somebody's going to notice that, sooner or later. And they'll make a fuss. Let me see if I can get it open. You got some stiff wire and a pair of pliers?"

"In the bag there, man."

Pike opened the bag, found the wire, took the pliers, and bent a small L on the end of the wire. Then he went back along the hall to the door with the padlock.

He had to rebend the wire twice before it was right; then he ripped up and down the tumblers and the lock popped open in his hand. He hung the lock on the shackle and opened the door for a quick look. The room was stacked almost to the ceiling with cardboard file-storage boxes. Leaving the door ajar, Pike went back to the room where St. Clair was waiting.

"It's open," Pike said.

"All right. Bring the tools."

By the time Pike got there with the tools, St. Clair was pacing among the boxes, muttering to himself.

"About there," he said. "You think? Help me move this stack of boxes."

When the boxes were dragged out of the way, St. Clair took a green cordless electric drill and a small battery-powered vacuum cleaner from the tool bag. He knelt on the floor.

"Here." He handed Pike the vacuum. "You hold this. Turn it on when I start to drill, and hold it close to the drill bit. Not touching, but close."

"What does that do?"

"You think there's alarms down there, right, or booby traps? Maybe a contact switch on the door. Maybe pressure switches under a mat inside. But maybe it's ultrasound, or a photocell. Something breaks the beam, and ring! There goes the bell. I drill through this stuff, there's chips, pieces of wood and shit, falls in the hole. Maybe that's not enough to break the beam, set the thing off. But you never know." A faint smile came and went on his face. "Better safe than sorry."

St. Clair kept the drill turning even after it broke through, pulling it back spinning out of the hole, making sure that it brought the chips and shavings with it. He handed the drill to Pike, bent and took a lumpy object from his camera bag. He held it up.

"This's fiber optic. Fits on the camera body, lets it shoot around corners. Or down in holes.

"I'm shooting this three times," he said. "Once with a strobe, change backs, shoot it once ambient light. Don't think there is much, but we'll give it a try. Fast film. Twelve hundred ASA. Then we change backs again, shoot it infrared. Probably not worthwhile, but you never know. Usually just comes up with a bunch of blurs, but sometimes it tells you something. This coupling on the side of the probe unit here, you can put on a strobe. Light comes out the end of the probe, doesn't need another hole in the floor to get a light in. Only trouble is, when you try to use it like a flood, see what you're gonna get, there isn't enough light comes through the probe, light things up very well. So it's hard to see."

He snapped a camera body onto the fiber-optic probe, lowered the probe into the hole in the floor, bent over, and put his face to the viewfinder. "Can't see shit," he said. "Maybe we're not through, or maybe there's an inner ceiling. Lemme turn the light on."

He fiddled with the strobe unit, then bent over again and peered through the viewfinder. "More like it," he said. "We're through, but can't see much." He began to trigger the camera, turning in small, precise increments.

When he had made a full circle he stood up. "Here," he said, handing Pike the camera and probe assembly. "Hold this while I get out the next back."

It took at least an hour, or maybe an hour and a half. Although when Pike looked at his watch as he was stowing the camera bag in the van, it had been just over ten minutes. Then they were inside the van and the doors were closed, and they were moving through the gate.

"I'll have the contact sheets for you this afternoon," St. Clair said. "Around five? That soon enough?"

"Yeah," Pike said. "That'll be fine."

Dossie looked in the drawers in the kitchen, found an apron. Poked around some more and found some pork chops in the freezer, and a couple of potatoes in the vegetable bin. There was a microwave and she put the pork chops in it to thaw. She washed the potatoes and pricked them with a fork, because Momma said they would burst if you didn't. Four hundred degrees, they'd take an hour. Too early to start cooking the pork chops yet.

Dossie walked around the kitchen. She caught sight of her reflection in the black glass door of the oven. She looked at herself and thought, Shit! Look at you, girl. Here you are in his house, feeling all sappy and goo-goo. Acting like you're living together, cooking him dinner, second night in a row. Thinking about how he'll come home, find dinner all ready, and you'll climb into bed again.

That part was a surprise. The bed thing was definitely a surprise. There'd been a couple of boys in Lubbock, at the junior college. But they'd been in a hurry—two minutes of heavy breathing and it was over, before it began to get good. And sneaking around, and feeling guilty, and being ashamed to look Momma in the eye, for fear she'd know. But now! Talk about night and day! He wasn't a boy, he was a man. Not in a hurry, sure of what he was doing. Taking his time.

Taking time for her. Making sure she was there, she was feeling it, until it all got too intense, and her insides melted and she lay there panting.

The bell rang as she was thickening the sauce from the pork chops, reducing it in the frying pan with a little cornstarch to make a nice gravy.

She could ignore it.

It wasn't her house, and nobody knew she was there. She could just keep on with the cooking, and let whoever it was get tired of standing there and go away. But Momma had taught her that you had to be polite to folks, to consider other people in what you did. Momma said it didn't matter whether it was a big thing like not asking embarrassing questions about your friend's brother who had just been sentenced to a year in the county jail for driving his pickup truck through the living room of his ex-girlfriend, or a little thing like keeping your shopping cart to one side of the aisle in the supermarket so other people had room to pass. Whichever, you had to think about other folks and be considerate. So Dossie really didn't have any choice. She had to answer the door.

Wiping her hands on the apron, she walked down the front hall, and because it was a strange house, and because Momma also said that while you had to be polite to folks, it didn't do to be stupid about it, she slipped the chain on the front door before opening it.

And as the door opened to the length of the chain, there, on the doorstep, was your typical urban cowboy. Boots, jeans, pearl-buttoned shirt, belt-buckle the size of a salad plate, and hat. He took off the hat, holding it in front of him, across his chest. Jimmy Stewart being the soft-spoken cowboy in some western. But not Jimmy Stewart. More swaggery. John Wayne maybe.

"Mr. Pike at home?" he said. And the accent was all wrong. It wasn't the twang of Texas or Oklahoma, or the flat, understated delivery of Montana or Wyoming. It was pure California and went with the hat and the rest of the getup about as well as a cow in church. The jeans were wrong, too. Not worn on the inside of the knees and calves the way they got from rubbing on a saddle.

"No," Dossie said. "No, he isn't."

"But you do expect him, don't you?"

It was only now that she realized that this was the *one*—the one Dave had told her about, that had done God knew what to the movie director, and had the fight with Dave. Unfortunately this realization came too late, because when Dossie tried to shove the door closed, the cowboy had the toe of one boot wedged in it and held it open.

Then he put his shoulder into the door, and the chain ripped from the doorframe, and the door was open.

Mickey lit a cigarette and blew out a stream of smoke. Not get the money back? What kind of crap was that? If they'd handed the stuff over when she gave Richie the money, she could understand then. That was like buying an ice-cream cone, then saying you'd changed your mind. Too bad for you. But when she'd given Richie the money ahead of time, well, that was like reserving a table at a restaurant. If you changed your mind, you canceled, and that was it.

He *had* to get the money back. With that goddamn lawyer getting all holier-than-thou, it wasn't going to be safe to have three keys of coke in her apartment. He *had* to get it back.

How to lean on him? I'll turn you in unless you give me the money? He'd laugh at that. Turn him in, he'd turn her in, too. Tit for tat. That wouldn't work. Not a stick then, a carrot. What did he want?

Her. He wanted her. Get me the money back and I'll marry you? Yecch! Only if he promised to commit ritual suicide at the reception. She could see it: the guests are all standing around sipping champagne. Someone hands her the knife with the little knot of ribbons on the handle to cut the cake. She hands the knife to Richie, says: Richie dearest, would you slit your wrists now?

Wouldn't that be lovely though? Life would be a lot simpler without Richie. It was like trying to live in Johannesburg and have a thing with a black. You couldn't take him anywhere, what he was stuck out a mile the moment he opened his mouth. Before that. Stuck out as soon as he walked into the room. A leg-breaker. A frightener. And jealous? Really. Always dropping little hints, asking suspicious questions. Maybe he'd pile up his stupid Jeep. He was a terrible driver.

But enough with the daydreams. Richard wasn't going to disappear. Besides, she needed him around to get the money back.

But wait!

He wanted the lawyer.

It was blindingly simple.

All he talked about was getting even. He tried to make it sound like he had it under control, but the strain was clearly getting to him.

So give him the lawyer.

Call and get the lawyer to be someplace. Give him some song and dance about a crisis of conscience—let's see, what would he believe? What would hook him good? Maybe if she couldn't decide what to do about Maurice's will. Considered herself partly responsible for his death. Didn't feel right about inheriting from him. Should the money go to charity? Or maybe just let his kids have it? He'd buy that for sure, if you leaked a few tears while you were explaining. Get him to come and discuss it.

And then call Richard and say, you want him, come and get him. Only there's a price. Bring my money back.

Tell him when the lawyer would be there, and have him wait at the bottom of the stairs with a blackjack—whatever they used, Richard would know.

When you thought about it, she only needed Richie as a pipeline to the Jap coke dealer, Nakamura. She'd seduced him just to make sure he stayed on her side and didn't try any funny stuff. But if she was going out of that business, well, who needed Richie? What would be really great would be if they'd take each other out, him and the lawyer. Yeah.

Like that oater Eastwood wanted her to do for him, only he got started on the Dirty Harry stuff instead and they never went beyond a screenplay. Gunfight at the O.K. Corral. Richie'd bring the money and he and the lawyer'd face off in the street, both draw, and shoot each other dead. Sure, Chuck. You wish. Might as well balance the budget, solve the troubles in Northern Ireland, and get the Arabs and the Israelis to sit down together while you're at it. Wish for solutions to everything.

If she could've been sure he'd behave himself, that could have been something else. He really could be kind of fun, the lawyer. Could carry on a conversation without saying huh? every time she used a word with more than four syllables. But to have him moping around, maybe interfering with her ability to do the film that was going to establish her reputation, put her right up there with the big names, no way, José.

He already *had* interfered. Didn't dare sell any more coke, that was interfering, and maybe he'd interfere with the money from Maurice's estate somehow. Lawyers did that. Everything looked fine, all nailed down, and then they did some tricky thing and it all went away. Like the alimony from her ex-husband when they found out she'd set up housekeeping with that cameraman.

The beauty of it was that it would kill two birds with one stone. Give Richie the lawyer, Richie'd get her money back, and he'd make the lawyer disappear.

Not bad. Not bad at all.

Pike got out of the elevator. Followed the wide linoleum corridor to a counter where two women in white uniforms sat talking.

"I'm looking for Mr. Stoddard," he said. "Coronary care unit?"

Both women looked at Pike. "You were here before," one of them said accusingly. "Night before last. Don't you remember where it is?"

"He wasn't awake," Pike said, "when I was here before. And I thought you might have moved him."

"Nope. He's still in the same place." The woman pointed to the left. "Third door down the hall. Visits limited to fifteen minutes, though, okay?"

"Sure," Pike said. "Whatever you say."

The door to the room was closed. Pike tapped on it and went in. Sid Stoddard, wearing a short-sleeved cotton gown, was lying on a hospital bed. A sheet and blanket covered his legs. His eyes were closed. A green plastic tube led from his nostrils to a fitting on the wall. An i.v. bag dripped colorless fluid into another tube that ended at a needle taped to Stoddard's arm.

Pike cleared his throat. Stoddard's eyes opened.

"David," he said. His voice was weak. "Can you believe this? One minute you're at your desk, next thing you wake up in here in a nightgown with no back in it. Hell of a thing. Rae gave you those files?"

"Yeah," Pike said. "Yeah, I got 'em. Look, Sid. I don't think this is such a good idea. Why don't I let you sleep, and we can talk about this after you're out of here?"

"Nonsense," Stoddard said. He pushed a button on a small box that was fastened to the rails on one side of the bed. An electric motor whined, and the bed moved into a more upright position. "Nonsense. I'm fine. Or will be, soon as they let me out of here. Besides, we got a couple of deadlines here. Got stuff that needs to be done. Let me tell you about this Poole thing."

He talked for almost ten minutes. Pike made notes.

"Then," Stoddard said, "there's Maurice's will. I'm named as executor. Don't know if you knew that?"

Pike shook his head. "I didn't even know there was a will. I looked for one and didn't find any file on it."

He debated telling Stoddard about firing Maurice as a client and decided it could wait until Sid looked a little stronger. Rae had said it had hit Sid hard, just hearing about Maurice's death. No sense in adding insult to injury.

"Funny duck, Maurice," Stoddard said. "Suspicious as the dickens about a lot of his business. Didn't want us to keep the original in the safe with the other wills. Wanted me to keep it. Me, personally. So I did. So it's there, in the wall safe in my office. Rae has the combination. We'll need to file a petition for probate, get the will admitted. You can tell Rae. She'll know what to do. Bring me the petition and I'll sign as executor.

"But," Stoddard said, "but I'll waive my fee as executor. That way the firm can bill for the probate. Otherwise we'd be getting two fees, and it'd get complicated. Should be pretty straightforward though. I think he left it mostly to that director. What's her name, Mickey?"

"The thing is," Pike said, "the thing Rae wanted me to be sure and tell you was that there's already a petition filed. To admit a will to probate. Filed by,"—he looked at his notes—"Doris Rosenblatt and Leonard something. I can't read my own handwriting."

Stoddard sighed and shook his head. "Those two never learn. That's his kids. Son and a daughter. They have an old will. Superseded by the one I wrote. Naturally they'll holler about undue influence and all that kind of thing, but they haven't a snowball's chance in hell. I videotaped the execution of the will. Maurie talked for half an hour about why he was leaving them what he left them, and not a dime more. The tape cassette's in the safe with the will. They're going to just shit when they see that tape played, I promise you.

"Only," Stoddard said, elbowing himself up a little higher in the bed, "we've got to get cracking here. Get our petition on file before theirs is heard. Otherwise one of them gets appointed executor and uses the estate's money to fight us on the contest. But if we file before their hearing date, then nobody gets any money out of the estate until the contest is resolved. They'll lose interest soon enough when they have to foot the bill for it.

"All right," Stoddard said, "I guess that's it." He looked even more frail and suddenly very tired. "Let me know how the Poole thing comes out at the hearing on the preliminary injunction."

He lay back against the pillows on the bed.

When the door flew open, Dossie landed on her tush on the floor, and slid several feet along the polished wood. But before she'd even stopped sliding, she'd rolled over onto her face and started a scrambling run on all fours across the living room.

Dossie knew she had to get out of there. Into the yard, the street, anywhere so long as it was out. By now she was back on her feet and had her balance, and she moved across the living room toward the hall, faster than she'd ever moved in her life. In her mind was no coherent thought, more like background noise, repeated so fast that the words ran together: Oh God oh God ohGodohGodohGodohGod.

She pushed the button on the knob when she slammed the hall door behind her—without any real belief that it would slow him down for long. Then she ran down the hall to the bedroom, still saying, OhGodohGod, in her mind.

On a second level, somehow going on at the same time as the litany, although she had never before been able to hold two coherent thoughts at the same time, was: Out. Got to get out. There were sliding glass doors from the bedroom onto the deck at the rear of the house. She didn't think about the doors, she just knew they were there and ran down the hall.

Behind her the door from the living room to the hall burst open, and she heard his boot heels clicking along the hallway. Not running, but coming quickly all the same.

She locked the bedroom door too, crossed the room, and snapped the catch on the sliding glass door and tried to slide the door open. But it had been blocked with a piece of wood in the track at the bottom, to keep it from being pried open by burglars.

The litany in Dossie's head had changed to a single word: Please. Please. Please. She couldn't have said what she was asking for— to get the door open, or to get out, or to get away from the cowboy. The word just ran through her mind, as meaningless and all-encompassing as a mantra.

Scrabbled with her fingers at the piece of wood in the track of the door. Broke a nail but didn't even feel it. Got one end up, pulled the whole stick free and threw it to one side. Grabbed the handle and tugged.

And the bedroom door slammed open, and he was in the room. He wasn't even breathing hard, just standing there, holding his hat in one hand, and in the other a small canvas bag, like a bag you'd keep your running shoes in. He was *huge*. His shoulders actually did fill the doorframe, and Dossie backed away from him, and away from the door, into the corner by the bed.

"Well," he said, putting his hat back on his head and tipping it forward over his eyes. "Well, little lady, my thought exactly. How nice that you went straight to the bed like that."

Dossie had one corner of the quilt back, feeling under the pillow, running her hands back and forth, where *is* it? Had it fallen on the floor? Was Dave just blowing smoke up her stack, talking to impress her when he'd said it was there?

Until finally her hand found the grip of the pistol, and she pulled it out from under the pillow, seeing as she pulled it free that it was a big revolver, but had those dinky little handles they put on eastern guns to make them small enough to hide in your purse.

That was the first good thing that had happened since the cowboy came to the door. Well, no, the first good thing was finding the pistol to begin with. But it was definitely a good thing that it was a revolver and not some complicated automatic, where she wouldn't know the safety from the magazine release.

She stood panting, next to the bed, sucking air and blowing it out. Why was it so hard to breathe? Holding the pistol down by her side, pointing at the floor, but held with the same fierce grip that a sinner uses to hold a Bible, as a shield against temptation and the devil.

He saw the pistol, but he just smiled and took a step closer, putting him halfway to the foot of the bed, nine or ten feet from Dossie. He tossed his canvas bag on the corner of the bed.

"You don't want to hurt someone with that," he said. "Just put it on the bedside table there. C'mon, sweetheart."

Taking a step closer, at the foot of the bed now as Dossie brought the pistol up in one motion, cocking the hammer with her thumb, her arm extended, shifted at the last second from the middle of his chest down to his legs, and squeezed the grip.

The noise scared her, as it always did, but she'd hit him, because he had turned around, faster than a man could turn by himself, and flopped onto the floor. Both hands on his leg now, holding the thigh, just above the knee, saying, in a voice that mixed pain with wonder, "Jesus Christ! Oh, Jesus Christ!"

Dossie had time to notice her own voice, and to feel a faint twinge of embarrassment. The north Texas twang she had worked so hard to lose was back. Being scared, or having her hand on a pistol, or just the whole situation, brought it back, as she said, "There's five more in this hogleg, asshole, and if you move from where you are I'll see if I can give you a forty-four caliber vasectomy. You hear me?"

Holding the pistol in one hand, aimed generally in the direction of the cowboy on the floor, she took the receiver off the phone, set it on the bed, punched 911, then picked up the receiver and held it to her ear. "Operator? I need the police. I've just shot a prowler."

It wasn't the kind of surprise she'd planned. That thought crossed her mind when Dave arrived home to find an ambulance, two sheriff's cars, and a CHP cruiser parked in his driveway, like someone had spilled a box of emergency vehicles.

The CHP had been having a cup of coffee down at Trancas. He'd been the first one on the scene. Seemed more concerned about getting the pistol away from her than anything else, although he did put handcuffs on the cowboy and a compress on his leg. Talked on his radio, told the other ones, the sheriffs, what was happening. At least Dossie thought that was what he did. He didn't exactly speak English, but some jargon full of *ten-four*s and *code-one*s and words like that.

Several times she caught him looking at her with a funny expression on his face. Like he might've looked at a snake, or a dog that had just bit someone.

He was looking at her like that when Dave got home. They had just put the cowboy in the ambulance, and it had driven away, and she saw the headlights coming up the hill, and it was Dave, driving this Ford Pinto that he had on a lease because his car had been blown up.

She moved so quickly that the CHP flinched. Then she was around the parked cruiser and across the driveway and had her arms around Dave as he got out of the car.

"Hey," he said. His face was serious, but when he looked down at her hugging him he had a little smile at the corners of his mouth, and she felt better, somehow, because he had a smile for her.

"Hey, take it easy. What is all this?"

She tried to explain, but the sheriffs came and got in the way. The CHP left about then. That was a good thing. About the only good thing. The sheriffs kept asking Dave all kind of questions, and talking to him, and she couldn't hardly get a word in edgewise.

Finally Dave yelled at them. Told them to shut up for a minute. They reared back then—looked like they didn't expect folks to talk that way to them. Dave told them to wait a minute, and he'd talk to them after. He started to take her into his house, but she wasn't going back in there, no way.

She made him walk her down to her sister's house. The sheriffs followed along, but at least they stopped talking. Dave left her in her sister's living room, and then he talked to the sheriffs outside on the porch for a long time.

She still hadn't cried when he finished talking to them and came inside, and she heard their cars drive by on the way down the hill. But she started then, and she cried while he looked in the cupboard where her sister kept the liquor, and poured her a drink of something, and made her drink it. Cried while he held her and made soothing noises.

She'd almost stopped crying, except for a little sniffle, when he carried her into her room and put her on the bed.

"Wait," she said, when he covered her with the bedspread and started to leave the room.

"What is it?" he said. "What's the matter?"

"Don't go," she said. "Don't leave me alone." And burst into tears again.

He turned around at the door of the bedroom. "What is it?" he said again.

"I don't know," she wailed, feeling scared and confused and angry and hurt all at once. "What is going on here? What would have happened to me if there wasn't a gun under your pillow? What if I didn't know how to shoot a pistol? Or if I couldn't find it? What would have happened then? Don't leave. I don't want to be alone."

He came back and sat on the side of the bed. Reached out with one hand and stroked her hair, just like her father used to do. "Ssh, ssh," he said. "Easy does it. Take it easy. I won't leave. And I'll fix it. I've already started. I'll fix it. I'll go tomorrow and arrange some things that'll fix it so he doesn't bother you again."

She felt a little better then, but she was still sniffling when she fell asleep.

CHAPTER

18

"APPRECIATE YOUR SEEING ME on short notice like this."

"No problem. Friend of Nico's is a friend of mine. All that shit. How is he, by the way, Nico?"

"I, ah, I'm afraid he's a little under the weather."

The office looked like a policeman's office. Bureaucratic gray steel desk. Three filing cabinets, one dark green, one beige, one gray. Asphalt tile floor, no carpet. Pistol-shooting trophy on the bookcase, next to a charging unit with a hand-held VHF sitting in it. Calendar from a plumbing supply company, featuring an impossibly luscious blonde wearing a lustful expression and not much else.

"Drinking again? Damn shame." Jan Bokkie paused and looked out the window, tugging at his earlobe, then turned back to Pike. The blue eyes were just as furious as Pike remembered them. "Oh well, can't live his life for him, can we. Do for you?"

"I've got some pictures I'd like you to look at. I'm not sure what they're of, and I thought maybe you could explain them." Pike slid the manila envelope across the desk.

"This involve my friend Richard? That you were asking about before?" Bokkie asked.

"I think so. Or at least the guy he works for. Nakamura."

Bokkie opened the flap of the envelope and slipped the pictures out. He went through them once, quickly, then went through again, pulled out two pictures and placed them side-by-side on his desk. He put the others back into the envelope.

"Nice clean shots," Bokkie said. "Guy's a professional, did these. Read the goddamn labels on the bottles."

"Yes," Pike said, "he is."

"Guy that owns this setup's a professional too," Bokkie said. "Look at this stuff! Here, you got mannitol. These containers, see? This's quinine, over here."

He looked up sharply at Pike. "You use those things to cut coke. Step on it. Dilute it down. You can use other stuff—B_{12}, baby laxative, lactose, dextrose, methamphetamine, procaine, caffeine, all kinds of shit. Whatever you use, you'd like the customer not to know it's there, think the stuff has the same taste and feel and effect as pure coke, which of course it never does.

"Anything," he said, "whatever you use, cut it with, it has a taste. The sugars mostly're too sweet, that's why they use quinine. It's bitter, same's coke. This here's a digital balance, to weigh the shit out. Shrink-wrap machine over here, package it up.

"That," he said, "that shrink-wrap thing tells you the guy deals in weight. He was dealing grams, or even pieces, eighths or quarters, he'd have like little plastic pill bottles, or paper, fold it up in that. The shrink-wrap, he's doing whole keys.

"Now this," he tapped an object in one of the pictures, "this's a high-pressure liquid chromatograph. You don't see that too much, but sometimes they got one. It's, you use it, do a very careful chemical analysis of what you got—how pure it is, and what it's cut with already, so's you know how much more you can step on it.

"Nice," Bokkie said. "Very nice setup. Where is it?"

"Can we just—do you mind if we slow down a minute here?" Pike said. "Maybe talk about a couple of things before we get to that?"

"Uh-huh," Bokkie said. "Had this feeling you were going to be cute about it. Where is it?"

"Wait just a minute," Pike said. "Let's suppose for a minute I tell you where this stuff is. What do you do then?"

"What d'ya think? I'm a cop. I call downstairs, get someone from

Narco, or OCU, they round up some uniforms, go out and bust the place open. Seize the stuff. That what you had in mind?"

"Not quite," Pike said. "How about the guys it belongs to?"

"Oh," Bokkie said. "That. Well. That's another matter. If they're there when the uniforms go in, most likely they're dead resisting arrest. Or maybe not. Maybe they decide not to try to shoot it out. So we arrest 'em.

"If they're not there when the uniforms go in, then we can't do much. Even if we find prints, get a good match, we don't have them in possession unless they're there, right in the room with the stuff. Circumstantial evidence, you know? Good defense lawyer—and the ones do dope, they're the best, ought to be, they get paid enough—good defense lawyer can make a reasonable doubt out of that easy."

"That's not quite what I had in mind," Pike said. "I'd like the people that own this stuff busted, tried, convicted, and put away."

"So tell me where it is," Bokkie said. "And we'll do that thing."

"You just got through telling me you can't, unless you just happen to find them there when you go in."

"Okay," Bokkie said. "So we'll stake it out. Wait around until someone shows up. Bust it then."

"I don't know," Pike said. "Is this going to be one of those stakeouts where a bunch of guys with short haircuts sit around in four-door sedans with blackwall tires and try to look inconspicuous?"

"You got a better idea?" Bokkie said. He was clearly getting riled. His habitually red face was redder, and there were little frown lines around the blue eyes.

"Not a whole lot better," Pike said. "But maybe a little. Suppose I arrange to find out when they're there, and give you a call. You could come and do it then, get them inside."

"Suppose," Bokkie said, switching to Official Police, "that I tell you that these photographs are evidence of the commission of a felony, possession of a controlled substance, to wit, cocaine, in

violation of section one-one-three-five-oh of the Health and Safety
Code. Suppose I further tell you that you, being aware of the place at
which said controlled substance is located, are in violation of section three-three of the Penal Code. Every person who, after a felony
has been committed, conceals or aids a principal, having knowl-
edge that said principal has committed such felony, is an accessory
to such felony. Suppose that."

"Suppose," Pike said, "that I tell you to take a flying fuck at a
rolling doughnut."

"I thought you might take that attitude," Bokkie said, writing on
a card. "Well, you're a friend of Nico's, so maybe you're straight.
And you're trying to nail Richard and his boss, sounds like. I like
that. I like that a lot. So I'll take a chance. This's my beeper number.
You call me anytime, day or night. I'll round up some uniforms and
we'll be there in five minutes. Well, maybe more like a half hour."

He held the card out across the desk. Pike took it. "Oh, and one
more thing," Bokkie said. His voice was not loud, but it was very
clear, and the pale blue eyes were as cold and hard as dry ice.

"Don't get the idea you can just forget about this stuff, and not
call. I got a job to do. And I want this stuff here," he pointed down at
the floor, "downstairs, in the evidence room. You got that?"

"Yes," Pike said, "I got it." Remembering his first meeting with
Bokkie. Thinking: this guy believes. He's on a crusade. So maybe
that means he'll show up when he says he will.

Pike walked into the office at the storage place. There was one
Naugahyde chair, with slashes through which the stuffing pro-
truded. A soft-drink machine hummed softly to itself. A counter
with a Formica top, disfigured by cigarette burns, divided the office
in two. Behind the counter one wall was taken up by a bank of
television monitors that showed different views of the outside of the
various buildings.

The same woman who had rented the storage room to Pike and

St. Clair was sitting behind the counter, idly looking at the TV monitors. She had a sad, middle-aged face and frizzy gray hair. She was making entries in a card index, tipping her head back to look through a pair of half spectacles as she wrote. She tipped her head forward and looked at Pike over the tops of the spectacles. "Help you?" she said.

Pike reached into his coat pocket and took out the leather case that held Nico's FBI credential. It'd been in Nico's briefcase. Pike had found it when he went through the checks and invoices, getting them organized the night Maurice had asked him to come explain them to Mickey. There hadn't been time to return it yet.

He held up the leather case and flipped it open, holding it so that his finger partly covered the photograph.

"I need to ask you a favor," he said, and he folded up the leather case and slipped it into his pocket. "I, uh, we need some information about one of your storage lockers."

"Space," the woman said, sitting back in her chair and biting thoughtfully at the nail on her left ring finger.

"I beg your pardon?" Pike said.

"Not locker. Space. We call 'em spaces," the woman said.

"I see," Pike said. "Well, space then. Some information about one of your spaces."

"Which one?"

"About halfway down on the other side of this building." Pike pointed out the window.

"Don't do me no good you telling me like that. You go down there, look at the number, and come back."

Pike did as he was told.

"B-18," he said when he returned to the office.

The woman slid open a file drawer and walked her fingers over the files. She pulled out one file, put it on the counter, and closed the drawer.

"What you need?" she said.

"Maybe if I could just look at the file?"

She looked at Pike for a moment, then slid the file across the counter.

The file contained a rental application, a signed rental agreement, and a payment record. The rental agreement was in the name of Stanley Tomlinson, with an address in Torrance. Neither the name nor the address meant anything to Pike. He closed the file and put it back on the counter.

"When Mr., uh, Tomlinson comes in to get into his locker, I mean his space, how long does he usually spend there?"

The woman raised her eyes and stared thoughtfully at the bank of TV monitors. The pictures flickered every thirty seconds or so as the view shifted to another camera. She shrugged. "I dunno. I never really paid attention. I think sometimes maybe just a few minutes, and sometimes over an hour. But like I say, I never really paid attention."

"Is it always the same people who come?"

The woman stared at the monitors and sighed. "Like I say, I never really paid attention. Probably two fellas. Or maybe three. That Oriental-looking one, and maybe two more. Anglos, the other ones."

"Now," Pike said, "now for the sixty-four dollar question. We need to know the next time when someone comes to get into Mr. Tomlinson's storage space. Particularly if the Oriental-looking man comes, or a big guy with blond hair, looks like a weight lifter. Is there a way you could phone me when that happens?"

"I suppose so," she said. "I'll have to tell the folks on the other shifts, have them keep an eye out. You want to give me a phone number?"

"Sure," Pike said, writing down his home and office numbers. Thinking: Nico's name had been on the FBI identification. Have to remember to tell the receptionist at work to route any calls for Nicolasiou to him.

"Oh," he said, "one more thing. The Bureau'd be real upset if Mr. Tomlinson found out about our conversation."

The woman tipped her head forward and regarded Pike coldly over the tops of her half spectacles. "Young man," she said, "go teach your momma to suck eggs."

"Didn't I tell you? Didn't I tell you to stay away from that turd?"

"But Dom, I . . ."

"Didn't I?"

"But . . ."

"Don't give me no buts. I told you. I told you and I told you. I asked you, had you repeat it. You understood. No questions. Stay. Away. From. Him. And you go, get yourself shot at the fucking guy's house! I mean, Jesus!"

Dominic had been pacing back and forth between the couch and the bookcase where the stereo was, in his office. He stopped and glared down at Richie, who was sitting on the couch. Richie's right leg, encased in plaster to the hip, stuck stiffly out and rested on the coffee table.

Glared at Richie, thinking, How can you run a business with people like this? Tell the guy do something, he goes, does the opposite. Gets himself in a situation where he is going to be a liability, can't use him for a good long time, and he wants to argue about it.

"Richard," he said. "How is, what is this gonna look like? You get shot in the fucking guy's house, and the next thing he ends up dead. Who the cops gonna come talk to? How smart they have to be, figure that out? Why do you think I told you, specifically, stay away from there? You think I said it to hear myself talk?"

"But, Dom," Richie said, pleading, "he was at the stash."

"Richard," Dominic said, "two things. First, I don't *care* where the fuck he was. Wherever he was, I coulda fixed it. You came and told me, I'da taken care of it. But you get yourself involved. Well, you see what happens. Now you got this cast on your leg, plus which, the cops got you on an assault beef, probably burglary too, entering an inhabited dwelling, intent to commit a felony therein.

"Now," Dominic said, "second thing. What the fuck were *you* doing there? Nobody. *No*body, is supposed to go there without doing the doubling back, car changes, all that stuff. And you just drive by? What is the point of having a secret place, if the cops can just follow any old employee and have him lead them right there? Can you tell me that?"

"Yeah," Richie said. "Yeah, well, you're right. I just thought, well, never mind what I thought. I'm sorry, Dom. Real sorry. I won't do it again."

He paused for a moment. "Uh, Dom," he said, "can I just ask . . ."

"What? Ask what?"

"Well, the movie lady would like to cancel her order, get her money back. And I told her I'd ask, and . . ."

Dominic shook his head, not believing what he was hearing. First the guy does what he's told not to do, and then he goes crazy to top it off.

"Oh no we don't," he said. "Richard, Richard, I don't know where you get these ideas. This is a business. She placed an order, paid for the product, that's it. She gets the stuff. We go around letting every customer change their mind, say they only want half, don't want it today, pay us next week, pretty soon there's no business left.

"So forget that," he said. "Now, as to this other stuff, this business with that turd of a lawyer. Take a month off. Go home visit the folks. Go get married like you said you were thinking about. Go somewhere stay in a hotel. Eat in restaurants. Charge things. Make a paper trail proves you weren't anywhere within a thousand miles of L.A.

"Call in," he said, "when you get there, wherever *there* is, call in and tell me where it is. I'll take care of things with the goddamn lawyer, and then I'll let you know when you can come back."

Thinking: enough was enough was enough. Maybe, just maybe, the best thing would be if *Richard* met with an accident. No, couldn't do that. Richard was useful, or would be when his leg healed up again. Useful, but God! was he difficult.

"Go on," he said. "Get out of here. Call me when you get someplace."

He watched Richie get to his feet and sidle toward the door, the cast thumping on the floor.

Mickey sat in the butter-soft leather of a high-backed Danish modern chair, swinging the chair back and forth in a short arc. The chair was where she did her serious thinking, if she was at home when there was thinking to be done. She'd been through it four or five times, and each time it worked out the same. If it took trading the lawyer to Richie to get her money back, then there was every reason to do it, and no reason not to. It was just that it was hard to *do* it, even after you'd decided it had to be done. Even after you'd already started to do it, talked to Richie. That had been the easy part.

She shook a cigarette out of the pack and tapped it firm on the arm of the chair. Sucked in a lungful of smoke and then blew it out. Took another drag, and then stubbed the cigarette out in an ashtray, picked up the telephone, and dialed.

"Mr. Pike please," she said. "Yes, I'll wait."

She stared vacantly across the room. "David," she said. "It's me, Mickey. Fine. Fine, and you? Uh-huh. Uh-huh. David, I, uh, well, I've been thinking about what we were talking about the other night." She sighed.

"I know," she said. "I think I understand how you feel. About Maurice and everything. And I've been thinking about it, and I had a couple of thoughts, about the will and all, and I'd like to talk to you some more. No. Not on the phone.

"Would it be possible to see you? Would that be possible? I'd really appreciate it. . . . Great. See you then."

She put the phone back into its cradle and took a deep breath. That had been hard. One of the harder things she'd ever done. She liked the guy. He was interesting to talk to. Amusing. Had a kind of skewed, off-center way of looking at things that was refreshing. Richard had been easy. Getting him to agree to come over. And when he heard the lawyer was going to be there, he was so eager it was comical. The hard part had been getting him to understand that she meant it. No money, no lawyer. He'd tried to sound hurt, getting that whiny edge in his voice.

Maybe he was hurt, but that was too damn bad. No tickee, no washee.

Nico looked like death warmed over. He'd lost weight, his skin was yellow, and his eyes glittered from deep in their sockets. He came to a jerky halt inside the door of Pike's office and looked around. Looked at Pike and licked his lips. Shambled across the room and came to another halt near Pike's desk.

"I think I know what you're after," Pike said. He opened a drawer of the desk and took out Nico's FBI credential case. Held the case out across the desk. "This was in your briefcase," he said.

"Uh-huh," Nico said. "Well." He reached out and took the leather case. Turned it over and then stood, holding it in his hand. "Tell the truth, I didn't know it was missing."

He looked around the office and licked his lips. "I, ah, wondered if I could get paid, little something on account, the work I did for you last couple of weeks? I'm a little short, and I need the dough."

Pike looked at him hard. "I suppose," he said, "that you'll spend it on booze."

Nico looked back for a moment, and then dropped his eyes and wiped the back of one hand across his mouth. Pike could hear the bristles of his beard scratching on his hand. Nico took a breath and looked Pike in the eye again.

"And if I do?" he said. "I earned the money, right?"

"Yeah," Pike said, opening a drawer and taking out a checkbook. "Yeah, I guess you did at that."

He finished writing the check and tore it out. Held it between two fingers and extended it across the desk. But as Nico reached for it, Pike pulled his hand back and rested it on the edge of the desk, still holding the check between two fingers.

"What the fuck?" Nico said.

"Just wanted to ask you to do one thing for me." Pike held up his hand. "Now calm down, I'm not going to say a word about what you're thinking. I'm not going to ask you to do or don't do anything with your life."

Pike stopped and shook his head, trying to get his own thoughts straight. Until the moment he'd reached out with the check he'd had no conscious thought of asking Nico to do anything. But she wasn't a bad person. At least, down inside she didn't seem bad. Sure, she'd taken Maurice's money, but it was really only a loan, and she had paid it back. And she was disturbed about it. Wanted to talk to him. Maybe she had been dealing coke, but that was the whole point. If there was something that could be done about that . . .

"Look, Nico," he said. "Mickey McDonald. The woman who's the movie director. The one that I had you doing this audit on. Go put a scare into her and get her to straighten up, okay? Make her think the feds are onto her dealing coke and she'd better straighten up and fly right. Can you do that for me?"

Nico leaned on the desk, reached across, and pulled the check out from between Pike's fingers. Folded it, and then folded it again and put it in his wallet. "You're crazy," he said. "You know that? Completely fucking cuckoo."

He crossed the room with his shambling step and paused at

the door. "On the other hand," he said, "what the hell. Why not?"

Pike walked down the hall to the library. Pulled the Continuing Ed book on estate administration off the shelf and looked up will contests. It was just like Sid had said. If a hearing had been held and one will was already admitted to probate before a contest was filed, then the executor was entitled to use estate money to defend against the contest.

But if no hearing had been held yet, and two wills were filed, then nobody was entitled to touch the estate until the court decided which will to admit.

Maurice's children had filed their version of the will. There were still ten or eleven days left before the hearing on admitting it to probate was set to take place. So there was plenty of time to file the will that Sid had in his safe and create a contest. Rae would have the forms to do that. He'd tell her to get started. He put the book back on the shelf.

The receptionist's voice came over the paging system. *"Mr. Pike, call on line three. Mr. Pike, line three."*

He picked up the phone and punched the button.

"This is Public Storage calling," the voice said. It was a man's voice, not one Pike had heard before. "Mr. Tomlinson drove in just now. He's unlocking the door on his space. He and another fella. Myrna said to call you."

"Okay," Pike said. "Thank you. Thank you very much."

Pike pushed the disconnect button on the phone. Took a card out of his wallet, punched an outside line, and then dialed the number on the card.

"Detective Bokkie, please," he said. "Dave Pike calling. Yes, I'll wait."

"Well," said Bokkie's voice. "Was wondering when I'd hear from you. You got something for me?"

"They're there now. Nakamura and one other guy."

"And where is there?"

"The storage place between the north- and southbound lanes of 101, near Vermont. Space B-18. First building on the left inside the gate."

"All right," Bokkie said. "I'm on the way. Oh, one little thing. I got the ball now, understand? The Los Angeles Police Department. We got it. You have any idea about going by there, watch what happens, forget it, okay? I don't want any fucking civilians in the line of fire. You got that?"

"Yeah," Pike said. "I got it."

So that was that.

Pike walked across to the window, looked down into the late afternoon. There was the usual coming and going of boats in the harbor, their sails and topsides golden in the late afternoon light.

He looked at his watch and sighed. Plenty of things to do. No reason to stand around daydreaming. Get the petition on Maurice's will dictated, wind things up at the office, swing by Mickey's place to talk about whatever was bothering her.

He'd probably read about it in the paper tomorrow. Three killed in drug shootout, or police arrest two, seize five hundred pounds of cocaine. Or maybe there wouldn't be anything. Maybe they'd get there too late.

If Bokkie hadn't told him to stay away, maybe it would have been different. What had he said? Something about stupid civilians getting in the way. Do I have to put up with that? Pike asked himself. Maybe, himself said. And maybe not. Depends on what you do about it. Don't forget you have places to be. Mickey's at six thirty.

On the other hand, she said "or seven." She said "six thirty or seven." He looked at his watch again and pressed the button that started the digital timer.

There'd still be time, if the traffic wasn't too bad. Just swing by, watch the cops do their thing. He picked up the phone and dialed the receptionist. "Heather," he said. "Call an elevator for me, will you? I need to get somewhere in a hurry."

Crossed the office to the cupboard where he hung his suitcoat. Pulled the coat off of the hanger. Hesitated a moment, and then took the Smith & Wesson Model 12 Airweight from the shelf of the cupboard. He had started carrying it, instead of leaving it under the pillow of the bed at home. Even with the two-inch barrel it made quite a lump in the pocket of his pants. But he could carry his coat folded over his arm. That would hide it pretty well. He hurried to the door.

The timer said twenty-seven minutes and counting when Pike made a slow pass by the driveway of the storage place. There wasn't a black-and-white in sight. Maybe they'd already done it. Maybe it was all over.

Pike scanned both sides of the street and the parking area, looking for the Jeep that Blondie drove, or Nakamura's black Mercedes. Then he remembered what Nico said about them changing cars. He parked, got out, and walked far enough into the driveway to see the door of B-18. The padlock was off the sliding bolt, but the door was closed. Didn't seem too likely that the cops would have left it unlocked if they'd been here already. And they would have plastered it with yellow "crime scene" tape besides.

Pike turned around and went into the office. Standing near the window, looking out into the driveway, was a stringy old man with rheumy eyes. Gray stubble sprouted on his wattles.

"You the FBI?" the old man said.

"Uh-huh," Pike said.

"Thought so. Recognized you from how Myrna said you looked."

"Well . . ." Pike said.

"What kind of gun you got?" the old man asked. "One them auto-matics?" He said it like that, two words: auto-matic.

"No," Pike said, not wanting to get into a discussion.

"What you gonna do, them fellers got guns and you don't?"

"Overcome them with logic," Pike said. Some logic, he thought. Six rounds of .38 special, and six more loose in his pocket.

"I know," the old man said. "Call for a backup."

"Beg pardon?"

"Call for a backup. You know." He made a microphone of his hand and intoned, "Calling all cars, calling all cars, officer needs assistance."

"Maybe you better pretend to be working," Pike said. "So they don't notice anything out of the ordinary. This is an undercover job."

"Oh," the guy said. "I'm sorry." But he continued to stand by the window.

Pike looked at his watch. The digital timer said thirty-one minutes. After a while it said thirty-four, and then thirty-five.

"You got a phone I can use?" he asked the old man.

"Sure, right there."

Pike extracted the card from his wallet and dialed. "Detective Bokkie please. Dave Pike calling.

"Oh," he said, "can you tell me if he's still in the building? Or if he's gone somewhere? It's urgent. Well, thank you all the same."

He put the phone down. If they wouldn't say where Bokkie was, he was probably on the way. That made sense. They wouldn't want to say where he was because that could tip someone off to something. So they'd just say he was unavailable. So what was the problem?

The problem was that the digital timer now said forty-one minutes. The woman had said they sometimes just stayed a few minutes, or sometimes an hour. That meant they could be leaving any time now. Get in their car, drive away, and that would be that. There was no way to control it now that Bokkie knew where the place was. The cops would come, bust the place open, seize the stuff, and be happy as pigs in shit.

Only Nakamura and Blondie would still be loose.

And presumably would be even less happy than they were now.

Pike took a deep breath. Opened the door of the office and walked out into the driveway. Felt sweat trickling down his sides, and his shirt sticking to his ribs. Took another deep breath and tried to relax. Nice evening. Asphalt still warm from the afternoon sun, but in shadow now, cool blue shadow from the elevated freeway. Noise of rush hour traffic sliding past above. No reason to be uptight. No reason at all.

Walked down the driveway beside the building to the door of B-18, lifted the padlock from where it hung on the shackle, and quietly slid the bolt home. Put the padlock through the shackle and clicked it shut.

Walked back to the office with the same feeling as the time he'd plugged up the entrance of a wasp nest. Fear and elation, separately and together, boiling inside. That should slow them down. Let's see them open that from the inside. They won't want to kick up a fuss, attract attention, so let's see them find a way to get that open.

Pike stood by the office window and watched. Forty-four minutes. Fifty minutes. Fifty-two minutes.

Around the corner of the building strolled Mister Wonderful. Oakley shades in iridescent beetle green, pushed up on top of not-quite-shoulder-length brown curls. Shirt by Side-Out, oxide-washed jeans tucked into high-topper basketball shoes.

"That's one," the old man said.

Pike looked at the old man.

"That guy there. That's one of the guys comes in for that Tomlinson space."

Pike watched Mister Wonderful stroll over to the parking area and eyeball the parked cars. Wander out to the street and look both ways.

"There. That's another one," the old man said.

From around the far end of the building Dominic Nakamura appeared, walking down the driveway toward the parking area.

It had been too simple. Of course they'd have a back way out. Probably rented the space that backed up to B-18 and just cut a hole in the wall between them. Pike swore and thought about calling Bokkie again. Fat lot of good that would do.

Mister Wonderful walked down the driveway to the door of B-18, unlocked the padlock with a key, and then started back around the building toward where he'd appeared from in the first place. Nakamura walked to a four-year-old Honda and got into the passenger seat.

Mister Wonderful had probably gone to close the back door. Then he'd go through from the inside, set their booby traps, or alarms, or whatever they had, lock B-18, and they'd leave.

Shit! The cops were on the way. They *had* to be on the way. And Nakamura was leaving. How to get him back inside? Scare him? Shoot at him? That wouldn't work. They wouldn't go back inside, they'd just split.

Pike took off his suitcoat and dropped it in a chair. Took off his tie and stuck it in his pocket. Ran out the door and around the corner of the building, in the direction Mister Wonderful had gone.

From the corner he could see down the alley between the buildings. Partway down, about as far down as B-18 would have been, a door was closing. Pike sprinted along the alley and came to a stop outside the door. Rapped sharply on the metal skin of the door. Rapped again.

"Who is it?" came a voice from inside.

"Office," Pike said. "We been waiting to talk to you. Got a leak upstairs. Need to be sure it isn't coming through."

"It's not," said the voice. "No problem."

"Hey," Pike said. "Look, this stuff is some toxic chemical some ding-a-ling stored upstairs there. The City is all over us like stink on shit. They say we gotta look."

"So, tell 'em you looked," said the voice.

"All right, it's your insurance premium," Pike said. "We can't be responsible for the safety of your stuff after we cut your lock off and take a look. You better plan to come down later, put a new lock on."

"Jesus Christ," the voice said. "Fucking bureaucrats!"

The door opened. The space inside was empty, except for a stack of boxes across the back wall. The door through to B-18 was probably behind the boxes. Mister Wonderful was standing at one side, and either his back hurt him, or he was keeping one hand on the grip of a pistol in a belt holster under his shirt.

Pike smiled at Mister Wonderful. "Sorry about this," he said. "Won't take a minute." He went into the space. Walked slowly around the walls, looking at the ceiling.

"Looks clean to me," he said. "Except for over here in this corner. What's that stuff there? Do you remember that stuff being there before?"

Mister Wonderful came and stood beside Pike. He craned his neck and looked at the ceiling. "What?" he said. "What stuff? Where?"

Pike pivoted and got quite a lot of weight behind a left hook that caught the guy just above the belt buckle. As the guy doubled up, Pike took the Airweight out of his trouser pocket and hit him again, on the back of neck, with the butt of the pistol. Mister Wonderful fell down and curled up into a fetal ball, making an odd gagging sound.

He had a Heckler & Koch VP-70Z and two spare magazines in a clip-on holster under his shirt. Fifty-four rounds of nine millimeter. Enough logic for a small war. Pike unclipped the holster, put it on his own belt, and took a minute to look around. No one was in the alley outside the door.

Pike took his tie out of his pocket (Countess Mara, twenty-nine ninety-five) and used it to tie the guy's hands behind his back. Took the guy's belt, looped it twice around his ankles and buckled it.

Stood up and took another look around. Still no one in the alley.

Digital timer said fifty-nine minutes. Where the fuck were the cops? Oh well, now to get Nakamura inside somehow. Pike went out into the alley and closed the door. He walked softly down the alley and looked carefully around the corner of the building.

The Honda was still there, but Nakamura was no longer sitting in it.

She heard footsteps coming up the stairs. Unequal footsteps, one hard and one soft. Sort of like somebody limping, but not exactly. The footsteps reached the landing, and there was a tap at the door.

Mickey crossed the room, clicked on the porch light, and peered through the peephole. Richie was standing on the landing, a cast on one leg. She opened the door.

"The fuck is he?" Richie said. "I been standing down there in the dark for an hour."

"I don't know," she said. "He's late. I told him six thirty or seven. What time is it now?"

"Almost seven thirty," he said. "Seven fifteen, seven twenty, around in there."

"Uh-huh," she said. "Richard, what happened to your leg?"

"Oh," he said. "Oh, that. Yeah, well, see it was this way . . ." And he began to tell a complicated story about seeing the lawyer somewhere and following him and being ambushed by some woman who lived with the lawyer, who shot him from behind. In the leg. None of it made any sense.

"So," she said. "Is this going to be a problem? I mean, you can still, well, do what you need to do tonight?"

"Oh yeah. No problem." He lifted his gym bag. "I got a little equalizer in here. No problem. That is, if he shows up."

"He'll be here," she said. "He promised me."

What she meant was that he'd *better* be there, because she didn't know what to do if he wasn't. "But since you're here, where's my money?"

"Soon as I got him," Richie said. "Soon as he's taken care of, we'll go and pick it up."

"Richard, goddamn it! I told you money first, and then you can have the lawyer."

"Hey, chill out," he said. "You think I'm going to stiff you? Dominic's got the dough. No problem." He licked his lips and looked away.

"Richard," she said. "What is going on? Are you lying to me? Look at me."

"Nothing. Nothing is going on." Looking up and meeting her eyes. Getting a sly grin on his face. "Only I got an idea. See, I'm going to be on vacation for a while. Take it a little easy. So suppose you and me take a few days off." His grin widened. "Maybe run up Vegas and get married. How about that?"

"Richard," she said, "aren't the cops after you?"

"For what? Why'd they be after me? Dope? Nobody knows I deal dope. They aren't after me."

"No," she said. "Not that. But if you got shot in somebody's house, aren't they after you for that?"

"Hey. No sweat, Dominic's lawyer got me out on bond. It's nothing anyway, just some crappy assault thing is all. It's no big deal."

"Don't you think," Mickey said, "that you'd better get back outside and wait? He may show up any time."

Thinking: Richard is going to go down. It looks like he doesn't know about it yet, but that's not surprising, because he isn't very smart.

Ever since the nasty little man with the complicated foreign name had come to the editing studio she'd had this feeling. Looked like he had a fever or some kind of sickness, dark circles under his eyes, sallow complexion. As soon as she'd seen him she knew he was trouble for somebody.

Film people were such bohemians. Or rather, to be completely truthful, they used bohemianism as a pose. Used it to excuse being careless, to excuse being behind on payments, or any failure to behave like responsible adults. Someone was always around, looking for one of the crew. Bill collector, process server, one of the unpleasant occupations.

That the nasty little man could be there for *her* hadn't occurred to her at first. She was sitting in front of a Steenbeck, had been rolling film from an eight-hundred-foot core, marking which takes to use. She'd just taken a break, made some notes, rewound the core and lifted it off the revolving stainless-steel plate of the Steenbeck. Reached around to turn on the lights and he was standing there.

"Jesus Christ!" she said. "Who the fuck do you think you are, sneaking in here like that?"

He didn't say anything, just held up a leather case with a green I.D. card, and the words leapt off of the card and hung in the air in front of her, like the dazzle from a flashbulb: Department of Justice, Federal Bureau of Investigation.

She'd lit a cigarette and waved out the match. Noticed that her hands weren't shaking, and was grateful for that. Saw him looking at the cigarette pack and held it out toward him. Keeping her voice under tight control, she said, "Smoke?"

"Thanks but no," he said. "I'm trying to quit."

"What do you . . ." she said. "How can I help you?"

"I just have a few questions to ask you," he said.

"About what?"

"It's just a routine matter," he said, and smiled. Smiling, he looked like death. Cheeks sunken in, eyes deep in their sockets. Skin shrunken tight against the bones of his skull. She was glad when he stopped smiling. She hoped he wouldn't do it again.

He had a technique she'd have liked to use in a film, if you could show how it worked. Four or five questions that sounded dull, easy, nonthreatening. And then casually, he'd slip one in, like: "How did you happen to meet Richard Morrissey?" Just casually assuming that she knew Richard, and that she'd known him for a while, and making it seem like it was no big deal.

Except that there could only be one reason the nasty little man would be asking her about Richard.

She'd given some kind of answers. Kept her voice level. She'd noticed at one point that she had her arms folded in front of her. That was the wrong body language. Be open, not defensive. She'd forced herself to unfold her arms and hook her thumbs in her belt.

When the nasty little man had gone, she'd collapsed into the chair in front of the Steenbeck and lit another cigarette. Too fast. It was all going too fast. Richard had promised her that he'd never tell. That no one would ever know she bought coke from him. So either he had lied, or someone else told. One of her customers maybe? But it couldn't be that. Her customers didn't know Richard. So maybe it was just routine, like the nasty little man said. But how could it be routine? Why would any routine investigation involve her? Something was definitely wrong. Maybe that goddamn lawyer. Maybe he told.

So when they got Richard on the dope charge, which they would certainly do, they'd offer him a deal, and he might take it. And it could lead to her. After all, there was this new policy, get tough on the users. She'd read about that. Or even without a deal, Richard was liable to tell everything he knew. He was so dumb they'd trick it out of him.

"Hey," Richie said, "what are you thinking about? I don't think he's coming."

"He'll be here," she said. "He promised."

"I don't think so. If he isn't here by now, something's happened and he isn't coming." Richie smiled. "But that's okay. Dominic will take care of it. I don't need to do it myself.

"So why don't you and me get packed, like I said, and head up to

Vegas. Find a wedding chapel. Maybe it surprises you, but I got quite a bit of money saved up. Almost three hundred thousand dollars in the bank."

Seeing her frowning, he hurried on, "That surprise you? That I got that kind of dough? I done it for you, you know. Saved it so I'd have something, and we could get married.

"So," he said, "let's do it, huh? That asshole isn't coming here tonight. Something happened, he had a flat tire or something."

Seeing Mickey still frowning, he bent, scooped her legs out from under her, and picked her up. For a moment Mickey thought he was going to overbalance with the cast and fall. But he leveled out. Clumped down the hall toward the bedroom.

She hammered on his chest with her fist. "Richard," she said, "goddamn it, put me down. He's coming. You've got to get back outside and hide. Put me down."

Richie clumped through the door into the bedroom and tossed Mickey on the bed. He opened the closet, took out a suitcase and put it on the bed.

As soon as he turned his back, Mickey was up off the bed like a shot and down the hall to the living room. She heard him coming behind her, the cast thumping on the floor.

She turned around in the dining area, with the table between them, and faced him across it, breathing hard. He stopped across the table.

"Michelle," he said. As far as she could remember, it was the first time he had ever called her by her full name. "You can pack some stuff, or you can not pack, but either way, you're coming with me, you got that? No more of this crap."

Mickey stood across the table from him and rubbed at her arms. "You hurt me," she said.

"We'll do it some more, you don't have that bag packed in about two minutes."

"All right," she said. "Calm down. I'll do it." She picked up her purse and opened it. Took out her cigarette pack, shook one out, and got it going. Put the pack back in.

"Get me a drink," she said. "There's some wine in the refrigerator."

She watched as Richie walked around the table into the kitchen, watched him open the cupboard and take out two glasses. Open the refrigerator. Pour the wine. Put the bottle back on the shelf.

It was too much.

It was all too goddamn much.

It all ran through her mind in less than the time it took him to close the refrigerator door. Not really in words, just feeling. Her body made certain motions, and she felt the motions, and knew what they were and why they were necessary, but there really weren't any thoughts that went with the motions.

If there had been thoughts, some of them would have been: that she could get away from the bastard. Ride along in the car, nice as you please, until they got somewhere. Walk up to a cop, or go in the ladies' room, not come out. There were fifty ways to ditch somebody. Fifty ways to leave your lover.

But then he'd be mad. And he was going to go down on the dope charge, no question about that. And you never knew what a rejected man would talk himself into doing, thinking it was the only thing there was to do.

Nakamura was setting Richie up. She could sense it. Getting some distance from him, sending him on vacation, ha! The Jap was going to turn him and his customers in. Maybe he was already working out some deal with the nasty little man from the FBI. The fact that Richard didn't know about the FBI man almost proved it.

Of course Nakamura'd have some neat way worked out where Richie couldn't get back at him. Some evidence Richie had murdered someone, something like that. Shut up, take the fall on the dope, or this will land on your back too.

And Richie didn't even see it coming.

But she could see it, and it meant Richie was dangling over her head like a 220-pound sword of Damocles. Unless there was a way to get rid of him and the lawyer both at the same time.

Her hands, without any conscious thought, felt around in the bottom of her purse and found it. One hand closed around the grip, and the other pulled the purse away, and she stood there holding the pistol she'd borrowed from the lawyer.

Pull it back and let go to load it, he'd said. There were kind of notches on the sides of the barrel at the back, where you grabbed to pull. She tugged on the barrel.

Nothing happened.

Tugged again, harder, and with an oiled, snicking sound the barrel slid back and forward again. There was a button and a red dot that was the safety. The red dot was showing. That meant it was ready to shoot.

But wasn't there some kind of lock that made it quiet? She'd asked about it, and he said not to mess with it. He'd called it a something-lock. She'd asked him what it was, and he'd looked funny, like he was remembering things that had happened to him a long time before, and said it was for if you were trying to shoot someone and not make any noise, and it was a something-lock, and it locked something so the something-else didn't do something, and there wouldn't be any noise from it.

It was a lever on the side of the pistol, above the trigger, kind of on the side of the barrel. She pushed on it, and it clicked into a slot on the barrel.

So. It was all set. Loaded, ready to fire, and set to be quiet. And he said it would cock itself and reload until all thirteen bullets were fired. Not bad.

Richie closed the refrigerator door. Turned from the counter with a glass in each hand. Came to a stop with a dumb expression on his face when he saw what she was holding in her right hand. "Sweetheart," he said, "what are you doing? What is this? I love you. I want to marry you. We don't have to stay here in L.A., we can move, if you're worried about what I do. I'm not married to Dominic. It's you I care about. Like I said, I got some money saved up, enough to live on for quite a while, if we're careful, in say Fresno or someplace. This is a joke, right?"

She saw the expression in his eyes; one that combined surprise with a terrible, pathetic yearning.

What was it the lawyer'd said? Don't mess with the sights, don't be fancy, just point with your hand at the middle of the guy's chest. Something like that. She raised her right arm.

"Richard," she said, "shut up."

And pulled the trigger.

Looking at the empty car, Pike felt the second half of the feeling that he'd had that time he'd stopped up the wasp nest—the sick horror after they got out. There was a cold, greasy sliding as sweat crept down his sides under his shirt. His mouth was dry and he could hear himself breathing.

Maybe Nakamura just got out of the car to stretch his legs. Maybe he just went to check the lock on B-18.

Stepping carefully, Pike walked along the end of the building. Looked around the corner, in the direction of the door to B-18. No one was in the alley on that side of the building. Pike turned and looked into the office. The old man was still in there, standing at the window. He raised his hand and waved to Pike.

Where had Nakamura gone? Would he just leave? Get spooked, split, and sort it all out later? That'd be the safe thing to do, if you were a big-time dealer. But if he left, would he leave on foot? Why wouldn't he have driven away in the Honda?

Pike crossed the alley to the parking area, squatted down, and looked under the parked cars. Couldn't see anything but tires. No feet. No one crouched behind a car.

Stood up. Walked to the end of the driveway, and looked into the street.

Nothing.

Went back to the parking area and looked into each of the half dozen cars standing there. No one was inside any of them.

The timer said sixty-five minutes.

Trotted down the alley to the far end of the building. Flattened himself against the wall and took a quick look around the corner.

Nothing.

Trotted around to the far corner and again took a careful look around. Now he was looking from back to front along the alley behind the building.

Still nothing.

Trotted back to the door of the space where he'd left Mister Wonderful. Stood carefully to one side and yanked the door up.

The room inside was as empty as before. More so, because Mister Wonderful was gone from the floor.

From behind the boxes at the back of the room came a voice. "Freeze, asshole," it said. "I said freeze!"

Pike froze.

"Come in," the voice said. "Close the door."

Pike went in and closed the door. Nakamura came around the pile of boxes at the back. He had an Uzi slung around his neck. Not the machine pistol, but the short-barreled carbine. On the barrel was a clumsy-looking silencer.

"Turn around, asshole," Nakamura said, "and lean on the wall. Farther. Move the feet back farther. Now spread 'em."

Pike did as he was told.

Nakamura's footsteps came across the floor. The holster with Mister Wonderful's Heckler was pulled off of Pike's belt. For a moment Pike thought maybe Nakamura would leave it at that, and not find the Airweight in his pants pocket.

No such luck. Nakamura had seen it done, or had it done to him.

He knew you didn't stop with the first thing you found. You kept looking until you'd looked in all the places. He found the Airweight and pulled it out of Pike's pocket.

"Stand up," he said. "Put your hands up. Walk around the boxes and go into the next room. Walk slow."

Pike did exactly as he was told. Nakamura's footsteps followed him.

Around the end of the boxes was a narrow passage, between the boxes and the back wall. Partway along the passage a hole had been cut into the back wall, making a doorway through into B-18.

Pike recognized the room beyond from the photos St. Clair had taken. The bottles of chemicals standing in serried rows on shelves. The shrink-wrap machine, with its rolls of plastic. The digital balance.

Laid out on the floor was Mister Wonderful. His hands and feet had been untied, and his head was pillowed on some rolled-up article of clothing. Pike was glad that he still seemed to be out, because he was probably going to be unhappy when he came around.

Pike slowed in the doorway. Felt Nakamura getting closer behind him. Close enough? It had to be real close before it was close enough. The instructor said it worked every time. The instructor said you could pivot and knock the gun off-line before the shooter could pull the trigger. The instructor had demonstrated with a cap pistol. The instructor hadn't offered to put on a demonstration with live ammunition.

Pike pivoted, sweeping his right arm out and around. Felt the funny bone on the arm whack into something hard, and the arm went numb.

Pike got both hands on the Uzi. Nakamura still had the sling over one shoulder. Tried to use his right hand to force the barrel up and back, so it'd hit Nakamura in the face. But there wasn't any strength in his arm, and his hand could barely grip the Uzi.

Nakamura hit Pike in the face with a looping overhand left, and kneed him in the groin.

Pike took a step back and yanked hard on the Uzi with both hands. The sling fell away from Nakamura's shoulder, and the Uzi flew across the room, hit the wall, and clattered to the floor in one corner.

Nakamura slid forward and hit Pike with a combination, left, left, right.

Things got very fuzzy then. Pike knew he was still on his feet, but they were a long way away. So far away that they did what they wanted to do, not what he thought they should do. But at least they did the most important thing, which was to keep him erect, and between Nakamura and the Uzi. That was important. Remember that.

Because he knew that if Nakamura got to the Uzi, he was going to die.

After a while, he could still remember that there was something he was supposed to be doing, but he couldn't remember what it was. Except maybe sit down. Sit down and take a rest. Get away from the punches that kept exploding into his head, into his stomach, graying his vision and taking his breath.

The damn thing must have been broken, the lock thing, because it was *not* quiet. It didn't even *start* to be quiet. In fact, it was the loudest noise she'd ever heard in her life. Well, almost. The loudest anyway since she did a public interest piece about the Air National Guard, and sat out there at some Air Force base in Wyoming, with a crew, freezing her ass, filming these fighter planes taking off, making a roar that was so intense it shook the world. This noise was as loud as that, but it didn't go on and on and on like the fighter planes. A lot of it was the surprise, because he'd said it would be quiet, and she'd heard guns before, on a set, and in the theater, and they didn't sound like this! But it was more than just surprise, because her ears were ringing, actually ringing, and it was almost a minute since the last time she'd pulled the trigger.

She put the pistol down on the table and just stood there. Picked up her cigarette from where she'd put it in an ashtray and let the thoughts run through her mind.

When the cigarette burned her fingers, she stubbed it out in an ashtray and walked over to where Richie was, shoved in the corner behind the bookcase, pushed up against the wall. He was lying on his left side, facing the wall, his left cheek flat against it. Listening for some noise in the next room, it looked like. His eyes were shut. That was something to be thankful for. If his eyes had been open, she didn't know if she could have done the next part.

She'd directed films about doctors. They did something with the eyelids, slid an eyelid up with one thumb, looked at something in the eye for a moment, and then turned around and delivered the next line, which was usually, "Dead," or "He's done for," or something like that.

But she didn't know what to look for, even if she could get herself to do that to Richard, slide up one of his eyelids, look into the eye. So instead she knelt by him, picked up his right arm, and held her forefinger across the inside of the wrist. Always the forefinger, because there's a pulse in your own thumb, she remembered that from somewhere.

Her fingers were cold, so cold that she'd started to shiver, but the skin on Richard's wrist was still warm, warmer than her fingers were, as she felt, and readjusted her hand, and felt again.

Nothing. Not a thump, not a bump, not a sound. Somehow it felt so final, so ultimate, so, well, *dead,* that she suddenly couldn't stand it, and dropped the arm, and Richard's body kind of settled, and rolled away from the wall a fraction. And she screamed, and jumped up, because he was dead but he was moving.

But then she saw that it was just the way the arm had pulled on the body when she dropped it.

After the body rolled, she could see, pretty much in the middle of the chest, but a little on the left side, a place where the shirt was black with blood. She couldn't see any other places where there was blood, but that one by itself would be enough.

That would make a nice ironic twist, if you were doing it as a film, big dumb cluck swearing undying love, and the lead shoots him in the heart twice, once with the pistol, and once on the symbolic level. How would you underline that, so the audience would see it? You could set it up with dialogue by saying . . . shut up! Shut up, shut up, shut up! Think. Don't babble. Where is the goddamn lawyer? He was supposed to be here, Richard was supposed to have taken care of him already, with his own gun, but he didn't, dumb shit.

It was self-defense, right? That'd work, right?

And then she thought, no, maybe it wouldn't work. There were too many stones that would get turned over, if the cops found Richie dead in her apartment, and she admitted shooting him, and they started asking questions. Why was he there? What was her relationship to him? Didn't she know he worked for Nakamura? Did she pay him protection? Or buy drugs from him?

The damn lawyer'd said they were both going to get caught in a shitstorm, Nakamura and Richie. And the little man had been to see her at the studio, asking about Nakamura and Richie. So the lawyer'd talked to somebody. And maybe he'd just happened to mention that she'd been buying from Richie. And he'd probably mentioned the porno film. And it could all unravel.

She could probably handle the dope part. If anyone even came to talk to her, she was pretty sure she could talk her way out of that. But even if they didn't find anything on her about the dope, they could stumble on the porno film. That dumb bitch of a lead was underage. Traci-something she called herself.

Hadn't wanted to use her, because she was only sixteen, even if she did have that fake driver's license that said she was nineteen. But somehow, she had a quality. . . . Some women could project inno-cence. Some could act, and project emotion. This dumb cunt could project *sex*. Get her slurping some guy's dong and looking sideways at the camera, it grabbed you somehow. You started getting hot and bothered, where some other woman doing the scene, better looking, better body, better everything, it just didn't come across.

So she'd used her. And now, if anybody looked, there was a kiddie-porn charge, sitting right there. No, no. Somehow Richie's body being in her apartment had to be worked out so that it didn't involve her.

But how?

Think!

Somehow he landed one punch that slowed Nakamura down. Gave him a second to get a breath. Right arm still felt numb, but coming back a little now. Got another breath in, and when Nakamura came close again, folded over and shot a side-kick at his head. Missed. Waste of time trying to kick anyone in the head anyhow.

Recovered and slipped a couple of punches, and then landed one of his own, a left to the head. Saw Nakamura's eyes go unfocused for a second.

Then the room was full of police in flak vests carrying M-16s. Without hesitation, two of them jumped on Nakamura, wrestled him to the floor, and handcuffed him.

Two more of them jumped Pike, wrestled him to the floor, and handcuffed him, too.

Bokkie arrived red-faced ten minutes later. Total elapsed time, one hour and eighteen minutes.

He untangled Pike from the uniforms.

"The fuck you doing here anyhow?" he said. "Who's got a key for these fucking things? Get these handcuffs unlocked."

"I told you," he said. "I told you to stay away. Didn't I tell you to stay away? Now get the hell out of here and let me do my job."

"All right," Pike said. He rubbed his arm. The funny bone still hurt like hell and the arm was numb. But everything else was sore, too, so the arm didn't seem to make too much difference.

"Don't do anything like this again, you understand?" Bokkie said. "You wasn't a friend of Nico's, I'd think about running you in. Obstructing an officer. Loitering. I'd think of something."

And then, as Pike turned to go, he put out his hand and touched Pike on the arm. Pike stopped. Turned back and looked at Bokkie.

"I'm not going to explain why it took so long," Bokkie said. "Doesn't really matter. It happened. Shouldn't have, but it did. Stupid turf dispute between the Narcs and OCU. Never did get it settled. Finally had to just get some SWAT troops and roll down here."

He shook his head and made a face.

"Thanks," he said.

The phone rang.

Her first instinct was to look around, see if someone was watching her. Stupid, she told herself. It's just the phone, not the doorbell. Stupid. She took a deep breath. The phone was still ringing. She took another breath, picked it up, and said hello.

"Mickey?" the lawyer's voice said. "I'm sorry for being so late. I got kind of tied up. I'm on the way now. I'll explain when I see you."

She supposed she said, "oh," and "all right" and "okay," and "good-bye" at appropriate places. At least he didn't seem to notice anything out of the ordinary. She put the phone down.

Think!

Get a grip on yourself and think!

Cut your losses. *Triage* they called it in a film she did for doctors about disasters. We got morphine for three cases, medicate the three we can save. These others will have to suffer, but they're going to die anyway, so what does it matter? They said the hardest thing was making the decision.

Do it, don't blither around, waste time, energy, end up saving none of them.

Richie was dead. She'd get away with it, self-defense, all that, but it'd generate too much curiosity. They'd sniff around the set, and either stumble into the dope, or into that damn underage actress. It had to be deflected somehow. Away from her. If only it were someone else that did it. Someone else that shot Richie, and she just came home and found it.

Well, why not?

Blame it on the lawyer—they'd believe that. After all, Richard had tried to off the lawyer twice as it was.

But the lawyer couldn't be around to prove he didn't do it, talk himself out of it.

So.

So the lawyer.

So the lawyer had to be dead too. He was supposed to've been. Richie was supposed to've already taken care of the lawyer for her. Dumb shit couldn't get anything right.

But it could still work. At least one of the lawyer's run-ins with Richie had been reported to the police, so they knew there was bad blood between them. So, if they both showed up dead, well, sure, that would play. Pop the lawyer and everything would be fine.

But this time, don't just let it happen like it had just happened with Richie. This time, think and plan it out. Set it up so it would play.

Think! Richie was dead, shot with the lawyer's gun.

So shoot the lawyer with Richie's gun.

She had the rag to use to wipe off the fingerprints, but not yet, not until after the lawyer showed up and she'd dealt with him. Then there'd be plenty of time to wipe the gun off, put it in the lawyer's hand. Yeah. Get the lawyer's fingerprints on it.

Triage. Useful concept.

Only, when she looked, Richie didn't have a gun.

He usually carried it in a holster that clipped onto his belt, at the back, on the right side. But the holster wasn't there. She felt in all his pockets, and it wasn't there either.

He *had* to have a gun.

Dear Lord, where was it? If if wasn't on him, maybe it was in his gym bag. What'd he call it? His bag of tricks. She yanked the zipper open and scrabbled through the contents.

Nothing but a couple of pieces of broom handle, tied together at one end. And rope and cloth. Down in the bottom, a knife, nasty-looking thing with an eight-inch blade. Well, that was no good to her. She had no idea how to kill somebody with a knife and she wasn't going to get a chance to practice. It had to go right the first time. Bang, you're dead.

Shit!

Think, don't blither. Think!

Maybe it could still work. Even with only one gun.

Eliminate the impossible, whatever is left is the thing to do. She'd have to use the lawyer's gun. It could still work. There were still plenty of bullets left. She couldn't say how many shots she'd fired at Richard, the noise from the first one was so sharp, so intense, that she must've gone into shock and lost count. But Richard had gone right down with the first one, and she'd stopped, so it couldn't have been more than maybe two, or at the outside three. So there were still plenty left.

She had been confused, worried, but now it was all clear. The way a scene that wasn't working would sometimes become clear. Something would click inside her head, and she would see it—see the underlying dynamic between the characters, see how that dynamic would drive their actions, and see how to change the script to show it.

Only this time there wasn't a script.

She could see them struggling. Richard has shot the lawyer, the lawyer is bleeding, but he's wrestling with Richard, the two of them straining and thrashing on the floor. But she needed to set the stage for the fight she saw them having. She walked around the room, blocking out the moves in her head, as if it were going to be a scene.

This lamp would go over. She pushed it down hard, so that the glass from the broken bulb would scatter out across the floor. And if they bumped into the bookcase, the things on the top of it would fall off.

She bumped the bookcase with her hip. Nothing happened. Bumped it again, harder. Well, maybe nothing would fall off. Forget that. But the candlesticks and the vase on the dinette table, something should happen to them. She gave the table a kick. It skidded a few inches, both candlesticks fell over, and one slid off the edge onto the floor. She picked up the vase and dropped it on the floor. It crunched and a couple of fragments skittered over the floor and ended up against the wall.

Stood back and surveyed the room. It looked about right. She might smash it up a little more, if she were filming it, but something told her to leave it understated, not overdo it. She could see it all in her head, see Richard and the lawyer, both with their hands on the pistol. The lawyer has been shot, but with desperate strength he bends Richard's hand back and back, and the gun goes off. The impact of the first shot stuns Richard, and the lawyer is able to pull the trigger again and again. Richard slumps into the corner, against the wall, as the lawyer bleeds to death on the floor.

Saw herself coming home later to find them both there, calling the police: "Something terrible has happened, there are two dead men in my apartment, or maybe they aren't dead, send the ambulance." Have to work on that line a little, it was weak, could stand polishing up. But something like that ought to work. It wasn't going to be as good as the way she'd planned it, for Richard to bring his own gun, and shoot the lawyer with it like she told him to do, but if there were a couple of loose ends, that wasn't her problem. It worked all the time in film. Keep up the pace, keep moving, and skate right across the thin places. People never even noticed. Besides, she wasn't even there, right?

She saw herself talking to the police. "No, officer, I'm sorry. I was at the studio working on some of the scenes we did last week, selecting which takes to use in the film. The guard saw me go in around five thirty. I don't know if he saw me come out, but I was there until almost eight, came home, and found this. Of course I recognize this man, he's the one that came to my apartment and threatened me about a film I was making. My producer, Mr. Baranowitz, knew all about it. Well, he's dead, but he must have mentioned it to someone. And this is Mr. Baranowitz's lawyer. How they got in? I don't know. I have no idea."

It was thin in a couple of places, but it would play.

She lit another cigarette and sat down on the couch. Why were her hands so cold? She was shivering and felt like she'd never be warm again. Was there time to get a sweater out of the bedroom? No. Somebody was on the stairs. Coming up the stairs.

She stabbed the cigarette out in an ashtray and stood up. Gave herself a little shake and walked to the door. Opened it.

"Where the *hell* have you been?" she said. "I don't appreciate being left hanging. When you say you'll be somewhere, damn it, you *be* there."

"I'm sorry," he said. "I got tied up. I couldn't help it."

"Sorry don't mean shit," she said.

"Take it easy," he said. "It's not something to get all worked up over."

He came in and looked around. "Jesus Christ!" he said. "Who's that on the floor?"

"That's Richie," she said. "Richard Morrissey."

"What happened? Have you called the police?"

She shook her head. "No. I didn't call them. Not yet. He was trying to get me to go away with him, Richard." She laughed. "As if I'd do a dumb thing like that."

She saw him looking at her. The laugh had been a mistake. Even to her, it had sounded like the edge of hysteria. "Forget it," she said. "Probably doesn't make a lot of sense you. Just forget it." She was still cold. Still shivering. She hugged herself and rubbed her arms.

"You know," she said. "I really liked you. I mean, it could all have come out differently if you'd liked me, too."

The pistol was on the couch, kind of tucked down between the cushion and the back. He was standing two steps away, just inside the door. She took a step to the couch and picked up the pistol. Pointed it at the lawyer and pulled the trigger.

Nothing happened, and she looked to make sure the red dot was showing, and it was, so she pulled the trigger again, harder, and still nothing happened. And then something hit her arm a numbing blow, and the pistol flew out of her hand and slid along the floor, and at the same moment something smashed into the pit of her stomach, and she lost all her breath and fell to her knees and then on her face on the floor, making a stupid, weak whining sound, unable to breathe. Her mind was clear, she could see herself, she knew he'd hit her in the stomach, or kicked her, or something, but she could not move, could not stop making the whining, whistling sound.

Until finally, when she wondered if she would ever breathe again, she got one breath in. And then another, and another. Pushed against the floor and got to her hands and knees, and then slowly stood up, feeling about a hundred years old. How did he move so fast?

He had the gun, but not touching it. He'd stuck a pencil down the barrel, and was holding it up like some kind of all-day sucker.

"What are you doing? What happened?"

"You probably know more about that than I do, but it looks to me like you put the slide lock on this thing. That means it only fires one shot, and then you have to cock it by hand to fire the next one. Which, thank goodness, you didn't do. Now, if you'll excuse me, I've had enough excitement for one evening. I think I'll be running along."

"Wait. What are you going to do about him?" indicating Richie's body in the corner.

"What am *I* going to do about him? I'll let you deal with that. He's not in *my* living room."

"But you can't just leave him there."

"Oh yeah? Watch me."

"But they'll think I killed him—the police."

"No! Why ever would they think a thing like that?" he said. He looked at her and seemed to be deciding if she was able to appreciate the sarcasm.

"But I'll tell you what I'll do," he said. "Since you killing him solves a problem for me, I'm going to do you a favor. But before you thank me, it's going to cost you. Lemme tell you about the favor first.

"The favor is," he said, "that I'll take this pistol along with me, and put it somewhere safe, and nobody but you'n me'll know I've got it. And I don't think you'll want to tell them about it, since it's got your dainty fingerprints all over it.

"And then I'm just going to watch," he said. "Maybe you can talk your way out of this, without the gun being around. I think you maybe could. It could go on the books as an unsolved homicide.

"Now," changing his voice, becoming confiding. "Now comes what the favor is going to cost you. I hadn't really decided, before, what I should do about Maurice's estate. You see, Maurice's kids have filed this old will. There's a new one around, the one Maurice gave you a copy of. But the only guy who knew about it, besides me, that is, he was in the hospital with a coronary, and he died last night.

"So," Pike said, "I wasn't sure what to do. Duty to file the will, testator's intent and all that. But on the other hand, would he have changed it? After he knew you'd made your little loan out of his production company? I don't know. So maybe I'd have filed the new will with the court. Let some judge worry about making the moral choices. But now?

"This," Pike said, "this is too much. We have this quaint statute in California. Says if you kill somebody, you can't inherit from him."

"I didn't kill Maurice," Mickey said.

"Maybe you didn't plant the bomb, but you caused the whole thing, set it all in motion."

She was looking down at her lap. She murmured something.

"What? I didn't hear you."

She looked up, glared at Pike, "No more than you did. The bomb was in your car. If you hadn't gotten mixed up with Richard, it wouldn't have happened."

"Yes, and I have to live with that. But who started the whole thing? Who took Maurice's money, so he got suspicious, asked me to look into it? It was because of that that I met Mr. Morrissey, and we had our little disagreement, he tried to off me, and got Maurie. So it was your fault he was there for me to get involved with. So the thought of your spending Maurice's money, after all that, well, it just doesn't go over big.

"Then there's this little *bagarre*. You've whacked Richard out, and you tried to whack me too. Now Richard I don't mind. You could have done that anytime, I wouldn't've let out a peep about it. Appreciate the favor. Very kind of you.

"But me," he said, "that's a different matter. That's a fellow I'm rather attached to. So I'll tell you what's going to happen. My briefcase is going to be stolen out of my car, and, what a shame, Maurice's new will and the videocassette of him signing it, and a bunch of other papers are going to be in there. And there're no copies, nobody even knows about it except you and me, so it's just gone. Too bad."

"You son-of-a-bitch!"

"If you say so."

"Bastard. Fucking bastard."

"Maybe that, too."

"Oh, you're so sure of yourself, so superior."

"Not superior. And not sure of myself. But there are *some* things I'm sure of. One thing I'm sure of is it'll all be pretty much over in a few months, in terms of the estate being closed, and the kids having the money. Another thing I'm sure of is if you even *think* about trying to claim a share of Maurice's estate, I'll have an attack of conscience and remember where this pistol disappeared to, and turn it over to a guy I know at the LAPD, and tell him all about what happened when I got here this evening.

"You know," he said, "or maybe you don't, they don't close the file on homicides. So it doesn't matter if you kick up a fuss now, or next week or next year, the cops'll still be interested in all this. Maybe you could get off with seven years. Maybe you could even get off entirely. But it'd be your problem. Have a nice evening."

It had all been there. All laid out so beautifully. Mickey'd done enough thriller-type films—spies, drugs, cops and car chases—to have had a pretty good idea how it was going to go down. An actor like maybe Charles Bronson would buy a screenplay, star in it himself, and want his name on the film as director—so he'd hire Mickey as A.D., and she'd really do the film, and he'd get the credit.

Like *Tequila Sunrise*, right? Guy played by Mel Gibson has been the biggest drug dealer in south L.A., but now he's quit and lives in this nice beach house, has a kid, little boy looks nine or ten, and he ends up with Michelle Pfeiffer, first just to fool around, but then for keeps. Couple of tight moments, like when the dumb DEA guy is trying to cover up his own mistakes and decides to kill Gibson, but overall, just enough bang-bang to put a nice edge on the romance.

And it had seemed to her (she had nothing else to judge it by) that that was the world, how it was. Sell coke for a while, and then retire. No one would care, no one would come after you, no one would try to lean on you later, use you or take advantage of you. Just step out clean, and go on to the rest of your life.

And that was how it was with shooting someone. The idea that the impact of a pistol bullet would actually knock someone off his feet, pick him up and *throw* him, so that he hit the wall, or knocked over some piece of furniture—until she'd seen it happen to Richie, that idea hadn't been part of her consciousness. It didn't work like that at all. Bang! Neat hole. Victim puts one hand over the hole, looks at the blood on his hand. Smiles this smile, wry and dumb, and slumps to the ground.

And as for what came after, the idea that it went on and on, police looking for who did it—well, hey, no, that's not how it was. You put the gun in someone else's car, or ditched it somehow, washed your hands, and that was it.

Kill with a smile.

Only with the lawyer having the gun, it didn't look like it was going to turn out that way.

Not at all.

The phone was ringing when Pike got home. He dropped his keys trying to get the door open. Fumbled with them in the dark. Finally got inside, and of course the phone had stopped ringing by then. And he'd forgotten to turn on the answering machine. He had a feeling it might be Dossie. He tried calling her but there was no answer.

He made dinner. Took something out of the freezer and stuck it in the microwave. Ate at the kitchen table and glanced at articles in the paper. Tried Dossie again. Still no answer.

He'd stiffened up pretty good during dinner. Ribs, arm, couple of places on his face, all were sore and bruised. Decided to take a hot shower, try to stop the various parts from aching so much.

Of course the phone rang again while he was in the shower. Continued to ring while he got out of the shower. Rang while he grabbed a towel. Rang while he left wet footprints on the professor's rug.

And stopped when he picked it up.

He tried calling Dossie again. Still no answer.

He'd been asleep for an hour or so when the phone started ringing again. He groped for it on the bedside table in the dark.

"Hello?"

"Dave? It's me. Dossie."

"Oh," he said. "Hi. How're you?"

"Okay, I guess."

She was silent for a long time, and there was no sound but the hiss and crackle of static on the line.

"Are you okay?" he said.

She sighed. "I'm in Dallas."

"Dallas? How in blazes did you get to Dallas?"

"Flew. I took an airport limo to the airport in L.A. and flew."

"Is something wrong? Is someone in your family sick?"

"No."

She was silent again for a long time.

"Dave," she said finally. "It wouldn't have worked, okay? I mean, I thought about it a lot, I really did. But enough is enough.

"You have," she said. "You lead a real exciting life. But it's just too much. I can't handle naked women showing up in the swimming pool, and bombs in cars, and urban cowboys dropping by to be shot.

"It's nothing against you personally," she said. "You understand? But it's just too fast for me. I can't handle it. Thank you very much, but no thank you."

He could feel her slipping away. Feel the wires stretching and her getting farther and farther away, until it was a million miles from where he was to where she was. He wanted intensely to touch her, talk to her. At least to stop the slipping feeling that was taking her farther away with every second of hissing silence on the line.

"Wait," he said. "Hold on here. Not so fast. I don't live like this. I mean like that. It was just something that happened to me. Happened the one time, I mean. It isn't any kind of usual thing, and I . . ."

"I'm sorry, David," she said, her voice made tiny by the ever-increasing distance. "Good-bye."